Spoiled Rotten

Spoiled Rotten

Brandi Johnson

www.urbanbooks.net

Urban Books, LLC
97 N 18th Street
Wyandanch, NY 11798

ISBN- 13: 978-1-62286-701-1
ISBN- 10: 1-62286-701-7

Fifth Mass Market Printing May 2010
First Trade Paperback Printing October 2008
Printed in the United States of America

10 9 8 7 6 5

Distributed by Kensington Publishing Corp.
Submit Wholesale Orders to:
Kensington Publishing Corp.
C/O Penguin Group (USA) Inc.
Attention: Order Processing
405 Murray Hill Parkway
East Rutherford, NJ 07073-2316
Phone: 1-800-526-0275
Fax: 1-800-227-9604

Acknowledgments

First and foremost there's a must that I thank my Lord and Savior. If it wasn't for Him and the power of prayer, there would be no me. I'm a firm believer of, with the Lord all things are possible, and He has showed me that every day of my life. Can I get an Amen?

Let me clear my throat!!! I gotta thanks my girls at Mans-field Correctional Institution for reading Spoiled Rotten when they know good and well they shoulda been making rounds. I'm not gon' name no names because y'all already know how they are out there.

Shout outs to my Man.CI family: Puella Jordan, Shirley (Momma) Briggs, Curtis (Pops) Johnson, Stan (Steady) Brown, Kevin Grier, F???? Miller, Curtis Hall, Damon Butts, JW. Windom, CW Adkins, Antonio Fletcher, Marvin Tanner, Charlie Graves, Onray Smoot, John Dunn, Pat Reed, Robin Garcia, Carnail Delk, Joseph Holmes, Terry (Ghetto) Melton, Jeff

Brokaw, Richard Almeda, Marlon Scott, James Beverly Jr., Andrea Young, Mary Miner, Annette Favors, John Cantrell, Elmer Hale, Bobby, Ricky and Boo-Boo Minard, Blindard Granger, Capt. Charlie Scott, Marvinetta Scott, Lt. Page, David Bond, Desiree Page, Mark Patton, Tara Brown, Jerry Powell, James Taylor. And for those of you I didn't mention, it wasn't because I don't consider you my family, I just had to make a cut off point somewhere, I got much love for y'all too. Oh, Dale Thompson, thank you for always keeping' tabs on the progress of my book. See, I didn't forget about you like you thought I would!

To Nikki Ajian, my friend, (Lord knows you can't give that title to everyone) thanks for being there for me every time I wanted to say forget it and give up. Only a true friend would keep reminding a person time and time again that all their hard work and dedication will pay off in the end. Look at me now, baby girl, I did it!!! You had my back from the beginning to the end. Thank you from the bottom of my heart, and God bless you. I could ask you to say the same, but He already blessed me once He put you in my life. You my girl, don't you ever forget that.

Jacqueline Chambers, you know I gotta give a big holla out to you, cuz if I didn't, I know you would never let me live it down. Thanks for all the "real" conversations we shared. We clicked from the beginning and that's only because real recognize real, so always remember you my girl. Now enough of the mushy stuff, you know a sista got an image to uphold. So git on up and go out and buy Spoiled Rotten and this time don't forget I wrote it! (Smile)

Barbara Cobb-Martin, you have been there since the birth of Spoiled Rotten. You were the one who gave me the ambition and determination to create my story. Thank you, thank you, and thank you for everything.

Alamo, you are my lover, my best friend, and even sometimes my enemy (Smile), but through it all you kept believing in me even when I had self doubt. You were the one who lifted me up every time I fell. You brought a smile to my face even when the tears flowed. I couldn't have prayed for a more loving mate, and even if I tried, I would be just plain greedy. I love you!!!!

To my niece Brittney, thank you for being my number one fan from the beginning to the end.

Sonya Mccrary, thanks for always being there to keep my hair intact when I needed it.

To the two people who loved me most. My mommy and daddy. You two have been by my side through it all. Y'all watched me grow into the strong woman I am today. Mommy, I've watched you work miracles. You probably thought I was too young to understand your struggles, but trust me, I wasn't. You managed to raise all six of us by ya' damn self. I look back sometimes and wonder where you got all your strength from. You always made sure we had what we needed, and if you couldn't get it right then, you had no problem with throwing a card party or two so you could. Mom, you have been nothing but the best. Daddy, put ya' eye on the wall and blink twice!!! I love you both . . .

My three sons, Montias, Brei'yonte, and Amir'aki, thanks for being so patient with Mommy. It's because of you three I can go on day to day without losing my mind, only because I have y'all to think about. I know we have had some rough times, especially when y'all demanded my time, but we made it through. I love you three more than anything. Y'all are my air, my being, my life, my everything.

Joylynn Jossel, my agent. Girl, I can't thank you enough. You have truly been a blessing. Thank you for all of your hard work and dedication. Without you, the world would know nothing about Spoiled Rotten. I can't explain how grateful I am to have you on my team. Good looking out for always keeping it 100%, no matter what. Like I said time and time again, you be doin' the damn thang!!! (Excuse my language.) Smile!

Big ups to my two favorite cousins, Nikki and Kiara Rife, thanks for everything. I love y'all!!! (R.I.P.) Aunt Elanda, I miss you so much!!! Aunt Mary, Uncle Kenneth, Uncle Bra', Rachel, Pam, Ronnie, Lisa, Edminston, Miranda, Grandpa Joe, and the rest of the family, thanks.

Joe and the rest of the family, thanks.

Shout out to my girl Tawanda Carrington. Keep ya' head up, cuz you know me and you got big dreams to accomplish.

I have to give a shout to all my brothers and sisters, just cuz my mom said to, psych, y'all know I love y'all. Stevie, Khayyam, Nayyohn, Rita, Chico, Andre, Darnell, Jim-Jim, Saquan and even Kim, thanks for always having my back.

Well, well, well, I gotta give a shout out to my home girl, Candra Carter, and my home boy Frank (Fat Daddy) Pointer, no matter how long we go without talkin', y'all know that we are still the best of friends. And as soon as it's all said and done, we are gon' kick it until the cows come home, just like we did in our Blue Room days. Much love!!!

Ralph Garrett, my body guard, you were the one who kept me informed about the book game, and when you found out any new info, I was the first to know. You also lead me to believe that I could do anything I put my heart and soul into . . . and check me out . . . I did it. Good looking out, Big brotha'.

To Trina Martin my own personal sales lady and friend. Thank you for everything you have done for me. You have been a blessing since day one. Believe me when I say this, God has something in store for you. You just have to let go and let God do his thing. I love you. Willie "Dynamite" . . . WELL HELL . . . I did it, baby boy. Much love Grandma Pearl, thanks for everything. Big ups to Judy Black, Lisa Petty and Rochelle Lee-El, Stacy Johnson, Janay Sudberry.

This book is dedicated to the backbone of my family: Big Momma and Poppa.

Prologue

"Get up, Jyson, I'm gon' be late for school," Trouble walked into the hallway and yelled into her sleeping brother's room.

"I'm up, damn, girl," Jyson yelled out into the hallway from his bedroom. Jyson sat up and wiped the cold out of the corners of his eyes. "Did you start the car yet?"

Shit, Momma should be the one takin' me to school instead of Jyson, Trouble thought as she walked back into her bedroom. *She's probably layin' in a crack house somewhere. That crack must be a bad boy.*

Trouble let her mind take her back ten years ago to the day she and her brother found out about their mother's drug habit.

Trouble was in the pint-sized kitchen of their apartment and opened up the bare refrigerator. "We don't never have nothin' to eat," Trouble whined as she slammed the door shut and leaned up against the counter.

"I'm hungry too," Jyson said as he walked into the kitchen. "What's in there to eat? Maybe I can whip us up somethin'."

"What you gon' make with a box of bakin' soda, a bag of hard sugar, and some old butter?" Trouble asked sarcastically.

"Hell, when you're hungry, you'll eat anything."

"I'm not eating," she huffed.

"Well, come on," he said, motioning to his sister. "Let's go see if Momma got some change in her dresser."

The two headed toward their mother's room. Once they got in there, Jyson opened up the top drawer. He moved a few pair of panties around and pulled out a long, thin piece of glass that looked burned on both ends.

"What's that, Jyson?" Trouble inquired.

Jyson ignored his sister's question. He couldn't believe his eyes.

"What is it, Jyson?" she asked again.

Jyson stood in disbelief, not knowing whether to tell his sister what the object was that he held in his hand.

"Do you hear me talkin' to you, Jyson?" Trouble said in a demanding tone, but she still got no response from him. And after a brief moment of silence, Trouble became worried as she stared at her brother.

"Jyson, please talk to me," she said as her hazel eyes welled up with tears.

"I'm sorry, sis. I didn't mean to scare you," he said, putting the glass object back into the drawer and slamming it shut. Jyson looked down at his little sister and hoped that she would understand what he was about to tell her. "Trouble, that was a pipe, a stem, and some even call it a glass dick. It's what people—or better yet, our so-called Momma—smokes crack out of." Tears of anger flowed down Jyson's cheeks as he spoke.

Trouble could not believe what she was hearing. A rush came over her entire body—hurt, deceit, and most of all embarrassment took control of her heart.

"You mean to tell me that our momma is a crackhead?"

Jyson closed his eyes and shook his head. "Yep, sis, Momma is a crackhead," Jyson said, grimacing. "Dig that," he sighed then exited the room. Trouble followed close behind in silence.

"That's a darn shame," Trouble said, walking into the kitchen behind her brother.

"I knew somethin' was wrong wit' Momma. I just didn't wanna say nothin' 'cuz I wasn't for sure, but now I have proof," Jyson said.

Trouble put her hands on her hips and walked over to her brother. "What do you mean you knew somethin' was wrong wit' Momma?" she asked. "Why you didn't tell me if you knew?" She let her hands fall down to her side as she waited for an answer.

"You should have known too, sis," Jyson said, grabbing two glasses from the cabinet and filling them up with water from the sink. "Here, drink this. It does a body good."

"I thought milk does a body good," she said, taking the glass of water from her brother's hand and drinking it down in one swallow, hoping it would fill her empty stomach.

"Milk, orange juice, Kool-Aid, water, it all does a body good when you're thirsty," he said, sitting down at the wooden table their grandmother had given them before she passed away.

"Jyson, how do you figure that I should have known that Momma was on crack?" Trouble asked as she sat down at the table next to her brother.

Jyson turned his chair around to face his sister and said, "All the stuff that has been comin' up missin' around the house, what do you think happened to it?"

Trouble shrugged her shoulders. "I don't know."

"What do you think happened to my PlayStation, the cordless phone, and the necklace that Daddy gave you last Christmas?"

Trouble thought for a brief second. "I don't know. I really didn't pay much attention to the phone or your Play-Station and I just figured that I lost the necklace."

"That's a shame that a woman could steal from her seven-year-old daughter."

"I looked everywhere for my necklace and I even asked Momma had she seen it. She said no, so I just figured I had lost it."

"You lost it, all right, and Momma found it and gave it to the dope man."

Jyson got up from the table, put his glass in the sink and looked at his little sister before walking out of the kitchen.

"I'm her daughter. How can Momma steal from me? It just ain't fair." Trouble laid her head down on the table as tears began to escape her eyes.

A few days later, Trouble was lying in her mother's bed watching an all-night marathon of *Moesha* when she heard her coming in. Trouble looked over at the clock and it was way past midnight. Trouble panicked and jumped up from the bed because she wasn't allowed in her mother's room when she wasn't at home. She ran to the closet and hid inside.

Her mother walked into the bedroom with a tall, dark-skinned brother with nappy locks in his head that hung to his shoulders. Trouble cracked the closet door just enough to be able to see her mother and her guest.

Trouble watched as her mother hurried over to the jewelry box on her dresser. *I wonder what she doin'?* Trouble thought as she peeked out through the half-opened door. Momma grabbed Big Momma's pearl necklace with the earrings to match and placed them in the palm of Dark Skin's hand. He looked the jewelry over as if he were an appraiser.

"This ain't shit. You gon' hafta come better than this, Denise," he yelled at Momma, loud enough to make Trouble jump. He laid the jewelry on top of the dresser and took a step back.

"Shhh, you gon' hafta keep the noise down. My babies are asleep," Momma warned.

"Look here, bitch, you said that you had some expensive shit. I hope you ain't wastin' my time 'cuz I can be somewhere gettin' my dick sucked, unless you gon' do it for me." Dark Skin smiled, showing off a mouthful of gold teeth.

"Nigga, please! I'm feinin', but I ain't suckin' no dick for no twenty-dollar rock and I really ain't suckin' no nigga's dick that ain't no older than my son!"

"Well, I'm outta here then," Dark Skin said as he turned for the door.

Denise was feinin' bad, so she thought for a second. "Wait! I got somethin' for you."

A mischievous grin came across Dark Skin's face as he reached for his zipper.

"No, nigga, I'm not suckin' ya dick I said." Denise reached back into the jewelry box, pulled out a diamond cluster ring that belonged to her father and put it in his hand. "You like it?" she asked as she shifted what weight she had left from one foot to the other. Denise looked bad. She went from looking like a brick house to a shit house. All of her long, thick hair had fallen out, and she now sported a short, nappy Afro. She once had a pretty smile that lit up the room when she walked in; now all she had were a few good teeth left in her mouth, and they looked like she hadn't brushed them in ages.

Trouble wanted to jump out of the closet and kick her momma's ass for being so stupid. She tried her best to stay still as she peeked out in between her momma's clothes that hung in plastic.

A huge smile came across Dark Skin's face as he repeatedly looked over the ring.

"Does that smile mean that you like what you see?" Momma asked.

"Yeah, this bitch here is sweet!" Dark Skin's blood-shot eyes glistened with excitement.

He placed the ring in his right front pocket and then dug his hand down in the front of his sagging Avirex jeans like he was about to pull a rabbit out of a hat. Instead, he pulled out a plastic baggy full of crack and handed her a piece.

Denise took the dope and examined it the same way he had done the jewelry. "You ain't got nothin' bigger than this? That's a diamond I gave you, not a cubic zirconia," she snapped.

"You got a fly-ass mouth to be a crackhead." Dark Skin laughed as he snatched the dope from her hand and put it back into the bag. He picked up the same piece again and gave it back to her.

Denise gave him a look that could kill. "Now, nigga, I might be smokin', but I ain't no dummy. I saw you pull that same bullshit back out that bag."

"A nigga can't get nuttin' over on you, now can he?" He laughed and pulled out a different piece. "Now they don't get no bigger than this. If you want somethin' bigger, go somewhere else," he said as he scratched his dry scalp.

"This piece is cool," Denise said as she rushed out of the bedroom and straight to the bathroom to smoke, leaving Dark Skin alone.

Dark Skin grabbed the pearl necklace and earrings and placed them in the same pocket as he had placed the ring before leaving out of the room.

"Shit, I can give this to my girl to make up for me stayin' out all night," he said out loud. He snickered and a few seconds later Trouble heard him exit out the front door.

Trouble waited for a few minutes to make sure the coast was clear. She jumped out of the closet and dashed into her brother's room.

"Jyson, get up," she yelled in a hushed tone.

Jyson jumped up with his heart beating a mile a minute.

"What's the matter?" he asked, still dazed and confused from the deep sleep he had been in.

"I just saw Momma give away Big Momma's and Granddaddy's jewelry to some black nigga wit' dreadlocks."

Jyson sat up on the edge of his broken-down twin-size bed that was being held up by encyclopedias. "You mean to tell me that Momma gave away our grandparents' jewelry?" He put his head in the palms of his hands.

"That's what I said, ain't it?" Trouble sat down on the bed next to Jyson and he placed his arm around her shoulders, pulling her closer to his side.

"Don't worry, li'l sis. Momma has a drug problem and there is nothin' we can do about it. She's gon' hafta get help for herself. Things will get better," Jyson tried to assure his sister.

"You think so, Jyson?" she asked as she grabbed a blanket and one of the two pillows from off of his bed and made a pallet on the floor.

"I know so, sis," he sighed as he lay back down and then stared up at the ceiling.

Deep down inside, Jyson knew things would only get worse before they got any better. *You know what they say*, he thought to himself, *it gets greater later 'cuz it was worse first*. "Try to get yourself some sleep," Jyson said as he closed his eyes and tried to find a comfortable position.

Trouble closed her eyes, but knew she couldn't sleep.

"Jyson, can I ask you a question?" Trouble fluffed her pillow and rested her head on it.

"Yeah," he sighed.

"Promise me that you'll never do drugs."

"I promise, sis. Now try to get some sleep 'cuz we got school in the mornin'." Jyson tossed and turned a few times before finally drifting off to sleep.

"Jyson, are you 'sleep?" Trouble nagged with no answer. "Jyson, are you 'sleep?" She got louder.

"I was," he said, yawning.

"Oh, my bad. I just wanted to say one more thing."

"What is it, sis?"

"When I get older I'm gon' be a millionaire and take good care of us. We ain't gon' hafta worry about nuttin'. We gon' have the tightest gear, all the latest tennis shoes, and all that. I can't wait," Trouble said, excited.

"You are so materialistic," Jyson said, smiling. "I'm gon' hafta break you of that."

"I can't help it if I wanna look good." Trouble smiled too.

"Well, I can't wait either. So just tell me, how do you plan on makin' enough money to buy us all these things?"

"I don't know yet. But by the time I turn eighteen, I'll have it all figured out. You just wait and see," Trouble said.

Jyson smiled at the fact that his sister wanted to take care of him. He loved his sister with all his heart because she was all he had. But he knew from witnessing it in other neighborhood families where drugs were involved that eventually the white folks would be all in their business and try to separate them, so he had decided right then and there that he would do something to keep them two together. He didn't know what, but he knew that he would eventually come up with something.

One

Everything had started falling into place for Trouble and Jyson. Trouble was now seventeen and her life was about to change drastically. Her wavy, jet-black hair had grown to the middle of her back, and when she walked it would bounce up and down like the girls in the Pantene commercials. Trouble's body was filling out in all the right places and she knew it too, right along with all the fellas at Mansfield Senior High, especially Dariel Daniels.

Trouble had a crush on Dariel, but no one knew, not even his cousin who was also her best friend. Trouble had known Dariel every since they were six years old. He would come to Mansfield from Chicago to spend the summer with his cousins, but since the GM plant that his parents worked at for years decided to close their doors, both his parents relocated to the plant in Mansfield, Ohio. It was hard at first for Dariel to adjust to living in a small city. To him Mansfield was like living in Mayberry, where everybody knew everybody, but eventually he got used to it.

Trouble looked forward to seeing Dariel's gorgeous face every summer, and even though they were just kids, she often fantasized about him one day becoming her husband. Dariel was now six feet tall with almond-colored skin. He wore his soft, brown hair in braids. He kept his hair intact. He was one of the finest brothas who walked the halls of Mansfield Senior and he knew it, but he was not the kind of person who was stuck on himself.

Dariel was the captain of the varsity basketball team. Baby boy had game! In addition, what attracted most girls to him was the fact that he was very respectful when it came to women. He rarely let the words *bitch* or *ho* come out of his mouth, especially when he was referring to a woman. Trouble was head over heels for this brotha, but there were two things that stopped her from pursuing her soul mate. One was that she had just gotten out of a relationship that went bad. The other thing was that Dariel already had a girlfriend, and Trouble would never mess with anybody's man under any circumstance.

Trouble lay in bed and began thinking about her life and how her momma was still up to her same old tricks, smoking like a chimney. She stayed gone for days, sometimes weeks at a time, not even coming home long enough to wash her ass.

Jyson had quit school in the beginning of his junior year and had taken to staying out late. Most nights he didn't even come home. To Trouble, one good thing was that her brother made sure that she had lunch money every day, that she wore all the top-notch designer clothes, and that she had all the latest tennis shoes and boots. She didn't know where he got all his money from, and as long as the clothes and shoes kept coming, she could not have cared less. Her biggest fear was that her brother was doing something he had no business doing, like selling weed, but she knew he was way too smart to be dealing crack. The checks that their father sent them every week for child support could only go so far, even if Momma hadn't been smoking them up. So Trouble knew that it was not those checks keeping the rent paid and paying for all the clothes and shoes. Jyson even bought a fifty-two-inch plasma television after their mother sold the one she used to have in her bedroom.

Trouble threw the comforter back and got out of bed as she thought about her favorite aunt, Rachel. *Good ole Aunt Rachel,* Trouble thought as she picked out her school clothes. *Most people tell me I look more like her than my own damn momma, which is a good thing, being that Momma went from lookin' like Halle Berry to Whoopi Goldberg.*

Trouble thought about her Aunt Rachel and how she never bit her tongue about anything. She remembered a few years ago when they were at their family reunion and the potato salad must have been nasty because Aunt Rachel stood up from her seat and went up to the DJ's booth and grabbed the microphone and started talkin' about how nasty the potato salad was.

Auntie Rachel don't play, Trouble thought. *She was never on the same shit as her sisters and she was always tryin'a talk Momma into checkin' herself into a drug rehab.*

Momma always agreed, but then she always came up with a reason why she couldn't go. Jyson and Trouble found out that their mother started smoking crack after their father left her for a woman named Miss Parker. But their mother wasn't the only one strung out in the family. Their father was strung out on something too, and it was called pussy! Their dad was one of the biggest whores that walked the face of the earth—at least that's what their Aunt Rachel would always tell their mother. There must have been some truth to it because those words were coming from his own sister.

"Why do you stay wit' his ass?" Aunt Rachel would always ask Denise.

"Because I love him, that's why. And love will make you do some crazy shit, like stayin' with a man that dog and disrespects you," Denise would say back.

"No! Only a damn fool would stay with a dog like my brother. He comes home from work on Friday, he shits, showers, and shaves, and you don't see his black ass no more until late Sunday night or early Monday morning. Honey, you need to wake the fuck up and take those two babies of yours and move the fuck on before that dog gives you fleas," Aunt Rachel would retort.

She wasn't intentionally saying those things to hurt Denise's feelings; she just wanted her to wake up and smell the coffee and realize that her brother was a dog. Trouble thought about her momma a little while longer before climbing back into bed for a few more minutes of sleep.

"Get up, Trouble," Jyson yelled as he walked into his sister's room.

"I don't wanna go to school today," she whined and rolled over, pulling the comforter over her head.

"Get yo' butt up and get ready for school, girl."

Trouble jumped out of bed and began yelling. "Didn't I tell you that I didn't wanna go to school today? You can't make me go because you are not my damn mother or father, so stop tryin' to act like you are! And I'm tellin' Momma that you dropped out of school."

Jyson gave his sister a puzzled look. "I don't give a damn who you tell, 'cuz I'm a grown-ass man. And do you think Momma gives a damn about you or me? Hell naw. 'Cuz if she did, she would be here to make sure we had clothes on our backs, shoes on our feet, and food on the muthafuckin' table. But where is she?" Jyson looked deep into his sister's eyes and she saw the pain in them as he stared at her.

Damn, he looks just like Daddy, she thought. Jyson was a very handsome young man. He was six feet one with hazel eyes just like their father's and hers. His teeth were as straight as a board and Trouble would hear some of the older women in the neighborhood say that he had a million-dollar smile.

And the waves that he sported in his hair were so deep that if you stared at them for too long, you were bound to get seasick. All of Trouble's friends had a crush on him, but he would never give them the time of day. Jyson would always say that her friends were too young and immature for his taste, and besides, he liked older women.

Jyson had women practically throwing themselves at him. Trouble knew in her heart that he would turn out to be a whore just like their father because at his young age, he was already following in his footsteps. Jyson had women from every neighborhood taking care of him. They were buying him clothes, shoes, and one older woman bought him his first car, and he didn't even have a license.

Jyson walked away from his sister, leaving her speechless. She wanted to call out to him so badly to apologize for her outburst. Trouble was upset about not being able to have her mother hug her when she needed one and not having her father around to tuck her in at night like he used to when she was a little girl. It wasn't Jyson's fault that their mother was strung out on crack and that their father didn't want to have anything to do with them. She knew what Jyson had said about their mother was nothing more than the truth. And she had to admit that her brother was the closest thing she had to a parent.

Trouble walked into the bathroom and got into the shower. She stood in the hot water for a long time before lathering her loofah with Caress body wash. She made up in her mind that she would apologize to her brother and promise him that she would never have another outburst like that again.

Trouble got dressed for school and then walked into the kitchen, hoping to find Jyson in there hooking up one of his famous entrées, but he was nowhere to be found. She picked up the plate of food he had left for her and read the note that laid on top of the counter.

Trouble, don't forget to do your homework and your chores when you get home. And yes, I'll accept your apology, just don't let it happen again. Love, Jyson.

Trouble smiled at the note and laid it back on top of the counter. She ran into the bathroom to check her teeth for any unwanted food and then headed out the door for the bus stop.

"Hey, Trouble," Ta'liyah yelled down the crowded hallway when she spotted her best friend.

Ta'liyah and Trouble had been best friends since first grade. They were tighter than Eddie Murphy's pants on *Raw*. They were so tight that they called each other sisters and for anyone who didn't know any better, they fell for it. Those two had a bond that could not be broken. They shared everything—all the latest gossip, clothes, and even their deepest, darkest secrets. The only thing they swore never to share was men.

Ta'liyah was short with dark skin. She was the kind of black that most people would have been ashamed to be. But not her—she was proud of her dark skin color. She reminded people of a very dark-skinned Kelly Rowland, but she was shaped more like Stephanie Mills. She kept her hair cut in a short style that brought out her high cheekbones. Ta'liyah was no virgin, either. She had been around the block a few different times and a lot of girls' mothers didn't let them hang around her because they said Ta'liyah was too fast. But it wasn't until she slept with Marcus Lindsay that she realized that men ain't shit, because after she slept with him, he went around and told everyone. So after that, Ta'liyah swore off sex.

Trouble adored her best friend because of her sense of humor. She was the real queen of comedy because Ta'liyah could make anyone laugh no matter what the situation was.

"What's up, girl?" Ta'liyah asked as she raked her fingers through her freshly done freeze curls.

"Not much. Oooohhhh girl, I love your hair. Who done it?" Trouble asked.

"Sonya did it," Ta'liyah replied.

"She hooked it up!"

"I know. She does a good job, but she be takin' all day," Ta'liyah said, running her fingers through her hair again. Ta'liyah looked nervously at Trouble. "I got somethin' to tell you but you got to promise not to get mad about it."

"It all depends on what you 'bout to say. I might get mad and I might not," Trouble admitted, truthfully.

"Well, I ain't tellin' you then." Ta'liyah turned to walk away but Trouble grabbed her by the arm and pulled her back.

"Okay, okay, okay! I won't get mad," Trouble said as she crossed her fingers behind her back.

"Promise me, Trouble."

"Okay, damn, I promise," she said, irritated.

"Uncross your fingers, Trouble."

"How did you know my fingers were crossed?"

"You act like I just met yo' ass."

"Okay." Trouble uncrossed her fingers and waited on her friend to talk.

"Okay. Word on the streets is Jameelah is talkin' about checkin' you because she thinks that you are messin' around with my cousin." Ta'liyah stood back and waited for a response.

"Who, Dariel?" Trouble asked, surprised.

"Who else could I be talkin' about? I guess she be seein' y'all talkin' in the lunchroom and now she thinks that y'all are fuckin'. Oh, and she said she don't want you braidin' his hair no more when Sonya is out of town."

Trouble opened up her locker and grabbed her English book. "Is that so? Well, I'm not thinkin' about that crazy-ass broad 'cuz Dariel is like a brother to me. Shit, I've been knowin' him ever since we were little kids, so I don't give a damn what she says."

Deep down inside, Trouble was furious but she didn't want to show it. *I really don't have no room to get upset 'cuz I do like her man,* Trouble thought, *and if she keeps on talkin' shit, I'll go against the grain and take him from her.*

"Dariel tried to tell her that y'all are like family, but she wasn't tryin' to hear all that. She keeps on insisting that you are tryin' to push up on him. I'm just givin' you the heads-up 'cuz you know how she gets down."

Trouble licked her lips then applied another coat of lip gloss to them. "If I wanted Dariel, I would have had him by now, don't you think? While she's talkin', she better keep an eye on him because the brotha is lookin' kinda propa' these days." She winked and smiled.

"Sounds to me like someone has a crush on my cousin," Ta'liyah joked.

"Girl, please," Trouble hissed as she rolled her eyes. "You know me and that nigga is like family."

"Un huh, I'm gon' hafta keep my eyes on you," Ta'liyah said, laughing.

You better, because the nigga is finer than wine, sweeter than candy, and juicier than a T-bone steak, Trouble thought.

"Do me a favor and tell your cousin-in-law that I don't want her man," Trouble said.

"Now you know I don't fuck with that big head–ass ho! That broad head is so big, she needs to soak the muthafucka in some Slim-Fast," Ta'liyah said, laughing.

Trouble laughed until her side began to hurt. "Well, where that bitch at then? I'll tell her myself."

"You promised, Trouble," Ta'liyah yelled.

"I know I did, but I can't stand when a bitch ain't woman enough to tell me what she wants me to know. If she was braidin' my man's hair or if I even thought she was pushin' up on my man, I would bring it to the bitch!" Trouble yelled, slamming her locker closed.

"Please, just calm down. You know if you get into any more trouble your mom is gon' hafta come up to the school for a conference and I know you don't want that, do you?" Ta'liyah emphasized strongly.

"You're right, I don't. I can't have my momma up here at the school lookin' all tore up from the floor up. But it really wouldn't matter if Mr. Granger did want to talk to my momma. Shit, he would have to go lookin' for her ass and ain't no tellin' where she's at," Trouble stated angrily.

"It doesn't matter. Just leave it alone. Jameelah must be insecure, 'cuz if she wasn't, she wouldn't accuse Dariel of messin' around with every girl she sees him talkin' to."

Trouble spotted Jameelah's best friend, Kassie, walking down the hallway. "Hey, Kassie, when you see your friend, Jameelah, tell her that I don't want Dariel and if I did I would have him!" Trouble stared as she leaned up against an empty locker and waited to hear what smart remark Kassie had for her.

Kassie walked up into Trouble's face and said, "Look, I don't have anything to do with what's goin' on between y'all, so leave me the fuck out of it! But um, I'll make sure I let her know what you said so she can kick yo' ass!" Kassie laughed and turned around to walk away.

"Bitch, please! You couldn't melt that ho down and pour her on me!" Trouble retorted.

Kassie turned back around and walked over to Trouble. "What did you just call me?" she asked.

"What? You deaf now? You didn't hear me call you a bitch, bitch?"

Trouble's heart beat faster than a jackrabbit's because she knew Kassie was not about to back down like the other girls she had the opportunity to punk out. Kassie was about to give her one hell of a fight and Trouble knew it too. How was she going to beat up this bitch that stood at least five feet nine and weighed every bit of 250 pounds?

Ta'liyah squeezed her tiny frame in between the two girls in order to keep them from fighting. But she knew that if anybody swung one punch, her tiny butt would have been tossed to the side with no problem.

"Ladies, is there a problem?" Ms. Jones asked as she stepped out into the hallway from her classroom.

"No, ma'am. We don't have a problem," Trouble said, taking a step back from the big Amazon beast that was breathing hot air in her face.

"Naw, we ain't got no problem, Ms. Jones," Kassie said, smiling. "Later for you," she said, pointing at Trouble.

"Yeah, whatever!" Trouble laughed as she walked down the hallway to her first-period class.

The fellas checked out her matured body parts as she strutted down the hallway wearing a pink-and-white Baby Phat shirt and a pair of Baby Phat jeans with pink stitching down the side of the pant legs. To top off her ensemble, she sported a pair of pink-and-white Baby Phat tennis shoes. Trouble knew she was the shit and she stayed dressed to impress. Jyson wouldn't have it any other way.

Trouble sat at her desk waiting patiently in her second-period class. She couldn't wait until Jameelah pranced her big-headed ass into the room. Finally, Jameelah walked through the door. As she was walking down the aisle, she bumped into Trouble's arm on purpose and then had the nerve to look at her like she dared her to say anything about it.

Trouble jumped up from her seat and got in Jameelah's face. "Bitch, I don't know what your problem is, but you better get some help before I beat the brakes off yo' ass," Trouble shouted loud enough for the teacher across the hall to stop his lesson.

"Fuck you, bitch. And you are my fuckin' problem," Jameelah spat. "You walk around this school actin' like yo' shit don't stink. But I got news for you, honey . . . it does."

"You played-out tramp," Trouble yelled and swung her fist, but Dariel grabbed her 125-pound body, and then Ms. Carter and the teacher from across the hall grabbed Jameelah.

Dariel walked Trouble to the back of the class. "Calm down, baby girl. She ain't worth all the stress," Dariel said, soothingly. "She be trippin'. Man, she think we be tryin' to holla at each other when you be braidin' my hair. I keep on tryin'a tell her that we are like family but she keeps on insistin' that I want you." Dariel let out a nervous laugh.

"Well, do you want me?" Trouble asked with confidence. She looked deep into his dark brown eyes and waited on an answer.

Dariel smiled and said, "I'll talk to you after school." He winked at her before walking back to the front of the classroom to deal with the drama queen. Jameelah was standing there crying like she had been in a brawl. "What are you cryin' for?" Dariel said, grimacing.

Jameelah cried so hard that she could barely speak. "I'm tired of her! I know that bitch wants you but she can't have you," she said, sobbing heavily.

"Stop trippin', girl," he said, grabbing a tissue from Ms. Carter's desk and handing it to her so she could wipe the snot from her top lip. "See, this is what I'm talkin' about. You think everybody wants me and every girl you see me talkin' to you accuse me of messin' around with. This shit is gettin' real old."

Jameelah looked up at Trouble. "It ain't over, bitch!"

"Shut yo' damn mouth, girl!" Dariel shouted.

"Do you have everything under control here?" the teacher from across the hall asked Ms. Carter.

"Yes. Thank you," Ms. Carter replied with a smile.

Trouble smiled at Jameelah as she walked back to her seat. *Jyson taught me to kill my enemies with kindness 'cuz a smile hurts more than any punch*, she thought as she opened up her English book. "I'm gon' get that bitch one way or another," she mumbled.

"Okay, class, settle down," Ms. Carter said. "May I start teachin' now that all of the commotion is done and over with? I need for you guys to turn to chapter five in your English books."

Ms. Carter was still out of breath as she spoke. She was a short lady with long hair that she always kept in a bun, who always wore the latest fashion and knew all the latest gossip before anyone else. She looked more like a student than a teacher. Her smooth caramel skin was flawless and she didn't look a day over thirty.

"I had ya back," Falisha, another girl in the class, leaned over Trouble's back and whispered.

"You know good and well I didn't need no help 'cuz that bitch couldn't bust a grape in a fruit fight." Trouble laughed. She turned around and noticed Dariel staring at her. Jameelah was so occupied with fixing her hair that she never noticed.

When the bell rang Ms. Carter yelled out, "Okay, class, don't forget to read chapter six because there will be a quiz on Monday. Study and have a safe weekend." As Trouble stood up and picked her books up off her desk, Ms. Carter said, "Wait one minute, young lady. I would like to speak to you for a minute."

The other students looked back and forth at each other as Trouble set her books back down on top of her desk. Ms. Carter waited until the classroom was completely empty before speaking.

"Sit down, Candria," she instructed. Trouble sat down slowly in her chair. Ms. Carter turned around and looked at her over the rims of her glasses. "Now you know what happened in class today was totally inappropriate, but I did see who started the whole ordeal."

"Well, if you saw who started it, why am I the one in here talkin' to you?" Trouble asked, rolling her eyes.

"You have to be the bigger person in this situation. Jameelah is obviously jealous of you, can't you tell?"

Trouble shrugged her shoulders. *She has the right to be jealous of all this beauty*, she thought.

"I know more than you think I know, Candria." Ms. Carter pulled her chair out and took a seat. "Jameelah is insecure. She feels threatened by you," she said as she picked up her coffee mug and took a sip of her cold coffee.

"But I—"

"But nothin'," Ms. Carter said, cutting her off in mid-sentence. "Whether you want Dariel or not, she still feels threatened by you. So the next time she says anything to you, just ignore her and remember that you got something she wants."

"What do I have?" Trouble asked, curiously.

"You got the three B's."

"What are the three B's?" Trouble inquired.

"You'll figure it out one day." Ms. Carter smiled, stood up, pushed in her chair, and started erasing the chalkboard.

Trouble smiled as she stood up and pushed in her chair.

"Hey, Candria," Ms. Carter called out without taking her eyes off the chalkboard.

"Yes, Ms. Carter?"

"Don't forget to read chapter six."

Trouble nodded with a slight smile and then exited the classroom.

Two

"Girl, what happened?" Ta'liyah rushed over to Trouble and asked as she spotted her coming out of the lunch line.

"Nothin'. We just had a talk, that's all." As she started walking over to their favorite lunch table, Trouble asked Ta'liyah, "You got your food yet?"

"No, I'm gettin' ready to get in line now," Ta'liyah replied.

"All right, I'll meet you at the table," Trouble said as she went and took a seat.

"What's up, girl?" Regina asked before taking a bite from her cheeseburger.

"Hey now," Trouble responded, smiling.

Regina was Trouble's girl too, but they weren't as close as she and Ta'liyah. Regina was fun to be around. She was a little on the chunky side, but she still had no problem getting a boyfriend. She was light-skinned with long, sandy-brown hair and dark freckles on her face. Regina was not the smartest person, but she was lovable as a teddy bear and girlfriend could sing like an angel.

Carla, one of Trouble's many enemies, looked over at her and turned up her nose.

"Don't hate," Trouble said.

"What you turn yo' nose up at Trouble for?" Regina asked before stuffing a French fry into her already full mouth.

"Who turned up their nose?" Carla asked.

"Who else?" Regina replied.

"I didn't turn my nose up," Carla said, lying, as she got up from the lunch table and walked away.

"Fuck her. The bitch can't whoop me," Trouble said.

"What's goin' on over here?" Ta'liyah asked as she sat down at the table across from Trouble.

"You know how ya jealous-ass friend be turnin' her big-ass nose up at me every time I come around, that's all," Trouble said, rolling her eyes.

"I know you ain't studyin' that shit, are you?" Ta'liyah asked.

"Do it look like I am?" Trouble replied.

"Anyway," Regina said, changing the subject. "I'm tired of school."

"Hey, girl," Carla said as she walked back over to the lunch table and sat down next to Ta'liyah.

"What's up?" Ta'liyah asked.

"Anyway," Trouble said, rolling her eyes. "Now what were you sayin?" she asked Regina.

"Never mind," Regina said.

"Don't stop talkin' on my account," Carla said, grimacing.

"Fuck you, Carla. You ain't nobody," Trouble snapped.

Trouble had had enough of all Carla's smart-ass remarks. The only reason why she tolerated Carla at all was because she was a friend of Ta'liyah's and Trouble thanked God that she only had to put up with her when they were at school. Carla was never allowed to go over to Ta'liyah's house because her mother was the main one calling Ta'liyah a fast-ass hefah.

"What cha'll gon' do tonight?" Ta'liyah asked, changing the subject before things got out of hand.

Carla leaned back in her chair and answered, "I don't know. Why? What you got planned?"

"Well, my parents are goin' out of town for the weekend and I was thinking 'bout havin' one of my old fashioned get-togethers."

"I'm game. Shit, it's been a long-ass time since you've had one of them." Regina smiled as she took a huge bite from her candy bar.

"Count me in!" Carla exclaimed.

"What about you, Trouble?" Ta'liyah asked.

Trouble shrugged her shoulders. "I don't know. It all depends."

"On what?" Regina asked Trouble with a mouthful of chocolate.

"Stop talking with your mouth full. And it depends on if I get my chores and homework finished."

"Girl, it's Friday. You ain't got no job, so you can kick it wit' us, smokey," Ta'liyah said, laughing.

"I don't know. Like I said, I need to study." Trouble opened up her English notes and looked them over.

"It's Friday. Homework can wait until Sunday," Regina said.

"I'm hip," Ta'liyah added.

"See, that's what's wrong wit' ya grades now. Ya always waitin' until the last damn minute." Trouble shook her head in disgust.

"You mean to tell me that you ain't gon' kick it wit' ya girls?" Ta'liyah asked. "My parents done fucked around and left my brother, Tico, in charge of the house again.

And you know what happened the last time they did some jackass shit like that?"

"Yeah, you had a get-together and someone burnt a cigarette hole in ya parents' brand-new carpet in their bedroom," Regina said, laughing.

"That shit wasn't funny! I got put on punishment for a whole month behind that shit," Ta'liyah snapped.

"I still don't know. I'll call you if I decide to come," Trouble said nonchalantly.

"Whatever," Ta'liyah said before spotting her cousin. "Hey, Dariel, come here," she yelled across the crowded lunchroom. He was sitting at the table with his boys, Charlie and Marcus, chopping it up about all the fly girls in the lunchroom.

"Man, look at Trouble over there lookin' all delicious and shit," Charlie said.

"She sho'll is the bomb. It ain't a broad in this school that looks better than her," Marcus added. "Too bad I had her best friend 'cuz I would be at her. What you think about her, D?"

Dariel didn't respond. He kept his comments to himself, not wanting to reveal how he really felt about the beautiful black princess with the hazel eyes. Jameelah wasn't slacking in the looks department, either. Her fivefoot-six frame was strapped in all the right places. Her hair hung neatly on her shoulders with Chinese cut bangs resting on her slightly enlarged forehead and green contacts to disguise her plain dark eyes.

"Oh, that's right. He can't talk about another girl, not while he's with Thunder Dome!" Marcus said as he and Charlie laughed.

Dariel laughed too. "Don't hate on my girl, nigga. You ain't got no woman, so shut the fuck up. She might have a thunder dome but she got a head game that's outta this world!" Dariel bragged.

"I bet she do got a good-ass head game. It's big enough," Charlie retorted.

"Fuck you, nigga," Dariel laughed. "Wit' yo' Dennis Rodman–lookin' ass." Dariel laughed his way over to his cousin and her girls. "What's up, 'cuz and ladies?" he said upon approaching their table.

"What's so funny?" Ta'liyah asked.

"Nothin'. Me and my boys was over there crackin' on each other, that's all."

"Anyway, I'm havin' a get-together tonight, so bring some of your boys. But do me a favor and leave Marcus's punk ass at home."

"Why can't he come?" Dariel asked. "Ah, yeah, that's right. I forgot after he tapped that ass he went around and told everybody about it." Dariel laughed, covering his sexy lips with his hand.

"Forget you, Dariel," Ta'liyah said, grimacing.

"My bad, 'cuz. You know I love you." He smiled. "Anyway, who all gon' be there?"

"Just a few people. It ain't gon' be nothin' spectacular," Ta'liyah said.

"Yeah, you always say that and it turns out to be some-thin' different," Regina said, adding her two cents.

Dariel looked down at Trouble and smiled. "You comin'?" he asked her.

I wish I was cumming, she wanted to say. "I don't know yet. I have a few things I have to get done around my house." Trouble didn't know why she felt nervous all of a sudden. She had talked to Dariel a million times before, but this time something was different.

"What could be more important than kickin' it wit' me?" he asked arrogantly.

Trouble took a deep breath. *This fine-ass nigga look so good!* she thought. "I don't know. Like I said, I might be there and I might not be," she replied nonchalantly.

Dariel reached down and massaged Trouble's shoulders. "Come on, quit bein' a lame and come kick it wit' us," he said, smiling.

Oh my goodness, please don't stop, she begged inside her head. Trouble enjoyed the warm feeling that Dariel gave her when he touched her body. "I'll see," she said, trying to remain cool.

"It's on then. Y'all supply the drinks and I'll supply the smoke," Dariel said. He looked back down at Trouble and winked before walking back over to the table to tell Charlie about the party that was about to jump off tonight.

"Ummm ummmp ummmp, he looks so damn good," Carla said, licking her lips as she watched Dariel walk away.

"I'm hip. That nigga looks good enough to eat," Regina added.

"Bitch, you'll eat anything. You always talkin' about food, wit' yo' greedy ass," Ta'liyah joked. Trouble and Carla laughed uncontrollably.

Regina had to laugh herself. "Fuck you, bitch."

"You know you my girl," Ta'liyah laughed and grabbed Regina's chubby cheeks. "Dariel is a fine young man. But hey, he can't help it 'cuz it runs in my family," she boasted.

"Shit, you a lie! If it runs in the family, it ran the opposite direction when it came to you," Regina joked.

Trouble, Carla, and Ta'liyah laughed until their sides hurt.

"Fuck you. You got me back," Ta'liyah said, wiping the tears from laughter away from her eyes. "I think Dariel likes someone at this table," she said, looking over in Trouble's direction.

"Yeah, Jameelah, but she ain't sittin' at this table," Trouble said, looking up from her English notes for a brief second.

"Naw, not her," Ta'liyah said, smiling.

Trouble thought for a minute and started smiling. "What we drinkin' on tonight?"

"Now that's what I'm talkin' about," Regina and Ta'liyah said simultaneously.

"I'm gon' have Tico go to the liquor store and get some Grey Goose, E & J, and all kinds of shit," Ta'liyah said, excited.

"I'm gon' bring some of my momma's whiskey," Regina added.

"And what you gon' bring, Trouble?" Ta'liyah asked.

"All I'm bringin' is my cup," she said and they all laughed.

Three

Trouble walked through her front door and threw her book bag on the brand new leather sofa. She ran into her room and opened up her closet to see what outfit she could wear to the party. *I got to wear somethin' new,* she thought. She sorted through all the clothes with the tags still on them and they just weren't right for tonight's party. *I need somethin' bangin',* she thought.

"Trouble," Jyson yelled.

"What's up?" she called out.

"Here," he said, entering her room and then handing her two shopping bags.

"What's this?"

"Open 'em up and see."

Trouble ripped through the first bag and pulled out a shirt and a pair of jeans. "This outfit is tight, big bra'," she yelled as she held up the pair of Akademiks Scorpio logo jeans with a graf-scipt print on the thigh. There was a whiteand-blue Akademiks shirt with the same print on the front of it. She quickly opened up the second bag. "Dang, these shoes just came out yesterday," she exclaimed, referring to the new Nike Air Coupe 2's Jyson had just bought her.

"I take it you like your outfit?" Jyson asked.

"Like it? I love it. I'm wearin' this to the party tonight."

Jyson looked at his sister. "What party?"

"Oh, Ta'liyah is havin' a party tonight," she said as she thought about how good she was going to look in her new outfit.

"Did I hear anyone ask if they could go to a party tonight?" Jyson asked playfully.

"Oh, yeah, may I go to Ta'liyah's party tonight, please?"

"I don't know. I don't think you've begged long enough," Jyson teased.

"Now you know you ain't gon' be home anyway, so I really didn't have to ask."

"You didn't ask. You told me you were goin' to the party," Jyson said. "Is there gon' be any niggas over there?"

Trouble didn't want to lie to her big brother, so she did what any other teenage girl would have done . . . she lied. "Naw, it ain't gon' be no niggas over there. It's just a chick thing."

Jyson gave his sister the evil eye. "All right now. You know what I told you about them knucklehead-ass niggas. All they want is one thing and if they get it from you, they might as well be gettin' it from me, and I don't like dick. You know what I mean?"

"Yeah, I know what you mean," Trouble said, rolling her eyes as she turned to go to the bathroom to try on her new outfit.

"And don't think I won't come over to Ta'liyah's house to see what's goin' on over there," Jyson said as his sister walked away. Knowing his sister like the back of his hand, he knew that there would be a houseful of niggas at the party.

"All right, come over," Trouble said before she was out of sight.

Trouble knew that her brother would be too wrapped up in all those women that be taking care of him to be coming to the party.

Jyson looked at his ringing cell phone and hesitated before answering it. "Who dis?" he asked with a serious attitude.

"Damn, nigga, this yo' brother. What's with the attitude?"

"Oh, what's up, bra'? Man, you know I don't like answerin' private calls. Shit, make a muthafucka think it's the police or somethin'." Jyson exited Trouble's room and headed for his own.

"Naw, man, you know I'm far from bein' the police," Big Mike said.

Big Mike was a solid 325-pound brotha with a lazy eye and a mouthful of platinum teeth. He put a lot of people in the mind of Debo and his reputation was of the same, but he was the best friend Jyson ever had. And even though Big Mike was eight years his senior, they still had a lot in common: bitches, money, and cars! Big Mike looked at Jyson as his little brother. Being an only child, Big Mike took Jyson under his wing, only because he reminded him of himself when he was young and buck-wild. Big Mike always wanted a younger brother but never had the chance to have one because his mother died from a drug overdose when she was seven months pregnant. The baby, which they later learned was a boy, didn't survive. It shattered his entire world. Big Mike took Jyson under his wing and loved and protected him like his blood sibling and dared anyone to fuck with him.

"What you gon' get into tonight?" Jyson asked. He pulled out his nightstand drawer and grabbed a bag. He then started rolling up his last bag of hydro.

"I'm 'bout to go to the club and get a couple of drinks. Feel like taggin' along?"

"Hell yeah. You know I haven't been in the spot since you remodeled it. And plus, I need a drink or two myself."

"You ain't got no problems, do you? You sound like you stressed-out about somethin'. You don't need me to grab my bitch and fuck one of these ho-ass niggas up around here, do you?" Big Mike was as serious as a heart attack.

"I'm cool, man," he said as he finished rolling a blunt and then lit it. "I'll tell you about it at the club." Jyson and his big brother talked a few more minutes before hanging up. He picked up his mother's Gladys

Knight album cover and proceeded to cut up an ounce of crack to give to one of his workers.

"Damn, this is some fire," he said after taking a pull from the blunt.

"How do I look, Jyson?" Trouble said as she walked into her brother's room. She went into a state of shock as she watched her brother blow smoke from the blunt out his nose.

"Don't you know how to knock?" he yelled after looking up at his sister.

She didn't respond. She just turned around and walked out the room, slamming the door behind her.

"Here we go," he said, carefully laying the album cover on top of his bed, trying not to spill any crumbs. Jyson walked to his sister's room and knocked softly on her door. "Trouble, can I come in?" he asked, pushing the door open before she could answer him. "Trouble, what's wrong, sis?"

"Nothin'," she snapped. She stared out her bedroom window and watched Ms. Lorraine from across the street as she struggled with a bag of groceries in one hand and her badass grandson, Marco, in the other.

"Well, why did you run out my room like you saw a ghost or somethin'? You've really been buggin' out on me lately. What's the matter with you?"

"You promised me, Jyson. You promised me when we were younger that you would never do drugs. Do you remember that?" Tears began to roll down the side of her soft cheeks.

Jyson took a deep breath. "I know, sis, but it's not like I'm smokin' crack," he said defensively.

"You might as well. It's all drugs," she shouted.

"Bud comes from the earth and crack comes from somethin' totally different," he tried desperately to explain.

"Whatever. And that explains where you be gettin' all your money from."

"How did you think I got it? I know you didn't think I had a nine-to-five and I know damn well you didn't think that little money Daddy sends us every week pays for all the bills, food, and puts all those expensive clothes on our backs. I wish it did so I wouldn't have to be out in them streets riskin' my life."

"Well, I just thought all those females that be blowin' your cell phone up be givin' you money or even sellin' weed, but crack, Jyson?" she said.

"They do give me money and lots of it, but a real man fends for himself. I can't have no woman take care of me. I would feel less than a man if I did some jackass shit like that. Come on, sis, you know me better than that."

"Well, sellin' drugs ain't gon' get you but two places, dead or in jail," she said furiously.

"That's just a chance I'm gon' hafta take, li'l sis. But for the time bein', sellin' drugs is payin' for this house, your expensive-ass taste, and everything else," he explained.

Trouble thought for a second because she knew that she did have an expensive lifestyle. She enjoyed spending money, and if it wasn't for her brother keeping her pockets filled, there's no telling what she would do to get it because she had an image to uphold.

"I'd rather you struggle than to have you out in them streets riskin' your life for the almighty dollar," she said sincerely.

"Sis, I don't know what to tell you, but I'm not gon' struggle no more. I had enough of that when we were growin' up. Remember how times use to be after Daddy left? There were many days where me and you didn't have nothin' to eat, remember that? And I used to go to E and B and steal us some hamburger and shit. How long has it been since you went to the refrigerator and it was bare? It hasn't been like that in a long time, now has it?"

Trouble shook her head no. She had no other choice but to accept the fact that her brother sold drugs, and no matter what she said, he was not going to stop. So she just hoped and prayed that he would stay safe in the streets. "Jyson, can I ask you a question?"

"Sure."

"Do you still love Momma?"

"Of course I still love Momma. Just 'cuz she's all fucked-up wouldn't give me a reason not to still love her. She is still our momma, regardless of her drug habit. Just give her some time, sis, she'll get it together. Momma is a strong woman," Jyson said, not believing his own words.

"Time ain't what she need. She needs to get her triflin' ass out that crack house and come home to be a mother to us," Trouble said. Jyson was shocked by Trouble's remark. "Look at us, Jyson. You dropped out of school; you sell drugs and you smoke 'em. Why does it seem like I'm in this bullshit all alone? I didn't even have Momma here when I started my period. I didn't even know how to use a tampon, and if it wasn't for Ta'liyah's mom showin' me how to use one, I don't know what I would have done. Momma shoulda been here for me."

Jyson felt bad for his sister and wanted to take her pain away so badly. He loved his little sister with all his heart because she was the only real family he had except for Big Mike. There was nothing in the world that he wouldn't do for her. If she would have come to him and asked him how to use a tampon, he would have done his best to show her how. Now that's love.

"Momma shoulda been here for you. You shouldn't have had to go through it alone. But that's what I admire about you. When shit starts to get rough, you know how to handle it. But me, on the other hand, I always look for the easy way out. Things will get better, Trouble."

"I sure hope so." Trouble forced a smile on her face as her brother grabbed her by the neck and held on tightly. They hugged for what seemed like an eternity. "Jyson," she called out.

"Yeah, sis?"

"I can't breathe," she said, laughing.

"Sorry." He laughed and let her go. "Okay, enough mushy stuff. I'm 'bout to get dressed and I'll drop you off over to Ta'liyah's." He headed toward the door.

"I don't need no ride. I'll walk 'cuz I wanna be late so everybody's attention will be on me when I walk through the door."

"Talk about conceited," he said as he went to his room.

"I'm not conceited, I'm convinced." Trouble nodded her head and smiled.

Jyson walked into his room to change his clothes. Twenty minutes later he walked out all dressed up and smelling good. "Okay, sis, I'm about to bounce," he said as his cell phone rang. Looking at the caller ID, he put it in his jacket pocket.

"Who was that?" Trouble asked.

"Damn, you are so nosy." Jyson playfully pushed his sister. "Now call me if you need me."

"I will. And be careful in them streets."

"I love you, Trouble," he said.

"Damn, boy, what's wrong wit' you? You act like you about to die or somethin'," Trouble said, coming out of her bedroom.

"You never know. And plus, I just want you to know that I love you," Jyson said.

"I already know. I love you too."

"Don't forget what I said, Trouble. Don't be nobody's fool and don't forget your curfew," Jyson said as he checked his image in the mirror one last time.

"I'm not gon' forget. I'll be home around four a.m.," she joked. She knew it didn't matter what time she came in the house because Jyson wouldn't be there anyhow . . . she hoped.

"All right, you can come in here at four a.m. if you want to," Jyson said, giving his sister the evil eye. "Have you seen my Usher CD?" he asked as he fumbled through his CD collection that he had neatly stacked on the shelf in the living room.

"It's in my room," she replied.

"I shoulda known. Okay, I'm out." Jyson walked to the front door, turned around, looked at his sister, and smiled.

Man, she is growing up, he thought as he walked to his car and jumped in his chromed-out brand new Grand Prix. Jyson loved his car almost as much as he loved his sister. His car was all black with gray leather interior. The tint on the windows was so dark that you could barely see who was driving. The twenty-two-inch rims he had on the tires set the entire car off. And every time he rode down the avenue, the females jocked his load and the small-time dope boys hated on it. Jyson always smiled at the haters as he rode by in his baby with the personalized license plates that read JOY RIDE.

Trouble went into the bathroom and jumped in the shower. She made sure she hit all the right spots because tonight just might be the night that she became a woman.

"I can hear my brother now," she said out loud. "Havin' sex doesn't make you a woman. Responsibility turns a girl into a woman."

Trouble shook those words from her head as she dried off. She sat on the edge of her bed and put lotion all over her body. She sprayed on a few squirts of Nanadebary Pink on her neck and behind her ears before slipping into her new Victoria's Secret panty and bra set. She smiled as she thought about what her momma used to say to her when she was a little girl as she watched her get dressed to go out.

"Always wear your best panty and bra set," she would say. " 'Cuz you never know what you might get into or what might get into you."

Trouble looked over at the picture of her father that sat on top of her dresser and instantly got an attitude. *I can't believe you left Momma for a nasty-ass ho,* she thought. *Momma was the only somebody who had your damn back. She was there when your own damn family didn't wanna be bothered with you.* Trouble began to speak out loud. "Momma stayed with you even when she knew you was fuckin' around with all different types of bitches and you repay her by leavin' her with two children to raise on her own! You fuckin' deadbeat-ass muthafucka," Trouble shouted at the picture of her father.

Trouble's mind wandered to when her daddy used to bring her and Jyson Christmas and birthday presents every year until he got with Miss Parker. After Miss Parker they got nothing. *I don't know what got into him,* Trouble thought. *But I don't give a damn no way. He ain't never got to call me or talk to me another day of his life.*

Trouble walked over and knocked the picture down on the floor. She walked back into the bathroom and checked her image in the long mirror that hung on the back of the door. "I think my butt gettin' big," she sung the verse from one of Nelly's songs. The phone rang as she stared at her big backside.

"Hello?" she answered.

"Hello, is Trouble home?" the caller asked.

"Who is this?"

"This is Dariel," he answered.

"Oh what's up? How you get my new number?"

"Does it matter how I got your number?"

"Not really. I was just curious 'cuz Jyson just got it changed the other day," she said.

"Now you know curiosity killed the cat," he teased. "But if you really must know, Ta'liyah gave it to me."

"It's cool," she said, smiling. For some odd reason she was nervous. Even though she had talked to Dariel a million times on the phone, this time something was totally different. "So what's your reason for callin' me? You gon' answer the question I asked you in school today?"

"First off, do I need a reason to call you? And secondly, I'm not gon' answer your question because you already know the answer to it. Anyway, have you made up your mind about comin' to the party tonight?"

"I don't know. Do you want me to come?" she asked as she laced up her new tennis shoes.

"Yeah. I wanna see you."

"For what? Inquiring minds wanna know," she said, smiling.

"Just be there," Dariel said, and hung up the phone without uttering another word.

Trouble lay back on her bed in disbelief. "No, this punk did not just hang up on me," she said to herself with a chuckle. "Shit, if it wasn't for me wantin' to show off my new outfit, I wouldn't even show up at the party."

She got up from her bed and went into the bathroom and brushed her teeth. She put some lip gloss on and sprayed her French roll with some spritz. "Damn girl, you look good!" she said to the image in the mirror. She went into the living room and grabbed her Perry Ellis jacket out of the closet because the weatherman said that it was going to get chilly tonight, but if she was lucky, she would have Dariel to keep her warm!

Four

"What's up, man?" Jyson asked, sitting down at the table across from his brother. "What's up, J?" Big Mike shouted over the loud music that the DJ was spinning.

"I like what you've done to the place," Jyson said, looking around at the newly remodeled night club. He admired the sunken dance floor, the animal cages, along with the big booty strippers that walked around scantily dressed.

Big Mike smiled at his own accomplishments. "Yeah, it's a little somethin' for the people." He looked around proudly. "Hey, Michaela, get me and my brother a double shot of Hennessy with no chaser!" Big Mike called out to one of his waitresses.

"No chaser? Who do you think I am?" Jyson said, giving Big Mike a distraught look. "I need somethin' to drink behind that shit, and by the way, who's the new waitress?"

"Who, Michaela? She's the new stripper I hired. She's only been here about a week. She came over here when she quit Showboat's. She came up in here talkin' 'bout she needed a job so she could finish payin' for school."

"She's in college too?" Jyson chuckled, shaking his head.

"Yeah. She's what you would call an educated stripper." Big Mike let out a hearty laugh and then finished off the rest of his drink.

"So you mean to tell me that your strippers are your waitresses too?"

"Why wouldn't they be? That way a muthafucka can get up close and personal with the strippers, and it's cheaper too."

Michaela walked over and sat two fresh drinks down in front of them. "Thank you," Jyson said, showing off his million-dollar smile.

"Thanks nothin'! It's about damn time!" Big Mike said.

Michaela rolled her eyes. "Whatever," she said, not paying any attention to the way Jyson was staring at her.

"Damn, she is double O.T.C.," Jyson said when she walked away.

"What is double O.T.C.?" Big Mike asked.

"One of the coldest," Jyson laughed.

"Yeah, she is fine as hell. Let me introduce y'all. Come here, Michaela," Big Mike yelled across the almost full club.

"Now I'm gon' warn you, baby girl is a big-ass freak. You think you can handle it?"

"How do you know she's a freak? Don't tell me that you fucked her too?" Jyson hoped his answer would be no.

"Naw. My boy Rudy used to fuck wit' the broad, and he said she could suck a bowlin' ball through a water hose!" Big Mike got excited and started pounding on the table.

"What's up?" she asked with her hands on her hips, looking down at Big Mike.

"I want to introduce you to my brother, Jyson."

"What's up, Jyson?" Michaela said, paying close attention to the fine young brother who sat before her. "Aren't you too young to be up in a place like this?" she asked.

Goodness, this brotha is so fine, with his sexy hazel eyes and a smile that could melt an iceberg, she thought.

"Give me thirty minutes alone with you and I'll show you young," Jyson responded with a sly grin.

Big Mike bounced up and down with laughter. "I guess he told you."

"Yeah, I guess he did," she said, blushing. "Look, I gotta go get ready for my show. Are you gon' be here for a minute?"

You think I'm gon' pass up a chance to see all that ass?

Jyson thought. "Yeah, I'm gon' be here."

Damn, it should be a law against looking that good, Michaela thought as she walked away and disappeared behind a long black curtain.

"I think she likes you, li'l bra'," Big Mike slurred.

Jyson smiled at the thought.

Ciara's "Goodies" came on and Michaela walked out on stage and worked the pole like a nine-to-five. She wrapped her long legs around the pole and made love to it while hanging upside down. Michaela was Jyson's type of girl. She was not too tall and not too short; she was just right for him. Her long, curly hair told Jyson that she indeed had Indian in her family. Her light complexion reminded him of Lynn's off of the sitcom *Girlfriends*, which was a plus in Jyson's book because he loved himself a light-skinned sista. Her eyes sparkled as she looked seductively at the men in the audience. Michaela moved her body like she was put on this earth to dance, never missing a beat. By the time her performance ended, she had all the men standing on their feet wanting to touch her voluptuous body and wishing they could be the one she laid with at night.

"Man, that broad is flexible," Jyson shouted over the loud cheers.

Big Mike smiled and shook his head in agreement.

Michaela walked off the stage and over to Jyson's table.

"You like?" she asked him.

Jyson smiled widely. "Yeah, it was cool," he said, trying to sound nonchalant. But in reality she made his warrior as hard as a brick with all those splits and twists she had done.

"Well, um, let me go get changed and I'll be back out here to talk to you," she said, smiling.

"You ain't off work yet," Big Mike said.

"My shift is over at eleven p.m., and by my watch it is officially eleven-oh-one p.m.," she said smirking, and walked away. She turned around and caught Jyson staring at her backside, along with every other man in the club.

"Damn, man, you haven't even held a real conversation with the broad and she's all over you. Boy, you got game," Big Mike said as he picked up his drink and took it to the head.

"Hey, what can I say? I've been known to have that effect on a lot of women," Jyson bragged.

"What type of effect do you have on women?" Michaela asked as she stood behind Jyson. She wore a cutoff T-shirt with *Fahairi* written in glitter on the front of it, and a pair of tight fitting Lady Enyce jeans that revealed her shapely rear end.

"Me and my brotha was just shootin' the shit, that's all," Jyson said.

Michaela looked around the club. The crowd was starting to die down since no more strippers were performing. The men loved the Friday-night strip shows. The line would be serried outside with men standing for hours waiting to see the big-booty women shake their asses.

Man, I gotta have this fine-ass brotha, even if it's only for one night, Michaela thought.

"I feel like the third wheel, so I'm 'bout to bounce on up outta here," Big Mike slurred. "My wife is waitin' on me, so I will see you two later." Big Mike stood up and staggered away. "Don't do nothin' I wouldn't do," he called over his shoulder.

"I ain't about to let my brotha drive home drunk," Jyson said to Michaela and got up and walked away to catch up with him. "Hey, you ain't 'bout to drive home, are you, man?" Jyson called to Big Mike.

Big Mike smiled with a drunken look on his face. "Hey, that's right, I forgot, friends don't let friends drive drunk."

Michaela approached Jyson and Big Mike.

"Do you wanna ride with me?" Jyson turned to Michaela and asked, not knowing she was already prepared to go before he asked.

I'm not lettin' you slip away, she thought. "Sure, why not?" She put her gym bag over her shoulder and followed them to Jyson's car.

"Come on, bra'," Jyson said, guiding Big Mike.

"This is a nice car," Michaela said.

"Thanks." Jyson shot Michaela another one of his million-dollar smiles before unlocking the car door.

"Naw, you get in the front," Big Mike slurred to Michaela. "I'ma sit my big ass in the backseat and get me some rest."

Michaela watched as Big Mike fumbled with the door handle.

"Here, let me help you." She opened the door and Big Mike got in and fell straight to sleep. "He is too drunk."

"I know. That ain't nothin' new. Just keep on workin' here and you'll see." Jyson took his Scarface CD out of the player and put on something nice and mellow.

Michaela moved her head to the beat of the music. "This is nice. Who is it?"

"This is Jean-Luc Ponty," he replied.

"Wow. I never would have imagined that you listened to stuff like this," she said, impressed.

"What? You thought all I listened to was hard-core rap music?" Jyson asked.

"To tell you the truth, yes I did," she replied honestly.

"I do got a soft side to me too," he said, smiling, making her melt in her seat.

Jyson pulled up in front of a gorgeous Victorian-style home with a four-car garage that had all four sections occupied with vehicles. Big Mike was living large. He went from selling rocks to boulders. But after a while he figured that he couldn't obtain the type of riches he wanted just by selling drugs, so he took the money he made and put it to work for him. He bought an abandoned building and turned it into one of the hottest strip clubs in town. He also bought several run-down houses and fixed them up and placed them on section eight. Big Mike invested his money wisely, plus he was still deep in the dope game, supplying all the big-time dope boys. Big Mike kept him a Cuban connect and he wouldn't let nobody know who he was, not even Jyson.

"My goodness. Big Mike lives here?" Michaela asked as they pulled in front of his house. She was amazed by the ritzy neighborhood and the size of the house.

"Yeah, this is where my brotha lives," Jyson said proudly.

Big Mike and his wife were the only real black family in their neighborhood. Yet they did have another black family, the Winstons, that lived a couple of doors down from them, but they didn't act black. They were white people trapped in black bodies. Big Mike called them blacaucasians. He said that he waved at the family one day, but they didn't wave back because Mr. Winston found out that Big Mike had tried to holla at their teenage daughter. He would have knocked her off if her mother wouldn't have threatened to call the police on him. Mr. Winston would always turn up his nose when Big Mike came home bumping rap music out of his truck stereo. He really knew something was wrong with them when Sherry, his wife, baked a sweet potato pie from scratch one Thanksgiving and took it over, and Mrs. Winston said she'd take it, but she'd rather had pumpkin.

Big Mike loved Sherry and all, but he just couldn't stop messing around on her. He gave her everything she wanted and he thought she was content with that, but she wasn't. His wife didn't have to work and they had no children, so she didn't have to share her money with anyone other than the daughter he had by some hood rat that used to work at the club.

Big Mike's philosophy was: I give my wife every-thing and I give the hoes I fuck with nothing but dick. He bought his wife the half-a-million-dollar house, thinking that it would keep her happy, but it didn't. It was a nice neighborhood and all, but the neighbors were too damn nosy for Big Mike. Some of them spoke and others turned their heads and pretended like they were occupied with doing other things. Most of the neighbors tried to figure out how a black man who wasn't not a doctor or a lawyer could afford to live in the neighborhood. No one really knew Big Mike's occupation. All they knew was he could afford to keep up with the Joneses.

"Hey man, you home," Jyson said to Big Mike, reaching back to shake him.

"All right, thanks, man," Big Mike yawned as he fumbled for the door handle.

"Here, let me help you." Jyson got out of the car and walked around and helped his brother out. He walked him to the front porch and rang the doorbell. Sherry must have been sitting by the door waiting on her husband because she opened it right away.

"Hey Jyson, how are you?" Sherry smiled. "I see my husband has been shootin' his regular."

"I'm doin' fine," Jyson said, giving her a hug and a kiss on the cheek. Jyson helped Big Mike to the living room sofa and took off his boots. "All right, man, I'll talk to you tomorrow," he said, but didn't get any response. Big Mike was sleeping like a baby.

"Thanks, Jyson, for drivin' him home. I done told him time after time, he's gon' get enough of drivin' drunk."

"Now you know Big Mike is hardheaded," Jyson said, smiling, giving Sherry goose bumps.

"How's Candria doin'?"

"She's growin' up," he responded.

Damn, this nigga is so fine! she thought as she tried to contain herself. "I bet she is." She untied her short red robe so that Jyson could admire her body a little more. "Tell her I said hello."

"I sure will," Jyson said, feeling a little uneasy because his best friend's wife stood before him with a short nightgown that revealed damn near all her action.

"I know she has all the boys chasin' after her," Sherry said, taking a step closer to Jyson.

He took a quick step back. "Yeah, she does and the little hefah is conceited as hell."

Sherry took another step closer. "Ain't nothin' wrong with bein' secure with yourself, is it? If you're not secure with the way you look, no one else will be either, am I right?"

Sherry looked at her husband's best friend with lust in her eyes.

"Well, um, I'm 'bout to go. Tell your *husband* that I'll see him tomorrow." Jyson made sure he emphasized the word *husband*. He looked over at Big Mike and headed for the front door.

Sherry grabbed him by the arm and said, "You gotta leave so soon?" The tone in her voice almost sounded desperate.

"Yeah . . . yeah, I do. I got somebody in the car waitin' on me."

"Oh, I see. Okay then. Well, feel free to stop by anytime, and I do mean *anytime*."

Jyson fumbled with the locks on the front door. He tried his best to get the door unlocked, but it was impossible because Big Mike had his house secured like Fort Knox.

"Here, let me help you," Sherry said as she walked past, rubbing up against him. She pretended like she dropped something on the floor and bent down in front of Jyson, revealing her pantyless rear end.

Oh my word! All that pussy and ass that's starin' me the face, he thought. Sherry was fine as hell and she had the body to go with it, which was rare in most cases. Jyson couldn't understand for the life of him how Big Mike could mess around with all those other chicken-heads when he had a black goddess at home.

Sherry gave Jyson a devilish grin before unlocking the door. "See you later," she said.

Jyson hurried out the door with his warrior on hard, nearly tripping over the huge statue that sat on the front lawn.

"I thought you forgot about me," Michaela joked when Jyson got back into the car.

"How could I do a thing like that? You look too good sit-tin' over there in that *fahairi* shirt. My sister-in-law was in there talkin' my head off."

"Oh."

"Where to?" he asked.

"I live on the south end of town, you know, over there by Prospect School." Michaela sat back and enjoyed the ride.

Jyson looked over at Michaela. "Can I ask you a question?"

"Sure, go ahead," she said, smiling.

"Now, I hope you don't get offended by what I'm about to ask you," Jyson said.

"Why would I do somethin' like that?" Michaela asked.

"I keep lookin' over at your shirt and wonderin' what *fahairi* means. It's buggin' the hell outta me," Jyson laughed.

"And all this time I thought you were starin' at my breasts," she teased.

I was doin' that too, he thought. "Now why would I do somethin' like that? I'm a perfect gentleman," he lied.

"That's good to know. Anyway, *fahairi* is Swahili and it means to have pride in oneself," she explained. "And this shirt best describes the type of person I am."

"Shit, I need to get my sister one of those shirts."

"How many sisters do you have, if you don't mind me askin'?"

"I have one sister. Her name is Trouble. Well, it's Candria, we just call her Trouble."

"I hope she doesn't live up to her name," Michaela said.

"Naw. She's a pretty good girl. She's a teenager and you know how teenage girls can get."

"No, I don't. Tell me."

"I'd rather not get into it. Let's change the subject. Do you have any brothers or sisters?" Jyson asked.

"Yes, I have two sisters, Sheila and Shannon. I'm the youngest."

"So you were spoiled?"

"I still am," she chuckled.

Jyson and Michaela rode around for hours talking about their families and their hopes and dreams. He didn't want the night to end and neither did she. He had to think of something and quick. "Are you hungry?"

"You must have been readin' my mind or listenin' to my stomach." Michaela put her hands on her stomach as if she was trying to calm the growling down.

"Let's go to Denny's then, 'cuz I need some pancakes to soak up all the liquor I drank."

"That sounds good to me," Michaela said, smiling.

"Then Denny's it is." Jyson returned the smile.

Five

Earlier that night . . .

"Hey, girl," Ta'liyah screamed as Trouble walked through the door.

"Hey, girl. Shit, I thought this was supposed to be a get-together?" Trouble asked, looking around at all the guests that were sprawled all around the house.

"I thought the same thing, but you know how it is when word gets out about a party."

"Let's just hope don't nobody start no shit 'cuz I ain't tryin'a get my outfit dirty," Trouble said.

"I feel you," Ta'liyah agreed. "Oh, Dariel has been lookin' for you." Ta'liyah smiled.

"And? I came here to kick it and to show off my new hookup, not to see Dariel." Trouble closed her eyes and asked God to forgive her for lying.

"Whatever."

"What do you mean, whatever?"

"Trouble, you act like I just met yo' ass today or somethin'. You just closed your eyes and asked God to forgive you for lyin'."

"All right, all right, maybe I did come here to get a little glimpse of him. But you know I don't mess with other ladies' men."

"I know you don't." Ta'liyah grabbed Trouble by the arm and led her into the kitchen. Tico and two of his friends walked through the front door with three cases of beer.

"I got that fire, that fire, that good shit," Dariel sang as he walked into the kitchen. He stopped dead in his tracks as his eyes met Trouble's. "What's up, baby girl?" He had one of the biggest Kool-Aid smiles on his face. "I see you couldn't resist kickin' it wit' me," he said, giving her a hug.

"Get it right. I couldn't resist kickin' it wit' my girl."

"Got blunts?" Tico asked, approaching them. "Damn girl, you look good," he said, looking over at Trouble.

"Thanks," she replied as if she didn't already know.

"I got blunts," Dariel answered. He reached into his book bag and pulled out a box of strawberry Swishers along with a fat-ass sack of bud.

"We 'bout to get blowed," Ta'liyah said, bobbing her head to Ice Cube's new song.

Damn near everyone in the house was getting their wigs blew back . . . getting high! Every corner Trouble turned, someone was blowing smoke in her face. Tico even had the nerve to try to pass one her way a few times.

"No thanks, I don't indulge," she said, waving the smoke out of her face.

"She's a square," Carla said.

"Keep talkin' and I'm gon' be squared off in yo' ass," Trouble retorted.

"Dang." Tico laughed.

"That was a good one." Ta'liyah laughed too.

Carla rolled her eyes without saying anything else because she knew that she couldn't win a fight against Trouble.

Trouble eyed Dariel from the top of his braids to the bottom of his shell toe Adidas he sported. She watched his mouth every time he wrapped his juicy lips around the tip of the blunt. *Shit, I wish those were my lips he was suckin' on and I'm not talkin' about the top pair either!* she thought. She got up and walked into the kitchen and poured herself a double shot of gin.

"I got this new mix CD," Dariel said, pulling it out of his book bag.

"Damn, what else do you got in that bag?" Ta'liyah laughed.

"Don't worry 'bout all that, 'cuz if I tell you I'm gon' hafta kill you."

People were dancing and bobbing their heads to the music while Trouble sat on the couch sipping on her gin through a straw. She could feel herself starting to get drunk.

Tico sat down on the couch next to Trouble. "You all right?" he asked.

"Yeah, I'm cool. I'm sittin' here on cloud nine," she said, smiling.

"Ahhh, that's my cut," Tico yelled loudly in her ear. "You wanna dance?" He stood up and extended his hand.

"Yeah, why not?"

Trouble stood up and walked into the middle of the living room floor and she and Tico danced while the sounds of T.I. blared out the speakers. Trouble moved her body like she was auditioning for a music video. She gyrated all over Tico's body. She wasn't sure, but she could have sworn that she felt his manhood jump a few times. She caught Dariel watching her every move, so she danced even freakier.

"Ahhh sulky sulky," Tico yelled as his warrior hardened.

Trouble walked back over to the couch when the song was over. But before she could take her seat, someone grabbed her around the waist.

"Hey," she slurred. "What are you doin'?" She turned around and smiled at Dariel as he firmly held her.

"Let's go," he said.

"Where we goin'?" Trouble asked as her head began to spin from all the secondhand reefah smoke she had inhaled.

"You comin' or not?"

"Damn, let me get my jacket." The night air was brisk for it to be the beginning of September and Trouble wasn't taking any chances on getting sick.

"Where y'all 'bout to go?" Ta'liyah asked, grabbing Trouble by the arm.

"For a walk. It's too smoky in here," Dariel replied.

"She need to walk 'cuz she is fried," Ta'liyah said. "See y'all later."

Trouble and Dariel walked down the dark street. There was no movement at all except for a couple of stray alley cats that were fighting over a scrap from the trash can.

"What's up wit' that?" Dariel asked out of nowhere.

"Up wit' what? I don't know what you talkin' about," Trouble played.

"What was up wit' Tico feelin' all over your ass?"

"We were just dancin', that's all."

"It looked like y'all was doin' more than just dancin' to me."

"It sounds like someone is jealous to me."

"I ain't jealous."

"Tico was just—wait a minute," she stopped in mid-sentence. "Who are you to be questionin' me? The last time I checked, Jameelah was your girlfriend, not Trouble," she said, rolling her eyes.

"Dang, I was just askin'. You didn't hafta bite my head off."

"My bad. I thought you were tryin'a check me."

"And if I was?"

"Well, you heard what I just said then. You got a woman and I'm not her."

"Not yet," Dariel said, winking.

Trouble's heart beat with anticipation. She couldn't wait to become Dariel's girlfriend, but she knew that it wouldn't be anytime soon because he already belonged to someone, for now.

"Where we 'bout to go?" she asked as she zipped up her jacket.

"Where do you wanna go?"

"I really would like to go home, 'cuz I'm startin' to get cold and it's makin' my buzz come down."

"It's only two a.m.. The night is still young."

"I know. But I promised my brother that I would be home by curfew, and it's already way past it."

"That's cool. To your house we go." Dariel wrapped his arm around Trouble's shoulders and pulled her close to him to keep her warm.

"Where's Jameelah?" she asked, enjoying the warm feeling Dariel gave her.

"There you go messin' up a perfect evenin' by askin' me about Jameelah. I guess she's at home. She got mad at me 'cuz I came to the party without her."

"How come you didn't bring her along?"

"You know Ta'liyah don't care for her that much."

"I don't blame Ta'liyah 'cuz yo' girl really be trippin' about stupid shit. And I don't understand why she's so insecure."

"I don't know either. But I do know that I don't wanna waste my evenin' talkin' about Jameelah."

"Have you ever messed around on her?" Trouble asked boldly.

"Let's get one thing understood. I don't mess around on my girlfriends. When I get into a relationship, I'm in it to win it. Now if the chick decides to mess around on me, then that's on her. As long as I don't find out, she'll be cool. What I don't know won't hurt me, but if I find out it will hurt her."

"Yeah, okay," Trouble said, smirking.

"Well, you asked, didn't you?"

"I guess I did."

"I talk a lot when I get high," Dariel said, smiling.

Trouble returned the smile. "I can tell." They walked the rest of the way in silence, making small talk here and there as they enjoyed each other's company.

"Here we are," Trouble said as they came to her house.

"Yeah, here we are." Dariel looked at Trouble and wanted badly to taste her lips. "Come on, I'll walk you to your front door."

"Thank you. Now if I can just find my house key," she said, digging through her Coach bag. She noticed that all the lights were out in the house, so that could only mean Jyson wasn't home. She stuck her key in the door, but before she could get it unlocked, Dariel kissed the back of her neck. She was in a state of shock, turning around to see what the reason behind the kiss was, but before she could open her mouth, Dariel pressed his soft lips against hers. She didn't know what to do—whether to slap the shit out of him or keep kissing his juicy lips. So Trouble decided to do the right thing with him having a girlfriend and all . . . she kept kissing him! He parted her lips with his wet tongue and she closed her eyes, letting his tongue explore her mouth. After about two minutes into the kiss, she took a step back and looked down at the porch.

Dariel took his finger and lifted her chin. "What's the matter?"

"Nothin'—it's just that you—I mean—we—" Trouble stammered. "Never mind. Just come in, it's cold out here." She unlocked the door.

I thought you would never ask, Dariel thought as he followed her inside. Dariel watched as Trouble walked over to the alarm to punch in a code. He enjoyed being around her and he watched her every move. She gave him the same warm-fuzzy feeling that she had for him.

"Make yourself at home," she said. Trouble walked into the bathroom to wipe the moisture from in between her legs. She brushed the stale gin taste from her mouth and walked back into the living room and took a seat next to Dariel.

He looked over at the bookshelf, noticing the large collection of DVDs and CDs they had. "Damn, y'all got a lot of movies and music," he said. "How many movies do y'all got?"

Trouble shrugged her shoulders. "I don't know. The only movie I watch is *Baby Boy*."

"*Baby Boy*? That's one of my favorite movies," he said, smiling.

"I see we got somethin' in common." Dariel took the movie off the shelf and put it in the DVD player.

"The only thing I don't like about this movie is that Jody kept on cheatin' on her and she always took him back, no matter what. Havin' a man ain't that serious!" Trouble rolled her eyes.

"Maybe not to you, but to some it's serious. Everyone don't like to be alone."

"Yeah, I guess. But bein' alone ain't always bad 'cuz you don't have to put up wit' some of the riffraff that comes along with havin' a relationship. You know how it is, shit, you goin' through it as we speak," Trouble said, smirking.

"Yeah, you're right about that. Sometimes it's good to be alone, but it also feels good to have someone to share your life with." Dariel looked into Trouble's eyes, hoping she could feel his vibe.

"I agree. Relationships have their good points and their bad ones," she said, feeling the vibe Dariel was letting off.

"What do you look for in a man?"

"For starters, I have three little rules: no cheatin', no lyin', and no keepin' secrets. If a man can do those three little things, then we won't have no problems. That's not too much ask for, is it?"

"Is that all a brotha gotta do to keep you happy? That's nothin'," he said, smiling.

"And I wouldn't mind goin' to the movies from time to time, gettin' my hair and nails done, and what would really make me happy is if he bought me a diamond tennis bracelet."

Dariel laughed. "Well, I enjoy spendin' time with my girlfriend and I enjoy makin' her feel special."

A rush of jealousy invaded Trouble's voice. "Oh, is that why Jameelah be trippin' all the time 'cuz she thinks that you are givin' her time and lovin' to some other chick?"

"To tell you the truth, I don't know why she be trippin' so hard. It ain't like I'm messin' around on her. But I can tell you one thing, I'm not gon' take too much more of her bitchin'. It's beginnin' to drive me crazy." Dariel shook his head in disgust.

Trouble and Dariel continued watching the movie until they both fell asleep. He woke up and looked over at the clock on the wall. "Damn, it's five a.m.," he said, looking over at Trouble, who was in a deep coma. *Dang, she's beautiful; even in her sleep,* he thought. "Trouble?" he called out, but didn't get any response. Dariel shook her shoulder and called her name again. "Baby girl, I'm gone."

Trouble lifted her head and squinted her eyes. "Okay, call me tomorrow," she said before falling right back to sleep.

"No, I'll call you today," he whispered and leaned down and kissed her on the forehead. *Damn, I'm diggin' the fuck outta that girl,* he thought as he headed home. Trouble was everything Dariel had ever wanted in a girlfriend. She was smart, funny, and beautiful. Not saying Jameelah wasn't pretty, but she didn't have shit on Trouble. Jameelah liked to argue and Trouble didn't. To Dariel, she seemed more laid-back.

When Dariel got home, he lay in his bed and stared up at the ceiling. He couldn't get Trouble off his mind. *Damn, what am I gon' do?* he thought, *and how come I'm just now realizin' that I'm in love with Trouble? I gotta kick Jameelah to the curb. The only thing is, she's the type of broad that stalk niggas after you break up wit' her ass.* Dariel thought for a minute. *The next time she gets to trippin', which I know will be real soon, I'm leavin' her ass alone.* After a few more minutes of thinking about Trouble, Dariel was finally able to get her off his mind and drifted off to sleep.

Trouble had opened her eyes as soon as she heard the front door close when Dariel left. She got up from the couch and went and got in her bed. She stared up at the ceiling and smiled as thoughts of Dariel filled her head. *Damn, I don't know what it is about Dariel; somebody else's man at that. It must be his looks, the way he acts, his sense of humor, or that body that's oh-so debonair! I gotta make him my man. I don't know how, but I'll think of somethin'. I don't even know why he's even with that chicken when he could be feastin' on steak!* Trouble rolled over, said her prayers, and drifted off to sleep.

Six

Trouble awoke to the smell of bacon. She got up and staggered into the bathroom to wash her face and brush her teeth. She walked into the kitchen and Jyson was bent over in the refrigerator. There was a skinny girl with big breasts sitting at the table wearing the shirt Jyson had on the day before.

"Good mornin', sis. It looks like you had a rough night," Jyson said, smiling.

"Mornin'," Trouble said in a dry tone.

"You must be Trouble?" Skinny Minnie asked, holding out her hand for Trouble to shake.

"I could be or I could be not. Who's to say?" Trouble said, imitating Mista off *The Color Purple*. "Who are you?" Trouble gave Skinny Minnie a dirty look. She was not feeling having to share her Saturday morning breakfast with a stranger.

"Sis, this is Michaela," Jyson introduced, placing his hands on Michaela's shoulders as if he was showing her off.

"How old are you, Michelle? You look a little too old to be messin' around wit' my brother."

"Trouble!" Jyson yelled.

"No, it's okay. I'll handle this myself," Michaela said to Jyson with a smile. She then turned to face Trouble. "The name is Michaela, not Michelle."

"Michelle, Michaela, it's all the same to me," Trouble retorted.

Michaela tried to brush off Trouble's comment with a fake chuckle. "Anyway," Michaela said, "sweetie, haven't you heard that it's not polite to ask a lady her age?" Michaela's voice was nice and calm as she spoke.

"Well, sweetie, haven't you heard that a closed mouth doesn't get fed?" Trouble smirked.

"Well, if you really must know my age, I'm twenty-five," Michaela confessed.

"Twenty-five? My brother is only nineteen! What the hell is wrong wit' you? You must be one of his hypes or somethin'?" Trouble could see that Michaela was getting upset and she loved every minute of it. Trouble was furious because Saturday mornings were the only day she got to spend quality time with her brother and Michaela was invading their time together.

"Trouble, that's enough!" Jyson yelled.

Michaela was furious. *No, this bitch did not just call me a fuckin' hype*, she thought. *This can never be the little sweet and innocent girl that Jyson told me about last night. This little smart-mouth hefah*, Michaela thought.

Without further insults to Michaela, Trouble got up from the kitchen table and went into the bathroom and got into the shower. "Who dis old bitch think she is? She probably ain't nothin' but a gold-diggin' ho," Trouble mumbled to herself. After showering, she walked into her room, dried off, and opened up her closet to see what outfit she would put on. She decided on a pair of Miss Sixty dark blue boot cut jeans with the extra low cut that made her booty stick out like Beyoncé's. She took her all-white Lady Enyce shirt off the hanger and slid it carefully over her head, trying not to mess up her French roll. Trouble fumbled through the numerous shoe boxes before deciding to wear her all-white Nike Impax TR2. When she finally finished gussying herself up, she walked into the living room, grabbed her purse off the couch, and headed for the door.

Jyson walked out of the kitchen. "Trouble, where you goin'? Breakfast is ready."

"Feed Michaela. She can use a meal or two with her frail ass. I'm out," Trouble spat as she opened up the door and walked out, slamming it behind her. "She ain't got no business here in the first place. Saturdays is our time," Trouble said to herself as she walked down the street.

Jyson walked back into the kitchen, mad as hell at his sister. "I don't know what has gotten into her," he said as a form of apology to Michaela.

"Well, you really need to be tryin' to find out," Michaela said, rolling her eyes. " 'Cuz somethin' is definitely wrong."

Trouble walked over to Ta'liyah's house and beat on the front door as hard as she could. She needed to talk. After about ten minutes, Tico answered the door still half asleep. She could tell that he had been in a deep sleep because he had a long white line of slob on the side of his face that led from the corner of his mouth to the side of his ear.

"Where Ta'liyah at?" she asked. Trouble walked in the house and looked at all the niggas that laid around on the couches and the floor. "Damn, it's a lot of niggas in here. They musta came after me and Dariel left," she said. The thought of Dariel made her smile.

"Just where did you and my cousin go last night anyway?" Tico asked.

"None of yo' damn business!" she snapped.

"Where yo' sista at, boy?"

"I don't know. I guess she's in her room. Hell, go look."

Trouble made her way up the stairs to Ta'liyah's room. She knocked on the bedroom door, but got no answer. She knocked again as she pushed the door open and walked in. Trouble got the surprise of her life. Ta'liyah was laying in bed, half naked, with Marcus. *I can't believe this. How dumb can this bitch really be?* Trouble thought as she put her hands on her hips and shook her head. She then tiptoed out the room and back down the stairs. Trouble walked out onto the porch and stood in disbelief.

Tico came outside on the porch and lit up a cigarette. "What's up wit' you?" he asked.

"Nothin'." Trouble tried hard not to look at the dried-up slobber on the side of his face.

"So, you ain't gon' tell me where you and Dariel went last night?"

"No."

"It's all good. Hey, I didn't know you could dance like that. Can I let you in on a little secret?" Tico leaned over and whispered into Trouble's ear. "You made my dick hard last night."

"Oh, is that right?" she asked, sarcastically. "Well, um, can I let you in on a little secret too?"

Tico smiled. "Hell yeah!"

Trouble focused on the slob on his face. "Lean closer 'cuz I don't want nobody to hear this," she said seductively. Tico leaned in closer, smiling from ear to ear. "You need to go in the damn house and wash that long-ass line of slob off the side of yo' face," Trouble yelled then walked off the porch laughing.

"Fuck you, Trouble! You ain't all that," Tico hollered at her back as she walked down the street. He ran into the house and looked in the mirror that hung on the living room wall and saw the slob. He shook his head and laughed at himself.

Trouble walked down the street heading nowhere in particular. Somehow she ended up walking past Dariel's house, but didn't stop. She wanted to, but she would never show up at his house uninvited. As she walked by, Jameelah passed her and shot her a dirty look. Trouble laughed and kept on walking as Jameelah raced to Dariel's doorstep.

Jameelah beat on Dariel's door until he answered it.

"Where the fuck was you at last night?" she snapped as soon as he opened the door.

Trouble heard the commotion and turned around to watch.

"Look girl, I don't have to explain nothin' to you, so don't be comin' over here questionin' my whereabouts, you understand?" he snapped.

"You was wit' Trouble last night, wasn't you?"

Trouble started to turn around and beat the brakes off Jameelah but thought about what Ms. Carter said, and decided against it. She shook her head and started walking again, not wanting to get involved with all the drama.

"Look, this is the last damn time I'm gon' tell you, if you keep accusin' me of messin' with Trouble or any other girl, I'm gon' kick yo' ass to the curb!" Dariel meant every word. "As a matter of fact, call me when you grow up, 'cuz I don't have time to be dealin' wit' no little-ass girls."

"I am mature. I just don't want no other broad pushin' up on my man, that's all," she whined.

"Why are you so damn insecure?"

"I'm not. And if you ain't messin' around with Trouble, why did I just walk past her?" Jameelah put her hands on her hips and waited for an answer.

"This is a free country, am I right? The girl can walk wherever she pleases." Dariel looked up and down the street, hoping he could still see a trace of Trouble.

"I'm leavin', Dariel!" Jameelah said and turned around to walk off the porch.

As bad as he wanted her to go, he still didn't want to see her upset. He grabbed her by the arm and kissed her on the forehead just like he had done Trouble earlier. "Let's go to my room. My parents are at work," he said, kissing her on the ear.

"Stop it, boy. You know that's my spot," she cheesed. "You do love me, don't you?"

Dariel didn't answer. "Just come on before my parents get home." All the talk about Trouble made him horny. And since he couldn't have her at the moment, he settled for the next best thing.

He led Jameelah to his bedroom and closed the door behind them. Dariel took off his shorts and sat up against his headboard. "You know the routine," he said to Jameelah as he pushed play on the stereo that sat next to his bed.

She danced to "Sugar Hill" by AZ. She moved like she should have been a professional stripper, turning Dariel on with every move. His warrior got hard as a brick because he imagined that Trouble was the one standing before him dancing. Jameelah seductively swayed her hips from side to side as she removed her clothes, trying her best to please her man.

"Turn around," he commanded. She turned around like she was told and bent over. She stood up again and made her cheeks clap to the beat of the music.

"Get over here!"

"Make love to me," she whispered as she straddled him.

Dariel moved Jameelah off of him and he then climbed on top of her and began stroking her hard and deep, only because he thought about Trouble being underneath him instead of Jameelah.

"Fuck me hard," Jameelah screamed.

"Would you shut up?" Dariel pulled his love muscle out and squirted all over her stomach as she rubbed it in like lotion.

"You do love me, Dariel!" Jameelah said as she sat up with a smile on her face and began to put on her clothes. "I'll be back over later on for some more, okay?"

Whatever, he thought.

"I'm out, baby," she said, kissing him on the cheek. *Yeah, bitches, he belongs to me. I done whipped this good shit on him,* she thought as she walked out his bedroom.

Dariel couldn't wait to hear the front door slam. He jumped out of bed and got into the shower. After he got dressed, he picked up the phone and called Trouble but no one answered.

Trouble walked up on the porch at the same time that Jyson pulled into the driveway with their mother sitting on the passenger side. She sure was glad that Michaela wasn't in the car with him, but her mother wasn't any better.

"Hey, girl," Jyson called out as Trouble unlocked the front door. Momma opened the car door and got out. She waved at Trouble, but Trouble ignored her.

"What?" Trouble snapped.

"What's your problem?"

"I don't got one," she said, as she continued walking into the house, going straight to her room and slamming the door behind her.

Denise sat on the couch eating leftover breakfast when the phone rang. "Hello?" she answered, smacking on a piece of bacon.

"Hello, is Trouble home?" Dariel asked.

"Hang on for a second."

"I got it, Momma, hang it up," Trouble yelled from her bedroom.

"Do you got the phone yet, Trouble?" Momma asked.

"Dang, I said I had it. So hang it up," Trouble snapped at her mother. She wasn't too enthused to have her mother around, but she knew it would only be for a few days, if that. Denise was only around to see what she could steal or borrow and Trouble hated that about her mother.

"Hey, baby girl," Dariel said as soon as Trouble's mother slammed down the phone.

"Who dis?"

"Who do you want it to be?"

"I would love for it to be Usher."

"I can be him if you want me to," Dariel laughed. "But for right now, I'm Dariel."

"Boy, I knew it was you," she laughed. "What's up?"

"I was wonderin' what you was gon' do today."

"I really didn't have anything planned. All I hafta do is study for my English test."

"Would you like to do somethin' when you get finished?"

"Somethin' like what?" she inquired.

"I want to see that new movie, *Meet the Browns*, you know, the one by Tyler Perry?"

"Yeah. I want to see that movie too. I heard it was good."

"It's a date then. I'll pick you up around six-thirty."

"All right, I'll see you then," she said, excited.

"Bet," Dariel said and hung up the phone without saying another word.

"I can't stand when he hang up on me!" she shouted. She rolled over on her back and smiled up at the ceiling. "A date? Wait a minute, it can't be a date, 'cuz he has a girlfriend," Trouble said to herself. "Oh never mind," she said, smiling.

"Trouble, come here for a minute," Momma yelled from the living room.

"What, Momma?" she huffed as she made her way to the living room.

"Who was that young man on the phone? It didn't sound like your boyfriend Markell, to me."

"Dang, you are so nosy! That's 'cuz it wasn't Markell. If you really must know, it was Dariel."

"Ta'liyah's cousin?"

"Yeah."

"He's a cutie," Momma said, smiling with her front tooth missing.

"Yeah, I know." Trouble smiled back.

"Well, what happened to Markell? He was a cutie-pie too."

"Markell and I been broke up. Where have you been?"

"Oh," Momma said, surprised. "Baby, can I ask you a question?"

"Yeah, only if I can ask you one too."

"Are you sexually active? 'Cuz if you are, I wanna take you to the Planned Parenthood and get you on the pill."

Trouble grimaced. "If you were here, Momma, you would know the answer to the question you just asked. But since you aren't, I don't feel that you need to know any of my personal business!"

"Well baby, I was just concerned."

"You should be concerned about yourself. Look at you, you look a hot mess."

Momma was embarrassed by Trouble's remark. She looked down at the outfit she was wearing. She had on a pair of old dirty Chic jeans that had to have been a size one and they were still sagging on her. She sported a filthy light blue sweater that she had found in one of the crack houses she had stayed in one night, and a pair of worn-out K-Swisses that Jyson had bought her about two years earlier. "I know I do," Momma said. "But Momma ain't always looked a hot mess. I used to look good, just like you."

Trouble could remember when her momma used to dress her ass off. She kept all the top designer clothes and got her hair done once a week and sometimes twice. That was Daddy's way of keeping her off his back about all the other bitches he was messing around with; just like Big Mike did Sherry.

"Momma, can I ask you a question now?"

"Yeah, go right ahead, baby," Momma said, twitching.

"When are you gon' get off of them drugs and come home to be a mother to me and Jyson?"

Momma looked at her beautiful little girl and said, "If you were out there in them streets, you would know the answer to the question you just asked. But since you're not, I don't feel that I should have to tell you any of my personal business," Momma said before turning around and walking out the front door.

"Bitch," Trouble said under her breath.

Seven

Trouble walked into the kitchen and sat down at the table. She pulled out her English notes and began to study. "Dang, it's five p.m. already? I better start gettin' ready for my date."

Trouble jumped in the shower again, so she could be nice and fresh when Dariel came to pick her up. *I gotta look extra good tonight,* she thought as she rambled through her closet for the second time that day. She pulled out an Adidas sweat suit and decided that she wanted to look sexy, not thugged out. So she pulled out a short denim skirt that came up to her thighs and a red Sass & Bide ruffle heron top.

"Look at me," she said as she slipped on her red Christian Louboutin stacks. "Damn, I look good!" She sprayed on a few squirts of her Blush perfume before walking into the living room to answer the ringing telephone.

"I know this ain't Dariel's ass callin' this early," she said as she looked at the caller ID and decided not to answer the telephone because she wasn't in the mood to talk to her loudmouth Aunt Loretta.

Instead she just chilled out and studied until it was time for her so-called date with somebody else's man.

"I'm 'bout to go back over to my man's house to get me some more of that good lovin'," Jameelah said to Kassie over the phone.

"Girl, you are so nasty," Kassie laughed. "Have you told him yet?" she asked.

"Naw, not yet. I plan on tellin' him when I get there," Jameelah answered.

"How do you think he gon' react?"

Jameelah really didn't know how Dariel would handle the news she had for him. "Dariel is my man, you know. So it really shouldn't bother him, much."

"I don't know, Jameelah. That's a big responsibility for two teenagers to handle," Kassie said. "Neither one of y'all got a job."

"So what?" Jameelah snapped, knowing what Kassie was telling her was the truth.

"Girl, you don't have a clue," Kassie said, rolling her eyes.

"I think you're just jealous 'cuz it's me and not you."

"Jealous of what?"

"Cuz I gotta man and you don't," Jameelah spat.

"So, what that mean? Does that make you better than me 'cuz you gotta man?" Kassie asked angrily.

"I see you startin' to act like all the rest of them bitches at school, so I'm 'bout to bounce on over to my man's house." Jameelah strongly emphasized *man*.

"That's why you ain't got no friends. Bye, bitch," Kassie said before hanging up the phone.

"These jealous-ass hoes kill me," Jameelah said out loud as she grabbed her jacket and headed over to Dariel's house to share what she hoped would be good news to him.

Jameelah sprayed on some perfume before ringing the doorbell.

"Who is it?" Dariel's brother Josh yelled.

"It's Jameelah. Is Dariel home?"

"Hang on a minute." Josh walked into the basement where Dariel was sitting on the couch playing *Madden 2008*. "Hey man, yo' psycho-ass girlfriend is at the door. Do you want me to tell her that you're not here?"

"Naw man," Dariel laughed as he laid the game controller down and followed his brother up the basement stairs.

Dariel opened up the door and smiled at his woman.

"Hey baby, I told you that I would be back to see you," Jameelah said, smiling.

"You didn't come back to see me. You came back for some more of Moby, didn't you?"

Josh grimaced before walking into the kitchen.

"You got me. Is your parents home?" Jameelah asked, looking around.

"Naw, not yet. They called and said that they wouldn't be home until around eight."

"That gives us plenty of time then." Jameelah smiled deviously.

"Yeah, I know." Dariel smiled back. "Let's go." He led Jameelah to his bedroom for round two.

Jameelah dug her nails deep into Dariel's back while she came and that turned him on. He moved faster and stroked deeper as sweat poured from his forehead onto her face. As he was about to reach his peak, he pulled his love muscle out and squirted on her stomach.

"Why did you pull it out?" Jameelah asked.

"What do you mean?" Dariel grimaced. "I ain't tryin' to have no kids," he said. "Is that what you're used to, niggas just skeetin' all up in you?"

Hearing that made Jameelah too nervous to tell Dariel what she came over to tell him. "No, Dariel. That's not what I'm used to," she lied. "I am your girlfriend, ain't I?"

Not for long, he wanted to say, but instead he asked, "What does that have to do with anything?"

"I been thinkin', Dariel; I want us to have a baby," Jameelah said after she built her confidence back up.

"Jameelah, get real! We're too young to be havin' kids and you know it!" This entire conversation was making him sick to his stomach, so he wanted her out of his room, his house—out of his life would have been even better!

"But, Dariel," she whined. "We're both mature enough to raise a baby."

"Jameelah, look, I'm not havin' no kids by you or nobody else, not right now. I'm goin' to college soon, so I don't need nothin' holdin' me back."

"Dariel?" Jameelah pouted.

"Look, Jameelah, I'm 'bout to take me a nap. I kicked it too hard last night, so I'll talk to you later."

"Dang, it's like you're tryin' to get rid of me or some-thin'," she said, pouting. "I can tell when I'm not wanted," she said, putting her clothes on. Dariel made no effort to respond to anything she said; he just wanted her gone.

After he heard the front door close, he jumped up and got into the shower. After a quick shower, he put on his black Sean John jeans, with a black Sean John shirt, and a pair of black Timberlands. He then walked over to the phone and called Trouble.

"Hello?" Trouble answered.

"What's up, baby girl?" Dariel asked.

"What's up, D?"

"Are you ready yet?" Before she could answer his question he said, "I'm on my way, holla!" and pushed end on the phone.

"I hate when he does that!" she screamed once again.

Trouble went into the bathroom and sprayed her hair with spritz, brushed her teeth, and put on some lip gloss.

"Damn, you look good, girl," she said to the reflection in the mirror. Fifteen minutes later, there was a knock at the door. Trouble looked at herself one more time before opening up the door.

"Damn, you look good," Dariel said as Trouble opened the door.

"Thanks," she said, blushing.

"I don't know if I can take you nowhere lookin' like this. I might hafta fight somebody."

"Oh stop it, you're embarrassin' me."

"There's no need to be embarrassed by the truth, baby girl."

"You don't think I'm overly dressed, do you?" she joked.

"Yeah, I do. Let me help you take some of those clothes off," he teased as they walked out the door.

"Damn, we're ridin' in style!" Trouble said as she checked out the new Escalade that was parked in her driveway. "Who truck is this?"

"Stop askin' questions and get in," Dariel said, opening up the passenger-side door. Dariel couldn't help but notice how short Trouble's skirt was and he watched as she kept trying to pull it down but it wouldn't budge.

"Can I ask you a question?" Trouble asked.

"You sho'll do ask a lot of questions," Dariel said, smiling.

"I just wanted to know where Jameelah at while you're takin' me to the movies. I'm startin' to feel guilty," Trouble said.

"Damn, it ain't like I'm takin' you to the Holiday Inn. We are friends, right?"

"Right."

"I am allowed to have friends, whether they are male or female. So, I'm just takin' my female friend to see a movie."

Trouble sighed. "Okay, whatever you say. I don't want no shit, though."

"Just sit back and relax," he said, patting her on the leg. Trouble did what she was told and leaned back into the plush seat and enjoyed the ride.

After the movie Dariel and Trouble rode around talking about the plans they had for the future. He learned that she wanted to become a dentist and she learned that he wanted to become a professional basketball player.

"I'm startin' to get hungry," Trouble looked over at Dariel and said.

"Me too. Let's get somethin' to eat," he said, smiling. "What do you have a taste for?"

"I don't care. I just need somethin' on my stomach."

Dariel pulled up in the Rally's drive-through and they placed their orders. As they sat eating in the truck, Dariel's cell phone began to ring.

"Hello?" he answered.

"What's up, D? Have you talked to Trouble today?" Ta'liyah asked. "I've been callin' her ass all day."

"Have I talked to Trouble today?" he repeated, waiting on Trouble to respond to his signal.

Trouble shook her head no.

"I haven't talked to her," Dariel lied. "I'll tell her to call you if I see or hear from her."

"Well, tell her that I'm havin' another party tonight since we had so much beer and liquor left over."

"Count me in," Dariel said.

"Bring some more of that bud you had," Ta'liyah said, feining for a high.

"It's on," he said, hanging up the phone.

Trouble looked over at Dariel as he laid his cell phone in his lap. "Why do you always be hangin' up on people?" Trouble asked.

"I don't be hangin' up on people. I be done talkin', so I hang up the phone," Dariel replied.

"Yes you do. Anyway, what did Ta'liyah want with me?" Trouble asked before sticking a French fry in her mouth.

"She told me to tell you that she's havin' another party tonight. You down wit' that?" he asked.

"I don't know. I'm pissed off at her right now." Trouble closed her eyes and thought about the sight she had seen earlier.

"What did she do, if you don't mind me askin'," Dariel inquired.

"I don't even wanna talk about it," Trouble said, turning to look out the window.

"Okay, suit yourself."

Trouble sat quietly as Dariel started up the truck and pulled out of Rally's parking lot. They pulled up in the King Street projects and Trouble looked over at Dariel. "What are we doin' out here?" she asked, puzzled.

"I'll be right back. I'm 'bout to run in my boy Brian's house and get some bud. If I ain't back in ten minutes pull off. Keep the truck runnin' and the doors locked," he said, getting out of the truck and looking around like someone was following him.

Trouble looked around at all the people that stood outside. A group of men were standing around passing a forty-ounce of Magnum back and forth. *How disgusting*, she thought. She watched as a group of kids played freeze tag while the smell of barbecue teased her nose. Trouble watched the clock closely, and after about seven minutes she started to get worried.

"I wish he would hurry up!" she said.

"Was you worried?" Dariel asked as he reappeared by the driver's-side door.

"Naw," she lied.

Dariel looked over at Trouble and smiled. "You still ain't gon' tell me why you mad at Ta'liyah?"

"Man, I didn't wanna say nothin' 'cuz it's her business. But I went over to her house today and saw her and Marcus all laid up in the bed naked."

"What? I know Ta'liyah didn't go back that route after that nigga dogged her the first time?"

"Yes she did," Trouble said, disgusted.

"Well, if he dog her again that'll be on her. I beat the nigga up the first time, but this time I'm not gettin' in it."

Trouble shook her head, hoping and praying that there wouldn't be shit to get into.

Eight

"Where have you been? I've been callin' you all day," Ta'liyah ran over to Trouble and said as she and Dariel walked through the door. "I've been busy," Trouble said as she pretended to be interested in all the guests.

"Too busy to talk to yo' sister? My, haven't we got nerve?" Ta'liyah looked at Dariel for some answers but all he did was shrug his shoulders.

She looked back at Trouble and then walked away.

Tico and a couple of his friends sat on the couch smoking a blunt. "I'm 'bout to go over there and hit the blunt," Dariel said to Trouble.

"Okay," she said before walking into the kitchen to pour herself a drink.

"Damn, man, baby in that short skirt is fine as hell," one of Tico's friends said.

"She sho'll is. I wouldn't mind hittin' that. But she look kinda stuck-up," another friend replied.

"I wouldn't mind gettin' a piece of that myself! But ain't you hittin' that, little cuz?" Tico asked Dariel.

"Naw, man, I ain't hittin' it. We're just friends."

"Well, won't you hook a muthafucka up wit' her then?" Tico said.

"No can do, my man. If you want her, you go hook yourself up!" Dariel felt a rush of jealousy, but soon shook it off after Trouble winked at him from the kitchen.

50 Cent's new joint came on and Dariel started dancing. Veronica walked out of the kitchen and started dancing with him. She rubbed her hand all over his chest and his warrior as they grooved to the music. Trouble stood back and watched as they danced.

Jealousy instantly took over. *Why am I so jealous? Dariel is not my man,* she thought, taking a double shot of gin to the face. Trouble walked over to the couch and sat in between Tico and one of his friends.

"What's up, Tico? You still mad at me?" she asked as she waved the refah smoke out of her face.

"Naw girl. We still cool," Tico said, grinning.

"That's good to know," she said, smiling.

"You sho'll do look good tonight," he said, eying her body.

"You sho'll do," his friend added.

"Thanks," she said, smiling.

"Can I take you to an early breakfast?" Tico's friend asked as he rubbed her thigh.

"Hey now, keep yo' hands to yourself," Trouble warned.

"I told you this bitch was stuck-up," Tico's friend said.

"You right, I am," she said, rolling her eyes.

Dariel watched as Trouble chopped it up with his cousin and his friends. He walked over to them and looked at Trouble and said, "Let's dance!"

"I'm 'bout to dance with Tico," Trouble said, pulling Tico to the middle of the living room floor.

Paul Wall's new song came on and Trouble shook her ass like she was dancing for money. She had moves in her that she didn't even know she had. She noticed Dariel standing on the sideline watching her. She winked and smiled at him and continued dancing. When the song went off, she wiped the sweat from her forehead and went into the kitchen to get herself something to drink.

"What's up, Trouble?" Veronica asked, looking her up and down.

"Nothin'. What's up wit' you?" Trouble replied.

Veronica sucked her buckteeth. "I guess the real question is what's up with you and Dariel?"

"What do you mean?"

"I saw the way he was watchin' you when you and Tico was in there dancin'. He looked like he wanted to beat the both of y'all up."

"And you're sayin' that to say what?" Trouble spat. "I don't care what look he gave me. Dariel has a woman."

"Whatever."

"Well, maybe he likes what he sees," Trouble said smartly.

Veronica turned up her nose. "Well, since there is nut-tin' going on between y'all, I'm about to invite him to my private after party," Veronica said, licking her crusty lips.

"Do yo' thang. Just remember he has a girlfriend."

"I don't care nuttin' about his girl. I'm not tryin' to fuck her, I wanna fuck him. And besides, I don't want no relationship; all I want is some dick."

Dariel walked into the kitchen to throw the tobacco away from the blunt he had just broke down. "Excuse me," he said to Trouble, who was standing right in front of the trash can.

"Hey Dariel," Veronica called out.

"What's up?" he asked.

"What you gon' do after the party?" Veronica asked.

"It all depends. Why, what's up?"

"I was askin' because my beaver is in need of some wood," she said, licking her lips in a seductive manner.

Trouble began choking on her beer. She couldn't believe how blunt Veronica was.

Dariel's eyed widened. "You okay, Trouble?" he asked as he patted her on the back.

"Yeah, I'm fine," she laughed. "Damn, you are blunt, Veronica."

"Well, if I see somethin' I want, I go after it," she said, winking at Dariel.

"Let me see. Trouble, what are you gon' do after the party?" Dariel asked.

"Why you askin' her what she gon' do? This is between me and you," Veronica said, smacking her lips.

"Well, if you plan on lettin' her beaver chop on yo' wood, I wish y'all would hurry up and get finished so I can get a ride home," Trouble said and walked back into the living room.

"Well? Are you comin' with me or not?" Veronica asked, folding her arms.

Dariel didn't know how to let her down easy. So he did the best that he could without hurting her feelings. "Well, Veronica, it sounds temptin' and all, but I got a woman and I couldn't mess around on her like that. It wouldn't be right, but thanks for askin'." Dariel walked back into the living room and stood next to Trouble.

"Come on, let's dance," he said, pulling Trouble by the arm.

Trouble smiled at Dariel.

"You knew she was gon' ask me to go home with her, didn't you?" Dariel asked Trouble.

"Yeah, I knew. What did you want me to say, no he can't go?"

"You coulda said anything! That broad is crazy."

"What did you tell her?"

"I told her that I had a woman and I couldn't mess around on her."

"You crazy."

"I'm crazy about you," he said, kissing her on the forehead.

"I'm about to go get me another shot of gin, would you like somethin'?" Trouble asked.

"Naw. I'm about to fire up this blunt."

Trouble walked back into the kitchen. Veronica was leaned up against the counter staring Trouble up and down. "I see why Dariel turned me down," Veronica said. "He must be goin' home with you tonight."

"He ain't comin' home with me, but he is givin' me a ride," Trouble admitted. "He has a woman and I respect that. I ain't tryin' to step on nobody's toes."

Veronica rolled her eyes. "You pretty bitches kill me. Y'all think y'all can have anybody y'all want," she hissed.

"What are you talkin' about, Veronica? I told you before that me and Dariel aren't messin' around," Trouble explained.

"Whatever. You can tell that to somebody else."

Trouble was tired of hearing Veronica go on and on, so she decided to have a little fun with her. "You're right, Veronica. Dariel is comin' home with me. Dariel, come here," Trouble called out.

Dariel came into the kitchen and stood next to Trouble.

"What's up, baby girl?" he asked.

"What are you gon' do after the party?" she asked.

Dariel caught on quick. "It all depends; why, what's up?"

"I was just askin' because my beaver is in need of some wood!" Trouble said, smirking.

"Well, give me a compass and show me the way to the forest and I'll be there!" They both laughed uncontrollably.

"Fuck both of y'all," Veronica yelled and walked out of the kitchen.

"I would, but yo' pussy got more miles than my grandpa's '68 Chevy," Dariel blurted out.

"You stupid, boy. Do you want a shot of gin?" Trouble asked, wiping the tears away from her face.

"Naw, girl. I don't drink and drive."

"Oh, but you smoke reefah and drive? That makes a lot of sense," she said sarcastically.

"It's almost three a.m. and I'm gettin' tired." Dariel looked at his watch.

"I'm gettin' tired too. I'm ready to go home," Trouble said before finishing off her fourth shot of gin.

Ta'liyah, with a pitiful look on her face, walked over to where Dariel and Trouble stood. "Can I talk to you for a minute?" she asked Trouble.

Trouble was a little hesitant at first. "Sure." She followed Ta'liyah up the steps and into her bedroom. The flash of her and Marcus lying in the bed popped back into Trouble's mind again.

"I know why you're mad at me. Tico told me that you came over this mornin'. And he said that you walked into my room and then walked right back out. He said it looked like somethin' was botherin' you when you were standin' out on the porch," Ta'liyah said.

"Why, Ta'liyah? After all the shit Marcus put you through."

"I know I'm stupid for goin' back that route. I was caught up in the moment. I guess we were on some drunk shit."

"Ta'liyah, don't blame it on the alcohol. The liquor is just a scapegoat. Just say you did it 'cuz you was horny."

"I know I fucked up! But that ain't the worst part." Tears began to fall down Ta'liyah's chocolate cheeks.

"Don't tell me y'all didn't use protection?" Ta'liyah shook her head no. "Ta'liyah? You know better than that! You better hope and pray that you come on your period."

The thought of becoming pregnant by Marcus made her skin crawl. "Are we still friends?" Ta'liyah asked.

"Fo' life."

Dariel walked into Ta'liyah's bedroom and wrapped his arms around Trouble's waist. "I been lookin' all over for you."

"I told you I'll be right back," she said, turning around and wrapping her arms around his waist.

"Ahhh, look at y'all," Ta'liyah said, smiling.

Trouble quickly let go of his waist. "What? We're just friends. He has a woman," Trouble said quickly.

"Don't pay Ta'liyah no attention," Dariel said to Trouble. "Here, take my keys and go start the truck."

As Trouble made her way out of Ta'liyah's room and out the door, she got dirty looks from some of the other broads at the party. They were mad 'cuz they wanted to be in her shoes.

"All right, cuz, I'm out!"

"Take good care of my girl. I'm not playin'," Ta'liyah said and playfully punched Dariel in the arm.

"Mos def! I'm 'bout to make her my girl."

"What? Y'all make a real cute couple. But what about Jameelah? You know Trouble ain't gon' play second for no bitch!"

"Jameelah is old news. I'm 'bout to kick that ass to the curb. There's a new sheriff in town and her name is Candria Lewis." They both laughed as Ta'liyah walked Dariel to the front door.

"You sure you don't wanna take me up on my offer?" Veronica asked as she blocked Dariel's exit.

"I'm sure. Look, I gotta go. I got someone waitin' on me." Dariel tried to walk around her, but she wouldn't move out of his way.

"Are you sure you want to pass up all this?" Veronica lifted up her halter top and revealed her C cups.

"Yeah, I'm sure. Now can you please let me get past?" Dariel became irritated.

"Look, broad. I understand that you horny and all," Ta'liyah jumped in. "But if you wanna get laid, crawl up a chicken's ass and wait!" she said, laughing.

Unamused, Veronica just stood there staring at Dariel, who was trying desperately not to laugh. "You'll be sorry," Veronica spat before walking away.

"Thanks, cuz. And just where do you be comin' up wit' the shit you be sayin'?" Dariel laughed.

"I don't know. It comes naturally, I guess."

"Damn, I thought you forgot about me," Trouble said, coming back through the door.

"How can I? You look too good to forget about," Dariel said, walking out the door with Trouble on his heels. "You gon' hafta drive 'cuz I'm wasted."

Trouble jumped in the driver's seat of the truck, put her seat belt on, and pulled off. She was nervous at first because she really didn't know how to drive all that well. But she wasn't going to pass up a chance on driving this nice ride, even if she didn't have a license.

"Whew, safe and sound," she said, pulling in her driveway. "Wake up, Dariel. We're here." She began nudging him.

Dariel woke up and looked around like he was lost. "Where are we?"

"We're at my house. I know you didn't think I was gon' drive you home then have to walk to my house."

Dariel laid his head back. "Whatever you say."

Trouble got out of the truck, walked over to the passenger side, and opened the door. "Come on," she said, smiling.

Dariel looked at her and then jumped out and slipped on some gravel.

"Are you all right?" She laughed.

"Do you see somethin' funny? I almost broke my damn ankle," Dariel said, steadying his balance.

They both staggered to the door. Trouble fumbled through her Prada bag for her house keys. She unlocked the door and then rushed over to turn off the alarm system. She tossed her purse on the sofa and told Dariel to make himself at home. Trouble walked into her bedroom to slip into something more comfortable.

Dariel walked into the kitchen and poured himself a glass of milk to bring his high down. He walked back into the living room and put *Baby Boy* in the DVD player and sat back and sipped on his drink.

"You all right in there?" Dariel called out.

"Yeah, I'm fine," Trouble said as she walked into the living room wearing a Nike T-shirt, some pajama bottoms, and some oversized Scooby-Doo house slippers. She sat down on the sofa next to Dariel and listened as he recited the movie word for word.

"Now this is how I want you to dress from now on," he lightly joked.

"Nigga, please! I ain't dressin' like this for you or nobody else."

Dariel stared deep into Trouble's hazel eyes. He wanted to grab her and kiss her soft lips before carrying her off into her bedroom to make sweet love to her, but then reality clicked in . . . Jameelah was still his girlfriend.

"Give me your feet," he said, grabbing her ankles and putting them on his lap.

"What are you doin'?" Trouble moved her feet and put them back on the floor.

"Relax and let me handle this." He grabbed her feet and put them back on his lap. He removed her house slippers and then began massaging the bottoms of her feet. "You have some pretty feet," he complimented.

"Thank you," she said, blushing. *Thank God I got a pedicure*, she thought as Dariel worked his magic.

"Let's talk," he said.

"What do you wanna talk about?" Trouble said, turning her attention from the movie to face Dariel.

"I don't care. I just want you to talk to me."

"I don't know what to talk about. Ask me somethin', then we'll take it from there." Trouble laid her head back and closed her eyes.

"Okay. How did you get the nickname Trouble?" he asked as he gently massaged her size sevens.

Trouble opened her eyes and stared up at the ceiling. "When my mom was carryin' me she had a lot of complications. She stayed on bed rest for the last four months of her pregnancy. She couldn't eat because every time she did it came right back up, and she couldn't drink anything but orange pop. My mom had to get fed through a tube in order for me to get the nutrients I needed. When she finally went into labor, I was breeched and the doctor couldn't get me turned around for nothin' in the world. So they scheduled an emergency C-section. And when I did finally decide to come out, the doctor took one look at me and told her, for all the trouble I was comin' into this world, that she should name me Trouble. That's who I've been ever since, Candria Ne'cole 'Trouble' Lewis."

"That's deep," Dariel said, nodding, very much into Trouble's story.

"And by the way, this massage feels good."

"This ain't nothin' compared to the way I can make your whole body feel. We learned a technique in basketball camp, it's called a deep body massage. It feels good while you're getting it, but your body feels sore and achy the next day. I'm gon' be massagin' muscles that you didn't even know you had."

"That sounds like what I need," she said, smiling.

"Well, come on then." Dariel placed her feet back on the floor and stood up and held out his hand.

"Where we goin'?" she asked nervously.

"To your room so I can give you that massage." Trouble shot him a nervous look. "Don't worry, baby girl. I ain't gon' hurt you, trust me."

He held out his hand for her to lead the way. She hesitated, but finally gave in and led him into her bedroom.

"You have a nice room," Dariel said as he looked around at the room that was decorated in pink and brown.

"Thanks."

"Do you have any massage oil?"

Trouble walked over to the dresser and picked up the bottle of massage oil that she and Ta'liyah used to soak their feet in.

"Here you go," she said, tossing him the bottle of oil. She walked around the room and lit the Juniper Breeze candles. "These are for tranquility."

"Oh. I thought we was about to have a séance up in this mug," Dariel laughed.

"Have you heard Fantasia's CD?" Trouble pushed play on the CD player and sweet music flowed from the speakers. She began swaying and bobbing her head.

"I heard a couple of cuts," he said, watching her every move. *How could someone so young have so much goin' for themselves? She is the closest thing to perfect,* he thought.

Trouble turned out the light and stood over by the dresser.

"Come here, baby girl. I can't give you a massage with you standin' over there."

"I'm comin'," she said.

"Here, let me help you," he said, walking up behind her and sliding her shirt over her head. Her entire body trembled with fear. "Don't worry, baby girl, I got you."

Dariel unsnapped her bra but she held it in front of her, afraid to let it fall away from her breasts. Dariel licked the nape of her neck, causing her to jump. When she did, the bra fell from her hands. She could feel his dick pulsating up against her ass. He gently pulled her pajama bottoms down and she stepped out of them slowly. He then removed her thong and lifted it up to his nose to get a whiff of her chocolate cave.

"Mmmm," he moaned and placed them in his back pocket.

Trouble stood still as a statue. She was afraid to move, and even more afraid to turn around to face him. Dariel took a step back and admired her shapely body by candlelight. He kissed the back of her neck and she jumped again. "Calm down. I ain't gon' do nothin' to hurt you, I promise."

His dick was as hard as the math section of the high school proficiency test. "Lay on the bed," he ordered her.

Dariel took his boots off and sat on the side of her. He poured the oil all over her back and began working his magic.

"This shit feels good," she moaned.

Dariel straddled her body, and sat on her lower back and continued with the massage. He slid down to the back of her legs.

"Am I too heavy?" he asked her.

"Unt unnn," she moaned as he massaged her ass.

"You ready for me to stop?"

"Please don't," she begged. No one had ever made her body feel this way before.

"Turn over on your back," he whispered.

Trouble did what she was told without hesitation. Dariel poured the massage oil on her breasts and began massaging her nipples. Her entire body shook with excitement. She didn't know what to do. *This nigga got a woman. What am I doin'?* she thought. *I can't tell him to stop; it feels too good*, she argued with herself. *I gotta tell him to stop*, she thought as he began licking her belly button. *Oh, no! Dariel, you need to stop. Put your boots back on and go home!* she thought as his tongue began moving down south.

What are you doin'? she asked him inside her head as she moaned.

He grabbed her legs and parted them like the Red Sea. He licked the inside of her thighs and then ran his wet tongue over her clit. Her body shook like a crap game.

"Dariel, please," she begged.

"I'm about to please you," he said, licking her chocolate waterfall.

She grabbed his head as he explored her chocolate cave. Her mind began telling her to push this nigga up off of her but her body was telling her something different. *Why am I lettin' this nigga do this to me?* she asked herself. Because you like him and the shit feels good, and only a damn fool would tell him to stop.

Dariel licked every inch of Trouble's womanhood. No crease or crevice was left untouched. He lifted her legs high in the air and let his tongue travel down . . . down in the delta.

"Dariel?" she moaned as she trembled and grabbed the sheets for support. He made his way back up to her chocolate cave and finished where he left off. Trouble moaned and called out for her mom as she lay in the bed shaking uncontrollably.

Dariel stood up with a hard dick and watched as her body did the Harlem Shake. He bent down and kissed her on the forehead before walking back into the living room to finish watching the rest of *Baby Boy*.

What in the world just happened to me? Whatever it was, it was the bomb! Trouble thought as she walked into the bathroom to wash up. She grabbed a wash towel out of the cabinet and ran it under some hot water and walked into the living room where she found Dariel reciting the movie.

"I hate you, Jody," he yelled.

"Here you go," she said, handing him the hot wash towel.

"I see somebody got some hospitality," he said as he wiped his face. "Are you okay?"

"Yeah, I'm cool."

"How does your body feel?"

"Which part?" she said, smiling.

"You tryin'a be funny?" he said, grinning.

"Now would I do a thing like that?" She batted her eyes at him as she took a seat next to him on the couch.

"That's okay, 'cuz I thought I was gon' hafta call nine-one-one for yo' ass. You was shakin' like you was havin' a seizure," Dariel laughed.

"Forget you," she said, punching him in the arm. "I tried to stop shakin' but I couldn't. I didn't know what was happenin' to me. When I stood up my legs felt real weak. I thought you gave me some of that date rape shit," she teased.

"Yeah right. You just experienced the best orgasm in your life, that's all."

"Is that all?" she joked.

"Whatever. I bet you one thing, if you decided never to speak to me again in life, you will always remember that orgasm." Dariel blew on his knuckles and rubbed them against his chest.

"You right about that," she said, yawning.

Dariel massaged the back of Trouble's neck. "You tired, baby girl?"

"Yeah. You wore my high off," she said, forcing a tired smile.

"Let me ask you a question," he said, putting his hand over his mouth and yawning. "What would you have done if I woulda tried to make love to you?" He watched her face for a reaction.

Trouble was now wide awake. "Let me start off by sayin' I wouldn't have let it get to that point, 'cuz of Jameelah. I already let myself down 'cuz I knew what we were doin' was dead wrong, and it was my fault 'cuz I should have stopped you, but I couldn't."

"That's because you didn't want me to," he cut in.

"Secondly, I wouldn't have let you, 'cuz in order to make love to someone, you have to love them, so therefore you would have been just fuckin' me."

"How do you know that I don't love you?"

"I really don't know."

"Well, next time say that, 'cuz you don't know how I feel."

"You're right, but the final reason I wouldn't let it go that far is 'cuz . . . I'm a virgin."

"A what?"

"You heard me. I'm a virgin and proud of it."

"Damn, baby girl, you a virgin?"

"Is there somethin' wrong with that?" she asked defensively.

"Naw. I don't see anything wrong wit' it. I heard you were a virgin, but I didn't believe it," Dariel admitted.

"Excuse me?" she said with an attitude.

"Naw, don't get me wrong, I'm not sayin' that you're lyin'. I just figured that somebody had tapped that ass before, that's all."

"Well, they haven't," she assured him. "A lot of people think I be lyin' when I tell them that I'm still a virgin. Niggas act like virgins are like dinosaurs, like we are extinct. I might be the last of the dyin' breed at school, but I ain't ashamed of it."

"But you've had a lot of boyfriends. How did they deal with your virginity?" he inquired. "I just knew Markell was knockin' that bottom out." Dariel laughed.

"That's the reason why Markell and I aren't to-gether anymore. He couldn't accept the fact that I was still a virgin, and I had no intentions on losin' my virginity no time soon. So I told him if he couldn't wait until I was ready, he could get to steppin', and he did just that."

"Man, that's deep."

"I was fucked-up at first 'cuz I thought I meant some-thin' to him. I thought we would have been together forever, and I had even planned on him bein' my first when I was ready for him to be." Dariel listened as Trouble rambled on.

"If it was left up to Markell, we would have had sex the first time we met. I guess he got fed up with takin' all those cold showers." Trouble laughed, thinking back.

Dariel laughed too. "I took plenty of cold showers back in the day."

"People don't realize how many niggas would love to have a girl that is still pure," she said.

"What are you waitin' on, Mr. Right?"

"Nope, I can't say that I am, 'cuz Mr. Right may never come. So I would be wastin' my time. I'm waitin' until Trouble is ready," she said.

"It's your choice, baby girl," he said, smiling.

"Yeah, I know. And I ain't gon' let nobody make it for me."

"You're not supposed to. And a man would be less than a man if he wanted you to."

That's why I like him, Trouble thought. "You know a lot of niggas at school think I'm stuck-up."

"Yeah, they do," he agreed.

"I used to let that bother me 'cuz I know that I'm not. I just don't fall for every line a nigga throw at me."

"So in other words, you don't fall for the banana in the tailpipe," he joked.

"That's right, I don't."

"I can respect you even more now. Not sayin' that I didn't already have mad respect for you. I mainly respect your decision on your virginity, along with your womanhood and everything else. You are one of a kind and a nigga would have to be a damn fool to let you slip away."

"Thanks," she said, blushing.

"When you do find what you're lookin' for in a man, he better treat you right or he's gon' hafta answer to me," Dariel said with a serious look on his face.

"I'm gon' hold you to that."

Trouble stood up and turned the television off and escorted Dariel back to her bedroom where they lay in her bed. He held her until she drifted off to sleep.

A virgin? I know I have to make her my girl. And when I get her, I promise that I'm gon' treat her like a queen, Dariel thought before turning his back toward Trouble because he felt his warrior starting to protrude again.

Nine

"Damn, it's six a.m.," Dariel said, opening up his eyes to check his watch. "I betta get up and go home, 'cuz I gotta get my clothes ready for church." He rolled over and looked at the clock that sat on Trouble's nightstand and made sure he had the correct time. "Trouble, get yo' butt up, 'cuz I'm 'bout to bounce."

"Okay. I gotta let you out." She crawled out of the bed and walked him to the door, still half asleep.

"I'll call you when I get outta church," he said, kissing her on the forehead.

"Okay." Trouble turned around and got back in her comfortable bed and fell back into a coma.

Damn, she still a virgin, Dariel continued to think as he drove home. He pulled into his driveway and shook his head. Jameelah sat on the front porch dressed in a pair of big sweatpants with a shirt to match. She wore a head scarf around her head, and she looked as if she hadn't been to sleep in days.

"Oh my goodness," he sighed. "Here we go again," he said as he jumped out of the truck, whistling Fantasia's new song.

"Where the fuck you been?" Jameelah walked up in Dariel's face and screamed.

"Look, you gon' hafta hold that shit down. This is not my damn house so respect my parents. And furthermore, I don't have to explain nothin' to you and I'm tired of tellin' you that!" Dariel said as he tried to walk past her to get into the house, but she would not move out of his way. "Move girl," he said, gently shoving her, but her feet stayed planted.

"Where have you been, Dariel?"

"Why?" he asked sarcastically.

"What do you mean why? 'Cuz I asked, that's why!" she shouted.

"Just 'cuz you asked me don't mean I hafta tell you. Now would you please get out of my face wit' all this bullshit? It's too early in the mornin' to be arguin'."

"You know what? Fuck you, Dariel!" she shouted.

"No, fuck you, Jameelah," he said in a nice and calm manner. "Now if you would excuse me, I would like to go into the house so I can get ready for church; if you don't mind," he said, smiling.

"How you gon' sit and say you're goin' to church, nigga? You done stayed out all night fuckin' and now you wanna go praise the Lord. Puhleeze!" she said, rolling her eyes.

"It doesn't matter what I was out doin' last night. You just mad 'cuz I wasn't out doin' it with you," he said, smirking.

Dariel looked into Jameelah's eyes and saw fire. And before he could open his mouth to say anything else, Jameelah had jumped on his back and began pounding her right hand on top of his head.

"What cha'll out here doin'?" Josh said, running out the door to pull Jameelah off of his younger brother.

"This muthafucka didn't come home last night," Jameelah yelled, out of breath.

"You gon' hafta hold that noise down," Josh warned.

"I tried to tell her that, man," Dariel said as he shook his head and laughed.

"Shut up!" she yelled and swung her arm around Josh's body, trying to hit Dariel again, but missed.

"Look, if you hit me one more time, I'm gon' kick yo' ass." Dariel laughed.

"You see somethin' funny, nigga? Why you was all laid up with that bitch, Trouble?" Jameelah shouted.

"You stalkin' me now?" Dariel asked. "You don't know where I was at."

"I saw your dad's truck parked over her house all night, and if it wasn't for the truck belongin' to your father, you would have been gettin' the bitch towed home."

"Look, man, it's cold out here. Are you gon' be okay?" Josh asked his brother.

"Yeah, man, I'm co—" Before he could finish his sentence, Jameelah had swung her fist full force and punched Dariel in the face.

"Now, you bitch-ass nigga! That's for fuckin' that bitch last night," she taunted him.

Jameelah had hit Dariel so hard that it stunned him for a minute. He grabbed her by the wrists and tried to squeeze the life out of them.

"I told you that I didn't fuck Trouble," he said angrily.

"Whatever! Who do you think I am? You stay at the bitch's house all night and you try to tell me that y'all didn't fuck? What y'all do, play dominoes all night?"

"I didn't fuck her, Jameelah," he said as he squeezed her wrists even tighter.

"Let go of me. You're hurtin' me," she whined.

"So what?" he said.

"Let me go, you punk-ass nigga," she screamed before spitting snot in his face.

"I can't believe you just did that," he said, pushing her off the porch and watching as she hit the ground. Dariel jumped off the porch and stood over her trembling body and contemplated if he should remember what his parents taught him about never hitting a female, or if he should just commence to kicking her ass.

Josh jumped off the porch and grabbed his brother. "Come on, man, she ain't worth it."

"You right, the bitch ain't worth it." Dariel stood over her again and looked down at the scared expression that was plastered on her face and laughed.

Jameelah was not all that worried because she knew that Dariel didn't hit on females, because if he did, he would have kicked her ass a long time ago.

"You know what, Jameelah? When I told you that I didn't fuck Trouble, I didn't lie to you. You chose not to believe me, so that's on you. I can't make you believe me and I ain't even gon' try to. And by the way, that was your last time accusin' me of anything 'cuz we're through," Dariel said calmly.

"Yeah, whatever. I know you fucked her," she said as she stared at the spit he had in the front of his hair.

"I didn't fuck her, but I'll tell you one thing, I ate the hell outta her pussy." He smiled in her face and turned and walked in the house.

Jameelah sat on the cold ground with her mouth hanging open, speechless, and watched as Dariel and his brother walked into the house high-fiving one another.

"Man, that broad is crazy. She gon' kill you." Josh laughed as he peeked through the blinds to make sure she didn't try to come and kick the door off the hinges.

"I know, man. I'm gon' hafta watch my back. I feel kinda bad for callin' her a bitch, but she shouldn't have spit in my face."

"The bitch deserved it. You act like a bitch, you get treated like a bitch," Josh said, giving his brother some dap.

Meanwhile, Jameelah finally picked herself up off the ground and wiped the wet grass from her knees.

"What are you lookin' at?" she yelled at the neighbors who stood on their porches, pointing and laughing. "I'm gon' get you, nigga, if that's the last thing I do! You done fucked over the wrong bitch this time," she screamed loudly, as she walked down the street.

"Dariel, what's wrong with that fast-tail gal?" his mother asked as she made her way down the steps. "I don't want no trouble over here. Now you know we live in a respectable neighborhood, and we don't need that girl comin' around here startin' no mess," Mrs. Daniels said, walking into the kitchen to fix breakfast.

"You heard ya momma, didn't ya son?" his father added, coming down the stairs. "That girl is nuttin' but trouble. I tried to tell you that from the giddyup," Mr. Daniels said as he picked up Sunday's paper and turned to the sports section.

"I'm finished with her. She won't be comin' around here anymore 'cuz she way too much for me to handle," Dariel said as he hugged his dad.

"Okay, Dariel, you better tell her before we do, and she ain't gon' like what we have to say to her," said Mrs. Daniels, sticking her head out of the kitchen.

"Now you know ya momma used to be a fighter back in the day," Mr. Daniels joked.

"Used to be?" Mrs. Daniels said, sticking her head back out of the kitchen.

They all laughed as Dariel went up to his room with a big smile on his face and packed up anything that had to do with Jameelah.

Ten

Trouble woke up and went into the bathroom to wash her face and brush her teeth. She walked into the living room and Jyson and Michaela were sitting on the sofa. Jyson was counting his money while Michaela talked on her cell phone.

"Good mornin', Jyson." Trouble smiled at her brother and rolled her eyes in Michaela's direction.

"I see somebody's in a good mood this mornin'," he said as he stacked his money into large piles.

"What time did you get in?" Trouble asked as she stretched her arms over her head.

"Time enough to see that Escalade parked in my driveway," he said, putting his money in a briefcase that was already full of money.

"And you're sayin' that to say what?" Trouble asked.

"Trouble, I have told you about them damn niggas."

"Look, Jyson, don't start with me. Okay?"

Michaela hung up her cell phone and gave Trouble a look of confusion.

"Dariel only stayed over here 'cuz he was too high to drive home," Trouble said.

"Well, how come he didn't sleep out here on the couch?" Jyson asked.

"Probably the same reason why Michaela didn't sleep on the couch," she said, rolling her eyes.

"Don't get smart, girl," Jyson warned.

"I'm not gettin' smart. I'm just tired of you sayin' the same old thing over and over again. We didn't do anything, I can assure you of that. I'm still a virgin, and gon' stay that way until I'm ready," Trouble said.

"I know this ain't none of my business," Michaela interjected.

"You're right, so stay out of it." Trouble cut her off.

"I just don't want you to get hurt, that's all. Because you know I'll kill a brick over you," Jyson said with a serious look on his face.

"I understand that. But why do you keep repeatin' the same thing to me? And besides, Dariel and I are just friends. He has a girlfriend."

"What does that mean? Most of the time niggas don't give a damn about havin' a woman. Niggas don't respect that shit no more. But the same goes for a broad too. They feel like 'What ya girl gotta do wit' me'," Jyson said.

"I know, but I ain't like that. I respect the fact that he has a girl," Trouble explained.

"I'm not so sure about that," Jyson said.

"Why you say that?" Trouble asked.

" 'Cuz if you respected the fact that Dariel had a girl, he would have slept out here on the couch and not in your room," Jyson explained.

Michaela nodded her head in agreement.

Trouble looked at Michaela and rolled her eyes. "Whatever," Trouble said as she threw her hands up in the air.

"Dariel is a cool li'l nigga though," Jyson said. "And the nigga can hoop. Who do that nigga mess around with?"

Trouble rolled her eyes into the top of her head because she was tired of talking about Dariel. "Jameelah Everson."

"Psycho-ass Jameelah? The one Li'l Joey was messin' around with?" Jyson asked.

"Yeah, that's her," Trouble replied.

"She was just at the hotel with my nigga, Shellmar. He said that bitch is crazy. He told me she be walkin' by his momma's house and shit. He said one day she saw him at the mall with his baby's momma and that Jameelah waited until she walked away and then rolled up on him and told him that if he didn't call her that night that she was gon' tell his girl all about them messin' around."

"Now that's some real live *Swimfan* shit there," Trouble said. "Dariel has been with her for about eight months, and if he doesn't know she's crazy by now, he'll know. He'll know when he comes home to find his rabbit boilin' on top of the stove like Michael Douglas did in that movie *Fatal Attraction*." Trouble and her brother cracked up laughing, and even Michaela had to laugh at that one.

"Well, Jyson, I'm about to go home," Michaela said, kissing him on the lips.

"Okay, boo bear," he said, smiling, kissing her back.

"Boo bear?" Trouble laughed and walked into the kitchen to pour herself a glass of milk.

"How come your sister doesn't like me?" Michaela asked. "I have never done anything to her."

"I don't know. Do you want me to ask her?"

"Naw. I ain't gon' even worry about it." Michaela stood up and walked toward the door. "I'll see you tonight, right?"

"It all depends if you really want to see me," he said, smiling, melting her heart.

"I can't wait." She winked and walked over to him and planted another kiss on his lips before leaving. *Damn, I'm feelin' this nigga. He's got a sista sprung*, she thought as she got into her brand new Mazda RX8 and sped off while Field Mob bumped out the speakers.

"Trouble, come here for a minute," Jyson called out after Michaela left.

"What's up?" she asked, standing in the kitchen doorway.

"How come you don't like Michaela? What has she done to you?"

Trouble shrugged her shoulders because she didn't have a real reason why she didn't like her brother's lady friend. "I don't know. It's just somethin' about her that I don't like," she answered.

"You got to get to know her, Trouble. She's a good girl. You haven't even given her a chance," Jyson pleaded.

"See, that's where you're wrong. I don't have to give her a chance; you do."

"That ain't fair, Trouble."

"Well, guess what, life ain't fair. Don't get me wrong. If you like her, I love her. I just don't have to deal with her; you do."

"What makes me happy should make you happy too," he said.

"Jyson, I am happy for you and what's-her-name. But I still don't have to deal with her," Trouble said, trying to get her brother to understand where she was coming from.

"She's gon' be comin' around a lot, so you might as well get used to it."

"It's all good. I still don't have to deal with her, though. I'll just stay in my room or go over to Ta'liyah's house."

"Trouble, you ain't right."

"She only wants you for your money." Trouble grimaced.

"So that's your problem with her? You think she's after my money?" Jyson asked.

"Well, what else could she want you for? She's way older than you are." *And plus I don't like that bitch cut-tin' in on my time with you*, Trouble thought.

"How come she can't want me for my good looks or my charmin' smile? Why does it has to be for my money?"

"I don't know. I just don't trust her. I bet you she has a shovel in the trunk of her car," Trouble said.

Jyson laughed and shook his head. "Michaela has her own money," he said defensively.

"Where does she work at?"

"Why?" Jyson asked, beating around the bush, not wanting his sister to know that his new lady friend was a stripper. "She works at the club," Jyson mumbled.

"What club? I know you ain't talkin' about Club Brittney's?" Trouble exclaimed.

"Yeah, I am."

"So you mean to tell me that Michaela is a stripper?"

"Yep. But she's only doin' it to finish payin' for college," he explained.

"So you mean to tell me that Michaela is like Diamond from the movie *The Players Club*?" she asked sarcastically.

"Whatever, man." Jyson waved his sister off and brushed past her and walked into the kitchen to get something to snack on.

Trouble sat on the couch and was rambling through Jyson's new CDs when the doorbell rang.

"Who is it?" Jyson yelled at whoever it was beating on the door.

"It's ya momma. Boy, open up the door," she screamed.

"Dig that." Trouble rolled her eyes and headed to her bedroom.

Jyson opened up the door and stared at his mother. Her mouth was twisted up and she had the same nasty clothes on.

"Hey, son. How are you?" She smiled and walked into the house taking a look around.

"I'm fine, Momma. How 'bout yourself?" Jyson's heart hurt from the sight he was looking at. His mother looked bad.

"I'm tired, son. Momma is tired of them damn streets. They beatin' me down, ya hear me?"

"Well, come home then, Momma," Jyson pleaded.

"I just wanted to know if I could get twenty dollars," she begged. "Ja'mario told me you was doin' big things. I asked that nigga for a twenty on credit and he told me to ask my son. I see you doin' well for yourself." She looked around the house. "It seems like you have somethin' new every time I stop by."

"Yeah, and?"

"I feel you, son," she said, smiling as she looked around the house to see what she could steal and take to the dope man.

Trouble walked into the living room and shook her head at the awful sight of her mother.

"How's my little girl?" her mother asked.

"Like you really care about my well-bein'. If you cared at all, you would be here instead of layin' up in them crack houses." Trouble was deeply hurt to see the woman she yearned for to be standing in front of her looking like she had just been hit by a bus.

"Trouble, I done told you to watch your mouth and show Momma some respect," Jyson said as Trouble walked back into her bedroom.

"Boy, what's wrong wit' ya sista?" Momma asked.

"Now you know damn well what's wrong with her. She misses you and she need for you to be here for her. And stop lookin' around my house 'cuz you can't get shit up outta here," Jyson said angrily.

"Come on, boy, let Momma have that cordless phone. I bet you I can take it to the pawnshop and get about forty dollars for it," she said.

"No, Momma."

"Then just give me the damn forty dollars."

Jyson didn't respond.

"Well, let me have that vase up there on the mantel. I probably can get about fifty for it."

Before Jyson could tell his mother no once again, there was a knock at the front door. "Who is it?" Jyson yelled.

"It's your Aunt Trina," someone yelled from the other side.

Jyson opened up the door and Trina walked in with Uncle Charlie and Aunt Loretta.

"What a surprise," Jyson said, smiling. "What brings y'all to my neck of the woods? And where's Aunt Rachel?"

"Yeah, what brings y'all over here?" Momma asked with little enthusiasm. Of all the times she decided to pop up, who knew there'd be a family reunion?

"Ain't no need to beat around the bush. You're what brought us over here, Denise," Loretta said.

"What about me?" Momma asked.

"Hush up, Denise," Uncle Charlie said. "Just listen."

"Denise, we have all been talkin' and we think that Candria should come to live with one of us," Aunt Trina said in a calm voice.

"Y'all gotta be kiddin' me," Momma said.

"Do it look like we're kiddin'?" Loretta spat. "Now look, we all know what's goin' on over here and we don't like it one bit. Trouble is almost finished with high school and we want to make sure she graduates and goes to college. We don't want her to get caught up in all the riffraff that's going on in this house. She's come too far."

"What are you talkin' about, Loretta?" Momma asked slowly.

"Don't play stupid with me. You know damn well what I'm talkin' about. You over here smokin' them damn drugs and yo' son is sellin' them," Loretta shouted.

Jyson's eyes got big. "How do you know what I do?" he said, butting in, no longer excited about the uninvited guests.

"Well, where else are you gettin' the money from to buy all these nice things around here? And you're drivin' a new car. You don't have a job," Loretta said enviously.

"You don't know what I do," Jyson huffed.

"And even if you did work, you still wouldn't be makin' enough money to pay for all this," Loretta said, pointing at all the expensive items around the living room.

Trouble stood in her doorway and listened to their conversation.

"We think that you should give one of us temporary custody of Candria. We also think you should check yourself into a rehab," Trina said hesitantly.

"I'll check myself into a rehab, but I'm not givin' y'all temporary custody of my daughter. I been strung out for all these muthafuckin' years and y'all just now decidin' to try to come and get her. Y'all gotta be outta y'all's damn minds. And I would appreciate it if y'all would get the fuck outta my damn house," Momma shouted.

"It's just temporary, Denise. Until you can get yourself together," Uncle Charlie pleaded.

"We just want what's best for Candria, that's all, Denise," Trina said.

"Y'all know what? Get y'all's sneaky, underhanded asses up out of here right now. You bitches think y'all nickel slick. I know what it is. Since y'all's daddy is dyin' and he's leavin' everything to Trouble, y'all think by y'all havin' custody of her it's gon' give y'all a chance to spend up her money. Y'all didn't think I knew about the insurance policy, did y'all?" Denise shouted.

"Why would you say a thing like that?" Trina gasped.

"What are you talkin' about, Momma?" Jyson asked.

"Y'all's grandfather made his only granddaughter his sole beneficiary because he never wanted her to have to depend on no man, and when he passes away she'll get over a hundred thousand dollars. He was gon' put it in a trust fund but he thinks she's responsible enough right now to manage the money. That cancer is gettin' the best of him so the doctor is givin' him about three months to live."

"Is that true?" Jyson looked at Trina and asked.

Trina shook her head yes. "But we're not tryin' to get Candria for the money. We just want what's best for her."

Jyson couldn't believe that his father's family was so greedy and conniving that they would try to use his sister like that.

"I would expect somethin' like that outta Loretta and Charlie, but not you, Auntie Trina," Jyson said as he shook his head in disgust.

"We really do want your sister to get a good education. It ain't all about the money, Jyson," Trina said. "But it will help pay for her college tuition."

"Yeah, along with payin' your bills, car notes, and ain't no tellin' what else," Trouble said, walking into the living room. "I don't want to live with none of y'all greedy bitches," she said indignantly.

"Trouble!" Trina shouted in disbelief. "I didn't know you had such a filthy mouth."

"See, I told y'all. This house is a bad influence on her," Loretta said.

"What? Did I say somethin' wrong or did I leave some-thin' out?" Trouble said, throwing her hands up.

"Well, I'm gon' tell you like this, you are gon' come to live with one of us whether you like it or not. And if you don't make a choice, children services will make it for you," Loretta said angrily.

Denise lunged over the ottoman at Loretta, but Charlie caught her frail frame in midair.

"Bitch, get the fuck outta my house and I ain't gon' tell you no more," Momma shouted. "Now I done told y'all that I'll check myself into a rehab, but don't fuck with my daughter. You think Charlie caught me in midair, well keep fuckin' with me and we gon' see if he can catch this bullet I got fo' yo' ass," Momma said with tears in her eyes.

"I done said what I had to say," Loretta said, backing up behind Charlie for protection.

"Candria, make it easy for all of us. Loretta has been threatenin' to call children services for a long time, but I kept talkin' her out of it. But now I don't think I can stop her, so please make up your mind and I'll call you tomorrow," Trina said.

"I know this came as a surprise to everyone, but it's best for Trouble. Now if Loretta calls children services they are gon' do a full investigation and there's no tellin' what might come out in the wash. And if they find out that Jyson is doin' what he's doin', they are gon' get the police involved and the shit is gon' hit the fan," Charlie said.

"Y'all get the fuck out please, and I ain't gon' tell y'all no more," Momma said in a calm voice.

"Denise, if you don't want no controversy in your household, I suggest you try to get Trouble to come live with one of us. And it's not for the money, either," Trina said as she tried to give Momma a hug, who was quick to push her away.

After everyone left, Momma walked over to the sofa and took a seat. She stared down at the floor as Trouble and Jyson looked at her. She stood up and walked to the front door without saying a word.

"Where you 'bout to go?" Jyson asked.

"I'll be back, son," Momma replied.

"Momma, they are talkin' about takin' your daughter and all you can say is you'll be back?"

"I need some time to think, son."

"You don't need no time to think. You tryin'a go get high. I can't believe a twenty-dollar rock is more important than your own damn daughter. I never thought I would say this to you Momma, but . . . you are fucked-up."

"Jyson, don't talk to me like that. I am still yo' mother, boy," she said, pointing her finger.

"I can't tell," he said.

"Look, I said I'll be back," she said, irritated.

"Momma, if you walk out that door, don't you ever step foot back in this damn house again, and I mean it," Jyson said with his chest going up and down as he tried to control his emotions.

Momma looked back at Trouble, hung her head to the floor, and walked out the door without looking back.

"You stupid bitch," Trouble yelled before walking away. She stormed into her room, slamming the door behind her, and then lay across her bed.

Jyson knocked on his sister's bedroom door.

"Come in," she cried, unable to control her emotions.

"Look, sis, we gon' get through this shit," Jyson said as he sat down on her bed.

"What am I gon' do, Jy?"

"I don't know yet, but we gon' come up with somethin'," he said, wiping her tears with the back of his hand. "Don't cry, sis." Jyson felt a lump forming in his throat. He tried to fight back the tears, but couldn't, and they flowed steadily down his cheeks. Jyson didn't know what he was going to do without his sister. She was all he had other than Big Mike. He wasn't going to let their no-good father's family keep them apart.

"Look, Jy, I don't want Loretta to call children services. They gon' try to get all up in yo' business and find out what you do for a livin'. So I think the best thing for me to do is go ahead and move with one of them greedy bitches. I know even though Poppy is leaving the money to me, I probably won't see a dime of it."

"Ain't that somethin'? My little sister will almost have as much money as me and she's never hustled a day in her life." Jyson smiled, trying to brighten up his sister's day.

"Whoever I choose to live with bet' not play me for my money, 'cuz if they do, I'm takin' them to court," Trouble said.

"Hold up before you get to callin' lawyers and shit. Wait until you get the money and see if they try to play you," Jyson suggested.

"Okay, I can do that."

Jyson's pager went off. He checked the number and then stood up. "I got some business I need to handle. Do you need anything while I'm out?"

"Yeah, I do. Could you pick me up a new mom?" Trouble said, smiling.

Jyson smiled back at his sister and gave her a hug before walking out of her room and out the front door.

Jyson got into his car and started it up. Yung Joc was blaring out the speakers. Jyson turned the volume down and dialed up the number that was left on his pager.

"Who dis?" he asked the person who answered the phone.

"Nigga, this Woo. What's up, li'l homey?"

"What's up, nigga?" Jyson said, smiling.

"Man, I need somethin'. My package is gettin' low," Woo yelled into the phone receiver.

"Damn, nigga, why you talkin' so loud? You tryin'a set a nigga up or somethin'?" Jyson asked.

"Can't you hear all these damn kids in the background?

That's why I'm talkin' so damn loud." *No, this bitch-ass nigga didn't say I was tryin'a set him up,* Woo thought.

"Yeah, I hear 'em. It sounds like you at a day-care center," Jyson laughed.

"I am. I'm over one of my baby's momma house and she got six kids," Woo said. "Might as well be a day-care center and shit."

"Damn, she's been doin' some serious fuckin'. They all yours?"

"Hell naw. I only got one by the hood rat. Anyway, nigga, what's up? I need a izounce of sizoft," Woo said.

"Meet me at the spizot in about a hizaf," Jyson said, hanging up the phone and driving over to his decoy apartment. All his so-called friends thought it was where he lived, except for Big Mike. It was no one else's business where he really laid his head as far as Jyson was concerned.

Eleven

Trouble walked into the bathroom, jumped in the shower, and put on a clean pair of pajamas. She was in no mood to leave the house; not even for a trip to the mall. Trouble never turned down a chance to go shopping, but the news her aunts and uncle dropped on her today was way too much to handle. She walked into the kitchen and sat down at the table, picking up her English notes in an attempt to study, but the words on the paper looked foreign to her because she had so much on her mind. Trouble laid the notes down and wondered which family member she should choose to live with. The phone rang and scared her out of her train of thought.

"Hello?" she answered in a noticeably depressed voice.

"Hey, baby girl, what's the matter?" Dariel asked.

"Too much." She closed her eyes and replayed the day's events in her head.

"It sounds like you've been cryin'."

"I'd rather not talk about it." Trouble felt like she was about to start crying again.

"I'm on my way over there," Dariel said and hung up the phone without saying another word.

"I hate when he hangs up on me!" Trouble shouted before jumping up and changing her clothes. She might have been depressed, but she damn sure wasn't going to let Dariel see her looking a hot mess. Twenty minutes later, Dariel was knocking at the front door. She opened the door and he planted a kiss on her soft lips.

"Ummm, minty," he said, smiling, and gave her another peck on the lips. "Now tell me what's the matter with you." Dariel walked over to the sofa and sat down. He patted the sofa and motioned for Trouble to come sit next to him.

"You are not goin' to believe this shit I'm about to tell you," she said as she sat down next to him.

"Try me."

"Okay, my aunts and uncle came over here today and told my momma that I had to come live with one of them until I graduate. They said that they didn't want me to get caught up in the riffraff that's goin' on over here. Anyway, to make a long story short, my poppy is leaving me some money and whoever has custody of me thinks they will have access to the money."

"Damn, that's deep. Don't your mom have custody of you or is that just automatic shit that whichever parent you live with is considered your legal guardian?"

"I don't even wanna talk about my mom right now," Trouble said. "All I'm concerned about is that they are makin' me leave my home." Tears began to form in her eyes. "And the messed-up part is that none of my family lives in the Senior High school district."

"Damn, that's messed-up," Dariel commented.

"Who you tellin'?" she said, wiping the tears away with the sleeve of her shirt. Silence filled the room as they both let the news sink in.

"What about us?" Dariel asked.

"Dariel, we haven't decided on us, furthermore, you have a girlfriend, remember? Earth to Dariel," she said sarcastically.

"Now that's where you're wrong. I had a girlfriend up until I got home this mornin'."

"What do you mean *had?* What happened?"

Dariel explained what had gone down earlier between him and Jameelah.

"Dang, that's crazy," Trouble said, amazed.

"She kept on and on about me fuckin' you and I told her that I didn't. She just wouldn't listen, so I went ahead and told her that I ate you out." Dariel watched Trouble's face for a response.

Trouble's eyes widened. "Oh my goodness. You gon' have that broad tryin'a kill me and you," she said, shocked.

"I had already started thinkin' she was crazy, but now I know that somethin' is really wrong with her.

You should have heard all the threats she made."
Dariel laughed.

"This shit is wild, man," Trouble said.

"Okay, enough about Jameelah," Dariel said, grabbing Trouble's hand and putting it into his. "What are we gon' do?"

"I'm not thinkin' about Jameelah, so I'm not gon' do anything."

"I'm not talkin' about Jameelah anymore, remember . . . Earth to Trouble." Dariel laughed. "I'm talkin' about us now," he said with a look of sincerity in his eyes.

"Look, Dariel, I'm gon' keep it real with you. I like you a lot, but—"

"There's always a but," he said, cutting her off.

"I don't wanna start somethin' that I can't finish. I will be livin' forty-five minutes away, and you know how long-distance relationships work . . . they don't."

"Look, Trouble, I'ma keep it real with you, like you better always do with me. I dig the hell outta you and have been for the longest time. But our timin' has always been off. You had a nigga and I had Jameelah, but now we are both single, so I don't see why we don't get together. It ain't like you gon' be livin' in another state.

"I looked forward to comin' to Mansfield every summer when I was younger 'cuz I knew you were gon' be over Ta'liyah's house. All I want to do is take care of you, pamper you, and most of all, love you," he said.

Trouble looked into Dariel's eyes as he spoke the most sweetest words she had ever heard.

"Dariel, you haven't even been out of your relationship for twenty-four hours, and you're already talkin' about us gettin' together," Trouble said.

"I love everything about you, Trouble. You're not like any other girl I've ever been with. And I know I want to be with you," Dariel pleaded.

Trouble's eyes began to water as she looked at him. She knew in her heart that she loved him too and wanted to be with him as much as he wanted to be with her, but she couldn't risk taking the chance of a long-distance relationship. She wasn't like Jameelah and needed to be in his face every second, but she didn't want to be that far away where she couldn't even see him in school. "I don't know, Dariel."

"Trouble, no matter how far we live from each other, we can make it work 'cuz we were meant to be together," Dariel said, smiling. Trouble was speechless. She didn't know what to say. "Will you give me the honor of becomin' my girl?" Dariel asked.

Trouble smiled widely, and before she knew it, she had said yes.

"Really?" Dariel said excitedly.

"Under one condition," Trouble said.

"Anything for you, baby girl."

"You gotta take me to the movies on Friday."

"That's cool with me," Dariel said, smiling.

"Did you study for your English test?" Trouble

asked, changing the subject now it was official that she was Dariel's girl.

"Not yet," he answered.

"Well come on, 'cuz I need my man to make straight A's." The idea of Dariel being her man made Trouble smile. "And you have to keep your grades up so you can go to a good college and be first pick in the NBA draft," she said, laughing.

They sat at the kitchen table and Trouble opened her English notes once again to study. No longer did the words look foreign to her.

"Damn, man, what took you so long to get here?" Jyson yelled at Woo.

"Man, I saw some fine bitches on my way over here and I stopped to talk to them," Woo replied. "They told me they were dancin' at Club Brittney's and they invited me to come watch their show tonight. Are you game or lame?" Woo asked.

"I'm game." Jyson smiled as he weighed up the ounce of powder that Woo came to purchase.

"I came over here last night, man. Where were you at?" Woo asked as he looked around the half-empty apartment.

"I was here. I just didn't feel like answerin' the door. I had a fine bitch up in here," Jyson lied.

"I'm 'bout to bounce. My moms is cookin' dinner," Woo said.

"I wish I had a moms to cook for me," Jyson said sadly.

Jyson had all his so-called friends thinking that he was an only child and that his parents passed away in a car accident. Big Mike was the only friend who knew Trouble existed. He made up that story just in case anything was to happen, so no one could ever shoot up his house or do anything to his sister. "Huh, man," Jyson said, handing Woo the plastic baggy with the powder in it.

"How many grams in this bag?" Woo asked.

"It's all there, nigga! Don't play with me," Jyson said angrily.

"How much I owe you?"

"Look, nigga, you doin' a little too much talkin' about shit you already know. Now the conversation is over." Jyson started getting paranoid as he watched Woo's actions.

Woo laid the eight hundred dollars on the kitchen table and nodded his head at Jyson before walking out the door without saying another word.

"Damn, that nigga act like he was wired up or some-thin'," Jyson said to himself.

Jyson grabbed the dishrag and wiped the leftover residue from the powder off the table. He then turned on a couple of lights before walking out the door.

Jyson got in his car and dialed up Big Mike's cell phone.

"Who dis?" Big Mike asked.

"Dis yo' brotha', nigga."

"Oh, what's up?" Big Mike laughed.

"Man, I think ya boy might be workin' for them people," Jyson spoke into the phone receiver.

"What boy and what people?" Big Mike asked.

"I'm talkin' 'bout ya boy, Woo, workin' for the police," Jyson replied.

"What would make you say a thing like that?" Big Mike asked.

"The nigga was askin' too many damn questions. He had me paranoid like a muthafucka," Jyson said, looking around for the police.

"Come to the club so we can talk in person. You know I don't like talkin' on these police-ass cell phones," Big Mike said before pushing the end button on his phone.

"It's seven p.m.," Trouble said, looking at the clock on the kitchen wall.

"It's late, and I'm starvin'," Dariel said, rubbing his stomach. "We have been studyin' for a long-ass time. Shit, we betta get an A on the English test."

Trouble laughed. "I'm starvin' too."

"Well, what you gon' cook?" Dariel asked.

"I ain't cookin' nothin'."

"Get ya coat and let's go to Nachelli's Chicken and Ribs."

"That sounds good." Trouble ran into her room and grabbed her jacket off the bed. "Wait a minute. I can't go anywhere lookin' like this," she said, referring to the old jeans and T-shirt she had put on before Dariel arrived.

"You my woman now and you don't need to impress anyone but me, and I think you look good no matter what you have on."

"Thanks. And I'm glad to know that it doesn't take much to impress you 'cuz I look a hot mess." They both laughed all the way to the truck.

Nachelli's Chicken and Ribs was jam-packed as usual, with people who wanted a good Sunday dinner but were too lazy to cook it. This was one of the best soul food joints for miles. Trouble didn't know anyone who could put their foot in some barbecue like Nachelli could, not even her Aunt Rachel, who was famous for her barbecue sauce recipe.

"Hey, Dariel," a heavyset girl wearing too much makeup said as she walked toward them.

"Hey, Jackie," Dariel said as he tried to hurry past her.

"Where's Jameelah?" she asked with a devious grin on her face. She looked Trouble up and down and then turned up her nose.

Trouble felt uncomfortable because of what she was wearing. *I can't believe I let him talk me into comin' out of the house in these old-ass clothes.*

Dariel pulled Trouble closer to his side. "I don't know where she at."

"Well, tell her that I said hello when you talk to her."

"I don't plan on talkin' to her," Dariel said. "So it looks like you're goin' to have to tell her yourself, Jackie."

"And why not? Y'all are still together aren't y'all?" Jackie asked, giving Trouble a halfhearted smile.

"No, they're not together anymore," Trouble spoke up. "He's with me now." She wrapped her arm around Dariel's waist and shot Jackie a fake smile. "Excuse us," Trouble said politely. Trouble and Dariel walked up to the counter to order their food, leaving Jackie standing there alone.

"Hey, Trouble," the girl behind the register said, smiling.

"Hey, Robyn. I didn't know you worked here." Trouble smiled even though she didn't want to. Robyn and Trouble fell out a while ago because they were supposed to be girls, until Robyn started messing around with Trouble's ex-boyfriend.

"I've been here for about two weeks," Robyn said, grinning.

"That's good." Trouble really couldn't have cared less.

"It was good seein' you. So what are you guys havin'?" she asked as her eyes were glued to Dariel's face.

"What do you want, baby girl?" Dariel asked Trouble, feeling uncomfortable because Robyn was staring at him like he was on the menu.

"I want a barbecue beef sandwich on wheat bread and a small water with a wedge of lemon," Trouble said.

Robyn kept her eyes on Dariel. If Trouble didn't know any better, she would have sworn that she saw a drip of slob drop from Robyn's lip.

"Did you hear me?" Trouble snapped.

"Uh, yeah, I heard you," Robyn stuttered. "You said you wanted a barbecue pork sandwich and a small lemonade," she said, smiling like she had just won the lottery.

"I didn't say that," Trouble snapped, then she repeated her order. "And if you wouldn't have been checkin' my man out, you would have heard me the first damn time!"

Robyn rolled her eyes at Trouble and addressed Dariel. "And what would you like, sir?"

Dariel placed his order and made the big mistake of smiling at Robyn.

"Would you like anything to drink?" Robyn asked.

"No, thank you," Dariel said, smiling, as he handed her a fifty-dollar bill.

Robyn made sure she touched Dariel's hand when she gave him his change.

"Who does your hair?" Robyn asked Dariel, admiring his braids.

"Sonya, but sometimes my girl does."

"Is she yo' girl?" Robyn had the audacity to ask, pointing at Trouble.

This bitch is bold! "No, I'm his fuckin' cousin! And what difference does it make if I'm his girl or not?" Trouble shouted, catching the attention of some of the other customers.

"It makes a lot of difference, 'cuz if he wasn't your man, I was gon' ask him out. You know, kinda like I did Markell," Robyn said, smirking.

"Don't get it twisted, bitch. I gave you Markell. It's not like you took him from me, 'cuz you don't have the ability to do that. But if you wanna keep thinkin' that you did, I ain't gon' bust ya bubble."

"Whatever, all I gotta say is that you betta keep a leash on ya nigga or I will have him tied up in my backyard! Next please," Robyn said.

Trouble and Dariel got their orders and walked over to an empty table and took a seat.

"What was that all about?" Dariel asked as he devoured his rib dinner.

Trouble took her napkin and wiped the corners of her mouth before she spoke. "When Markell and I broke up, she started messin' around with him even though she was supposed to be my girl. I kicked her ass and then I asked her was we still cool. I wasn't mad 'cuz she messed around with my ex, I was mad 'cuz she was supposed to be my friend," Trouble explained.

"She sure acted like y'all were friends when we first came in," Dariel said.

"Trust and believe, it was all a front. Now would you mistreat someone who beat your ass and then asked you if y'all were still cool afterward? And the bad part about it, the stupid bitch said yes that she was still cool with me," Trouble laughed.

Dariel licked the barbecue sauce from his fingers. "Damn, you must have put a whoopin' on that ass," he said, laughing.

"I did." Trouble laughed too. "And I started to bust yo' head when you kept smilin' at the broad."

"Damn, baby girl. I was just tryin'a be courteous."

"Whatever. 'Cuz every time she said somethin', you just had to show off that 'hey Kool-Aid grin,'" Trouble joked.

"Whatever," Dariel laughed. "I can see somebody's jealous."

"I'm not jealous. I was just tryin'a get my point across."

"Excuse me for smilin'. From now on, I'll walk around with a dog look on my face," Dariel said with a fake mean mug.

"Just don't say nothin' when I skin and grin up in another nigga's face and show all thirty-two of my teeth."

"Oh, don't worry, I ain't gon' say nothin', 'cuz if I catch you grinnin' in a nigga's face, you won't have thirty-two teeth in ya mouth 'cuz at least six of 'em gon' be on the ground." Dariel laughed.

Twelve

Jyson walked through the club doors and spotted his big brother sitting at a table getting drunk, as usual. "What's up?" Big Mike said as Jyson got closer to his table. He stood up and gave his little brother a firm handshake and a hug.

"What's up?" Jyson said, sitting down at the table with his brother and an unfamiliar girl.

"Jessica, this is my little brother, Jyson," Big Mike said.

"Nice to meet you," Jyson said, smiling, extending his hand.

"Nice to meet you too." Jessica smiled back. "I don't mean to sound desperate or anything, but has anyone ever told you that you have a beautiful smile?"

"I tell him that all the time," Michaela said, walking up behind Jyson and wrapping her arms around his neck. Michaela kissed Jyson on the cheek to let Jessica along with the other bitches in the club know that this piece of meat belonged to her. Michaela kissed Jyson on his other cheek and then shot Jessica a dirty look.

"Don't get it twisted, bitch. I was just givin' the nigga a compliment on his smile," Jessica spat. "It wasn't like

I asked him to come home with me, but if you don't keep a close eye on him, he will be sleepin' in my California king-size bed tonight." Jessica pushed herself away from the table and walked to the dressing room.

"Damn, Jyson, you got broads fightin' over you and shit," Big Mike laughed.

"Ahh man, it ain't like that," he said, smiling, wanting to laugh himself.

"Ain't nobody thinkin' about her. She needs to go home and take care of all them damn kids of hers," Michaela said.

"I think she can whoop you," Big Mike joked.

"Shut up, nigga," Michaela said and threw the towel she had hanging over her shoulder at him. She then walked toward the dressing room.

"Damn, man, you fuckin' Jessica too?" Jyson asked Big Mike.

"Naw, nigga, I ain't messin' with her. That's my wife's youngest sister. Remember I told you that Sherry had a sister that used to live here a long time ago, but her mother made her move to Atlanta to live with her daddy?"

"Old girl is stacked like a deck of cards! She got ass like the broad on that OutKast video," Jyson said. "When you told me Sherry's little sister was movin' back to Mansfield I was expectin' some little girl with ponytails, not some-thin' that looks like that."

"She all right. I can't stand the bitch, though. She got a son, Li'l Tony, by Woo, that's why her momma sent that ass to Atlanta. But that didn't do her no good, 'cuz she went down there and had five more babies by four different niggas," Big Mike said.

"Damn."

"Man, you betta go'n and hit that," Big Mike said, smiling. "I saw the way you was starin' at that ass."

"Shit, she got too many damn kids for me," Jyson said, waving his hand as if to say he was passing up on that one.

"It doesn't matter how many kids she got. You ain't got to take care of none of 'em. All you got to do is take care of business in the bedroom," Big Mike laughed.

"You sho'll right about that." Jyson laughed too and gave his brother some dap. "Hook a nigga up on the down low."

"You got that comin'," Big Mike said and ordered them both a shot of Hennessy with no chaser.

"What you wanna watch?" Trouble asked Dariel as she walked over to the shelf of movies.

"You already know what I wanna watch," he replied, sitting down on the couch.

Trouble put the movie on and sat down on the couch next to Dariel and let out a deep sigh.

"What's wrong with you?" Dariel asked.

"I just can't believe that so much has gone wrong today. This has been one of the worst days of my life. What else can go wrong?" Trouble laid her head back on the couch.

"Nothin' else is gonna go wrong, not as long as you're with me. I'm gon' make sure that everything in your life falls into place, I assure you." He leaned over and kissed her lips.

"I hope so." She kissed him back. "I don't think I could handle any more bad news," she said, laying her head on Dariel's shoulder. "I feel so comfortable with you."

"I feel the same way with you," he stated.

Trouble and Dariel enjoyed each other's company for hours. They laughed and talked about everything they could think of.

"Damn, it's goin' on midnight," Dariel said, looking at the time on the cable box.

"Funny how time flies," Trouble said, stretching her arms.

"Well, we should ace our English test tomorrow." Dariel stood up and stretched too. "I'm about to go, baby girl."

"Wait!" Trouble grabbed him by the arm. "Stay with me tonight. I would like some company since my mother and brother are never home."

Dariel agreed without hesitation. Trouble turned off the television, set the alarm, and then led Dariel into her bedroom.

"I'll be right back. I'm goin' to wash my face and brush my teeth," she said before disappearing into the bathroom.

Dariel walked around Trouble's bedroom and looked at all the pictures she had hanging on her walls. He thought it was rather strange that she had only one picture of an older couple and the rest of the pictures were of her and her brother. Dariel walked over to her bed and took a seat. He picked up her dirty brown teddy bear and threw it in the corner with the rest of her stuffed animals.

Trouble jumped in the shower and washed up real quick. She brushed her teeth and tied her hair in a silk scarf before walking back into her bedroom.

"Dang, it took you long enough," Dariel joked.

"Excuse me for wantin' to be clean. Hey, where's my teddy bear?"

"I threw it in the corner with the rest of the stuffed animals," Dariel said, pointing.

"That one doesn't belong in the corner with the rest of 'em. I hold on to him at night." Trouble walked over to the corner and picked her teddy bear up and laid it back on her bed.

"Well, I'm here tonight, so you don't have to hold on to your teddy bear." Dariel grabbed the bear and tossed him back into the corner.

"Come here, Jessica," Big Mike yelled over the loud music.

"What's up, Big Mike," she yelled back as she made her way over to the table and took a seat, never once taking her eyes off of Jyson's gorgeous face.

"My nigga wanna fuck you tonight," Big Mike said, grinning.

"Ya nigga can't speak for himself?" she asked, putting her hands on her hips and looking over at Jyson. *Damn, he looks a lot like one of my baby's daddies.*

"What's up, are you game or lame?" Big Mike asked, ignoring her last comment.

"I'm game. But uh . . . what about Michaela?" she said, smirking.

"What about her? If you won't tell, I won't tell," Jyson said, winking.

"Call me. Here's my cell phone number," Jessica said, then quickly jotted her number down on a napkin and slid it over in Jyson's direction.

Jyson picked up the the napkin and memorized the number. "I'll call you in an hour."

Jyson watched Jessica as she walked away.

"Ya just a playa playa," Big Mike sang.

"I ain't no playa. You the one," Jyson laughed and then looked around to make sure Michaela hadn't been watching him talk to Jessica.

"Where you gon' take her?" Big Mike asked as he took his fifth shot of Hennessy to the head.

"I'm takin' her to the Merritt Inn. She ain't worthy of nothin' else," Jyson said as he drank his fifth and final shot.

"Now what was you sayin' about Woo?" Big Mike slurred, changing the subject.

"I'll tell you tomorrow. You too damn drunk for me to be tellin' you tonight. Come on and let me take you home so I can go ahead and stick and move on this hood rat." Jyson got up from the table and he and his brother stumbled to his car.

Jyson pulled up in front of his big brother's house. "You home, man," he said, shaking Big Mike's shoulder.

Big Mike lifted up his head and looked around. He rubbed his eyes and shook his head. "Good lookin' out, man," Big Mike said as he desperately tried to climb out of the car. "Oh, and bust a nut for me," he said, smiling. And stumbled to his front door and banged on it like he was the police. Jyson waited on Sherry to open the door for her drunk husband, and after about five minutes of banging, she finally opened the door and waved at Jyson. He acknowledged her by blowing his horn three times and then sped down the avenue blasting Keyshia Cole.

"Ahhh shit!" Jyson yelled as he saw the police lights flashing behind him. He looked in his rearview mirror and fumbled in his jacket for a Listerine strip. *I know I wasn't swerving,* he thought to himself as the cop got out of his car and approached the car.

"Sir, could you please step out of the car," the officer said as he held one hand on his gun and the other hand on his flashlight, shinning it in Jyson's face.

"Look, man, I'm gon' save you the time," Jyson said, throwing his hands up. "I'm drunk, so check my car, license, and registration and go'n on and read me my rights and put me in the back of your car," Jyson slurred. The officer did what Jyson told him to do and hauled him straight to the city jail.

"How are we gon' make our relationship work? Not goin' to the same school anymore; not bein' able to see each other like we want to because we live so far away?" Trouble asked.

"Dang, girl, you act like you're about to move to another country." Dariel laughed.

"I know. It did sound like that," she said, chuckling.

"Don't let me hear about you messin' around with these tack-head-ass hoes in Mansfield, 'cuz you know if you do, Ta'liyah will tell me," Trouble said, laying her head on Dariel's chest.

"I know she'll tell you. But you bet not let me hear about you messin' around wit' them tired-ass niggas in Marion either. You know I got a few homeys over there," Dariel informed.

"Who are they?"

"Don't worry 'bout all that."

"Thank you for stayin' with me tonight," Trouble said.

"No, thank you."

Dariel found himself a comfortable position as Trouble did the same. He wrapped his arm around her waist as she said her prayers in silence. Before they both fell sound asleep, Dariel thanked God for sending an angel his way.

Trouble jumped up from a deep sleep. Something didn't feel right to her. She had a bad feeling that something was happening to someone close to her. She closed her eyes and prayed for God to watch over and protect her brother, and for him to return home safely. Surprising herself, she even prayed for her mother and that her poppy was okay. Trouble lay in bed, staring up at the ceiling. She couldn't go back to sleep, so she got up and turned the water on in the shower and got in. She let the hot water run down her body as she continued to pray.

"Can I get in?" Dariel said as he pulled back the shower curtain, nearly scaring Trouble half to death.

She looked at his naked body standing before her, and after seeing the big package he carried, how could she resist?

"Sure," she said, smiling. "Can you wash my back for me please?" She handed him a soapy loofah pad.

Dariel did what was asked of him. He washed in a circular motion and made his way down to her ass cheeks. He dropped the loofah and began to rub her soft behind with his bare hands.

"My turn," she said, bending down, picking up the loofah and washing his chest.

Trouble rubbed in a nice and slow motion before working her way down. She grabbed his almost erect love muscle in one hand and washed it with the other.

Dariel let out little soft moans. "What can you do wit' all this?" he asked.

"I don't know, why don't we find out?" Trouble said, without thinking first.

"What?" Dariel thought he was hearing things and asked her to repeat herself.

"You heard me," she said, surprising herself as much as him. She stepped out of the shower and walked back into her bedroom with Dariel close behind.

Dariel sat his soaking wet body on her bed and leaned back against the headboard. "Let me see what you workin' wit'." He reached over and pushed play on the CD player and sat back for the private show he was about to receive.

"What? You want me to dance?" Trouble asked coyly.

"Yes, dance for me please," he begged. A woman dancing was a big turn-on for him.

"How do you want me to dance?" she asked nervously.

"Anyway you want to, just as long as you do it."

Trouble was afraid at first, but once she began imagining that she was one of Usher's background dancers, she got into the groove of things. She moved her hips like she was in a reggae video. Dariel took in every move she made with his warrior standing on hard. He motioned her to come to him, and she obeyed.

I don't know what I'm about to get myself into, she thought as she walked over to the bed. *This nigga's dick looks like a ruler!*

Dariel stood up from the bed and pressed his naked body against Trouble's, kissing her forehead. "Lay down, baby girl," he whispered.

She did what she was told without hesitation. Her heart beat a mile a minute as R. Kelly sang softly in her ear. *Oh my goodness, what am I doin'?*

Dariel stood over her and bent down and kissed her soft lips. He climbed in the bed and parted her legs with his knee. He laid on top of her and began kissing her neck nice and slow. He worked his way down to her perky nipples. He sucked on one after the other as Trouble moaned quietly as she could because she didn't know if Jyson was home or not, but the way Dariel was making her feel at that moment, she couldn't have cared less if the entire neighborhood heard her. Dariel moved his way down and dug straight into her chocolate cave; his warm, wet tongue made Trouble moan like a banshee. He spread the lips that led to her stairway to heaven and gently ran his tongue across the split. He sucked every juice that flowed from her waterfall, making sure he didn't leave any behind. Dariel took his middle finger and attempted to stick it in her drenched waterfall, but it was much too tight, and plus Dariel knew it was making her feel uncomfortable by the way her body squirmed and jerked. Dariel went back to tasting her bodily fluids like he was eating soul food. His lips worked their way back up her beautiful body as he kissed it nice and slow.

"Are you sure you're ready for this?" he asked. Trouble shook her head yes, and then closed her eyes. "Now you know I'm not pressurin' you into this, right?"

"I'm doin' this 'cuz I want to," she said.

"Okay," he said, smiling down at her. "You ready?"

"As ready as I'm gon' get."

Dariel leaned down and picked up his blue jeans and pulled a condom out of his back pocket. He ripped through the plastic and slid it on. Trouble's heart beat fast as she watched his every move.

"Ohh wee, this is gon' be just like puttin' a summer sausage inside a Cheerio," he said, trying to make her laugh to take away some of her nervousness.

Trouble let out a nervous chuckle and then closed her eyes.

Dariel was almost as anxious and as nervous as Trouble. The way his heart pounded, you would have thought that it was his first time too. "Spread ya legs," he whispered softly in her ear.

Oh my goodness, she thought as her legs parted on their own.

"Ain't no turnin' back now." Dariel put the tip of his warrior in the opening of her waterfall and tried to work it in. He felt her entire body tense up. "Are you okay?"

"Yeah, I'm fine. I'm just a little scared, that's all." She took a deep breath and tried her best to relax, but every time he tried to work it in, she got tense.

"Don't be scared. I won't hurt you, or least I won't do it on purpose." He attempted to put the head back in and this time she grabbed ahold of the sheets.

"Relax, and let me handle this." This time Dariel managed to work his warrior into her cave.

"Ahhh," Trouble moaned loudly.

I'm makin' progress, Dariel thought as he began diving deeper with each stroke. He tried like hell to open up the locked walls that only he had a key to.

"Dariel, please," she begged.

"Ahhh, this shit feels good," he moaned with each stroke.

It had been a long time since Dariel had felt a cave this tight around his warrior, and boy did it feel good. "You like this, Trouble?" he asked as he made fuck faces. Dariel stroked harder and deeper as Trouble began warming up to the sensation of being made love to.

"Dariel!" Trouble screamed.

"Yeah, baby," he stroked and moaned at the same time. "Oh, this is some good shit," he moaned as he was about to explode.

"Dariel, please."

"Do you want me to stop?" he asked, slowing down, but never coming to a complete stop. Trouble shook her head no, so he picked back up the pace and began putting in work. After about five more minutes of work, Dariel let out one of the loudest squeals Trouble had ever heard before collapsing on top of her chest. Dariel breathed heavily as he spoke. "Are you okay?"

"Yeah, I'm fine. I'm in pain, though," she admitted without shame.

"So how was it?" Dariel asked.

"Painful, but in a good way," she said, smiling.

"I asked you if you wanted me to stop, and you said no so I kept goin'."

"It sounded like you were havin' too much fun, so that's why I didn't stop you."

"Was it anything like you imagined?" Dariel asked.

"Ta'liyah told me that it would be painful, but I didn't think she meant excruciatin' pain," Trouble said.

"I almost forgot you was a virgin."

"Well, you can't say that after today." Trouble was exhausted and wore out and all she wanted to do was go back to sleep, but she couldn't because she had to get up and get ready for school. "Can I get a ride to school?"

"You sure can. I'll be back around seven-fifteen a.m.," Dariel said as he put his clothes back on. He leaned down and kissed Trouble on her forehead and headed out the door.

Trouble lay in bed smiling to herself. *I can't believe I just lost my virginity. Niggas has been tryin'a get this shit for years and here this nigga has been my man for less than twenty-four hours and got a piece of this sweet potato pie.*

As Dariel drove home, similar thoughts invaded his mind. *Damn, niggas been tryin'a get at Trouble for years and here I come along and get her in twenty-four hours. You the man, Dariel,* he thought.

Thirteen

"Lewis, you made bail!" the CO yelled into the holding cell that Jyson slept in.

"All right," Jyson yawned as he sat up. He had to lay back down in a hurry because his head felt like someone was beating it with a hammer.

"Come on, Lewis, if you wanna go home," the CO yelled again.

"I'm up, damn." Jyson slowly lifted himself off the hard bench and followed the CO down a long hallway. *Damn, I don't even remember comin' to jail. I gotta stop drinkin',* he thought, rubbing his head.

The first face Jyson recognized was Big Mike's.

"You all right, man?" Big Mike said and then gave his little brother a hug.

"Hell naw," Jyson said. "I feel like I've been hit by a semitruck." He began rubbing his temples. "How did you know I got arrested?"

"Sherry's nosy ass be listenin' to the scanner all the damn time to see if she hears my name. She done got slick, 'cuz when I used to stay out all night, I would tell her I got arrested for DUI. I can't tell that lie no more," Big Mike laughed, and patted his brother on the shoulder, which made his head pound even harder.

Big Mike and Jyson walked out of the county and headed to his truck. "You look bad, man," Big Mike said.

"I feel bad too," Jyson replied. "Take me to get some Tylenol," he whispered.

"You don't need no pills. All you need is another shot of what you were drinkin' on last night," Big Mike said, opening the truck door for his sick brother to get in.

"Whatever it takes to get rid of this headache." Jyson climbed in the truck and laid his head back on the headrest and closed his eyes.

"You know Jessica's tramp ass called the house for you all night," Big Mike said as he checked his messages on his cell phone.

"Man, I ain't thinkin' about that ho. I just checked my pager and I see where she done paged me about fifteen times. Is she a stalker or what?" Jyson laughed.

"How did she get yo' number?"

"I don't know, man."

"All that bitch want is some dick in her life," Big Mike laughed.

"All them damn kids she got, she done had enough dick to last her ass a lifetime!" They laughed as they drove off.

"Damn, my shit is bleedin'," Trouble said as she washed up. She walked in her room and pulled out a navy blue Mecca sweatsuit and a pair of navy blue Timberlands and got dressed. Five minutes later there was a knock at the door.

"Well, don't we look thugged out?" Dariel said when Trouble opened up the door to let him in.

"I need to feel comfortable 'cuz my stuff is hurtin'. I had to wear dark colors 'cuz my stuff is bleedin' too."

"Yo' stuff?" Dariel laughed. "I ain't heard that word in a long-ass time." "Shut up." "Baby girl, I sure can go for some pancakes, bacon, and eggs," Dariel said, rubbing his stomach. "You know what . . . I can too." Trouble laughed. "Let's go," he said, walking out on the porch with Trouble by his side. "What's that on your dad's windshield?" Trouble asked. "I don't know. It wasn't there when I pulled up five minutes ago." Dariel jumped off the porch and figured it was a letter from Jameelah and he was right, it was. He began reading it to himself.

Bitch, you thought I was playin' when I said that it wasn't over? Nigga, you tried to play me, but in reality you played yourself! Oh! Don't fall in love with the bitch just yet, because you are about to be a daddy! I know you are just so ecstatic about the good news. I am too. So go on and pick your face up off the ground and I'll holla at you, if not today, in about seven months! Love Jameelah and baby!

"What's the matter, Dariel?" Trouble asked as he stood frozen. "Nothin'. Let's go," he said, looking around as if someone was watching him. "Let's not go to school today." "Boy, please. What is wrong with you? You know we have a test today. Why are you actin' so damn nervous?" "Ain't nothin' wrong wit' me. Let's just go to my house and chill for a second, 'cuz we need to talk."

Damn, this nigga is actin' strange. I wonder what was in that letter? Trouble thought. "Dariel, what was in that letter if you don't mind me askin'?"

"Nothin'," he snapped.

"Hold up, nigga, don't be gettin' irritated with me. You need to be mad at the person who left the letter on your windshield. And furthermore, it ain't cool for you to be keepin' shit from me. If it's gon' be like that, we might as well end this shit right here and right now," Trouble snapped back.

"Look, baby girl, I'm sorry if I seem to be irritated, but it's some deep shit in this letter. I'm not tryin'a keep anything from you. I just got to find out if the shit in this letter is true before we discuss it."

Trouble and Dariel got in the truck and buckled their seat belts. "What is it, Dariel?" Trouble asked. *I hope this nigga ain't got AIDS or some other STD!* All kinds of crazy shit ran through Trouble's mind as they rode to school in complete silence.

"Here, take the keys and pick me up from basketball practice," Dariel said, handing Trouble the truck keys as they walked into the school building.

"Okay," Trouble said, taking the keys from him and walking in a different direction.

"Girrrlll, have you heard the news?" Regina said, walking up to Trouble.

"What news?" Trouble replied. She couldn't wait to hear what was goin' on now. If there was anything that needed to be known, everyone knew to ask Regina, aka News Center 8.

"Jameelah is muthafuckin' pregnant!" Regina said as she jumped up and down. "Can you believe she's pregnant by Dariel's fine ass?"

Trouble's heart began to race as her head spun in circles. Her chest became tight and it felt like her air had just been cut off as she fell up against her locker.

"Trouble, are you okay?" Regina panicked.

"Yeah, I'm okay. I just need some water." Trouble stumbled over to the water fountain and took a sip of the lukewarm water. "Who told you Jameelah was pregnant?"

"Shit, she's been showin' off the paperwork she got from Planned Parenthood." Regina noticed the sick look on Trouble's face. "Trouble, you ain't lookin' too good. You need to sit down." Regina helped her friend to the rusty bench that hung from the wall.

"I'm okay." Trouble forced a smile to hide the hurt and pain.

"What just happened to you?"

"I don't know. I just got dizzy all of a sudden. I guess it's because I didn't eat any breakfast this mornin'," Trouble lied.

"I know what you mean, 'cuz I get like that too when I miss a meal." Regina had just opened herself up for a wisecrack because Trouble knew good and well that her friend never missed a meal, but Trouble was in no mood to crack jokes.

"Speakin' of food, I'm 'bout to go to the cafeteria to see what they're havin' for breakfast. You gon' be okay?" Regina rubbed Trouble's back and headed off, after Trouble assured her that she would be just fine.

"Okay, Trouble, you can do this," she told herself as she raised herself off the bench to go look for Dariel. She roamed the halls desperately looking for her so-called man, finally spotting him leaning up against a vacant locker talking to Ta'liyah.

"All I wanna know is if what I'm hearin' is true?" Trouble blurted in anger as she approached Dariel.

"Trouble, I don't know," he said, reaching out to her.

"Is it true, Dariel?"

"I don't know," he said, grabbing her wrist.

"Let me go, nigga. Is that what the letter was about? 'I'm gonna make sure everything in your life stays intact, you don't have to worry about nothin' as long as you're with me,' " Trouble said, imitating Dariel's words. "That's bullshit and you are too. I gotta give it to you, you got hella' game, Dariel, and I can't believe I fell for the shit. I hate you!" she cried and turned and walked away.

Those three words stuck in Dariel's head like an ax.

"Trouble," he called out, but she kept right on stepping.

"Damn, what was that all about?" Ta'liyah asked her cousin.

"I'll tell you about it later," Dariel said before walking away to go find Trouble.

I can't believe this shit, Trouble thought as she stomped down the school hallway. *First I find out that I have to move, then I find out that my own damn momma cares more about smokin' crack than her own damn daughter's well-bein', and now my man of two days is about to be a fuckin' daddy! What next?*

"Trouble," Dariel called out, but didn't get any response.

Trouble walked into her homeroom class and took a seat at her desk. "Trouble, why don't you answer me?"

"We don't have shit to talk about," Trouble said.

Jameelah walked into the classroom and smiled at Trouble. But instead of getting up and kicking Jameelah's ass, Trouble got up and walked back out of class.

"Trouble," Dariel shouted.

"Let the bitch go," Jameelah said, chuckling.

Dariel shot Jameelah a look that could kill. "Why don't you shut the fuck up? The baby probably ain't even mine."

"Oh, trust and believe it's yours. I was gon' tell you the other day that I was pregnant, but you rushed me outta yo house so fast," Jameelah said.

"Well, I need a blood test," Dariel said before walking out of the classroom to catch up with Trouble. "Trouble, don't do this to me," he called out when he caught up to her.

Trouble stopped and turned around. "What am I doin' to you? I didn't do a damn thing to you, Dariel. You did it to yourself when you had unprotected sex with Jameelah." Trouble shook her head in disgust and walked away.

"Trouble, please. I'm just as fucked-up about this as you are," Dariel begged and grabbed her by the arm. "We don't even know if the shit is true."

"Let me go," she shouted. "And you sound stupid. How can you be just as fucked-up as I am?"

"Do you actually think I want a baby by Jameelah? I'm not ready to be a father and she knew that. That broad tricked me. She knows that I'm tryin'a finish school and go away to college. I got a chance to go to any college I want to on a full scholarship, do you think I wanna blow that?"

"Look, Dariel, I completely understand where you're comin' from, but I have a lot of shit on my plate, and there's no more room for baby momma drama."

"There won't be any drama," Dariel tried hard to assure her of that.

"Whatever. I know how Jameelah is and she's gon'
use that baby to her advantage any way she can, and I
don't have time for games."

"There won't be any games, I promise. I love you,
baby girl." Those three words rolled off of Dariel's
tongue with no problem, because he really did love
her.

"Puhleeze, what could you possibly know about
love?" Trouble said, grimacing.

"I know that I love you. And I might be young, but
I know some of the things I want outta life and you're
one of 'em."

"I'm sorry, Dariel, there can be no us." Tears
streamed down Trouble's cheeks as she handed Dariel
back the keys to his father's truck before walking
away.

"Now, what was you sayin' about Woo?" Big Mike
asked, pulling into his driveway. The neighbor's
daughter was standing outside with some of her
friends smoking cigarettes. Big Mike shot a smile over
at the young ladies, and they giggled like the little
schoolgirls they were before running into the house.
"I'm gon' get me some of that young stuff," Big Mike
said.

"Man, you betta go'n on and leave them cotton
panties alone before you fuck around and be in the
penitentiary," Jyson said as he closed the truck door.

"Man, I ain't worried about that young ho tellin' on me, 'cuz she too scared of her father. What you think her daddy would do if he found out she gave a nigga some of that snappy nappy? He gon' throw that ass out the house and cut her out his will." Jyson shook his head and laughed. "All you gotta do is take them young hoes to the mall a few times, get their hair and nails done, and they all yours. You can do whatever you want to as long as you kick the bitch out a couple of ends from time to time," Big Mike said, sticking his house key in the front door.

"Hey, baby," Sherry said, smiling and kissing her husband on the lips as he walked into the living room.

"Hey," he said with little enthusiam as he sorted through the bills that laid on top of the mantel.

"I don't get no hug and kiss?" she said with her lips poked out.

"I'm sorry, baby," he said as he walked over and kissed her on the lips.

"Now that's what I call love," Jyson said, smiling, before taking a seat on the couch and closing his eyes.

"What's wrong wit' you, Jyson?" Sherry asked.

"He got a headache," Big Mike answered for him. "Why don't you go get him somethin' for it?" he said, patting his wife on her round backside.

"We got Tylenol and Bayer. Which do you prefer?" Sherry asked.

"It doesn't matter, you choose," Jyson said, opening his eyes. "I see y'all got some new furniture."

Jyson looked around at the newly decorated living room. It was finished with cognac-color top-grain leather sofa and love seat, and there was an oversized leather chair sitting in the corner to match. The sixty-two-inch television that sat in the other corner with hundreds of movies stacked in the DVD slots set the entire living room off. Sherry had what seemed to be about sixty or more black figurines sitting around the room. They were the expensive ones, not the ones you get from the dollar stores.

"Yeah, man, my wife had to have this furniture," Big Mike said as he sat down on the couch before admiring his wife's taste. "So you ain't feelin' Woo, huh?" he said before picking up one of the five remotes that sat on the coffee table.

"Man, I think that nigga is the police," Jyson said.

"Why would you say somethin' like that about him? If you would have said that about anybody else I probably would have believed you. Woo has been one of my most loyal soldiers, man. I've been dealin' with him too long for him to dime me or you out," Big Mike said, turning to BET.

"Man, he was askin' way too many damn questions when I served him last night. He was actin' all nervous and shit." Jyson focused his attention on the half-naked women on the video they were watching.

"Maybe he was high or somethin'," Big Mike said in Woo's defense. "You know niggas think y'all kinda resemble one another. Y'all do favor a little," Big Mike laughed.

"He could have been high, but I know one thing, I ain't sellin' him shit else," Jyson said. "And me and that nigga don't look shit alike, I'm tired of hearin' that!"

Sherry walked into the room with Tylenol in one hand and a big glass of orange juice in the other. "What are you fellas in here talkin' about?" Sherry sat down on the couch next to her husband and rubbed his thigh.

"Stop bein' so damn nosy, woman," Big Mike said.

"My sister told me that y'all was supposed to hook up last night, Jyson. As a matter of fact, she's on her way over here as we speak," Sherry said, grinning.

"Why don't you mind your own damn business?" Big Mike snapped.

"What are you talkin' about?" Sherry asked, confused.

"Why did you call that bitch and tell her Jyson was over here?" he yelled, slamming the remote down on the coffee table.

"I didn't even call her, she called me," Sherry lied.

"I didn't hear no phone ring, did you, Jyson?" Jyson sat in silence, not wanting to get in the mix. "And I bet you the one that gave that ho Jyson's pager number too."

"Whatever," she said.

"Let's go, man." Big Mike stood up and motioned for Jyson to follow.

"Where you 'bout to go?" Sherry snapped.

"I'll be back later on," he said, walking toward the door.

"You get on my fuckin' nerves. You always out in the damn streets. We don't never spend no time together. But you know what they say, what you won't do, there's always another nigga that will," she retorted.

And before she knew it, the back of Big Mike's hand was across her face. "Fuck you, bitch! Go ahead and let another nigga do what I won't do. Matter of fact, get yo' shit and get the fuck up outta my house," he snapped, then walked out the front door, leaving Jyson awed by his reaction.

"You all right, Sherry?" Jyson asked after an awkward silence. He listened as Sherry poured out her heart.

"Yeah, he bought me that forty-thousand-dollar car, a fivethousand-dollar ring, and this half-a-million-dollar house," she continued, "But I didn't want any of it. He bought this shit just to keep my mouth shut about all them bitches he's out there fuckin'." Tears formed in her eyes. "I would have settled for an apartment, a Pinto, and a ring from the bubble gum machine just to be able to spend time with my husband. I meant what I said, Jyson, about me findin' somebody to spend my time with," Sherry said convincingly.

Jyson looked into her soft brown eyes and felt sorry for the woman that stood before him. She was crying out for help, but he didn't know how to help her.

"Sherry, I don't want to get in the mix of y'all shit, 'cuz both of y'all are like family to me," he said. "So all I can say is do what's gon' make Sherry happy."

Sherry understood that he didn't want to get in between their marital spat, and she thought about what Jyson had just said to her. "Thanks," she said, smiling, and gave him a hug and a kiss on the cheek.

"Anytime." He smiled back and then walked out the door.

"What are you doin' here?" Trouble asked Dariel as she walked up on her front porch.

"We need to talk," Dariel said.

"We talked already, and there's nothin' left to say."

"Look, just give me ten minutes of your time and then I'll leave."

"Okay, but you betta start talkin', 'cuz you have already wasted thirty seconds," she said sarcastically.

"Trouble, don't let this break us up. The news about the baby is a big shock to me too. I just found out about it this mornin' myself. That's what the letter was about."

"I figured that much out," she said, cutting her eyes.

"I love you." Dariel tried to kiss Trouble but she backed away.

"We already established how we felt about each other, and it still doesn't change the fact that Jameelah may be pregnant by you."

"I know," he said, closing his eyes and wishing this was all a dream.

"Look at it like this, you done got somethin' from me that no other nigga can ever say he got. Congratulations," she said sarcastically.

"Do you think all I wanted from you was a piece of ass? I coulda got some pussy from anywhere. I told you that I love you, and yeah, I might have a baby on the way, but that still doesn't change the way I feel about you. I've never loved Jameelah, and I've never once led her to believe that I did."

"Whatever. You mean to tell me that she didn't think that you loved her?"

"I ain't gon' lie, in the beginnin' all I ever wanted from Jameelah was sex. You women don't understand that sex is like crack, it's very addictive, especially when it's good. And old girl put it down on me. She had one of the coldest suck games. I cared about her a lot, but I didn't love her. I've never told any woman that I loved her, other than my mom and my grandma, because I've never been in love until now," he said sincerely.

"Okay, Dariel, your time is up. I'm about to go in the house," Trouble said.

"It's like that?"

"It's like that," Trouble said, walking into the house and closing the door behind her.

Fourteen

"Where are my damn house shoes at?" Jyson yelled as he let his feet hit the cold hardwood floors.

"You don't have no house shoes over here. You ain't at Michaela's house, remember?" Jessica said with an attitude.

"Well, if I'm gon' be comin' over here, you are gon' hafta buy me some then," he said, grabbing a blunt from off the nightstand and lighting it up.

"If you want me to buy you some house shoes, you gon' hafta take me and the kids to Disney World," she said, taking the blunt from his fingers.

"How many times do I gotta tell you that I ain't takin' no other nigga's kids to Disneyland, Disney World, or not even the Disney store?"

"Well, you know I'm a total package. If you do for me, you got to do for all six of my kids," Jessica said, inhaling the blunt.

"Who said I was gon' do somethin' for yo' ass? Shit, I am doin' somethin', I'm comin' here dickin' you down real good," he said, smirking.

"Whatever, nigga. The dick is good, but it ain't made of gold, 'cuz I done had better," Jessica said.

"I can't tell you done had better, 'cuz you keep blowin' my damn pager up," he laughed while taking the blunt from her.

"You need to give me your cell phone number."

"No can do." Jyson never gave his cell phone number out to any females other than Michaela. He didn't give it out because he didn't want to get caught up in no drama, like Michaela deciding to answer his phone while he was sleeping or something. "I'm takin' a hell of a chance comin' over here to fuck wit' yo' ass. I got a good girl at home," he said, blowing the blunt smoke in her face.

"She must not be that good, 'cuz if she was, you wouldn't be over here with me."

"Trust me, she's good. I just wanted to try you out," Jyson said. "You're like a new toy to me right now."

"You need to go on and leave her ass and get wit' me."

"Bitch, please. You got a baby by Woo and you know how sensitive that nigga can get over a broad," Jyson said, laughing.

"So, I ain't wit' Woo. He's just my baby's daddy."

"One of many, and I don't want you, girl. What do you have goin' for yourself? Absolutely nothin'!"

"Fuck you," Jessica said, rolling her eyes.

"My cell phone is ringin', hand it here," Jyson said as he heard his phone ringing.

"Can I answer it?" Jessica asked as she picked it up off the floor.

"Hell naw," Jyson yelled, snatching the phone from her hand.

"Who dis?" he answered.

"Who do you want it to be?" the voice on the other end asked.

"I wouldn't mind it bein' my boo bear," Jyson said, smiling, as Jessica shot him a dirty look.

"Are you still goin' to get a tattoo today?" Michaela asked.

"Yep," he answered, before blowing smoke from the blunt into Jessica's face again.

Jessica rolled her eyes and began kissing Jyson's stomach. She saw that it wasn't fazing him one bit, so she grabbed his love muscle and wrapped her wet lips around it and began sucking it.

"Whoa," he said.

"What's wrong wit' you?" Michaela asked.

"Nothin', ain't nothin' wrong wit' me at all," he said, holding his head back with his eyes glued shut.

"Where are you at?" Michaela asked suspiciously.

"I'm over Big Mike's house. Why?" he whimpered.

"Look, I'll see you at the tattoo shop, 'cuz I got some errands to run," Michaela said.

"Be there around five. I love you."

"Yeah, I love you too. Oh, and by the way, bust a nut for me," she said before pushing the END button on her cell phone.

That must be what they call a woman's intuition, Jyson thought. *I feel bad and all about gettin' my dick sucked by somebody else, but hey, if Jessica wants to do it, shit, I ain't gon' stop her.* Jyson laid his head back and enjoyed the pleasure Jessica was giving him. Fuck it, if he had to explain himself to Michaela, he might as well make it worthwhile.

"Trouble, why are you doin' this to us?" Dariel whined over the phone.

"What am I doin', and stop accusin' me of doin' some-thin' wrong when I know that I haven't. I'm the one who's hurtin' here," Trouble said.

"I'm hurtin' too."

"Why are you hurt, Dariel? You're the one who might have a baby on the way," she shouted into the phone receiver. "You should be ecstatic . . . *daddy.*"

"Don't you know my parents are gon' flip out, Trouble, when they find out that Jameelah might be pregnant by me?"

"And?"

"What about the other mornin'? Didn't that mean anything to you, baby girl?" Dariel asked.

"Dariel, stop, please. There is a baby involved here."

"I know. And if it's mines we want you to be a part of our lives," Dariel said.

"Who in the hell is *we?*"

"Me and my child."

"Dariel, I don't know. I have more important things to think about. I don't have time to be plannin' to spend time with you and some child that hasn't been born yet."

"I still don't want us to break up over this. You said you loved me," Dariel said.

"Bye, Dariel," Trouble said, slamming down the phone. "Now how does it feel to be hung up on?" she said, smiling.

"You all right, sis?" Jyson asked, walking into her bedroom.

"Yeah, I'm fine."

"You're not fine. What's the matter?" Jyson asked, concerned.

"Everything, Jyson," Trouble said, bursting into tears.

Jyson wrapped his arms around his sister and pulled her into his chest. "What's wrong, sis?"

"I don't want to move, Momma doesn't give a damn about me, and my boyfriend that I've only been with for about a week might have a baby on the way," she cried.

"By you?" Jyson asked.

"Naw, boy!"

"Whew," Jyson said, relieved. "You talkin' about Dariel?"

Yeah," she said in a childlike voice.

"Damn, that's deep. So Dariel might have a baby on the way. When did y'all start goin' together anyway? The last time we talked, you told me that y'all were just friends."

"We were just friends. But if you woulda been lis-tenin' to me, you would have heard me say that we've only been together for about a week. If you wouldn't be in the streets all the damn time, you would know what's goin' on in your little sister's life."

"You never cease to amaze me. No matter what mood you're in, you always find a way to slip in a smart remark." Jyson laughed. "Now correct me if I'm wrong, but you said y'all only been together for about a week, right?"

Trouble shook her head yes.

"Well, I ain't tryin'a make no excuses for the nigga, but if y'all only been together for one week, Jameelah had to have been pregnant before y'all got together," Jyson said.

"I know," she said, hanging her head down. "But it ain't fair. Why is all this bad stuff happenin' to me?" she cried.

"You don't even know if the baby is really his. I told you about all them niggas she was fuckin' wit," Jyson said, hoping to lighten his sister's mood. "You know how scandalous bitches be tellin' a nigga she's pregnant, thinkin' that's gon' keep him around," he continued.

"I know, Jyson. It's still a fucked-up situation."

"I don't know either, baby sis. But everything is gon' be all right," Jyson assured his sister. "I got somethin' for you."

Trouble smiled widely. "What is it?"

Jyson lifted up his shirt and revealed the new tattoo on his back. "This is for you."

"*Love has no boundaries,*" Trouble said, reading the tattoo out loud. "That is so sweet," she said as more tears rolled down her cheeks. Trouble wrapped her arms around her brother's waist and hugged him like the world was about to end, and Jyson held on to his sister, never wanting to let her go.

"I love you, sis."

"I love you more," she said, smiling.

"No, I love you more," Jyson said as he playfully punched her in the arm.

"I love you more," she said, putting Jyson in a headlock.

"Okay, I'm 'bout to go take a nap," he said, yawning. "If the phone rings and it's for me, tell them I'm not home."

"Even if it's Queen Michaela?" Trouble said, smiling.

"Even if it's my queen." Jyson walked into his bedroom, got into his bed, and fell straight to sleep.

Thank you, Jesus, for Jyson, Trouble thought. *He's my everything and I don't know what I would do without him. Lord, you made him my brother for a reason, and it was a very good one, I know. And Lord, right now I'm messed up over Dariel's situation, but I'm gon' put it in your hands and let you deal with it, because there is nothin' I can do. It's all yours, Lord. In the name of Jesus. Amen,* Trouble prayed before crying herself to sleep.

Fifteen

For the next few weeks, Trouble's life was in shambles. She didn't know whether she was coming or going. She couldn't eat, sleep, or concentrate in school.

"Trouble, girl, you gon' hafta eat somethin', 'cuz you gon' make yourself real sick," Ta'liyah said, brushing her best friend's hair.

"I know," Trouble cried. "I don't have an appetite, though, and all I do is sit around the house all day in my pajamas." Tears fell from Trouble's eyes, and as she wiped them away, more followed.

"I know, girl, and that ain't healthy at all. But you are the one who hasn't talked to Dariel in three weeks. He sends you flowers, you throw them away. He sends you cards, you write *return to sender* on the envelope. He calls you and you hang up on him."

"What else can I do? This shit hurt, and I don't know if I can forgive him."

"You only got two choices, Trouble. You can forgive him and move on, or not forgive him and still move on. You don't care about anything anymore. Have you took a good look in the mirror lately? You haven't gotten your hair done or your nails, and you throw on any old thing and come to school." Ta'liyah shook her head in disgust.

"I just haven't had the energy to dress myself up. All I do is come home from school and try to do my homework and lay around the house," Trouble said.

"I know Dariel is my cousin and all, but he ain't worth killin' yourself over. I can't believe you are lettin' him get you down. You must really be in love," Ta'liyah said.

"I am."

"You are gon' hafta get it together, girl. Come to school lookin' your best, hold your head up high, and forget about all the dumb shit. I hope you know that Jameelah is the only one gettin' some satisfaction out of you bein' hurt. She knows you're miserable and she's lovin' every minute of it."

Trouble thought for a minute. "Yeah, you right. I'm gon' come to school tomorrow lookin' cute as hell. Let's go to the mall so I can get me somethin' new to wear, and then I'm gon' stop to get my nails done and I might even spring for a new hairdo," she said, smiling.

"Now that's what I'm talkin' about. That's the Trouble I know," Ta'liyah cheered as Trouble stood up and put on her coat.

"Wait a minute," Trouble said, stopping in her tracks.

"What now?" Ta'liyah sighed.

"I can't go to the mall lookin' like this. I look a hot mess," she said, smiling, and changed her clothes.

The next morning Trouble couldn't wait to get to school. She got up bright and early and got dressed. She decided that she wasn't going to let Dariel get her down any longer. It was time for her to move on with her life.

Trouble got out of the shower and put on her new tan suede jacket with a coffee cream V-neck sweater. She slid on her tan suede skirt and topped the ensemble with a pair of camel Gianni Bini boots. She checked herself over in the mirror twice and was pleased both times.

"Damn, girl, you look good," she said to the reflection in the mirror. Her hair was intact, and her nails were all done up in a French manicure. Trouble was now ready to face the world with her head held high. She grabbed her things and headed to school.

"Hello, class. Today we are going to do something a little different," Ms. Carter said. "I want each and every one of you to stand up and tell the class about what you have accomplished so far in high school. It's real important because some of you—and I do mean *some*—will be graduating next year and going off to college. So if you didn't accomplish anything while you were in high school, you sure aren't going to accomplish anything in college," Ms. Carter said to the class. "Now who's going to go first?" She looked around the room for volunteers.

"I'll go first," Dariel said as he stood up and walked to the front of the classroom. He cleared his throat before speaking. "My biggest accomplishment in high school was that I had the chance to find true love. It has been the best feelin' that I have ever experienced. And I know it's more than just a phase because me and my true love are no longer together and it's drivin' me crazy. I can't eat, sleep, or concentrate in school. It has been three long weeks since she last spoke to me, and I want her to know that bein' in love alone is very lonely, and I wish that she would allow me to come over to her house after basketball practice so we can settle our differences, and before I go I would like for her to know that even if she doesn't take me back, I still love her no matter what. Thank you," Dariel said and walked back to his seat, relieved that he finally got a chance to let Trouble know how he was feeling without her being able to hang up on him.

"Well, that was deep," Ms. Carter said. "Does anyone have any questions for Dariel?"

"I do," Sharlena said, raising her hand. "Why did you and your true love break up?"

"We broke up because I might have a baby on the way by somebody else," Dariel said.

"She needed to leave your dog ass, then," Sharlena retorted, and some of the other girls in the class agreed with her.

"Now wait a minute. The other girl got pregnant before me and my true love got together, and I don't even know if it's mine, so I'm not a dog for real," Dariel explained, but he still got dirty looks from some of the girls in the class.

"Okay, class, settle down. Now, who would like to go next?" Ms. Carter asked.

"I'll go," Trouble said, walking to the front of the class so everyone could see how good she looked in her new outfit. "My biggest accomplishment in high school was comin' to my senses. I too have found true love and almost let him slip away because of my childish antics. I'm glad to know that he still loves me after all the times I've hung up on him and said all those mean things to him. I would also like for him to know that he is not in love by himself because I am there too and I would love for him to come over after practice so we can talk. I haven't been able to sleep, eat, or concentrate either. So, the best thing for us to do if we don't want to repeat the same grade again is to get our stuff together and move on. Thank you." Trouble smiled at the class and walked back to her seat.

"Well, you answered my question that I had for Dariel, and I bet the class is glad to know the answer too." Ms. Carter laughed.

The rest of the school day went by slow, and Trouble couldn't wait to get home, so she decided to skip her last period class and headed straight home. She hurried into the house, freshened up, and lay on the couch and turned on *Baby Boy* to kill some time, because she had another three hours before Dariel would be arriving.

"What's up, sis?" Jyson asked as he and Michaela walked through the front door. "What are you doin' home so early?"

Spoiled Rotten   191

"I didn't feel like stayin' for my last class. And anyway, it's nothin' but a study hall," she said, smiling.

"Is that a smile I see on your face? What are you so happy about?" Jyson asked.

"Shoot, boy, I'm always happy," Trouble said.

"Just yesterday I thought I was gon' hafta make arrangements for your funeral," he joked. "I take it you and Dariel are back together?"

"You take it wrong. Me and Dariel are not back together, but he is comin' over after he gets out of practice so we can talk."

"Hallelujah! You are givin' the poor brotha somethin' to hope for, 'cuz for a minute there you was hangin' up on him every time he called. You threw away all the flowers he sent. Shit, I know he almost went broke over you." Jyson laughed.

"Ain't nothin' wrong with a brotha spendin' a little money on a sista, especially if he claims to love her," Michaela intervened. She looked over at Trouble for agreement and hoped she didn't get any lip from the smart-mouth hefah, because she was not in the mood for no shit.

"You're right, it ain't nothin' wrong with a brotha spendin' money, especially after he done fucked up," Trouble said, smiling and nodding at Michaela.

"That's how you know they done somethin' wrong; they start bearin' gifts and shit." Michaela laughed.

"Yep, you sho'll right about that." Trouble laughed too.

"Hey, y'all females ain't gon' be gangin' up on a nigga." Jyson laughed. *This could be the start of a friendship,* he thought as he watched his girl and his sister joke together. Jyson was impressed by how his little sister and his girl came to an agreement without Trouble chopping her head off.

Trouble and Michaela stopped laughing when they heard the doorbell ring.

"Who is it?" Jyson yelled.

Trouble rushed over to the door, nearly tripping over the ottoman that sat in front of the leather chair. Trouble opened up the door to find Dariel standing there looking good as usual. "What's up?" she asked.

"What's up?" he said, smiling. "Can I come in? It's cold out here."

"I'm sorry, come in," she said, opening up the screen door to let him into the house.

"What's up, Dariel?" Jyson said, nodding his head.

"What's up, Jyson?"

Trouble was all smiles. She introduced Dariel to Michaela and they all sat around laughing and talking. Jyson was surprised at how polite his sister was to Michaela. Trouble talked to her like they had been the best of friends since day one. His little sister was finally maturing and he sure was glad.

"Show Dariel the tattoo you got for me," Trouble said, excited.

Dariel watched as Jyson lifted up his shirt to show off his artwork.

"Man, that's deep. I think it's cool to be able to have a good lovin' relationship with your family," Dariel said.

"Me too," Michaela added. "I wish me and my sisters could have a relationship like theirs," she said, smiling at Jyson.

"Me and my brother is tight, but not as tight as we should be," Dariel stated. The room got quiet and no one said anything. They all just sat back and enjoyed the peaceful moment.

"Hey, Trouble, I heard you were goin' to Howard University," Michaela said, breaking the silence and taking a chance on Trouble giving a smart remark.

"Yep. I was gon' go to Atlanta A and T, but I changed my mind," Trouble said.

"May I ask why? I've always wanted to go to Clark Atlanta, but I never had the chance to, somethin' always came up that hindered me from goin'. Right now I'm attendin' North Central State College takin' classes until I'm able to transfer to Atlanta," Michaela said. "I wanna be a pediatrician," she continued.

"I'm attendin' Howard University because they have awarded many degrees in all fields and it's proven that more blacks have gotten more PhDs and MDs than any other university in the whole world. Then I want to finish off at Meharry College of Dentistry," Trouble explained.

"Damn, you mean to tell me that you want to be a dentist? Lookin' all in people's tore-up mouths?" Michaela asked.

"They just kicked us out the conversation," Jyson said to Dariel as he got up and walked into the kitchen.

"This is girl talk. Y'all wouldn't know anything about it," Trouble said.

"What do you plan on doin' after you graduate, Dariel?" Michaela asked him.

"I plan on attendin' Ohio State University and then transferrin' to Howard to finish my degree in engineerin'."

"That's if he doesn't go pro first," Trouble said, gloating.

"I heard about you and your basketball skills. My cousins talk about you all the time," Michaela said.

"I do a little somethin'," he said, smiling.

"Oh well, I gotta get home and get some sleep. I gotta work tonight," Michaela said, getting up from her seat.

"Nice meetin' you," Dariel said.

"Same here," Michaela said, smiling. "Jy, baby, I'm gone," she hollered into the kitchen.

"Okay, here I come," he yelled back.

"What do you do for a livin'?" Dariel asked Michaela.

Michaela looked at Dariel nervously and didn't know what to say.

"She got a job, that's all that matters," Trouble interjected.

"That's cool. Ain't nothin' wrong with a woman with a job," Dariel said.

"I wish someone else would take heed," Jyson said, walking out the kitchen with a bologna sandwich in his hand.

"Whatever. I'm gon' get me a job, one day," Trouble said.

"That was rude of you not to ask anyone else if they were hungry," Michaela said.

"I'm sorry, baby, are you hungry?"

"No, and if I was, I wouldn't want no bologna sandwich," she answered.

"I know that's right," Trouble laughed.

Jyson put his food on the coffee table and walked Michaeala out to her car.

"What's the matter with your sister?" Michaela asked as she opened up her car door.

"I don't know. Somebody else has taken over her body," Jyson said, getting in the car.

"Well, I'm glad that we had a decent conversation without her gettin' fly." Michaela started up her car and the music blared out her speakers.

Jyson reached over and turned the volume down on the radio. "I'm glad too. My baby sister is finally growin' up," he said, smiling. "I'm gon' hafta go in there and thank her," he said, and leaned over and kissed Michaela's soft lips.

"Am I gon' see you tonight?"

"I don't know, do you wanna see me?" he teased.

"Get outta my car askin' them stupid-ass questions," Michaela huffed.

"My poppy once told me that there was no such thing as a stupid question," Jyson said.

"Get outta my car, Jyson. You can come over if you want to, I'm not gon' beg you, though," she said, smiling.

"I love you," he said, opening up the car door and getting out. Michaela didn't respond. "I said I love you."

Michaela turned the music all the way up and pretended not to hear him.

"I said I love you," Jyson yelled over the loud music.

"Whatever, close my damn car door," she huffed and pulled off with the passenger-side door still opened.

Mission accomplished, Jyson thought to himself as he walked back into the house. *Now I can go over to Jessica's house so she can give me one of her good old head jobs!* "Trouble, can I talk to you in the kitchen for a minute?" Jyson asked when he walked through the door.

"Sure," she said as she got up from the couch and followed her brother into the kitchen.

"I just wanted to say thank you and ask, why now?" Jyson asked.

"Your welcome, besides, I had to face the fact that you really like Michaela. You have to trust her because she's the only female that knows where you really live, and plus, I see the way she makes you smile when she's around. And if you're happy, I don't have no reason not to be. I was just bein' immature and I want to apologize to you and to Michaela when I get the chance," Trouble said, making her brother proud.

"I love you, Trouble," Jyson said.

"I love you too, Jyson." Trouble gave her brother a nice warm hug before walking back into the living room to finish her conversation with Dariel.

"You know the semester is almost over?" Trouble said to Dariel as she sat back down on the couch next to him.

"Yeah, I know," he said, looking down at the floor and feeling a lump form in his throat.

"I don't wanna go."

"And I don't want you to go." Dariel moved closer to Trouble and grabbed her hand.

"Have you decided which family member you're goin' to stay with?"

"All of 'em stay about the same distance. But I decided to move in with my Aunt Loretta, only because the bitch can cook her ass off," Trouble said.

Dariel smiled. "Well, at least I know you won't be hungry."

"You know I wish there was a way that I could stay at Senior High without my aunt findin' out," Trouble said.

Dariel thought for a minute. "There is."

"How?"

"All you hafta do is call your aunt and tell her that Jyson is gon' sign you up for school over there in Marion and I'll come over there and stay with my nigga Orlando, and I can come pick you up for school every mornin'," Dariel plotted.

Trouble picked up the phone to call her Aunt Loretta. "You do love me, don't you?" she said, smiling as she dialed the phone number. "Hello, auntie?"

"Yes, is this you, Candria?" Loretta asked.

Who the fuck do you think it is? Trouble thought. "Yes it's me," she answered.

"So, have you decided who you're goin' to live with?" Loretta asked.

"Yes. I've decided to move in with you."

"Oh, that's wonderful," Loretta said, smiling, as she started seeing nothing but dollar signs. "Candria, I can't wait until you get here. I've got a lot of excitin' things for us to do," Loretta said.

I just bet you do, and with my money too. Trouble could read her aunt like a book. "I can't wait until I get there, either," Trouble lied. "I was just callin' you to tell you the good news. Oh, and Jyson is goin' to sign me up for school tomorrow if that's okay with you?" Trouble closed her eyes and crossed her fingers.

"It's okay with me, 'cuz I have to work in the mornin' and I didn't have the slightest idea when I woulda been able to sign you up for school," Loretta said. "Tell ya brother I said thanks. I can't miss no more work for a while," Loretta added, relieved that Jyson would be signing her niece up for school . . . so she thought.

"Well, I'll talk to you later," Trouble said, hanging up the phone before Loretta could say anything else.

"What did she say?" Dariel said in anticipation.

"It's on, baby," Trouble said, smiling from ear to ear.

Sixteen

The end of the semester was only two days away and Trouble hated the idea of having to go stay with her Aunt Loretta. Even though she would be staying at the same school, she didn't want to be away from Jyson.

Jyson woke up and looked around his bedroom. He couldn't remember how and when he had got home because he was so drunk off the Hennessy he and Big Mike drank on the night before. He rubbed his eyes and looked out into the hallway and noticed his sister's bedroom light on. "What's up, Dariel?" Jyson said, walking into his sister's bedroom.

"What's up?" Dariel said.

"I see you helpin' my sister pack all those damn clothes," Jyson said, taking a seat on his sister's bed.

"Naw, man, she has too many," Dariel said, chuckling. "I'm sittin' back watchin' her!"

"What cha'll gon' do since y'all gon' be goin' to different schools?" Jyson asked Trouble as she walked out of the bathroom and into her room.

"Who said we were goin' to different schools?" Trouble asked as she struggled to get her suitcase closed.

"Here, let me help you," Dariel said, closing the suitcase with no problem.

"What cha'll gon' do then if y'all not goin' to different schools? Dariel gon' be livin' with Loretta too?" Jyson joked.

"I told Loretta that you had signed me up for school already. Oh, and she said thanks," Trouble said, smiling.

"Thanks for tellin' me," Jyson said sarcastically. "Now what if she would have called and asked me about signin' you up for school?"

"I'm sorry, it slipped my mind," Trouble said, shrugging her shoulders.

"Ummm huh," Jyson said. "You still didn't tell me how you were gon' get back and forth to school every day?"

"One of my niggas that lives in Marion is gon' be stayin' in Columbus with his girlfriend, so he's gon' let me stay at his house and I'm gon' take Trouble back and forth to school every day," Dariel interjected.

Jyson shook his head. "Well, what your parents gon' say about you stayin' over in Marion?"

"I got that under control," Dariel said. "Their not gon' care as long as I go to school every day, keep my grades up, and play basketball. Anything I do is all right with them."

"See, it all worked out," Trouble said, smiling. "I don't have to transfer schools now and I can come over here every day to check on you," she said to Jyson.

"That's cool," Jyson said, grabbing the two suit-cases off the bed. "Y'all ready? 'Cuz it's gettin' late and you know how ya aunt is."

"Yeah, I know how she is," Trouble said, rolling her eyes. "And don't be callin' that witch my aunt. She's your aunt too."

"She's not only your aunt, she's your favorite aunt," Jyson laughed.

"Whatever," Trouble said as she grabbed her purse off her bed and walked slowly to Dariel father's truck.

Trouble and Dariel pulled up in front of Loretta's house twenty minutes before Jyson and Michaela.

Trouble got out of the truck and walked over to Jy-son's car. "What took you so long to get here?" she asked as she opened up the door. "Hi, Michaela," Trouble said.

"Hi," Michaela replied.

"I had to stop by and pick up Michaela before I came over here," Jyson responded.

"I see. I don't wanna go in there," Trouble whined.

"Well, sis, you gon' be stayin' over to the house every weekend," Jyson said, walking over to the truck and grabbing two of Trouble's suitcases.

"I know, man, but who's gon' take care of you? Who's gon' make sure you take your vitamins like you're supposed to?" Trouble asked with a demure look on her face.

"Don't worry, sis, I'll be okay." Jyson felt a lump form in his throat. "And I'm not gon' forget to take my vitamins."

"I won't let him," Michaela said as she got out of the car and joined Jyson and his sister.

"Y'all come on in here, it's chilly out here," Loretta yelled from the front porch after spotting them outside.

"We're comin'," Jyson yelled back.

Dariel, Michaela, and Jyson stayed for dinner and sat around for a couple of hours and talked.

"Well, sis, we're about to go," Jyson said, getting up from the sofa.

"Why y'all gotta leave so soon?" Trouble whined.

"I got some business to take care of. I'll come see you tomorrow—better yet, I'll drive down here and take you to school in the mornin'," Jyson said, winking at his sister and giving her a warm smile.

"Okay," Trouble said.

"I'm gon' too, baby girl," Dariel said, standing up.

"Dang, everybody is leavin'," Trouble said, pouting.

"You know we got school tomorrow, bright and early," he reminded her.

"I know. Let me walk y'all to y'all's cars," Trouble said, putting her jacket on.

Trouble followed as Dariel, Michaela, and Jyson walked out the door to their cars. "See you later, sis," Jyson said, giving his sister a hug before getting into his car.

"See ya," she said with tears in her eyes.

"Bye, Trouble," Michaela said as she opened up the passenger-side door.

"Bye." Trouble waved and watched as her brother started the car and pulled off. Trouble walked over to where Dariel was standing outside the truck and wrapped her arms around his waist.

"I'm gon' miss you tonight," Dariel said, kissing Trouble's chattering lips.

"I'm gon' miss you too," she replied, fighting back tears.

"Okay, baby, I'm gon' get on over to Orlando's before he goes to bed," Dariel said, opening up the truck door. "I'm gon' call you in about an hour or so." Dariel hugged Trouble tightly.

"Dariel?" Trouble said as Dariel held her.

"Yeah, baby girl," he answered as he held her closely to his body.

"I can't breathe," she laughed.

"I'm sorry." He laughed too as he released her. "You were feelin' so good in my arms, I didn't wanna let you go."

"I'll see you in the mornin'," she said, walking toward the porch.

"I love you."

"I love you too," she said, smiling, as she ran up on the porch and waited for Dariel to pull off in his dad's truck. She waited and watched until the truck disappeared around the corner before going back into the house.

"Trouble?" Loretta called out from the hall bathroom.

"Yeah?" Trouble answered in a dry tone as she made her way toward the bathroom.

"Why did they come in two different cars?" Loretta asked as she wrapped her hair around some big pink sponge rollers.

" 'Cuz Jyson is not goin' straight home, that's why,"
Trouble replied as she rolled her eyes. *Damn you nosy!*

"Okay, well, I'm goin' to bed and I'll see you in the
mornin'," Loretta said while wrapping a black satin
scarf around her head.

Trouble didn't respond. She just stood there and
looked at her aunt before walking into her new bedroom. Trouble looked around her new room and
shook her head. It was nothing like her other room.
This room had no color at all. The walls were decorated with a floral wallpaper that was torn in several
places. It had cobwebs in every corner and the carpet
looked like it hadn't been cleaned in years.

"I can't live like this," Trouble said out loud. "The
least she could have done was cleaned this damn
room up. She knew I was comin'," she said, hoping
Loretta could hear her complain about the filth.

Trouble sighed and flopped down on the bed and
stared up at the ceiling. Drifting off to sleep, she was
awakened by the ringing of the phone.

"Hello?" Loretta said, quickly picking up the phone.

Trouble sat up on the edge of her bed and waited
just in case it was Dariel on the phone.

"May I speak to Trouble?" Dariel asked.

"Honey, it's after nine p.m. and Candria is in bed.
And for future references, she's not allowed no phone
calls after eight p.m.."

All Dariel heard next was the sound of the dial
tone. "She's one stupid broad," Dariel said, staring at
the phone.

"Stupid bitch," Trouble said as she laid back down on her bed. *I gotta get outta here. I don't know how, but I gotta go!* she thought as she drifted back off to sleep.

"Candria, it's time to get up," Loretta yelled as she pulled the pink rollers out of her hair.

"I am up," Trouble said, walking out of the bathroom with an attitude. She had been up for over an hour after waking up at around five o'clock in the morning.

"Oh, you're up already? You must be anxious about goin' to your new school?" Loretta asked as she stood in the hallway trying to loosen up her tight curls.

Trouble ignored her aunt and continued on to her room to finish getting dressed.

"You're just like your daddy. He used to have an attitude when he had to get up early too," Loretta laughed as she walked into Trouble's room behind her. "That's why I think your bedtime should be eight-thirty, so you won't be so cranky in the mornings."

"You must be outta your mind if you think I'm 'bout to go to bed that early," Trouble snapped.

"Well, Candria, I just thought—"

"You thought nothin'," Trouble said, cutting her off. "You just want to run my life, but I'm not gon' let you 'cuz you are not my mom."

"I'm not tryin'a be your mom," Loretta said defensively.

"Why didn't you let me talk to Dariel last night when he called?"

"It was late, that's why. And I already told him that you're not allowed on the phone after eight," Loretta said, combing through her hair with her fingers.

"Why?" Trouble shouted.

"This is my house, that's why," Loretta said as she turned and walked out of Trouble's room.

"And you're sayin' that to say what?" Trouble asked.

Loretta stopped in her tracks and turned to look at Trouble. "I'm sayin' that to say that this is my damn house and I pay the bills. Now, I done told that nigga that I don't want him callin' here after a certain time and I meant it," Loretta said angrily.

Trouble rolled her eyes as she tied up her tennis shoes.

"I don't know what you're used to," Loretta continued. "But it's about to be some changes goin' on," she said.

"You're right, don't even worry 'bout it." Trouble shook her head in agreement. "I'll just get me a cell phone and he can call that anytime he feels like it," she yelled victoriously.

"I don't think so, 'cuz I don't want no damn cell phones in my house . . . they give you cancer," Loretta said between clenched teeth.

"Whatever." Trouble laughed and threw her hands up in the air. Trouble heard a horn blow so she hurried and grabbed her book bag off her bed.

"Just where do you think you're goin' so early?" Loretta asked. "And who is that outside of my house blowin' the damn horn like we called for a taxi?"

Trouble ignored her aunt as she rambled on. She grabbed her jacket out of the closet and walked toward the door.

"Did you hear me talkin' to you, young lady?" Loretta snapped.

Trouble turned around, looked at her aunt, and smiled before walking out the front door.

"What's up, baby girl?" Dariel asked as Trouble got into the truck with him. "Did you sleep well last night?" Dariel leaned over and kissed her on the cheek.

Trouble sighed. "Not really. It's gon' take a lot of gettin' used to. I gotta do somethin' to that dusty-ass room," Trouble said.

"Your aunt really be trippin'," Dariel said, pulling off.

"I know. And I wasn't in the bed last night when you called," Trouble said.

"I didn't think so," Dariel said as he concentrated on the early morning traffic.

"Me and Loretta got into an argument this mornin'. She said that she wanted me in bed by eight-thirty and that I wasn't allowed on the phone after eight."

"She need to get some help," Dariel said. "You gon' hafta get you a cell phone."

"We argued about that too. She said I wasn't allowed to get one 'cuz they give you cancer," Trouble said, giggling.

"Hell, now days almost anything will give you cancer. So how we gon' talk then?" Dariel asked, pulling into a gas station.

"We gon' get me a cell phone, that's how," Trouble said with a mischievous smile. "I don't care what that broad says."

"Okay, we'll go get it when we get outta school today," Dariel said.

Trouble smiled widely. "That's fine with me."

After getting gas Dariel drove onto the highway and then pulled off at the Richland County exit and looked at Trouble. "It's too early to be goin' to school."

"Let's go to my house then," Trouble suggested.

"Yeah, let's go," he said, grinning.

"Not for that, boy," she said, laughing, as they headed for her house.

"I can't believe Jyson is home," Trouble said as they pulled in front of the house. She jumped out of the truck and rushed up on the porch with her house keys in hand, unlocked the door and rushed over to push the code into the alarm, but it wasn't turned on. "Damn, Jyson is slip-pin', and look at this damn house; it looks like he threw a party or somethin'," Trouble said, looking around.

Jyson had a pile of dirty dishes left in the sink, the pillows from the couch were thrown all over the floor and he had left the television on all night. "Jyson," Trouble called out as she walked down the hallway and into his bedroom. Jyson and Michaela were both lying in the bed sound asleep. "Jyson," she called out again, and this time he woke up.

"Yeah," he answered with a groggy voice. "What's up, sis?"

"What's up with you?" she asked as she looked around the room at the piles of clothes that lay in the middle of his bedroom floor.

"I've been gone for one night and I come back to find the house in shambles," Trouble said.

Jyson sat up and shook his head. "Do me a favor and wait for me in the livin' room. I'll be out there in a few seconds," he said, rubbing his eyes.

"Hurry up," Trouble said, loud enough for Michaela to hear her, but she didn't wake up, she only moved into another position.

"Shhh," Jyson said as he covered up Michaela's half-naked body.

Jyson walked into the living room with his robe on and took a seat on the couch next to Dariel. He pulled a bag of bud from his robe pocket and picked a blunt up off the table and began breaking it down. "What's up, Dariel?" Jyson asked as he emptied the tobacco from the blunt into the ashtray that sat on the coffee table.

"What's up?" Dariel said, nodding his head.

Trouble was standing over at Jyson's CD collection rambling through them. "Don't be over there takin' my CDs, Trouble," Jyson said as he rolled the blunt like a professional.

"I'm not," Trouble said as she stuffed Mary J. Blige's *What's the 411?* into her jacket pocket.

"You think you're slick," Jyson said as he lit his blunt and took a long pull. Jyson got up off the couch. "You wanna hit this?" he asked Dariel. Dariel took the blunt from Jyson's fingers and began to smoke it. Jyson walked over to his sister and put her in a headlock. "What CD you got?"

"I got *What's the 411?*, damn," she said as she struggled to keep his hand out of her jacket pocket. "You don't even listen to this anymore."

"So what? Yo' ass don't know how to return shit," Jyson said.

Trouble rolled her eyes. "Whatever. You hurt my neck," she said, rubbing it.

"You know better than that. You know I wouldn't hurt my favorite sister." Jyson laughed as he walked back over to the couch and sat back down.

"Dummy, I'm your only sister." Trouble laughed too.

"So, how do you like livin' with Loretta?" Jyson asked.

"Dang, I just moved yesterday. You act like I've been gone for about two months."

"It sure feels like it," Jyson said.

"I don't like it at all. I can't stand that woman," Trouble said. She told her brother about the incident with Dariel calling the house and about the cell phone, and he couldn't believe that Loretta was still miserable after all these years of being alone. Loretta used to be one of the sweetest people you could have ever ran across, but she always had to try to boss someone. Her ex-husband, Jimmy, was a big pushover. He did everything Loretta told him to do, from cooking to cleaning the entire house. He went grocery shopping and sometimes she even made him do the laundry. But after ten years of marriage, Jimmy got fed up with Loretta's bossy ways and decided to leave her.

Loretta came home one day from work after a long, hard day, planning on Jimmy running her some bathwater so she could soak her tired body. But when Loretta got home, Jimmy had taken almost everything out of the house. The only thing he left was her clothes, one plate, one fork, a frying pan, and a note telling her how tired he was of her trying to be the boss of everything. He told her that he couldn't take it anymore, and ever since then, she been one of the angriest women you could ever come in contact with.

"Loretta needs to get some help." Trouble laughed.

"More like some dick." Jyson laughed too.

"That too." Trouble laughed harder.

Jyson put the remainder of the blunt out in the ashtray and sat back on the sofa. "I'm glad you decided to stop by here, 'cuz Momma came over last night and said she was ready to check herself into rehab." Jyson was ecstatic about the news. "She's supposed to talk to some lady by the name of Elizabeth Reynolds so she can get started in the program."

Trouble held her head down because she was embarrassed. *How could he tell me this shit in front of Dariel?* Dariel looked around the living room like he wasn't paying any attention to their conversation, wondering why Trouble never told him her mother was strung-out. "That's nice," she said with little enthusiasm.

"*That's nice* is all you can say?" Jyson exclaimed.

"After all these years Momma has been—"

"Okay, Jyson," Trouble said, cutting him off. "I'll call you after school and we can talk more about it, okay?" She then turned her attention to Dariel. "C'mon, let's go."

"Don't forget to call me when you get out of school," Jyson said, walking them to the front door.

"I won't. Oh, where's my lunch money?" Trouble asked with her hand out.

"I know Loretta left you some money this mornin'," Jyson said.

"She left me five dollars on the table, but I was in such a big hurry to get away from her, I forgot it." Trouble admitted. "And besides, what can a sista do with five dollars?"

"You gon' hafta get you a job," Jyson said as he walked to his bedroom to get his sister some money. Jyson walked back out into the living room where Trouble stood waiting. "Here," he said, handing her a fifty-dollar bill.

"Thank you very much," she said, smiling.

"Don't mention it," Jyson uttered with a smile.

Trouble and Dariel walked to the truck hand in hand. "Your brother sure does spoil you," he said, opening up the passenger-side door for Trouble to get in.

"I'm not spoiled," she said, climbing into the truck and putting her seatbelt on.

"What do you call it then?" he asked.

"I call it lucky," Trouble said, pulling down the visor and checking her hair in the mirror.

Dariel and Trouble pulled up in the student parking lot. They got out of the truck looking like Will and Jada. Dariel grabbed ahold of Trouble's hand as they walked past a group of senior girls sitting at a picnic table smoking cigarettes. Trouble knew that they couldn't wait to start hating on her by the looks they shot her way as she and Dariel walked past them. Trouble didn't let the mean stares bother her; in fact, she kept her composure and kept on stepping with her man by her side. Marcus was the first person Dariel ran into when they entered the school building.

"What's up, man?" Marcus said, holding out his fist for Dariel to give him some dap.

Dariel smiled and gave Marcus fist a pound. "What's up with you?"

"Nuttin', just movin' in slow motion, that's all," Marcus said. "What's up, Trouble?"

Trouble shot Marcus a fake smile. "I'm about to go to my locker, Dariel. I'll catch up with you later on."

"All right, baby girl, I'll see you in English class," Dariel said.

"I don't know how many times I have to tell you this, but you are one of the luckiest niggas alive," Marcus exclaimed.

"Why you say that?" Dariel gloated, already knowing the answer to his own question.

"'Cuz man, you got one of the baddest broads in the entire school district."

"I know," Dariel agreed.

"I know you ain't hittin' it. As a matter of fact, I know ain't nobody hittin' it. Word on the street they call the bitch Ms. Tight Pussy," Marcus said, laughing, but soon realized he was laughing alone.

"Watch ya mouth, man," Dariel warned. "If you don't do nothin' else, you gon' respect her!"

"My bad. I didn't mean no harm," Marcus said as he held his hands up in the air like he was being arrested. "So have you hit it yet?"

Dariel smiled.

"Yeah, nigga, you done hit," Marcus said, smiling.

"I didn't say that."

"You didn't have to. You know actions speak louder than words. Man, you know how many niggas been tryin'a hit that?" Marcus asked.

"I can imagine," Dariel replied.

"Man, you lucky," Marcus said, giving his nigga some dap. Marcus cleared his throat. "Speakin' of lucky, you know that ho, Veronica?" Marcus asked with a mischievous grin.

"Yeah, I know her."

"I hit that ho the other night. She said she been checkin' me out ever since Ta'liyah's party," Marcus said, smiling widely.

"Along with everybody else," Dariel said smartly.

Marcus ignored Dariel's comment and went on with his story. "So I went ahead and put it down on the trick."

"Well, I hope you protected yourself, 'cuz that broad's reputation is destroyed," Dariel said.

"I ain't gon' lie, I didn't use nothin'," Marcus admitted. "She said she was clean."

"Okay, nigga, you gon' fuck around and catch somethin' you can't get rid of, or you gon' be some-body's maybe baby daddy, just like me." Dariel shook his head in disgust and hoped like hell he could talk some sense into his friend.

"Naw, man, I ain't gon' end up like that. I know I was slippin', but the bitch head game was so raw, I got in a rush to get in the pussy and forgot to put a condom on," Marcus said.

"Keep on, nigga. I don't care how good the broad's head game is, that still don't explain not usin' a condom," Dariel said.

Marcus rolled his eyes, wishing he would have just kept his mouth shut about his encounter with Veronica. He was glad to share his news with his boy, but he just wished he would have left the part out about him not using a condom. Ever since Dariel found out about Jameelah being pregnant, all he did was preach about safe sex. He could have been the prime spokesmen for the "wrap it up" commercials on BET.

Dariel shook his head at his friend and hoped and prayed that he had took heed to everything he had just told him.

Trouble was bent over in her locker searching for her Spanish book when someone came up behind her and grabbed her ass.

"Stop it, Dariel, I'm lookin' for my Spanish book," she said, smiling, keeping her eyes glued to the inside of her locker.

Once again she felt someone squeeze her ass. "Stop, Dariel." She smiled and turned around and looked into the face of her ex-boyfriend, Markell. "What do you want?" Trouble said, grimacing.

"I want your tight pussy," Markell said, smiling wickedly.

"Well, you can't have it 'cuz it's already taken."

"So what I've been hearin' about you is true?" Markell asked.

"It all depends on what you've been hearin'," Trouble smirked.

"I heard you was fuckin' that chump, Dariel."

"If you would stay your ass out of juvenile, you would know who I was messin' around with. And besides, why are you so worried about who I'm messin' with? You didn't want me when you had me."

Markell blew Trouble's last comment off. "You let Dariel hit that shit?"

"Why?" Trouble snapped.

"'Cuz, only thing you let me do is play wit' the pussy," Markell snapped back.

"And that was too much," Trouble said, smiling.

"Is that so, tight pussy?" Markell became aggravated. "Bitch, I paid for you. I put yo' hood rat ass on the map," he retorted.

"Only thing you paid for was my shoes, clothes, and got my hair and nails done. And all that means is that I'm a muthafuckin' playa," Trouble said and then laughed in Markell's face. She must have struck a nerve with that remark because before she saw it coming, Markell grabbed her by the arms and threw her up against her locker.

"Ouch," she screamed. "Let me go, nigga," she shouted as she struggled to get away from Markell.

"Shut up, bitch! And do you actually think I care that I'm hurtin' you?" he said, spitting in her face as he spoke words of anger.

"Markell, get off of me," Trouble shouted even louder.

"Bitch, I'm tired of your smart-ass mouth. I don't hear you gettin' smart now," he said, pulling her away from the locker and slamming her back against it, making her hit her head.

"Get off her," Ta'liyah yelled as she ran down the hallway and jumped on Markell's back and started swinging like a madwoman. She probably would have accomplished something if it wasn't for him throwing her off of his back.

"What the fuck?" Dariel and Marcus said simultaneously as they ran toward the commotion.

"Get yo' hands off her, nigga," Dariel snapped.

"What you gon' do if I don't?" Markell retorted.

"I'm about to kick this nigga's ass," Dariel said.

"No, Dariel, he ain't worth it," Trouble yelled as Markell let go of her arms.

"Fuck that, that nigga put his hands on you. I don't hit you so I'll be damned if I let another nigga put his hands on you," Dariel snapped angrily.

"Man, I ain't about to fight you over this bit—." Before Markell could get the entire word out his mouth, Dariel had swung his fist full force, hitting him in the jaw, knocking him against the lockers. A crowd of people had gathered to watch the fight. As Markell slid down the lockers, laughter roared throughout the crowd.

Ta'liyah stood over Markell's lifeless body and said, "You got knocked the fuck out!" The crowd of bystanders laughed even harder, and as mad as Dariel was at the moment, he had to laugh at his cousin's quip.

"You all right?" Dariel wrapped his arm around Trouble and asked.

"What about me? I'm the one who got tossed to the floor," Ta'liyah said, pouting.

"Are you all right, Ta'liyah?" Dariel asked as he turned his attention from Trouble to his cousin.

"Yeah, I'm cool. You know I had to help my girl out. Even if it did mean gettin' tossed to the floor," Ta'liyah said, smiling.

Trouble smiled too. "Thanks, girl."

"Anytime," Ta'liyah replied and gave her best friend a hug.

"Let's go. I'll walk you to your first period class," Dariel said, grabbing Trouble by the waist and walking her away from the crowd of people. "I'll see you in English class," he said, kissing her on the lips before walking away to his own class. *Damn, I think my hand is broke.*

Seventeen

"Do you love me, Jyson?" Michaela asked as she dried the specks of water off her body that were left behind after the long hot shower she and Jyson had just taken together.

"Why you be askin' me that all the damn time when you already know the answer?" Jyson asked, irritated.

"Because sometimes a woman needs to be reminded from time to time."

"Girl, you be comin' up wit' some crazy-ass shit to say," Jyson laughed.

"No, I be sayin' some for-real-ass shit. Y'all niggas just can't comprehend the realness of a woman's feelings," she snapped. Michaela put her clothes on and walked out the front door, slamming it behind her.

"Damn, what did I do to her?" Jyson asked himself, confused by Michaela's actions. Jyson picked up the telephone and dialed her cell phone number.

"Yeah," she answered with an attitude.

"What was that all about?" he asked, feeling sick to his stomach.

"I'm just tired of messin' around with niggas that can't express their true feelins."

"What are you talkin' about, Michaela?" Jyson was fed up with the mood swings she had been having lately. One minute she was happy and smiling, and the next she was ready to take his head off. "I tell you that I love you all the damn time. What more do you want?"

"Stop yellin' at me, Jyson," Michaela whined.

"Yellin'? Michaela, you have lost your damn mind," he screamed into the phone. "What the fuck is wrong with you? Matter of fact, call me back when you get ya mind right."

Jyson slammed the phone back into its cradle and ran into the bathroom, throwing up everything he had in his stomach and then some. *Damn, it must have been some-thin' I ate*, he thought as he staggered back to his room and climbed under the covers.

It seemed like first period would never end, Trouble thought as she headed out of her classroom and down the crowded hallway. Dariel walked up behind her and wrapped his arm around her waist.

"Boy, you scared me," she said, holding her chest.

"I'm sorry, baby girl, I didn't mean to," he said, smiling. "I think my hand might be broke."

"Let me see," Trouble exclaimed as she examined his hand.

"Dang, why you so rough?" he said, snatching his hand away.

"Dariel, I think you need to go see the nurse," Trouble suggested.

"What is she gon' tell me? The broad probably didn't even hafta go to college to become a school nurse, so why waste my time?" Dariel laughed.

Trouble wasn't amused by Dariel's comment. "Just go show her your hand, Dariel."

"Okay, calm down. I'll go after English class," he said.

"No, you need to go right now," she demanded.

"All right, stop bein' so damn bossy," he said, smiling. "Tell Ms. Carter where I went, okay?"

"Okay," Trouble said as she walked toward her English class and watched as Jameelah rubbed her flat stomach. *I wonder where this crazy bitch been at? She haven't been at school for almost a week.*

Ms. Carter walked into the classroom wearing a pair of khaki Guess? pants with a brown long-sleeve Guess? shirt. "Good morning class," she said, smiling. *Cute outfit,* Trouble thought. Class flew by rather quickly, and when the bell rang, Trouble was the first one out of her seat and heading out the door. She headed straight to the lunchroom to meet up with her girls. When she walked into the crowded lunchroom, she spotted Ta'liyah sitting at their favorite table smiling as Regina talked.

"Hey, Trouble." Ta'liyah smiled as Trouble approached the table.

"Hey," Trouble responded in a sullen tone, along with a disturbed look in her eyes.

"What's wrong with you?" Ta'liyah asked.

"Yeah, what is wrong with you?" Regina asked as she took a huge bite from her slice of pizza.

"I feel so bad, 'cuz Dariel thinks his hand might be broke," Trouble answered.

"Where he at now?" Ta'liyah asked, concerned.

"He went to see the school nurse." She sank deep into her chair.

"You mean the school drunk," Regina said, giggling.

Trouble looked in Regina's direction with a serious look on her face, letting Regina know that she was not in the mood to laugh. "Come on, Regina, he's got a game on Friday and he may not be able to play and it's all my fault," Trouble said.

"It's not your fault, girl. Didn't nobody tell Markell to put his hands on you. Dariel did what he was supposed to had done," Ta'liyah assured her.

"Yeah," Regina agreed. "What type of man would Dariel be if he let another nigga put his hands on you?"

"I guess y'all right," Trouble said, feeling a little bit better about the entire situation. "I'm 'bout to go see if he's okay. I'll talk to y'all later," Trouble said as she got up from the table and made her way to the nurse's office to check on her man.

Dariel smiled when he saw Trouble peek her head through the door.

Trouble smiled back when she saw him smiling. That let her know that he wasn't mad at her. "Are you okay?" she asked, making her way past the other sick students and taking an empty seat next to Dariel.

"Yeah, I'm fine," Dariel answered. "The nurse doesn't think it's broken, but she called my mom to have her make me a doctor's appointment just to make sure," Dariel said, pulling his swollen hand out of the bucket of ice it had been resting in for the past hour.

"Put your hand back in there," Trouble snapped.

"Calm down, baby girl, the ice is cold," he said, putting it back into the ice after about twenty seconds.

"I'm sorry. It's just that I feel bad like it's all my fault that your hand is messed up." Trouble let her eyes fall to the floor to keep from looking at Dariel's swollen hand.

"Look at me, Trouble," Dariel said, pulling his hand back out of the ice and wrapping it up in the towel the nurse had given him. "It's not your fault. It's Markell's fault for puttin' his hands on you."

"I know, but—"

"But nothin'. What type of nigga do you take me for? You think I was supposed to stand there while he had you pinned up against them lockers?"

"No, but what about your game on Friday? Aren't you mad 'cuz you might not get to play?" Trouble asked.

"Trouble, you're more important than a game of basketball, don't you ever forget that. I might have to sit out a few games. It ain't like it's the end of my basketball career," he said, smiling, giving her a sense of comfort.

"Okay, I feel a lot better now." She gave him the same comforting smile. "I'll see you after school," she said, leaning over, planting a kiss on his cheek, and then walking out of the nurse's office.

Jyson rolled over and answered the telephone still half asleep after it had rung about fifty times back-to-back. "Hello," Jyson snapped at the caller.

"Damn, what's the matter with you?" Michaela asked. "Did I interrupt somethin'?"

"Naw, why you ask that?"

"'Cuz it took you long enough to answer the damn phone," Michaela snapped.

"Well, common sense shoulda told you that I didn't wanna talk to nobody," Jyson spoke as he yawned.

"Anyways. Jyson, I have somethin' to tell you," Michaela said, nervously.

"What's wrong?" Jyson asked as he rubbed his eyes.

"Are you sittin' down?"

"Just tell me, dammit!"

"Okay, just stop yellin'. Jyson, I'm pregnant," she blurted out and then closed her eyes and waited for a response.

Jyson sat up, not believing what had just came out of Michaela's mouth. *How did this happen?* "Are you sure?" he asked, not knowing if that was the correct response.

"What do you mean, am I sure?" Michaela snapped at his insane response. "Hell yeah, I'm sure. I just took my second pregnancy test."

"Well, what are we gon' do?" Jyson asked as he stood up and paced the floor.

"What do you mean *what are we gon' do?* I'm still in school, Jyson, and I done came too far to be havin' a baby right now. And besides, it's not in my ten-year life plan," she added.

"Calm down, Michaela. We are gon' think of somethin'," Jyson said, yawning.

"I have already thought about what I was gon' do before I even called you. I'm gon' have an abortion and I didn't think it would be fair for me to have one without you knowin' that I was pregnant first."

"What? I'll be damned if you kill a baby of mines," Jyson hollered into the phone. "Now, we need to sit down and talk about this some more. You're just in a messed-up state of mind right now. I'm gon' jump in the shower and I'll be over in about twenty minutes."

"There's no need, Jyson, 'cuz I have already made up my mind."

"What about me and my input on the situation?" Jyson asked.

"All I'm sayin' is that I don't have room in my life for a baby right now. I'm in college and I'm not gon' drop out just to raise a baby. I've been payin' my own way through school since I started. Do you actually think I like shakin' my ass for a livin'? But I gotta do what I gotta do to make things happen for myself," Michaela explained as tears rolled down her cheeks.

"Don't you think you're bein' a little bit selfish?" Jyson asked.

"No, don't you think you're bein' selfish?" she asked, and lay across her bed. "Look, Jyson, I'll talk to you later."

"No, I'm not done—" before Jyson could say anything else, all he heard was the dial tone. "Fuck!"

Jyson paced back and forth across his bedroom floor, wondering if he should go over to Michaela's apartment or if he should just let her cool down and get her thoughts together. "Fuck it, I need a drink," he snapped. Jyson picked up his cell phone and called his big brother.

"What's up," Big Mike asked, answering his cell phone.

"What's up, bra'? I need a drink," Jyson said.

"What's goin' on? You don't need me to get my bitches together, do you?"

"Naw man, it ain't nothin' like that. Where you at?"

"I'm in the truck on my way to the club. I'm about to drop this fine honey off and I'll be over to swoop you up, bet?"

"Bet," Jyson said, hanging up the phone and rushing into the bathroom to vomit. *I must be havin' some symptoms of her pregnancy myself. That explains why I can't keep anything down and why I been sleepin' all the time,* Jyson thought as he got undressed, slipped into the shower, and let the hot water run down his well-built body for what seemed like eternity.

"Jyson, where are you?" Trouble called out as she entered the house. "Jyson?" she called out again.

"I was in the shower, what's wrong?" he called from the bathroom.

"I just wanted to know where you were at before me and Dariel went into my room to make love," Trouble joked and then laughed.

Jyson walked into the living room with a towel wrapped around his waist. "I ain't in the mood, Trouble," he said with a long face.

"What's the matter, Jy?"

"Michaela called me and told me she's pregnant."

"Congratulations. What are you upset for?"

"She said that she wasn't keepin' it. She's gettin' an abortion," he said painfully.

"Why would she do somethin' like that?" Trouble asked. She could hear the hurt in her brother's voice as he spoke.

"I don't know. She was talkin' about she ain't ready for no baby and she needed to finish school before she even considered havin' kids." At that moment Jyson could feel himself about to break down in tears.

"Jy, y'all need to talk and come to some type of understandin'," Trouble suggested. "Remember when I found out that Dariel might have a baby on the way, and you said you weren't takin' his side?"

Jyson nodded his head yes.

"Well, I'm not tryin'a take Michaela's side, but she has invested so much time and money into payin' for her own education, and maybe she doesn't have the time it takes to raise a baby. Don't get me wrong, I strongly disagree with her choice on havin' an abortion. How come she can't give the baby to us just until she finishes school?"

"I don't know, Trouble. I tried talkin' to her, but she said her mind was already made up." Jyson walked into his room to get dressed. He put on his brown Akademiks jeans, a brown sweater to match, and a pair of brown Jordan boots and went back into the living room and sat on the couch to wait for Big Mike.

"Somebody's at the door," Trouble yelled when she heard knocking.

"I'll get it. It's probably Big Mike." Jyson opened up the door and Big Mike walked in.

"You all right, man?" Big Mike asked, giving him some dap.

"Not really," he sighed.

"What's up, Big Mike?" Trouble asked as she walked out of the kitchen and into the living room.

"What's up, sis?" Big Mike gave Trouble a hug. "Man, you growin' up too fast. I bet you got all the li'l niggas chasin' you, don't you?" he said, smiling, showing off his platinum fronts.

"Not since I got a dude," Trouble said, grinning.

"What dis nigga do for a livin'? He betta keep chedda in his pockets," Big Mike said.

"He keeps money or I wouldn't be foolin' with him."

"All right now, don't be fuckin' wit' no broke-ass niggas 'cuz they don't do nothin' but bring you down," Big Mike said, trying to school his little sister to a game that she was already too familiar with.

"I won't." She then changed the subject. "Do you think I can get a job at the club?" she asked.

Jyson and Big Mike both shot Trouble a dirty look. "Hell naw, and you bet not let me hear about you tryin'a get a job at nobody else's club, either," Big Mike warned.

"Dang, I wasn't talkin' about becomin' a stripper. I could be a barmaid or somethin'."

"His barmaids are his strippers," Jyson laughed.

"Oh well," Trouble said, disappointed. "You can't say that I didn't try to get a job," she said to Jyson.

"Get a real job," Jyson stated.

"Nice seein' you, Big Mike," Trouble said. "I'm 'bout to go in here and study for my history test while I wait on Dariel to come from basketball practice. He's gon' take me back over to the wicked witch's house," Trouble said, laughing.

Jyson shook his head and laughed.

"Nice seein' you too, Trouble," Big Mike said, smiling, as he pulled a wad of money out of his pocket and handed Trouble a hundred-dollar bill.

She accepted it with a smile and then walked into her bedroom.

"She's somethin' else," Big Mike said, laughing.

"Don't I know it," Jyson agreed.

Big Mike and Jyson walked out to Big Mike's truck and got in. "Fire that blunt up in the ashtray," Big Mike said, pointing to it.

Jyson pushed in the lighter and held the blunt in his mouth until the lighter popped out. Jyson lit the blunt, took a long pull, and passed it to his brother. He laid his head back on the headrest and waited for a few seconds before letting the smoke escape through his nostrils.

"Man, what's goin' on with you?" Big Mike asked, taking a pull himself.

Jyson closed his eyes and shook his head. He replayed the entire conversation before speaking. Big Mike smoked on the blunt while his little brother got his thoughts together.

"Man, Michaela is pregnant," Jyson finally said after a brief moment of silence.

"Is it yours?" Big Mike asked.

Jyson shot Big Mike a dirty look. "Hell yeah, nigga, it's mines."

"My bad. Shit, you gotta be careful these days. You know these bitches will blame a baby on a nigga in a heartbeat. You watch Maury Povich, don't you?" Big Mike laughed.

"Believe me, nigga, it's my baby."

"Okay. It's your baby. Well, congratulations," Big Mike said, passing the blunt back to Jyson.

"The broad said she's havin' an abortion." Jyson looked over in his brother's direction to see what his response would be.

"There it is. You don't have to worry about payin' no child support," Big Mike said.

"Nigga, it ain't all about that. She's talkin' about takin' my child's life," Jyson snapped. "You know what, man, fuck it! I don't even wanna talk about it no more."

Big Mike continued the ride to the club in silence. The only noise was the sound of the music bumping out of his speakers. He pulled up in front of Club Brittney's and as usual it was packed. People were there for the Wednesday after-work dollar day. Everything was a dollar, even top shelf.

"Man, let it go for right now," Big Mike said as they made their way through the crowd of people. "You out with me to have some fun, so get Michaela off your mind," Big Mike said to Jyson.

"Bet." Jyson and Big Mike sat at an empty table close to the bar. "Give me two double shots of Hennessy," Jyson yelled to one of the barmaids. After two shots, Jyson was ready to take on the world. He stayed on the dance floor. Every time a song would go off, he would head for his seat, but another fine honey would pull him back on the dance floor. After dancing to six songs back-to-back, he headed for his seat.

Jessica walked over to where Big Mike and Jyson were sitting and leaned down and whispered into Jyson's ear. "You comin' home with me tonight?"

Jyson was so drunk he didn't even know who was talking to him. "Let's go."

"Man, you betta hold that shit down. You know these hoes talk around here. All it's gon' take is for one of these bitches to see you leave with Jessica and they gon' beat down Michaela's door just to tell on you," Big Mike said.

"You right, man," Jyson slurred and stood up. "Man, I gotta piss," he said, stumbling over to the men's room.

Jessica put her hands on her hips and looked at Big Mike. "I don't wanna be waitin' on him all day either, nigga."

"Thirsty-ass bitch," Big Mike retorted. "I'll drop him off if he doesn't find anyone else to go home with first," Big Mike said, smirking, pissing Jessica off and loving every minute of it.

"I'm not worried about that. I know I got some good pussy, and only a fool would pass up the chance to get a piece of this, if you know what I mean," she said, winking at Big Mike before sashaying back to the dressing room to freshen up.

I might be drunk, but I think that bitch is offerin' me a piece of that pussy! Big Mike thought as he threw back another drink.

Trouble lay across her bed and waited on Dariel. She sat up when she heard a horn blowing outside.

"Oh, no this nigga ain't in front of my house blowin' like I called a cab or somethin'," she snapped as she walked into the living room and snatched the blinds open. She looked out the window and it was someone else blowing for her next-door neighbor. "It bet' not hadda been Dariel," she said. She then went and sat on the couch. Twenty minutes had passed and there was a knock at the door. Trouble smiled and answered it.

"Hey, baby," Dariel said, smiling, as Trouble unlocked the screen door. "Are you ready to go get your phone?"

Trouble had totally forgotten about going to get a cell phone. "Oh, yeah," she said, smiling. "How's your hand feelin'?"

"It still hurt a little. I got a doctor's appointment after school tomorrow, so I hope you don't mind waitin' over here for me?" Dariel asked.

"No, I don't mind. I can't believe your coach still makes you come to basketball practice even though your hand is messed up," Trouble said.

"Hell yeah. Coach Ephraim wants his players at every practice. Even if your momma dies, he wants you to show up right after the funeral." Dariel laughed.

"You silly, boy." Trouble laughed too.

"I'm serious." Dariel's smile turned into a look of concern. "Jameelah called me today."

Trouble's heart beat faster. "Oh, that's nice." *What the fuck that bitch call you for?* is what she really wanted to say. "Is everything okay with the baby?" Trouble asked, trying to sound concerned, even though she couldn't have cared less.

"Yeah, everything is cool wit' the baby. She was tellin' me that the prenatal vitamins she's takin' is makin' her sick, so she asked me what do I think she should do."

"What is she askin' you for? You're not a damn doctor!" Trouble snapped.

"I know." Dariel quickly changed the subject before their conversation turned into an argument. "Come on, let's go get your phone," he said, opening up the front door.

Strike one! The baby isn't even here yet and the baby momma drama is already in the works! What advice would Dariel have to give about a fuckin' prenatal vitamin? Trouble thought as she followed Dariel to his father's truck.

Jyson woke up and looked around the room. He couldn't remember where he was at. He rolled over and looked down at Jessica, who was still sound asleep. He shook his head, then he grabbed his cell phone out of his pants pocket and called his big brother.

"What's up, Big Mike?" Jyson asked.

"Sup, nigga? You make it home all right?" Big Mike asked.

"Naw. I'm still over this hood rat's house."

"That's why you wasn't answerin' your phone."

"Man, I didn't even hear my phone ringin'; that's how drunk I was."

"I left you about six messages to let you know that li'l Robbey got robbed last night."

Jyson laid his head back on the pillow, digusted about another one of his little soldiers getting robbed again. "That's crazy! This is the second time this month one of our soldiers got robbed. Call me paranoid if you want to, but I seriously think it's an inside job," Jyson said.

"So you sayin' that you think it's someone in the clique that's settin' up these robberies?"

"Hell yeah. As a matter of fact, I'll put my momma's best Sunday panties on it."

"I don't know. You could be on to somethin'. 'Cuz when I talked to Robbey last night, he said that he had just left some bitch house and was about to go to the crib to drop the shit off, and supposedly a blue minivan pulled up in front of him and blocked him off. He said he tried to back up, but a black Intrepid pulled up behind him so he couldn't move," Big Mike said.

"Was he in the car by himself?" Jyson asked.

"He told me Tight Moe was in the car with him, and they took all ten of 'em."

All of a sudden Jyson felt sick, but this time it wasn't no pregnancy symptoms. "Ummmp, ummmp, ummm, it sounds like some shady shit in the game to me," Jyson said.

"I'm hip." Big Mike grabbed the Listerine out of the medicine cabinet and swished it around in his mouth.

"I'll tell you what, Robbey's punk ass is gon' hafta work extra hard to pay me my money or I'ma take him out the game . . . for good!" Jyson said angrily.

Big Mike spit the Listerine in the bathroom sink. "I feel you on that, dog. That's one helluva loss. But it's all part of the game," Big Mike said as he smiled at himself in the mirror.

Jyson became angry with that snide remark. "Man, you think I don't know that? This is my money we're talkin' about. When dem niggas got you for them hundred gees, you didn't think it was a part of the game then; you did what you had to do to get yo' money back," Jyson said.

"Yeah, I did. But listen to what you just said; I did what I had to do to get my money back, now you take heed to that."

Jyson didn't want to discuss the matter any longer. "All right, man, I got a lot of things on my mind right now. I'm out," he said, hanging up his phone before Big Mike had the chance to say anything else.

The months had passed by rather quickly. Snow had covered the ground like a clean white sheet. Winter was Trouble's favorite time of the year, but this winter gave her the blues because it meant only one thing: Jameelah's due date was getting closer!

"What you gon' do for a nigga's birthday?" Dariel asked as he and Trouble walked into the cafeteria for lunch.

"I don't know, yet. Your birthday isn't until February, and if I'm not mistaken, it's only December. So I got plenty of time to decide on what to get you," Trouble stated.

"I got what I want right here," he said, smiling.

Trouble and Dariel walked over to the table where Ta'liyah and Regina sat. "What's up, y'all?" Ta'liyah asked.

"Y'all look so cute together," Regina said, smiling.

"We know, don't we, Trouble?" Dariel joked.

"You so crazy, boy," Ta'liyah laughed along with her cousin.

"What we gon' do after school, Trouble?" Dariel asked.

"Don't you have basketball practice?"

"I'm talkin' about after practice," he said, smiling.

"What do you wanna do?" Trouble smiled back at him.

"You know what I wanna do," he said, winking.

"Uhhh, you are so nasty," Regina said. "My girl doesn't get down like that."

"For real! 'Cuz if she did, we would be the first to know," Ta'liyah added.

"I know she don't get down like that," Dariel lied, not wanting to put their business out there, especially with News Center 8 sitting at the table. "And you wouldn't be the first to know, I would," he said, laughing. "Oh, Trouble, don't forget to pick me up after practice, but don't leave until I get my uniform out of the truck."

"You gotta be one of the luckiest girls alive, and I'm jealous," Regina said as Dariel walked away to meet up with Marcus.

"I don't know what for," Carla said, sitting down at their table.

"You're the only bitch I know that be drivin' a brand new car and don't even have a license yet," Ta'liyah said.

"Well, what can I say?" Trouble said, smiling. "Some of us got it like that!"

Carla rolled her eyes.

"I see Regina's not the only one jealous of me," Trouble said, smirking.

"Puhleeze, jealous of what?" Carla responded.

"I know what and you know what, so we'll just leave it at that," Trouble said as she stood up from the table, leaving Carla speechless.

"Why you always gotta start shit?" Ta'liyah said, grimacing.

"I didn't start nothin'," Carla replied.

"Grow the fuck up!" Ta'liyah said before getting up and walking away from the table with Regina on her heels.

Fuck them! I don't need them bitches anyways. I'm gon' show them hoes how lucky Trouble is, right after I fuck her man, Carla thought as she sat alone at the lunch table.

"Damn, what's takin' Dariel so long to come get his uniform?" Ta'liyah asked.

"I don't know," Trouble answered as they walked to the truck. "I'll just take it to him so we can leave."

Trouble pushed the alarm on the key chain and grabbed the uniform out the backseat. An envelope fell on the floor and she picked it up and read the letter that was in it.

Dariel, I know that we have been goin' through a lot, but we can work this shit out. I know I used to argue all the time and accuse you of bein' with different girls, and now I realize that I really was bein' insecure. I don't know why it took me losin' you to realize it, but now I know. But look at it now, my insecurities have become reality; you really was messin' around with Trouble.

"No, this bitch didn't," Trouble screamed. Ta'liyah and Regina ran over to Trouble's side. "What's wrong with you?" Ta'liyah asked. "Here, read this letter from Jameelah," she said, handing them the letter.

Regina and Ta'liyah read the letter together. "No, she didn't," Regina said, handing the letter back to Trouble. "Let's go find Dariel," she said.

"Let's go," Trouble said.

Trouble and her girls walked into the gymnasium and spotted Jameelah and Dariel talking by the bleachers. "Just the two people I've been lookin' for," Trouble said as she and her girls made their way over to them. Trouble cleared her throat. "Am I interruptin' somethin'?" she asked.

"What's up, baby girl? I was just about to come to the truck to get my uniform," Dariel said. "Ummm huh," Regina said, rolling her eyes. "Well, I guess

I can kill two birds with one stone," Trouble said, handing Dariel his uniform and then throwing the letter into Jameelah's face. "I would appreciate if you would not leave my man any more love notes. You had your chance with him, and now it's my turn. I'm assumin' you want him back."

Jameelah bent down and picked up the letter and held it tightly in her hand. "Well, you know what they say when people assume shit," she said, smirking.

"Anyway, what are you two discussin'?" Trouble asked, folding her arms.

"We ain't talkin' about nothin' really. She was just tellin' me that she has a doctor's appointment on Friday, so she wanted to know if I had practice on that day," Dariel said.

"Are you gon' miss practice to go to her appointment?" Trouble quizzed.

"What do you think?" Jameelah butted in.

"I think I was talkin' to Dariel," Trouble snapped. Trouble knew deep down inside that Dariel should go to the appointment with Jameelah. As much as it hurt her to agree with Jameelah, Trouble knew it would be the right thing on the chance that this might be his baby.

"Yeah, I'ma go," Dariel said.

He knew that going to the doctor with Jameelah would hurt Trouble's feelings, but after all this might be his baby whether Trouble liked it or not.

Jameelah rubbed her protruding belly and smiled. "Well, did you think he wasn't gon' go? This is his child, you know?" Jameelah said.

"You hope," Trouble said, smirking. "It could be anybody's baby. Why you playin'?" Trouble retorted, wanting to bust her out about the shit Jyson had told her, but hating was not in her nature.

"Come on now, Trouble, please don't start," Dariel begged, because he knew once Trouble got started, there was no stopping her. And as much as he couldn't stand Jameelah, he didn't want to see her get her ass kicked.

"Yeah, listen to my baby's daddy, and don't start no shit, 'cuz we don't want to upset the baby, do we, Dariel?" Jameelah stated.

Fuck you and that baby, Trouble thought of saying, but her conscience wouldn't let her. "I'll see you later, Dariel." Trouble walked away, leaving Dariel feeling trapped between a rock and a hard place while Jahmeelah felt victorious.

"Trouble, wait!" Dariel called out, but she kept on walking until she spotted someone she knew.

"Hey, Rondell," Trouble said, smiling, and gave one of her ex-boyfriends a quick hug.

"What's up, girl?" Rondell responded with his smooth voice. Rondell was fine too. He reminded a lot of people of Taye Diggs, but he was much too possessive for Trouble's taste, which is why their relationship didn't last but two months.

"I haven't seen you around school lately. Where have you been?" Trouble asked. She had only sparked up a conversation with him just to make Dariel jealous.

"I've been around. I've been keepin' my eye on you," he said, smiling. "I heard you got a new nigga."

Trouble didn't respond. She just smiled.

"You know I really miss bein' with you," Rondell said sincerely.

Trouble instantly felt sick to her stomach. "That's nice," she said, when she really couldn't have cared less if he missed her or not. Trouble smiled and laughed as much as she could as Rondell spoke. She made sure she made some type of noise to make Dariel think she was enjoying Rondell's boring conversation. "Well, I'll see you around," she said, smiling.

"All right. Why don't you give me a call one day? My number is still the same," Rondell said.

"I just might do that," Trouble lied.

No, she didn't just have that nigga all up in her face, Dariel thought while Jameelah rambled on about baby cribs and strollers.

"Dariel, I just wanna say this before I go," Jameelah said seriously. "I know you're probably with Trouble just to teach me a lesson and I have to admit, I'm sufferin', so the game is over now. I think it's time for you to be a part of this pregnancy."

"I said I was goin' to the doctor with you," Dariel said. "And I hope you know that as soon as the baby comes out, I'm havin' them swab our mouths so I can know if the baby's mine," he said, not caring if he hurt Jameelah's feelings or not.

"That's cool wit' me. I know who the father of my child is," she said, rolling her eyes. "I can't fuckin' believe you."

"Look, I'm sorry, but like I said, I need to know if it's mine."

Tears formed in Jameelah's eyes as she spoke. "You always said that if you had a child that you would be in its life no matter what, so here's your chance," Jameelah said.

Dariel felt bad for Jameelah. And she was right, he did say those words. His father had never turned his back on his mother, so he knew it was time for him to step up to the plate and be the man his father was, after he got the results back from the DNA.

"Now you know you ain't right," Ta'liyah said to Trouble as they exited the gym.

"What are you talkin' about?" Trouble asked as they headed back toward the truck.

"You know damn well what I'm talkin' about. Can me and Regina get a ride to the crib?" Ta'liyah asked. Trouble didn't answer. "What? All I did was give Rondell a hug. Was I wrong for that?" Trouble said as they opened the truck door and got inside. "Ta'liyah, I don't know if I can go through with this baby shit. I'm tryin', but it's hard. And I be tryin'a keep my cool with the little smart remarks Jameelah be puttin' out there. One of these days I'ma forget she's pregnant and I'ma kick her ass," she said as she drove off.

Regina kept quiet the entire time because she didn't have any advice for her friend. "You might need to cool things off between you and Dariel for a while. It's not like y'all fuckin'," Ta'liyah said. Trouble didn't respond. "It ain't like y'all fuckin'," Ta'liyah repeated. Trouble still didn't respond. "Oh my goodness! Girl, you and Dariel are fuckin'!" Ta'liyah shouted. "How come you didn't tell us?"

"And here I was takin' up for you at lunch today, and come to find out y'all have been doin' the nasty the whole time," Regina said, laughing.

"I was gon' tell y'all," Trouble said.

"Bitch, you haven't told us in all this time, you wasn't plannin' on tellin' us," Ta'liyah said loudly.

"Did it feel good, girl?" Regina asked curiously.

"It felt real good," Trouble said, gloating.

Trouble pulled up in front of Ta'liyah's house and they got out. Ta'liyah stared at her best friend and smiled.

"What? I gotta booger in my nose or somethin'?" Trouble asked.

"I been wonderin' why you've been glowin' for the past few months," Ta'liyah said.

Trouble's smile slowly faded away. "That's another reason why I'm so confused about this whole pregnancy ordeal. I gave your cousin my virginity. You know I must care a lot about him, 'cuz I've always said

I wasn't havin' sex until I found the right guy, and I thought I found him in Dariel."

"Whatever decision you make, you know I gotcha back," Ta'liyah assured her and Regina agreed.

"Thanks." Trouble gave each one of her girls a hug before jumping back in the truck and heading for home.

Trouble didn't want to be bothered with anyone, not even Jyson. All she wanted was to go to Loretta's house, climb into bed, and cry herself to sleep, but she couldn't because she had to pick Dariel up from basketball practice at four p.m.

Trouble walked into her room and lay across the bed. She thought about what Ta'liyah had said about cooling things off with Dariel for a while. She argued back and forth with herself until she drifted off to sleep. She was awakened by a knock at the door. She pulled herself up off the bed and staggered into the living room and opened up the door. Dariel stood on the other side of the screen door, smiling.

"How did you get here? I thought you didn't get out of basketball practice until four p.m.," Trouble asked when she unlocked the screen to let him in.

"It's after five. I've been callin' your cell phone for about an hour, but I got no answer," he said. "So I had to call my dad to come pick me up."

Trouble walked over to the couch and lay down. "My bad. I fell asleep and my phone is still in my book bag," she said, yawning.

Dariel walked over to the couch and tried to sit down beside Trouble, but she opened her legs so he couldn't fit. "Are you gon' move your legs so I can sit down?" Dariel asked.

"Sit over there," Trouble said, pointing to the chair.

"Trouble, you can't be mad about me goin' to the doctor appointment with Jameelah," he said.

Trouble sat up. "That's not what I'm mad about. I'm mad about the letter she left you. How come you didn't tell me she wrote you a letter? Was you tryin'a hide it from me?"

"I wasn't tryin'a hide shit. I just didn't wanna start no argument," he explained.

"Whatever. And I thought you never told her that you loved her?"

"I have never told that girl that I love her. She told me that I loved her. It never once came outta my mouth," Dariel clarified. "And furthermore, that letter didn't have anything about love in it."

"Whatever, Dariel," Trouble sighed. "I'll tell you one thing, I'm tired of Jameelah's fly-ass mouth. She gon' fuck around and make me go up in it and it ain't gon' be pretty when I do."

Dariel sat down on the couch next to Trouble, not knowing what else to say. He looked at her and did what he thought was best: He picked up the remote, pushed play, and held his girl as *Baby Boy* popped up on the TV screen.

Eighteen

"Jyson, it's been two and half months since I had that damn abortion and you still act like you're mad about it," Michaela said.

"What? You don't think I should be mad about you takin' my child's life ?" Jyson said. "Shit, I was beginnin' to think the baby wasn't even mines."

"Who else baby could it have been, dummy?"

"I don't know, you tell me? If it was mines, why in the fuck you kill it?" Jyson asked suspiciously.

"I told ya black ass that I wasn't ready for a child just yet," Michaela said as she got dressed. She put on her red suede skirt, a white satin top, and a pair of red suede boots that came past her knees.

"Oh, but you was ready to have unprotected sex, but you wasn't ready to be a mother? Broad, please," Jyson lashed out.

"It wasn't my idea to have unprotected sex in the first place. You're the one who didn't have any more condoms left, 'cuz you used 'em all up on all those other bitches you be fuckin'."

"Shut the fuck up!" Jyson said, climbing out of bed and walking into the bathroom so he could shower. He

was actually running away from the argument because
that last remark Michaela made was nothing more
than the truth. Jyson was turning out to be just like Big
Mike, fucking everything in a skirt. He had been thinking about keeping it real and being with just Michaela,
but after she had the abortion he had lost all respect for
the woman who would have one day become his wife.

Michaela walked into the bathroom. "I don't think
you want me to go to Big Mike's New Year's Eve party,
that's why you started this argument," Michaela
said as she grabbed her eyeliner out of the medicine
cabinet. "But I'ma tell you like this, I'm goin' and I'm
gon' have a good time whether I have one with you or
not," she said, storming out of the steamy bathroom.

Jyson loved to make Michaela mad, because it all
paid off in the end when they made up. Jyson got out
of the shower and got dressed up in a brown Snoop
Dogg sweater, a pair of brown Snoop Dogg jeans, and
his brown Timberlands. They both checked themselves
over and over in the mirror before jumping into Jyson's
brand new Envoy and driving to the party in silence.

"Happy new year!" everybody in the big house yelled
at once. The house was decorated with thousands of
Christmas lights. Big Mike thought it was a good idea
because it reminded him of a childhood he would
have loved to be a part of. Christmas always made him
feel like a kid again because he never got a chance to
experience that part of his life. When he was younger
his mother never had the time to put up a Christmas
tree, because she was always out in the streets trying

to find a way to make a quick twenty dollars to buy her a hit of dope. Big Mike could remember spending one Christmas at a crack house. The house reeked of piss and there was no furniture, but they did have an old shabby tree that looked more like a branch. It was decorated with one strand of lights and at the top of it sat a star made out of paper. Big Mike was amused by the blinking lights on the tree. He could still remember that tree and he promised himself when he got older that every Christmas he would buy the biggest tree he could find and it would have a real star at the top.

Everybody walked around hugging one another, glad to have made it to another year. Jyson smiled when he saw Trouble and Dariel walk through the front door.

"Happy New Year's, big brother," Trouble said, giving him a hug.

"Same to you, little sister," he said, hugging her back. Jyson gave Dariel a hug and a firm handshake before walking off to mingle with some of the other guests. As the guests sang the traditional New Year's song, Jyson made his resolution. He promised himself to let the past stay in the past and move on with his relationship because he didn't want to lose Michaela over something he could not change; the baby was gone.

Big Mike kept the same resolution that he made every year. He told himself that he was going to start being a better husband for Sherry and try to leave all those other broads alone. Sherry's New Year's resolution was to file for a divorce if her husband didn't straighten up by June. This was her third year of making that same resolution, but this time she was serious, just like all the other times.

Trouble's resolution was to try to get over the fact that Jameelah might be having Dariel's baby in four months. And last, Dariel's resolution was to love and take care of Trouble as much as he possibly could.

"Hey, party time!" Jessica yelled as she walked through the door with two of her friends.

"Oh, my goodness," Big Mike said, grimacing. "The queen of hood rats has arrived." Big Mike laughed. Jyson laughed too.

"Who let the dogs out?" Trouble whispered to Michaela and they both giggled.

"Hey, sis, how are you?" Sherry asked, walking over to her drunk sister and giving her a hug.

"Happy New Year's to you too," Jessica slurred as she scanned the room for Jyson. *I see he brought his bitch wit' him*, she thought when she spotted him. Jessica pressed the wrinkles out of her fake leather pants before walking over to where Jyson and Big Mike stood. "Happy New Year's, Jyson, and you too, Big Mike." Jessica held out her arms for a hug but didn't get one from either of them.

"Same to you," Big Mike replied with little enthusiasm.

"Damn, y'all just gon' leave me hangin' on the hug?" Jessica asked. "I said Happy New Year's, Jyson," she said again.

"Yeah, whatever," he said.

"Damn, don't sound so enthused," she said to Jyson.

"I'm not, at all," he replied.

"Fuck you," Jessica said.

"I did. But ya pussy smelled like salmon," Jyson retorted.

Jyson hadn't dealt with Jessica in a couple of months, since she had lied to him and told him she was pregnant by him. Jyson made her take a pregnancy test and it was positive, only to find out she used one of her pregnant friend's pee. Jessica tried to have Jyson give her money for an abortion, and he would have given it to her with the quickness if it wasn't for one of her jealous-ass friends getting mad at her because she wasn't the one being dicked down by him. He was so grateful for her friend telling him that he took her to a cheap motel and put it down on her and never spoke to her again. Birds of a feather truly flock together!

"Bitch, you ate this salmon-smellin' pussy!" she spat.

"Bitch, I wouldn't eat yo' pussy with someone else's mouth, let alone my own." Jyson laughed, hoping to piss her off to the extent that she would just walk away.

Jessica wasn't backing down. "You limp-dick bitch," she said.

"Go'n girl, with that bullshit," Big Mike warned.

"Naw, fuck that nigga! He thinks he's all that!" Jessica said.

By this time they had caught the attention of all the guests. Michaela had stopped talking to Trouble and walked over and stood by Jyson to watch Jessica make a fool of herself.

"What the hell is goin' on over here?" Sherry rushed over to her husband and asked.

"Why don't you ask your crazy-ass sister?" Big Mike laughed.

Sherry shot Big Mike a dirty look before turning her attention toward her sister. "What's goin' on, Jessica?"

"Ya husband and his friend is over here talkin' shit. Jyson betta shut the fuck up before I tell his bitch that me and him was messin' around!" Jessica said out of spite. "Oops, too late, I already did." She laughed.

Jyson couldn't believe what had just came out of Jessica's big-ass mouth. He wanted to run and hide, but first he wanted to slap the shit out of her for opening up her mouth. Jyson watched as Michaela's smile quickly turned into a frown.

"Is this true, Jyson? You've been fuckin' this nasty-ass ho behind my back?" Michaela asked as tears formed in her eyes. But she had promised herself a long time ago that she would never cry over another man, at least not in front of him. And she damn sure wasn't about to let Jessica's stank ass see no tears fall.

Jyson stood motionless. He didn't know what to say. He wanted to reach out and comfort Michaela and beg for forgiveness but he couldn't. Most of all, he wanted the entire night to start over, but it couldn't. All he could do was hold his head down, walk down the hallway into the bathroom, and close the door behind him.

"You gotta go, bitch," Big Mike said as he grabbed Jessica, picked her up, holding her over his head, and throwing her out the front door, just like Philip Banks used to do Jazz on *The Fresh Prince of Bel-Air*.

"I'ma get you back, bitch-ass nigga," Jessica screamed as the door closed shut. "You just wait and see, it's on, bitch!" Jessica got up off the ground, dusting the snow off her fake leather pants. She limped to her car and took off, leaving her pride along with her two friends behind.

"Jyson, you okay, man?" Big Mike yelled through the bathroom door.

"Where Michaela at, man?" Jyson asked.

"She's gone. She got a ride home with Melissa."

Jyson slowly opened up the bathroom door and let his big brother in. Big Mike grabbed him and hugged him tight. For the first time in his life, Jyson cried over a girl. "I didn't mean for it to happen like this," he said.

"I know, man. We never mean for it to happen the way that it does. It's all a part of the life, baby boy," Big Mike explained.

"I hurt her, man. I could see it in her face." Jyson cried even harder. "I didn't mean to hurt her, Big Mike."

"Jyson, you all right?" Trouble asked as she peeked through the cracked bathroom door. Trouble watched as her brother cried, and she began to cry herself. She knew that even though her brother messed around with a lot of different girls, Michaela was number one in his life.

"I'm okay, sis. I'm ready to go home and go to bed," he said, hugging his sister.

"Let's go," she said, hugging her brother back and wanting to take his pain away.

"Michaela, don't hang—" Jyson yelled into the phone receiver before he heard a click in his ear.

"She still not talkin' to you?" Trouble stood in his doorway and asked.

"Nope. I feel like Dariel did when you kept hangin' up on him." Jyson shook his head and let out a little chuckle.

"Just keep tryin'. She'll give in eventually, just the way I did," Trouble said, smiling, and then walked away.

Jyson heard a knock at the front door and jumped up and ran into the living room, hoping it was Michaela at the door. "Oh, what's up, Dariel?" Jyson asked, sounding depressed once he opened up the door.

"What's up, Jyson? Are you ready to go?" Dariel asked Trouble.

"As ready as I'm gon' get," she said, smiling. She then turned to her brother. "Are you gon' be okay, Jyson?"

"Yeah, I'm gon' be okay. I'm about to get dressed, 'cuz I got some business to take care of," he said.

Trouble gave her brother a hug and a kiss on the cheek before leaving out the door.

"Man, your brother sure is takin' this breakup kinda hard, ain't he?" Dariel asked as they walked to the truck.

"Yeah, but what goes around comes right on back around. You can't keep mistreatin' a person and expect good things to happen to you. He knew he shouldn't have been messin' around with that bitch with all them damn kids in the first place," Trouble said angrily. She got into the truck and buckled her seat belt while Dariel messed around in the trunk.

"I'm sure he regrets it now," Dariel said, opening up the driver's-side door.

"Huh?" Trouble's mind had wandered elsewhere.

"Jyson. I bet he regrets messin' around on Michaela," Dariel said.

"Oh, yeah. Well, he should have thought about the consequences beforehand. Y'all niggas kill me. Y'all think y'all can do any damn thing yall wanna do to us, and we supposed to sit back and take it. But it doesn't work that way," Trouble snapped.

"Calm down, baby girl," Dariel said, starting the truck and putting it into drive. "You act as if I cheated on you."

"I'm sorry, but stuff like that makes me so mad. And if Jyson wasn't my brother, I would say the same thing to him."

Dariel pulled off and drove Trouble to her aunt's. When he pulled in front of the house, he got out and opened up her door. "I love you," he said, giving her a long, passionate kiss. "I'll call you as soon as I finish my algebra."

"Okay," she said, unbuckling her seat belt and climbing out of the truck. "I love you too," she said, smiling and walked up on the porch and watched as Dariel drove away.

Michaela sat on her bed crying and listened to Mariah Carey's "Shake It Off" over and over again. She lay there wondering how she let herself get dogged by a man once again. It had been two weeks since the terrible incident and she still wouldn't speak to Jyson. All she did all day was sit around the house and wait on Jyson to call, just so she could hang up on him.

"I told you, girl, that he was no good," Sheila said while comforting her younger sister.

"I'm tired of fuckin' around with these no-good-ass niggas," Michaela cried. "I sit at home, just to see if he's gon' call, and when he does I hang up on him. I feel satisfied when he calls; it makes me think that he really is sorry and that he really does love me."

"He's supposed to call you. He's the one that fucked up, not you. If you messed around on him and he found out, you would be the one callin' him, beggin' for forgiveness. But see, men and women are totally different when it comes to breakin' up," Sheila explained.

"How are we different?" Michaela inquired.

"Take for instance: we females sit around the house all day and wait for them to call, and when they do, we tell them to stop callin' and hang up on 'em. Even though we're glad they called, we feel that if they don't call, they don't care. Now if a man caught us cheatin', it would be totally different. I'm not sayin' he wouldn't be hurt, but he would just move on to the next chick. He wouldn't be sittin' around no damn house waitin' on us to call, I'll tell you that," Sheila said to her grieving sister.

"I wish it were that easy for us," Michaela said.

"It can be. All you gotta do is get up and get dressed and I'll show you how easy it can be to move the fuck on."

"I really don't feel like goin' anywhere. I'm too tired," Michaela said.

"You're not tired, you're depressed. Now get up and get dressed, 'cuz we are goin' to Club Brittney's tonight. It's dollar night." Sheila stood up from her sister's bed and walked into the bathroom to get ready for the club.

Michaela smiled and got out of bed and walked over to her closet to find herself something to wear. She was not going to let Jyson get the best of her. Ever since the breakup, she had not been to work, but now it was time to get back into the groove of things because her cash flow was starting to get low.

Michaela showered and put on a cream sheer organza blouse, the one that Jyson hated for her to wear because he said that it showed too much cleavage. She put on a brown suede skirt that zipped up the front with her cream suede boots.

"Watch out, world!" she yelled as she looked at her reflection in the full-length mirror that hung on the back of her bedroom door.

"Look at you! Now that's the Michaela I know," Sheila said, smiling, as she walked into the room. "We are gon' get some free drinks tonight, and if a fine nigga ask you for your phone number, you betta give it to him or give him mines instead," Sheila laughed.

"Thanks, Sheila," Michaela said with tears in her eyes.

"No problem. That's what big sisters are for. Now stop your cryin' and let's go to the club."

"Let's go," Michaela said, grabbing her keys and her purse off the couch and they both headed to the car.

I hope Jyson be at the club tonight, Michaela thought as they drove to the club, bumping the sweet melodic sounds of India Arie. Michaela pulled up into the crowded parking lot and the first car she noticed was Jyson's. She wanted to smile and jump for joy, but she didn't want Sheila to know how desperate she really was.

"You ready?" Sheila asked, grabbing for the door handle.

"Ready as I'm gon' get," Michaela said, smiling, as she got out the car. They walked into the club feeling like a million bucks. The music was sounding good, people were on the dance floor, and Jyson was sitting at the table with Big Mike, shooting their regular.

Jyson watched as Michaela and Sheila walked into the club. Men flocked to them like flies on shit. Jyson watched as Michaela laughed about something one of the men said to her. He was furious and wanted to go over there and tell that nigga to back the fuck up off his girl, but she no longer belonged to him.

Michaela spotted Jyson watching her and pretended not to pay him any attention, even though she was happy to see his sexy face.

Michaela and Sheila took a seat at the bar and they both ordered fuzzy navels. "The place is packed tonight,"

Sheila said, sipping on her drink.

"It sure is," Michaela agreed.

"I see your ex is over at that table watchin' your every move," Sheila said to her sister.

"I ain't thinkin' about that nigga," Michaela lied. She was so glad that someone other than herself noticed Jyson watching her.

"Would you like to dance?" a tall, light-skinned brother with curly hair and a face full of acne asked Michaela.

Uhhh, this nigga is in need of some Proactiv, she thought. *Didn't you see P. Diddy and Alicia Keys's results?* "No thanks. Maybe later," she said as Light-skin turned to walk away.

"Michaela, dance with him," Sheila demanded.

"Oh all right," she said, getting up from the bar stool. "I'll dance with you." Light-skin stopped dead in his tracks and turned around and walked back over to Michaela. She pushed her drink over to her sister. "Watch my drink for me." Michaela pressed the wrinkles out of her skirt and followed Light-skin to the dance floor. She was only dancing with him to make Jyson jealous. She moved her body like she was onstage performing for money and Light-skin loved every minute of it. He was too stupid to know he was being used.

"Don't you work here?" Light-skin asked.

"Yeah," Michaela answered. *Just dance and shut the fuck up 'cuz yo' breath smells like you ate some ass for dinner,* she thought.

"You got a nigga?" he asked.

"Yeah, I do," she lied.

"My name is Leon, what's yours?"

"Beverly," Michaela lied.

Jyson watched as Michaela moved her body like a sex feind.

"Man, you see your girl over there dancin' wit' that nigga?" Big Mike asked Jyson.

"Yeah, I see her," he responded. "I don't even know why Sheila brought her ass out; she supposed to be at home studyin' for her finals."

"How you know Sheila brought her out? It could have been her idea to come to the club tonight," Big Mike said, striking a nerve.

"Naw. I know Michaela didn't wanna come out. Her sister talked her into it. 'Cuz she don't come out unless she gotta work," Jyson said.

"Shit, she ain't been to work in a long-ass time," Big Mike said, adding more fuel to Jyson's fire.

"I know."

Big Mike took a sip of his Hennessy and said, "It looks like she's enjoyin' herself to me. You see the way she's dancin' wit' that cat?" Big Mike instigated.

Jyson rolled his eyes. "Do you think I'm blind, nigga? Yeah, I see how she's dancin'!" Jyson had stopped drinking after he and Michaela broke up, but he couldn't stand the sight of his girl out on the dance floor shaking her ass up for free. "Give me a double shot of Hennessy wit' no chaser," he said to the barmaid that was walking past.

"I thought you quit drinkin'?" Big Mike asked.

"I did. I need somethin' to calm my damn nerves down so I won't go over there and pull that nigga off the dance floor and beat his ass." Once the barmaid brought his drink over Jyson took it to the head and slammed the glass down on the bar just like they used to do in the old western movies.

Big Mike could see the fire in his little brother's eyes. "Man, don't do nothin' crazy," he said as Jyson started to get up out of his seat.

"I'm cool. I ain't gon' do nuttin' stupid." Jyson walked over to the dance floor and pulled Michaela by the arm to get her attention.

"What do you want?" Michaela asked when she turned around.

"I need to talk to you for a minute," Jyson said.

"Don't you see me dancin'?" she said with an attitude, but she was happy that he wanted to talk to her.

"It ain't gon' take long. Hey, my man, do you mind if I cut in and talk to her for a minute?" Jyson asked Leon politely.

"Can't you wait till we're done dancin', nigga?" Leon replied.

"What the fuck you mean? Nigga, this my girl!" Jyson spat.

"I'm not your girl, Jyson. We broke up, remember?"

"You heard her, nigga, she don't belong to you no more! So git on befo' you get spit on," Leon said and then laughed in Jyson's face.

"What yo' ugly ass just say?" Jyson walked up into Leon's face.

"Y'all please," Michaela begged.

Big Mike saw what was about to go down, so he picked up his drink and took it to the head before walking over to his brother. "What's goin' on over here?" Big Mike asked.

"This nigga just told me to git on befo' I get spit on. He don't know who he fuckin' wit," Jyson yelled.

"Nigga, I don't bar you! Fuck you, wit' yo' gangsta wannabe ass," Leon said.

"Nigga, you betta back the fuck up befo' you get smacked the fuck up!" Jyson warned Leon.

"Yeah, dog. You betta go'n and get out his face," Big Mike said, getting angry himself.

"Fuck you too!" Leon shouted before hitting the floor. Big Mike swung his gigantic fist, knocking him out cold with one punch.

"Oh my goodness! Someone call an ambulance," some old drunk lady screamed when she saw all the blood gushing from Leon's nose and mouth.

Three of Big Mike's bouncers walked over to the scene and stood beside him.

"Shut up, old bitch. This nigga all right," Big Mike said. "Pick this trash up and take him outside my establishment. He's a troublemaker and we don't need none of them in my place of business," he said to one of the muscular men.

"Jyson, that wasn't even called for," Michaela huffed.

"Well, I said I needed to talk to you," Jyson stated.

"That's what's wrong with the world today, everybody wanna go to heaven but don't nobody wanna die!" Michaela snapped.

"Huh?"

"Oh never mind, Jyson."

"What's goin' on over here?" Sheila asked, rushing over to her sister. "Are you okay, Chaela?"

"Yeah, she's fine," Jyson interjected.

"I'm not even talkin' to you. I'm talkin' to my sister," Sheila snapped.

"I'm okay," Michaela said.

"Can I please talk to you, Michaela?" Jyson asked, almost in a begging manner.

"Talk to her about what?" Sheila intervened .

Jyson shot Sheila a dirty look. "I'm not talkin' to you, Sheila, damn!"

"Aren't you the one who hurt my sister? And now you wanna talk yo' cheatin' dog ass back into her life. I don't think so. Come on Michaela, he's a waste of your time. You can do better than him." Sheila grabbed her sister by the arm and tried to lead her off.

"Let Michaela be the judge of that," Jyson said, removing Sheila's hand from Michaela's arm.

"Come on. I'll talk to you, but only for a minute," Michaela said.

"Michaela, don't play yourself," Sheila begged.

Michaela put her hand up as if she were trying to stop something. "Let me deal with this on my own, Sheila, please. All I'm askin' is for you to let me handle this my way."

"Suit yourself, dummy. But when the nigga dog you again, don't come cryin' to me," Sheila snapped and walked away.

"Sheila," Michaela called out.

"Let's go. She'll be okay," Jyson said as he guided her to the club's exit and over to his truck.

Jyson unlocked the truck doors and they got in.

"What do you wanna talk to me about?" Michaela asked, fastening her seat belt.

"First, I wanna say I'm sorry for hurtin' you." Jyson looked at Michaela for a response but got none. "Did you hear me?"

"Yeah, I heard you. What do you want me to say?"

"Say somethin'. Don't just sit here like I'm talkin' to myself," he said as he drove past Mifflin Lake.

"You know, I really don't have too much to say right now. You really hurt me, and I just can't up and forgive you just like that," Michaela said, snapping her fingers. Michaela had already forgiven Jyson before he asked for forgiveness. She wasn't about to let him know that, though. The last thing she wanted was for him to know how bad she wanted him back in her life.

"I don't expect you to forgive me, just yet. Let me make it up to you, 'cuz I owe you," he said sincerely.

"What about Jessica?" Michaela asked, not knowing if she really wanted to know anything else about him and Jessica.

"What about her?"

"How is she gon' feel about you tryin'a make up with me?"

"Fuck Jessica. I'm not messin' with that hood rat no more. As a matter of fact, I haven't been messin' around with anyone since we broke up. What about you?"

"Oh, now she's a hood rat? She wasn't a hood rat when you was fuckin' her, was she?" Michaela hissed. "And it's none of your business if I've been fuckin' around with someone or not. Just remember one thing, I wasn't fuckin' him while we were together." Michaela could see the surprised look Jyson had plastered all over his face. She smiled at her accomplishment and laid her head back and listened as her "man" begged for forgivness.

Nineteen

"I can't wait until Dariel's birthday party," Regina said as she danced around in the lunchroom chair. "I can't wait either. He said his boys, Dante and Darius, are comin' to town," Ta'liyah said. "Who are they?" Regina inquired before taking a bite of her baked chicken. "They all grew up together in Chicago," Ta'liyah answered. "I hope they fine. I need some water, 'cuz my well has ran dry," Regina laughed. "You are so silly, girl." Trouble and Ta'liyah laughed.

"Dariel told me about Dante. He said he done some time in juvenile for murder when he was twelve," Trouble said.

"Dang," Regina responded.

"I remember that," Ta'liyah said. "He killed the nigga that murdered his mother and sister."

"Dariel said he only done three years behind it," Trouble said.

"I used to love kickin' it with them when we went to Chicago. Darius is the reason I started smokin' bud," Ta'liyah reminisced.

"You started smokin' 'cuz you wanted to. Don't blame it on Darius." Trouble laughed.

"You sho'll right about that," Regina agreed.

"Hey, baby girl," Dariel said to Trouble as he walked over to the lunch table.

"Hey," Trouble said, smiling.

"Don't forget we gotta go to the mall today. I gotta get fitted for my suit and find you a dress," Dariel said.

"What colors are y'all wearin'?" Regina asked.

"My suit is lavender and I got a cream silk shirt to match. And Trouble gotta find her somethin' that matches my suit," Dariel said.

"Do you need help with anything?" Ta'liyah asked as she coated her lips with gloss.

"Naw, not really, 'cuz Nachelli's gon' cater the food, Josh is in charge of gettin' the DJ, so there's nothin' left for you to do but have fun," Dariel said.

"I didn't get invited to your little party," Carla said.

"I invited everyone, so don't be afraid to come," Dariel replied.

"Where is it gon' be at?" Carla asked.

"I'm havin' it at the Seven Eleven hall," he answered. "Come and enjoy yourself."

"I wanna cum all right," Carla said, smirking, before getting up from the lunch table and walking away.

"Ta'liyah, I know she's your friend and all, but if she keeps playin' me like she doin', I'ma give that bitch just what she's lookin' for," Trouble said, heated.

"Don't pay her no attention, she's just jealous," Ta'liyah said.

"Like I said, the bitch is gon' get just what she's lookin' for."

As the school day started to come to an end, Trouble became eager to get to the mall to pick out a dress. She loved shopping, especially when someone else was spending their money. Jyson had given her six hundred dollars to purchase something to wear and Dariel's parents had given him their Discover card and told him to get everything he needed. Trouble and Dariel shopped until they nearly dropped. They bought purses, shoes, jewelry, and Trouble even had Dariel pay for her to get a third hole in both of her ears while they shopped at the mall.

"I wonder what Loretta is gon' say about these other holes in my ears?" Trouble said as they pulled up in front of Loretta's house.

"Why would she say anything about you gettin' your ears pierced?" Dariel asked.

"'Cuz she's ignorant like that," Trouble said.

"Is your aunt home?" Dariel asked, looking in the driveway to see if her beat-up car was parked there.

"Naw, she doesn't get home until around seven o'clock, 'cuz she be havin' a lot of paperwork to do at the end of each day," Trouble answered.

"Well, can a nigga come in then?" Dariel said, smiling, hoping she would agree because with all the party planning, he needed to relieve some stress.

"I think not," she said, smiling back.

"You can't blame a brotha for tryin'." Dariel leaned over and kissed her soft lips.

Trouble gathered all of her shopping bags and got out of the truck. "I'll call you later on," she said, smiling.

Dariel smiled back. "Okay." *Man, I know a relationship ain't built on sex, but I sure could use a little bit right about now,* Dariel thought as he drove to Orlando's.

The school week flew by rather quickly. It was Friday, and for February the weather felt rather nice. All the snow had melted and turned into slush, and the sun even had the nerve to be shining brightly.

What a good day for a party, Dariel thought as the school bell rang and he headed to his first period class.

"What's up, Dariel? Tonight's the big night," Charles said, excited.

"Fo' sho'," Dariel said, smiling.

"I know it's gon' be some fine hotties up in there tonight," Charlie said, rubbing his hands together as if he were putting lotion on them.

"You already know!" Dariel walked up and down the halls looking for his girl. "There you are," he said once he spotted her talking to Ta'liyah. "I shoulda known you were somewhere around here runnin' your mouth," he said, hugging her from behind.

"I was just tellin' Ta'liyah and Regina about your suit and my dress," Trouble said.

"I know y'all gon' be so cute tonight," Ta'liyah said.

"And you know this, man!" Dariel laughed as he thought about the wonderful evening that was in store.

"Come in," Trouble yelled at whoever stood outside her bedroom door knocking.

"What are you doin' in here?" Loretta asked, entering. "Oh, I see you got your hair done today." She began looking around Trouble's bedroom at all the shopping bags that were laid all around.

"Yeah, I did. Tonight is Dariel's seventeenth birthday party." Trouble smiled happily, laying her dress out on the bed and her new lavender panties on top of it.

"Oh, that's nice," Loretta responded with little enthusiasm. "But you know I already made plans to go over to your daddy's house for their housewarmin' party. And guess who's gonna be there?" Loretta had a huge smile plastered on her face.

"Who?" Trouble asked, even though she couldn't have cared less. She just wanted Loretta to tell her and get the hell out of her room so she could start getting ready.

"Your granddaddy, that's who. His nurse said he won't be able to stay long, and you know this might be the last time we all get to party with him," Loretta said sadly.

Trouble felt sad about the fact that her grandfather was dying of cancer, but she still wasn't going to miss Dariel's birthday party to go to some housewarming party with her father's fake-ass family and in-laws. "Oh well, enjoy yourself, and tell my father I said hello and give Poppy a kiss for me," Trouble said, grabbing her bathrobe off the back of her closet door and throwing it across her shoulder.

"You can do all that yourself, 'cuz you are goin' over there with me. Now I have already told your daddy and your grandfather that you would be there and they were so happy."

"No, I'm not goin'. I'm goin' to Dariel's birthday party. He's my boyfriend and I wouldn't miss his party to go to a man's party that doesn't give a damn about me," Trouble said calmly, even though things were about to get real ugly.

"How could you say that about your daddy?" Loretta screamed. "I'm appalled that you would even let that part your lips." Loretta was furious because of Trouble's comment about her brother, but Trouble couldn't have cared less.

Trouble became angry too. "That nigga ain't never been no father to us. All he's ever been was a sperm donor, that's all! You think by him sendin' us a check every week and callin' once or twice a month, he should be considered for the father of the year award? I don't think so!"

Loretta stomped over to Trouble and stood in her face. "He's been nothin' but good to you and your brother. Y'all are just—y'all are just ungrateful," she stammered.

"Where have you been? On Mars? If that man cared anything about me or Jyson, he would have never left us!" she yelled. Before Trouble could see it coming, Loretta's hand landed across her cheek. Trouble held the side of her stinging face, in shock.

"Don't you ever disrespect my brother by callin' him that man! *That man* loves you and your brother. And he didn't leave y'all. Ya triflin' mammy started smokin' them drugs so he had no choice but to leave!"

Trouble's right hand came up from out of nowhere and landed on the left side of Loretta's face. "Bitch, if

you ever call my momma anything other than Denise,
I'll kill you! Ronnie was a muthafuckin' ho, and if anything, that man pushed my momma to smoke crack.
All the shit she took from his dog ass. So you speak on
what you know, and shut the fuck up about the shit you
think you know," Trouble said angrily. "Now if you'll
excuse me, I need to finish gettin' ready for my man's
party." Trouble gave Loretta the evil eye as she walked
past her to get to the bathroom.

Once Trouble got into the bathroom, she took a
long hot shower, and to her surprise, when she came
out Loretta was standing in her room with a leather
belt in hand.

"Let me tell you one thing: as long as you live in my
house you will abide by my rules. And look at that short
dress you got on. You look like a five-dollar whore. And
like I said before, you ain't goin' to no damn birthday
party, so you might as well take off that short-ass dress
and put on somethin' more appropriate."

"I'm goin' to Dariel's party. I don't care what
you say," Trouble huffed. "And by the way, for your
information, a five-dollar whore could only wish to
look this good," Trouble bragged.

"We'll see if you party tonight. The only partyin'
you'll be doin' is over to your dad's house," Loretta
said, walking out of Trouble's room and slamming the
door hard enough to make the eight-by-ten picture of
her and Jyson fall to the floor.

This bitch ain't said nothin' but a word, Trouble
thought as she picked up the phone to call her brother.

"Get off my damn phone," Loretta screamed into the receiver.

Trouble slammed the phone down in hopes of breaking Loretta's eardrum. She reached in her book bag and pulled out her cell phone and called her brother's cell.

"Hello?" Jyson answered on the very first ring.

Trouble started crying as she told her brother what went down between her and Loretta. She din't leave anything out and Jyson was furious.

"Tell me you playin' about that bitch slappin' you," Jyson said. "Look, be ready, 'cuz I'm on my way over there to get you. That bitch can stop you from goin' to Dariel's party, but she can't stop you from comin' with me. And if she tries to, it's gon' be hassle in the castle," Jyson said, hitting the expressway.

"Who is it?" Loretta yelled as she looked through the peephole after hearing someone knock on the door.

"It's me, Jyson," he said.

Loretta opened the door and let him in. When Trouble heard the door she hurried and gathered her belongings and walked down the stairs. Loretta looked at Trouble and said, "Just where do you think you're goin'?" She put her hands on her hips and walked over to Trouble. But this time Trouble was prepared for her aunt to hit her again; she was gon' mop the living room floor with her ass.

"She's goin' with me," Jyson answered. "I'm takin' her to dinner and to a movie, so don't wait up, 'cuz she's spendin' the weekend with me."

"But I told her that she couldn't go anywhere, 'cuz we're goin' over to ya daddy's house for his and Mary's housewarmin' party. Ya granddaddy is gon' be there, so you need to come along too," Loretta suggested.

"Naw, I'll pass," Jyson replied.

Loretta rolled her eyes at Jyson. "Well, Trouble ain't goin' to Darnell's party," she said.

"Dariel," Trouble said, correcting her aunt.

"Whatever his name is. I don't want her at his party," Loretta said.

"Whatever you say. I'll just go to dinner and the movies with Jyson," Trouble said, smirking.

"You think you so slick," Loretta huffed.

"I am. Thanks for noticin'," Trouble said, smiling, and she walked out the door behind her brother.

"Thanks Jy," Trouble said, once they got into the truck.

"Don't mention it," he said, starting the truck and pulling off.

"Jyson, we haven't had a brother-sister talk in a long time, and I think it's time we had one. I've been keepin' somethin' from you, and I hope you don't get mad when I tell you."

"Don't tell me if it's bad. I don't have time for no more bad news right now. So what's up?"

"Never mind, it can wait," she sighed. Trouble sat back and listened to George Howard on the radio as her brother coasted down the expressway.

Jyson pulled up in front of Dariel's house and looked over at his sister. "Be careful tonight, and here," he said, pulling five twenties from his coat pocket and handing them to Trouble.

"What's this for? I thought you said you weren't givin' me no more money."

"Don't I always say that to you? And besides, I gave it to you so you can buy yourself something nice and a box of condoms."

Trouble didn't know what to say. Her brother's comment surprised the hell out of her. *How did he know? I didn't tell him and I know Dariel didn't tell him. Maybe he's psychic,* Trouble thought as she got out of the truck and stood beside it. "Okay," she said, stuffing the money into her clutch purse.

"I love you, sis," Jyson said.

Trouble had closed the door to the truck, still in shock. "I love you too, Jyson," she uttered, but he was already gone. She strolled up to the house and rang the doorbell, still in shock about her brother already knowing that she was no longer a virgin.

"Who is it?" a sweet voice hollered out from the other side of the door.

"It's Candria," Trouble stated.

"Come on in, chile. How you doin'?" Dariel's mother asked, giving Trouble an inviting hug.

"I'm fine," Trouble answered as she took off her short suede coat and hung it up on the coatrack.

"You sure are fine," Dariel said, walking up behind her and checking out the rear view.

"Boy, I don't want no grandbabies around these parts. You might already have gotten Looney Tune pregnant," Mrs. Daniels said.

"Look at you. You wearin' the heck outta that dress," Josh said, walking down the stairs and into the living room.

"Hold on, nigga, that's my girl you checkin' out," Dariel teased.

"Boy, what have me and ya daddy told you about usin' that word in this house?" Mrs. Daniels said, slapping Dariel on the arm.

"My bad, Momma."

"Yeah, it's always yo' bad," she laughed. "They look so good together. Go get me the camera, Josh, and tell ya daddy I said come look," Mrs. Daniels said as she smiled from ear to ear while waiting on her husband to come downstairs.

Dariel wore a lavender Versace suit. The suit jacket came a little past his knees, and he sported a cream silk shirt underneath it. He laid the entire ensemble out with a pair of checkered lavender-and-cream Gators. He was dressed to kill and he knew it. Trouble had to represent and sport the same color her man sported. It wouldn't have been right if she didn't. She had on a lavender strapless, tight-fitting DKNY dress that came right above her knees, and she had on a pair of DKNY wraparound, open toe heels. Her fingernails were all done up in a French manicure and she had the pedicure to match. Her hair was swooped in a French roll with a piece of hair hanging on the side.

"You two sure do look good together," Mr. Daniels said as he strolled into the living room.

They took pictures for what seemed like hours.

"Who is it?" Josh yelled at whoever was knocking on the door, interrupting the photo shoot.

"Come see who it is," the person yelled back.

Trouble started getting worried.

"Look, man, I don't have time to be playin' no games," Josh said angrily, before snatching the door open and getting bum-rushed by two very handsome young men.

That must be Dante and Darius, Trouble thought, relieved.

"What's up, nigga?" Dante shouted as he embraced Josh.

Dariel wiped a tear away from his eye as Darius hugged him.

"How y'all been?" Darius asked with a light southern accent and a mouthful of platinum teeth.

"It's just like old times," Mr. Daniels said, smiling as he watched the longtime friends reunite.

"Hey, Ma and Pops," Dante and Darius said, giving Mr. and Mrs. Daniels a hug.

"How y'all boys been?" Mr. Daniels asked.

"Y'all stayin' outta trouble," Mrs. Daniels asked before they could respond to her husband's question.

"Yes, ma'am," they both answered.

"And who is this fine young honey over here?" Darius asked, referring to Trouble.

"I know this can't be you, Dariel?" Dante joked.

"She's all me, baby boy," Dariel boasted.

"Hi, I'm Trouble," she said, extending her hand.

"Trouble," Dante repeated. "Now that's an interestin' name for a beautiful young lady like yourself."

"It's just a nickname. My real name is Candria."

"Nice to meet you, Candria," Darius said, wrapping his arms around her and giving her a warm embrace.

"Nice to meet you too," she said, smiling widely.

Dante took Trouble's hand and kissed the back of it. "Nice to meet you, Trouble," he said, smiling.

"Same here," she responded.

Trouble's cell phone rang as the men proceeded to reminisce.

"What's up, girl?" Regina asked. "What they look like?"

Trouble excused herself and walked into the kitchen to talk on her phone. "Girrrl, they are both fine with a capital *F!* Dante reminds me of Nick Cannon and Darius kinda looks like Omarion but with a mouthful of platinum teeth," she whispered into her phone.

"I can't wait to see 'em," Regina exclaimed.

"I bet you can't, old ho," Trouble laughed.

"Okay, I'll see you at the party," Regina said, pacing the floor while waiting on Ta'liyah to come pick her up.

"All right." Trouble hung up her phone and walked back into the living room. Dariel and his friends were still laughing and reminiscing about the old days.

"Y'all ready to roll?" Josh asked, putting on his coat.

"Trouble, you can take the truck and Josh, we can ride with Darius and Dante so they won't get lost," Dariel suggested.

"The four amigos back together again," Mr. Daniels laughed.

"I guess it's okay. I mean, if you want me to drive the truck I don't have no problem with that," Trouble said, disappointed because she wanted people to see her and Dariel make a grand entrance into the party, just like they did on that show *My Super Sweet 16*. Dariel would be making his grand entrance, but it wouldn't be with her by his side, instead, he would be with his boys.

Dariel handed Trouble the keys and he and his boys walked out the door. Trouble walked out after them and got into the truck. She called Ta'liyah's cell phone. *I can't believe this nigga didn't want to ride to the party with me,* she thought as Ta'liyah's phone rang. "Fuck him!" she said as Ta'liyah answered her phone.

"Excuse me?" Ta'liyah asked.

"Oh, my bad. I was just thinkin' out loud. Y'all left yet?"

"Not yet. My brother's Pinto keeps actin' like it don't wanna start, but we're about to try it again in a few minutes. Thank God I made it to Regina's house."

"Well, don't leave yet, y'all can ride with me. I got the truck," Trouble said.

"That's what's up," Ta'liyah said. "Hey, we about to ride in style," she said, dancing around Regina's bedroom.

"You call Tico's beat-up Pinto ridin' in style?" Regina asked as she sprayed some oil sheen in her hair.

"No, dummy, Trouble is comin' to pick us up in the Escalade."

"Hey, we 'bout to be ridin' in style." Regina danced too.

Twenty

"This muthafuckin' Seven Eleven hall is packed," Regina said as they pulled into the crowded parking lot and searched for a close parking space. Once they found a parking space in the back of the hall, Trouble and her friends got out of the truck feeling like a million bucks. The parking lot was still packed full of people that were trying to fix themselves up before going into the party. A group of girls getting out of a small blue Nova gave them dirty looks as they strutted past.

"They think they somethin'," one of the girls said.

"They sho'll do," another one of the girls answered.

"Jealousy," Trouble retorted as she and her girls walked through the parking lot.

Regina and Ta'liyah were both on cloud nine. They had smoked a blunt while waiting for Trouble to arrive. They walked through the doors and people were everywhere.

"Damn!" all three of the girls said. They walked in, handed their coats to the coat-check lady, and went straight to the dance floor.

"Damn, baby, you wearin' the hell outta that dress," Alex, an old friend, walked up to Trouble and said.

"Thanks," Trouble said, smiling.

"You wanna dance?" he asked.

"We're both out here on the dance floor, so we might as well," she said, smiling.

Trouble and Alex began dancing to the new 50 Cent joint. Trouble looked for Dariel as she grooved to the music.

"Are you lookin' for someone?" Alex asked, noticing Trouble's attention was elsewhere.

She shook her head no and continued to dance. She noticed a bunch of people crowded around the door like a celebrity had just entered the building. She slowed her dancing down to see who had come in. The niggas was shaking the mystery man's hand, and the women was screaming like Usher had just walked in. She watched as Dariel and his boys walked out of the crowd. Dariel and his crew walked over to a table that was set up only for the birthday boy and his close friends. They took a seat and began laughing about something.

Trouble continued to dance until the song went off. "Thanks," she said.

"No, thank you," Alex replied. Trouble's favorite song by Keyshia Cole came on and she asked Alex would he like to dance again. He agreed and they slow danced as Keyshia crooned through the speakers.

"Ain't that Candria on the dance floor?" Dante asked Dariel.

"Yeah, that's her." Dariel got up and walked over to the dance floor and began dancing behind Trouble.

"What's up, baby girl?" he asked, kissing her cheek and ignoring the fact she was dancing with someone.

Alex gave Dariel a dirty look.

"Nothin'. Can't you see I'm dancin'?" she replied.

"May I cut in?" Dariel asked Alex.

Alex took a step back, but Trouble grabbed his arm. "You can get the next dance," she said to Dariel. *Now, that'll teach you to put your friends before me*, she thought as she wrapped her arms back around Alex's neck.

Dariel was outdone. He couldn't just let that ride so he tapped Trouble on her shoulder. "Don't play wit' me, Trouble," he said.

"I'll dance with you later, Alex," Trouble said, giving in.

"What's this attitude all about?" Dariel asked.

"What attitude? Are you talkin' about the attitude I got 'cuz you couldn't ride to the party with me?"

"I—"

Trouble threw her hands up and walked off the dance floor, leaving Dariel standing alone surrounded by a large crowd of people.

Trouble and her girls sat in the VIP section with Josh and his boys while Dariel mingled with some of the other guests.

"These shoes are startin' to hurt my feet," Ta'liyah complained.

"You knew they were too little when you bought 'em," Regina laughed.

"I'm bored. I think I'm 'bout to go home," Trouble said out of nowhere. She started feeling sad when she looked around at all the couples who were hugging and kissing one another.

Ta'liyah gave Trouble a crazy look. "Don't be spoilin' our fun just 'cuz you beefin' with Dariel over somethin' so stupid and childish."

"I'm hip. We're havin' fun, and if you wanna go home, go ahead and go. We'll find another way home, but if you gon' stay, you are gon' hafta cheer the fuck up 'cuz you're startin' to mess with my high," Regina said.

"With your spoiled ass," Ta'liyah stated.

Trouble sat quietly. She knew her girls were telling her the truth. She was spoiled and she knew it. "I'm sorry y'all. I hope y'all will forgive me for tryin'a spoil y'all's fun."

"We'll forgive you under one condition," Ta'liyah said, smiling.

"Anything," Trouble replied.

"If you'll find Dariel and make up with him," Ta'liyah said.

"I don't know. He made me feel so left out," Trouble said, pouting.

"Trouble, he wasn't tryin'a make you feel left out on purpose. He haven't seen Darius and Dante in a long-ass time. He sees your ass every day," Ta'liyah said.

"I guess you're right," Trouble agreed.

"These are for you," a tall light-skinned brother with an Afro said, handing Trouble a dozen roses.

"Oh my goodness!" Ta'liyah and Regina screamed.

"They are so beautiful. Who are they from?" Trouble asked.

The light-skinned brother pointed over in Dariel's direction. Trouble stood up from the table and walked over to her man. He bent down and kissed her on the lips.

"Thanks for the roses, and I'm sorry for actin' so immature," Trouble said, smiling.

"It's okay. Just understand one thing, Darius and Dante are only here with me for the weekend, but you'll be with me forever. Now let's dance," Dariel said, pulling Trouble to the dance floor.

"Damn, they look so good together," Regina said, smiling.

"Don't they?" Ta'liyah agreed, feeling a little bit jealous because she was without a man.

"I'm about to go sit down 'cuz my feet are startin' to hurt," Trouble said, wiping sweat from her forehead.

"We only danced to four songs," Dariel laughed. "Go ahead. I'm about to go over here with Darius and Josh." Dariel led Trouble over to the table before heading over to meet up with his boys. Darius and Josh were standing around checking out all the fine girls at the party. "What y'all talkin' about over here?"

"We talkin' about all the fine chummies up in here," Darius answered. "I know I'm about to make somebody's parents real upset tonight, 'cuz I'm takin' one of these broads to the hotel, and I ain't takin' 'em home 'til six in the mornin'," Darius said.

"I feel you," Josh laughed.

"Dariel, you can't hang out with us, 'cuz wifey ain't gon' have that shit," Darius joked.

"You damn right she ain't," Josh teased.

"I know she's fine as hell. You always keep the baddest bitches in your stable," Darius said, finishing off the Corona he snuck in.

"I have to agree with you, but Trouble is far from a bitch," Dariel said. "She's a classy young lady."

"I have to agree with my brother on that note. How many girls you know gon' stick with a nigga that might have a baby on the way by another chick?" Josh asked.

"In the hood it's a whole lot of 'em," Darius laughed.

"Well, well, well, what do we have here?" Jameelah said, approaching the young men while looking at Dariel.

"Speakin' of the devil," Josh said.

"How nice of y'all to be discussin' me. I hope y'all had some good things to say," Jameelah said.

"What do you want, Jameelah? And who invited you here in the first place?" Dariel said, grimacing.

"Aren't you gon' introduce your baby momma to your friends?" she asked.

"You gotta be kiddin' me," Darius laughed.

"Y'all, this is Jameelah. Jameelah, these are my boys from back home. Are you satisfied?" Dariel asked sarcastically.

"I've heard a lot about y'all," Jameelah said.

"Upp, Trouble is on her way over here. The shit is about to hit the fan," Dante said.

"Let me step back, 'cuz I don't wanna get hit by a stray fist," Darius joked.

"Catfight," Dante joked.

"Naw, it ain't goin' down like that. Trouble knows she's my one and only," Dariel assured his friends and prayed at the same time that Jameelah didn't start no mess.

"Bet a hundred," Dante said.

"Bet," Dariel quickly said before Trouble walked up.

"I don't know what y'all bettin' for, 'cuz she's got sense," Jameelah said, putting her hands on her wide hips.

"What's going on, baby?" Trouble asked when she walked up.

"Nothin'," Dariel replied.

"We gon' dance in a few minutes, Dante," Trouble said.

"That's cool with me," he said, smiling.

"What's up, Jameelah?" Trouble asked.

"Don't perp. You know you're jealous because I'm pregnant by your man and that I'm at his party," Jameelah said, smirking.

"Now why would you say somethin' like that, chubby girl?" Trouble said, smiling.

"Don't hate. I know you're just jealous, and you have the right to be," Jameelah retorted.

"Better you fat than me. And I have no reason to be jealous because if the baby is even his, he or she will be around me all the time anyways," Trouble said.

"I don't want my child around her, Dariel," Jameelah screamed hysterically, making a fool of herself.

Darius and Dante watched as Trouble handled the situation like the classy lady that Dariel said she was.

"Girl, calm yo' ass down," Dariel said, grimacing.

"And why we even discussin' this here? If the child is mine what you say is irrelevant."

Trouble smiled. "Let's go, Dante, this is my song." Trouble led Dante to the dance floor and left Dariel there to handle his baby momma drama!

"That nigga owes you a hundred dollars. I can't believe Trouble didn't trip out like most broads would have," Darius said to Dariel.

"I tried to tell y'all that she ain't like that. She ain't on all that trip shit."

"Now that's how I like my women, I can't stand a woman that likes to argue all the damn time. If a bitch wanna argue, she'll be doin' it by herself, 'cuz I'll leave her ass standin' alone," Darius said.

"I'm leavin', Dariel," Jameelah said.

"Bye," Dariel shot quickly as she stormed away.

"Man, you had to have been outta yo' mind to fuck with that crazy-ass broad," Darius said, laughing.

"If I would have known then what I know now," Dariel said. "The more I think about it, I know she got pregnant on purpose. Don't get me wrong, I know I should have used a condom, but I still think it was some shady shit in the game."

"Shit, she thought if she got pregnant by you, you would be with her ass forever. That's what you call a keep-a-nigga baby," Darius teased. "Oh, and by the way, you betta go over there and get Dante away from yo' girl."

"Yeah, you right. They look like they havin' way too much fun over there on the dance floor," Dariel said, walking over to the dance floor with Darius and Josh behind him.

"Damn, nigga, you and Trouble dancin' like y'all on *Soul Train* or some shit," Josh joked.

"She's freakin' the shit outta me," Dante laughed.

"That's okay. She might be freakin' you on the dance floor, but after the party she'll be freakin' me in the bedroom," Dariel replied.

"I'm gone," Trouble laughed, and walked away, leaving the fellas alone on the dance floor.

"Hook a bitch up with Darius," Regina said once Trouble made it back to their table. Trouble nodded at her friend.

Dariel and his friends made their way over to the table with Trouble and her girls. They all sat around laughing and kicking it while passing around the half gallon of Rémy Martin that Dante had snuck in. They all got drunk as the night went by smoothly.

"What time is it?" Darius slurred.

"It's two o'clock, and I have to go to the bathroom," Regina slurred, standing up from the table.

"What time is the party over?" Trouble asked Dariel.

"In thirty minutes. I have someone to clean up, so I'm ready to roll," Dariel said. "I'm goin' home with Trouble, I don't know about y'all," he said to everybody.

"I'm takin' Ta'liyah with me," Dante said, smiling.

"I'm goin' home with Nikki," Josh slurred. "I'll see y'all tomorrow afternoon." Josh gave his brother and his friends a hug before departing.

"I guess that leaves you and Regina," Trouble said, smiling at Darius.

Darius hesitated and thought for a moment before responding. *I ain't never messed with a chubby girl before, but like they say, big girls need love too.* "I guess it does," he said, grabbing Regina by the arm as soon as she walked back over to the table. They all walked outside to their vehicles and said their good-byes before going their separate ways.

"I really like your friends," Trouble slurred as she climbed into the Escalade. "Darius is really funny."

"Yeah, those are my boys," Dariel said. "Darius keeps everybody laughin'." He put his seat belt on and checked his rearview mirror before pulling out of the half-empty parking lot.

"Do you think Jyson is home?" Dariel asked.

"Hell naw," Trouble said before closing her eyes and praying that he wasn't.

"What we gon' do at your house?" Dariel said, grinning.

"I have somethin' in store for you," Trouble said, smiling. Trouble had a big surprise for Dariel. She had been reading up on different sex positions for the past couple of months, and had decided to give a few of them a try.

"What is it?" Dariel asked.

"You'll see." Trouble had also planned on returning the favor Dariel had done for her the first time they had engaged in a sexual activity. She was nervous as hell, but she kept repeating what she had read in the books. *It's nothin' to it but to do it*, she thought for the rest of the ride home.

Dariel pulled up in front of Trouble's house and let out a sigh of relief because her brother's truck wasn't there.

Trouble jumped out of the truck and hit the ground. "Ooooch!" she screamed in pain.

"What's the matter with you?" Dariel asked as he ran over to the passenger side of the truck and saw Trouble on the ground. "What happened?" he asked, trying not to laugh.

"What does it look like? I fell, nigga," she said.

"Here, let me help you up," Dariel said, snickering, before grabbing her by the arm.

"Get off me. I see you laughin' at me," Trouble said, trying her hardest to keep a straight face, but couldn't.

She got up, dusted herself off and limped to the front door. As Trouble opened the door, Dariel scooped her up in his arms and carried her off to her bedroom and laid her on top of her bed. He took off her shoes and threw them on the floor.

"I don't need no help gettin' undressed," Trouble said.

"Shut up and let me do this." Dariel unzipped Trouble's dress and began undressing himself. He threw his suit on the arm of the chair and climbed in the bed and started kissing Trouble with every bit of passion he had for her.

"Wait," Trouble said, stopping him. "I need to get my scarf and tie my hair up." Trouble climbed out of bed and dashed into the bathroom and found her scarf.

"Girl, you know you will mess up a wet dream," Dariel said.

"Shit, I can't have you messin' up my hair."

"Who paid to get it done? All right then, I can mess it up."

"Okay, I'm ready," she said, climbing back into bed after putting on her scarf. "No, wait."

"Now what?" Dariel asked. It had been a long time since he and Trouble had made love, and he was long overdue.

"It's your birthday, and I have a surprise for you," Trouble said, smiling.

Dariel smiled. "Okay, I'm ready for it."

Trouble hit play on the CD player and Omarion's new song came on, and she moved to the rhythm of the music. She watched as Dariel's love muscle grew. He took in each movement her body made without missing a beat. She swayed her hips like she should have had a starring role on *Fame*. She danced her way over to the bed and began kissing her man. Dariel wanted her so bad. He wanted to skip the foreplay and go straight to the lovemaking. She straddled his body, kissed his neck, and moved her way down to suck on his nipples, which drove him bananas. She kissed her way down to his washboard abs before going all the way down south. She massaged his love muscle with her small hands. And to Dariel's surprise, she put it between her lips and began to suck it like a pro.

"Oh my goodness!" he moaned with clenched teeth.

Trouble thought about all the things she read in them books. She pulled his erect love muscle out of her mouth and began licking and playing with it with the tip of her wet tongue. She worked her magic like she'd been doing it all her life.

"This shit feels so good," Dariel said, excited. He grabbed the back of her head, forcing her to go deeper.

"Hold on, nigga, don't be touchin' my hair. I done told you once and I ain't gon' tell you again," Trouble said.

"My bad, damn, come on and finish," Dariel said anxiously.

Trouble went back to work. She sucked and licked until her jaws got tired.

"Don't stop, baby girl." Dariel moaned like a banshee. "Please, don't slow down," he begged, as his toes curled before reaching his peak.

Trouble sucked harder and faster until an explosion erupted from the tip of his love muscle and shot straight into her mouth with full force. She remembered on page forty-nine in the book it said if you swallow, it turns your man on even more, so she did what the book said and swallowed all that she could as the rest ran down her hand.

"Happy birthday," she looked up at him and whispered.

"Thank you," he said, out of breath.

"Did you enjoy your surprise?"

"Let me show you just how much I enjoyed it. Turn over and get on your knees."

Once Trouble did so, Dariel stood up and got behind her and placed his hands on her hips as he guided his erect love muscle into her chocolate waterfall. He moved vigorously, in and out without skipping a beat. Trouble let out soft moans, one after the other and that turned Dariel on even more.

"Dariel, please slow down, you're hurtin' me," Trouble begged.

"I can't help it," he moaned as he stroked deeper and deeper.

"Dariel?" she called out in ecstasy.

"Relax, baby girl, and let me hit my pussy." Dariel slowed down the motion so she could stop complaining. But when she began to moan louder and beg for him to hit it harder, he did just that. Before long, Dariel had exploded all up in her insides and collapsed on the bed. He wrapped his arms around his girl's waist and they both fell asleep peacefully.

Twenty-one

"Jyson, I'm seriously thinkin' about movin' to Atlanta to finish off my major," Michaela stated as she stood in front of the stove cooking breakfast for her man. "How do you feel about that?"

Jyson sat at the kitchen table in silence. "I think it's a wonderful idea," he finally said. "I'm gon' hafta start usin' my American Express card to get me some frequent flyer miles, so I can come see you at least two or three times a month."

Michaela thought about only being able to see her man two or three times a month and decided to stay in Mans-field.

"I said I thought about goin'. I didn't say that I was," Michaela snapped. She became so angry with herself for putting another man before her future, once again.

"Why are you so mad at me? You act like I told you not to go." Jyson stood up and walked over to Michaela and wrapped his arms around her waist, gently pressing his lips against the nape of her neck.

"I know. I'm sorry. It's just that I keep puttin' everybody else before me," she said.

"You can't be talkin' about me, 'cuz I want you to go to Atlanta to finish school. You said it has been a dream of yours and I want you to fulfill it," Jyson said, kissing her neck again.

I want you to be there, dummy, Michaela thought, but didn't have enough nerve to say it because she didn't want to hear a negative response. "I'll get there; it's just a matter of time. Now let's change the subject." She smiled and piled Jyson a plateful of bacon, eggs, hash browns, and pancakes.

"Thank you," he said, smiling, and sat down at the table.

Jyson bowed his head in prayer as Michaela led. He looked up and saw the pain in her face as they sat in silence. The only noise was coming from the clinging of the forks against the plates.

I'm about to turn my life around for this girl, Jyson thought as he stared at her. *I hope it'll be the right thing for me to do.* "You wanna go to a play on Saturday?" he asked, breaking the long silence.

"Sure." She smiled at Jyson as she continued to eat breakfast.

"Tylenol," Trouble woke up mumbling. She crawled out of bed and stumbled into the bathroom and opened up the medicine cabinet. *My head is poundin'*, she thought. She walked back into her bedroom and watched Dariel as he slept peacefully. She kissed him on the forehead and walked back into the bathroom, turned on the shower, and slid in. She let the feeling from the hot water take her to another place. "Let me get outta here before I mess up my hair," she said. As she dried off it dawned on her that Dariel didn't use any protection last night. "Oh no! Dariel, get up," she yelled as she stormed back into her bedroom.

"What's wrong?" he asked as he jumped up from a deep slumber. "Can you please let down the blinds, the sun is killin' my eyes."

"You ain't got to worry about the sun killin' you, 'cuz I'm about to," Trouble said.

"What did I do now?"

Trouble walked her naked body over to the blinds and pulled them up as far as they would go.

"Damn, baby girl, I'm sorry for whatever it was that I did," Dariel said, pulling the comforter over his head. "Come sit next to Daddy and tell me what I did."

Trouble sat down on the bed next to Dariel and tried to pull the comforter from over his head, but he wouldn't let it go.

"Okay, what's the matter?" he asked, sticking his head from under the comforter.

"Your ass didn't use any protection last night," Trouble said as she stood up and put her hands on her hips and walked to the other side of the room.

"Why you yellin' at me? You act like it's all my fault. You didn't make me put no condom on," Dariel said.

"Dariel?" Trouble squealed. "We can't be careless like that anymore. You might already got one baby on the way, nigga."

"You're right. From now on we will be more careful," he said, getting out of bed.

"Can we go to the mall today? I need some new shoes," Trouble said as she rambled through her closet, looking for something to wear.

"Didn't you just buy some new shoes?" Dariel asked, walking up behind Trouble and wrapping his arms around her waist.

"Yeah, but my brother gave me some money last night and told me to buy myself somethin' nice and a box of condoms."

"What did you just say?" Dariel asked.

"You heard me," Trouble said as she continued searching through her closet.

"You told Jyson you were sexually active?"

"No, I didn't tell him. I don't know how he found out," Trouble said, pulling out a pair of Rocawear jeans that she forgot she had.

"Well, since we don't have to hide anymore, make it two boxes of condoms," Dariel said, pulling Trouble over to the bed and pushing her down on top of it.

"Dariel, stop it and go get in the shower so we can go to the mall," Trouble said, getting up and walking back over to her closet to find a shirt to match her jeans.

Trouble heard the shower come on as Dariel's cell phone started ringing. "Dariel, your phone is ringin'," she hollered into the bathroom.

"Answer it," he yelled back.

Trouble smiled and then answered the phone. "Hello?"

"Hello, may I speak to Dariel?" the girl on the other end of the phone asked.

Trouble's jaw hit the floor when she heard a female's voice. *Maybe it's one of his cousins,* Trouble thought as she walked toward the bathroom with the phone still stuck to her ear. She wanted to ask who the hell it was on the other end of her man's phone, but didn't want to sound nosy, so she did what any other trustworthy girlfriend would have done. "May I ask who's callin'?"

"This is Shirl," the female said in the most pleasant voice.

I don't remember him havin' a cousin named Shirl, she thought.

Just then Dariel walked out of the bathroom, drying off. "Who was it?"

"It's some girl named Shirl, and she's still on the phone." Trouble handed Dariel the phone and walked to the other side of her room.

"Who is Shirl?" Dariel scrunched up his face.

"Shit, I don't know. It's your phone she's callin', not mines," Trouble snapped. Trouble pretended to look for something on top of her dresser, but the entire time she was listening to Dariel's conversation.

"Who dis?" Dariel answered the phone.

"It's Shirl. You don't remember me, do you?" she asked.

"No, I'm afraid not. Refresh my memory," Dariel said.

"I talked to you at the mall about nine months ago and you told me to call you when I got rid of my boyfriend. I got rid of his no-good ass, so now I'm givin' you a call," she said.

"Okay, now I remember. You work at the Footlocker in the mall. What took you so long to get rid of your man?" he asked, without intentions.

If looks could kill Dariel would have been dead from the look Trouble shot in his direction.

Dariel caught Trouble's drift quick and hurried up and changed the subject. "Well, Shirl, I have a girlfriend, and as we speak, she is about ready to kill me. So could you please do me a favor and don't call me anymore?" Dariel said, trying not to sound rude.

"Okay," Shirl replied before hanging up.

"What was that all about?" Trouble asked as soon as Dariel tossed his phone on the bed.

"Shirl is a girl I met at Foot Locker about nine months ago. I only talked to her so I could use her discount. The broad had a man that was doggin' her and I told her when she got rid of him to give me a call. She just told me that she got rid of him, so she called me," Dariel explained.

"Is that so?"

"Man, that was a long time ago. You see I had forgot who she was." Dariel laughed as he grabbed Trouble's round backside.

"Whatever. And would you please stop touchin' my ass?" Trouble said, rolling her eyes.

"You wasn't sayin' that last night when I was all up in it." Dariel laughed, grabbing her ass once again.

Trouble slapped Dariel's hand. "That's okay, 'cuz it'll be a long-ass time before you be all up in it again," Trouble hissed, rolling her eyes.

Dariel pulled up in front of his parents' house and noticed an unfamiliar black Infiniti parked in the driveway with North Carolina plates.

"I wonder who this could be? Come in for a minute," Dariel said, as he got out of the truck. Trouble got out and followed Dariel inside the house.

"Here he is right here. Just the man we've been lookin' for," Mr. Daniels said, smiling, and waved for his son to come over to him.

Trouble walked in and took a seat on the couch.

"Hello, I'm glad to finally meet you in person," the tall slender white gentleman said, holding out his hand for Dariel to shake. "I'm Jackson Meehan, a scout from UNC," he said, smiling wickedly. "You know we have had our eyes on you ever since you were in the seventh grade."

"Is that so?" Dariel said without taking his eyes off of Mr. Meehan. "How did you know I moved to Mansfield?" Dariel asked suspiciously.

"We've got our ways of finding out about everything in North Carolina, and I do mean *everything*," he said, winking. "You know, if you come to UNC we could make you the next Michael Jordan."

Dariel rolled his eyes into his head. *Here we go again,* he thought. "I haven't decided on what college I'm attendin', but when I do decide I will call you and let you know." Dariel reached down and picked up a piece of peppermint out of the candy dish that sat on top of the mahogany coffee table and stuck it in his mouth.

"Well, maybe this'll help you make up your mind a little bit faster," Mr. Meehan said with his country accent as he handed Dariel a check.

Dariel shook his head no. "No thanks, no money is needed." Dariel handed the check back without looking at the amount.

"Okay, I see you drive a hard bargain, but I heard you would," he said, winking again. "So I'll tell you what, I'll give you some time to think on it, but in the meantime, the check is on me." Mr. Meehan laid the check down on top of the candy dish before putting on his coat and hat.

Dariel shook his head in disgust.

"Nice to meet you, Mr. Daniels," Mr. Meehan said, shaking his hand firmly before walking toward the front door.

"Same here." Mr. Daniels waved as he walked over to his son. "So what do you think, son?" he said when Mr. Meehan walked out the door.

"I don't know, Dad. Like I told Mr. Meehan, I'm not sure what college I'm goin' to," Dariel answered.

"It's your choice, son. I just hope you make the right one. I don't want you to have to work hard all ya life like me and ya momma, boy."

Trouble felt so uncomfortable as Dariel and his father talked.

"I know Dad, but—" Dariel started.

"But nothin'," Mr. Daniels cut his son off. "Don't be no fool. You got talent and everybody who knows you, know it. And furthermore, you can't keep acceptin' these gifts from them scouts. You gon' mess around and get yourself in a whole heap of trouble."

"Dad, you know I be tryin'a tell them no. They insist that I take whatever it is they have to offer. Shoot, I'm not gon' argue with 'em," Dariel said.

"I know, son. I just want you to do what's best for you." Mr. Daniels gave his son a hug before disappearing into the kitchen. "I'm so sorry, I done lost my manners somewhere," Mr. Daniels said, walking back out of the kitchen. "How are you doin' today, Ms. Candria?" Mr. Daniels said, smiling.

"I'm fine," Trouble answered.

"That's good," Mr. Daniels said before walking back into the kitchen.

Trouble turned her attention to Dariel. "What are you gon' do with this money?" Trouble asked, picking up the check to see how much it was for.

"I don't know. I guess I'll do what I did with all the rest of the checks, I'ma put 'em in my dad's savings account."

"Can't you get in trouble for acceptin' money and gifts from scouts?" Trouble inquired.

"What money?" Dariel asked, looking around. "I look at it like this, if these clowns wanna give me money and gifts 'cuz they think they stand a chance of gettin' me to play at their college, then that's on them. Look, girl, I got a brand new Escalade from one scout and I was sixteen."

"I knew that wasn't your dad's truck," Trouble said. "'Cuz you're always in it."

"I have to tell people that, how many teenagers you know drive a brand new Escalade?"

"None, unless he's on TV," Trouble answered. "What if they catch you?"

"For starters, I put everything in my father's name. And anyway, if I get caught, I just get caught. I don't worry about it 'cuz playin' in the NBA is my father's dream, not mines."

"You mean to tell me with all the talent you have, you don't wanna go to the NBA?" Trouble asked.

"I'm just tellin' you that it doesn't matter if I go or not. I'm good at basketball, Trouble, but I'm also good at makin' love but you don't see me goin' out tryin'a become a porno star, do you?" Dariel said, his voice dripping in sarcasm.

"It's your life, Dariel."

"I'm glad you recognize that, 'cuz my dad sure doesn't."

"He just wants what's best for his son, that's all."

"But he wants me to eat, sleep, and shit basketball. I don't really wanna be a professional basketball player, I wanna be an engineer. And I don't see why he can't get that through his head."

Trouble studied Dariel's face and could tell that he was serious. All this time she thought her man wanted to be a professional basketball player only to find out otherwise.

Twenty-two

Big Mike and Jyson sat at the bar sipping on their favorite drinks. The club was empty except for a couple of white businessmen sitting at a nearby table, checking out the black barmaids that were serving drinks.

"The white men sho'll be tippin' a sista swell," Jessica said to Chocolate Ice, another stripper who worked at the club.

"They sho'll do. Them niggas be comin' up in here per-pin' like they all broke and shit. They be wantin' to touch all on the booty, but don't wanna give ah bitch no looty." Chocolate Ice laughed.

"Girl, you crazy," Jessica said as she headed over toward Jyson and Big Mike.

"I can't stand this bitch," Jyson said, grimacing, as Jessica walked over to them.

"I can't stand the ho, either. And if it wasn't for her being my wife's sister, I would have fired her ass for playin' you like she did," Big Mike said.

"Hello fellas. Would y'all like another drink?" Jessica asked politely as possible.

After the incident that happened on New Year's Eve, she knew she was treading on thin ice with her brother-in-law. Big Mike had already made it clear to her that if it wasn't for Sherry her ass would have been in the unemployment line a long time ago.

"Only thing I want you to do is get the fuck outta my face," Jyson yelled at her.

"Jyson, I apologized for what I did. I know I was dead wrong. But when I saw you at the party with Michaela, I got jealous, and you know people do stupid shit when they get drunk," Jessica pleaded.

"You knew what it was between us from the get-go. You knew that you could never compete with Michaela. Bitch, you knew you were only my tip drill," Jyson lashed out.

Jessica's feelings were crushed. She at least thought that Jyson had some type of feelings for her, being he did spend a lot of nights over to her house.

"And don't blame it on the alcohol, ho!" Jyson continued with his tongue-lashing. "You tried to fuck up my relationship with Michaela 'cuz you thought I would come back to yo' scandalous ass. I wouldn't fuck you again on my worst night," Jyson spat angrily.

Jessica wanted to take off running out of the club, but what little pride she had left wouldn't let her. She then tried another approach . . . she got ghetto!

"Fuck you, nigga, with yo' tired ass! You think you all that, but nigga you ain't shit," Jessica screamed, catching the attention of the white businessmen.

"What's all the commotion about?" Madame Margaret asked as she ran out from the black curtain.

Margaret was one of Big Mike's first strippers. She'd been around a long time. Ever since he used to throw strip shows in his basement back in the day. She was the one who kept all the girls and the money intact for him. If any one of the strippers got out of pocket, Madame Margaret was there to put them back in their place. Margaret was in her late thirties and gave up stripping a few years back. She told Big Mike that her ass-shaking days were over with, so she retired to let the young girls make some money. Margaret and Big Mike were close friends and even Sherry liked her. Big Mike would never mix business with pleasure; that's why he never tried to fuck Margaret, even though he knew he could have hit her too.

"This ho-ass nigga thinks he can talk to me any kinda way he wants to, but I ain't havin' it," Jessica screamed loudly.

"Margaret, you betta get this broke bitch out my face before I forget my home trainin' and mangle this ho," Jyson said, balling up his fist.

Madame Margaret grabbed Jessica by the arm. "Let's go, Ice Cold," Margaret said to Jessica. "You need to start gettin' ready for your show."

Jessica yanked her arm away from Margaret and shouted, "No, fuck that nigga. And what type of boss are you? You let your customers talk to your employees any kinda way," Jessica screamed at Big Mike.

"Fuck you," Big Mike shot back. "This nigga ain't no customer, this my brother. And furthermore, this is my club and I do what I wanna do. And if you don't like it, take yo' ass home and don't come back!"

"Ain't nuttin' wrong with bein' broke, Big Mike, 'cuz nigga you ain't always had money. You think money makes you? Well it don't, 'cuz you still ain't shit." Jessica walked away and disappeared behind the black curtain, furious. *I'ma get them stankin'-ass niggas, if that's the last thing I do,* she thought as she sat and waited for Madame Margaret to come and tell her off some more.

"You always got my back," Jyson laughed after he watched Jessica storm off.

"You my little brother, I'm supposed to."

"I'm really gon' miss you, man," Jyson said, finishing off the rest of his drink.

"Where am I goin'?" Big Mike asked with a confused look on his face.

"You ain't goin' nowhere, but I am. I'm movin' to Atlanta in a few months," Jyson said, trying not to make eye contact with Big Mike so he didn't have to see his response.

"What?"

"Yeah, man. Michaela wants to finish school at Clark Atlanta, but she won't go unless I go. And I wouldn't feel right if she didn't get to live out her dream," Jyson said.

"Damn, man. You movin' all the way to the ATL?" Big Mike asked again just to make sure he heard his brother right. "What am I supposed to do without you?" Big Mike asked glumly.

"I'm gon' have a room ready for you and Sherry, so y'all can come down and stay with us anytime y'all want to," Jyson said.

"What you plan on doin' when you get down there? I know you gon' set up shop," Big Mike said.

"Naw, man, I'm about to sign up for a GED class so I can go to college to get my degree in criminal justice," Jyson said.

"That's cool. Michaela has touched you in a good way."

"Man, I love her, and didn't realize how much until we broke up," Jyson said, finishing off the rest of his drink.

"I'm happy for you, man. Well, we gon' celebrate before you leave. I got some business to handle so I'll holla at you later on," Big Mike said as he stood up and gave his brother a hug. He then walked out the door, trying his hardest to hide the emotion of knowing that soon he would no longer have his little brother around.

"Where are you gettin' your shoes from?" Dariel asked as he pulled up into the crowded mall parking lot.

"I'm goin' to Foot Locker," Trouble said, smirking, in hopes of Shirl being at work.

Dariel shook his head as he locked up the truck and trailed behind Trouble as she hustled inside the mall. "I'm goin' over here to the tape store, I'll catch up with you in a minute," he said.

"You don't wanna look at shoes with me?" Trouble asked, laughing.

"I'll be over there in a few minutes," he said, walking into the tape store as Trouble headed toward Foot Locker.

"Hello, may I help you?" the tall dark-skinned girl asked as Trouble walked into the store.

"I'm just lookin' right now," Trouble answered. Trouble tried hard to read the name tag on her shirt, but the girl walked away too quickly. She browsed around the store for about fifteen minutes before Dariel finally decided to join her.

"Hi, Dariel," a short brown-skinned girl said, coming from the back of the store.

"What's up?" he replied.

"What brings you to the store?" she said, smiling. "Just admit it, you wanted to see me," she joked.

Trouble stopped in her tracks and turned around as the female flirted with her man. Trouble waited until the other workers were busy with other customers and yelled, "Can I get some help over here?" as she walked over to Dariel and the female he was talking to.

"What can I help you with?" she asked politely.

Trouble read the name tag on the girl's shirt. "Oh, so you're Shirl?"

She gave Trouble a confused look. "Yeah. Do I know you from somewhere?" Shirl asked.

Dariel shook his head and hoped that things weren't about to get ugly between the two girls.

"We met this mornin' when you called *my man's* cell phone," Trouble said.

"Look, I didn't mean no disrespect. I didn't know he had a woman, so now that I know, you don't have to worry about me," Shirl assured Trouble.

"Worry? Honey, you are the least of my worries," Trouble said before walking off, leaving Shirl standing with Dariel. Trouble walked through the store and looked at a few more pairs of shoes before walking back over to Dariel. "Where did your little friend go?" Trouble asked him.

"I guess she had work to do. And she's not my friend, I hardly even know the girl, Trouble."

"I can't tell. You were standin' over here still talkin' to her after I walked away," Trouble hissed.

Dariel didn't feel like arguing so he decided to change the subject. "I thought you came here to buy some shoes."

"I did, but I changed my mind." Trouble looked back at Shirl as she waited on another customer. "I didn't see anything I liked, did you?" Trouble said, smirking.

Dariel rolled his eyes into his head as he followed Trouble out of the store, not bothering to respond to her question.

Trouble had Dariel drop her off over to Loretta's house so she could get her homework finished and her school clothes picked out for the next day. When she finished, she decided to make herself a ham sandwhich and lay around on the couch and watch television. And even though she had watched this episode of *Good Times* a million times before, she still laughed as J.J. yelled *dynomite!* Trouble's show was interrupted by a loud knock at the door.

"Now who the hell could this be?" Trouble asked, getting up off the couch to answer the door, not wanting to miss any of the show. She looked back at the TV while walking toward the door. "Ouch," she yelled, bumping her knee on the edge of the coffee table. "Who is it?"

"It's yo' brotha', big head, open up the door," Jyson yelled.

Trouble smiled. "What brings you to my neck of the woods?" She asked as she unlocked the door.

"You, what else?" Jyson said, walking into the door and taking a seat on the couch. "Where's your aunt at?" Jyson asked, picking up the remote and changing the channel.

"Hey, turn back," Trouble said, plopping down on the love seat across from her brother. "She's at work."

Jyson stared at the television like he was in a trance.

"What's on ya mind, Jyson?" Trouble asked as she watched her brother's trancelike state.

Jyson stood up from the couch and paced back and forth across the living room floor. "Michaela wants to finish school in Atlanta, and even though she didn't come right out and say it, she won't go unless I go too," Jyson replied. "Look, sis, I don't want to be the cause of her not bein' able to fulfill her dream. I wouldn't be able to live with myself if she didn't go because of me."

"So what you gon' do?" Trouble asked.

"I'm gon' get my GED and move to Altanta with her so I can go to college too," Jyson responded.

Trouble smiled. "I am so proud of you." She knew that Jyson wasn't only doing this for Michaela, but for himself also. She could sense that her brother was getting tired of the streets. Trouble could remember when they were younger, Jyson used to talk about going to college to become a probation officer. She knew that their parents were to blame for Jyson not finishing high school and turning to the streets for a means of support and comfort. Trouble also knew that Jyson missed their mother more than she ever would, but she continued to tell her big brother that you can't help someone who doesn't want help. Jyson didn't want to believe that old saying; he still felt their mother could be saved.

"You really think I can do it, sis?" Jyson asked.

"Jyson, you can do anything you set your mind to. If you want to go to college, you can do it," Trouble said, smiling.

Jyson had a huge smile on his face, but it disappeared as soon as Loretta walked through the door.

"Oh, I see you're home," Loretta said to Trouble.

"It's not by choice," Trouble replied smartly.

Loretta sorted through the pile of bills she had in her hand and looked up for a brief second. "How are you, Jyson?"

"I'm cool," he answered.

"You hungry, Jyson?" Loretta asked as she headed toward the kitchen to prepare supper.

"Naw, I just ate, thanks, though," he said.

"Well, sis, I'm 'bout to roll on up outta here," Jyson said to Trouble.

"Why you gotta leave so soon?" Trouble whined.

"I gotta go pick up some money. I'll call you later on." Jyson kissed his sister on the cheek and walked out the door with a huge smile on his handsome face.

"Bye, Jyson," Loretta yelled out of the kitchen, but he was already gone.

My big brother's goin' to college, Trouble thought as she gathered her schoolbooks and made her way up the stairs to her bedroom. "I'll be damned!" she spoke out loud with a huge smile on her face.

Twenty-three

"You know you still want this," Jessica said as she walked out of her bedroom dressed in a red negligee. She sat down on the couch and rested her hand on Woo's knee.

"Bitch, you all used up. Ain't no way I would ever mess with you again, unless you was payin' me," Woo laughed, taking a pull from the blunt he was smoking.

"Whatever!" Jessica said, rolling her eyes as she moved closer to her baby's daddy.

"What did you call me over here for anyways?" Woo asked. "My son ain't here, so what could you possibly want with me? I don't got no money, either."

"I told you it was some top-secret shit so I couldn't talk about it over the phone." Jessica looked around the room as if someone else was there besides the two of them. She leaned in and whispered. "I got somebody else we can set up and they got a lot of money."

Woo put the blunt out in the ashtray. "Who?"

"I wanna set Big Mike's bitch-ass up," she stated, and then sat back and waited on a response.

"Yo' sistas husband Big Mike?" Woo asked, just to be sure his ears weren't deceiving him.

"Yeah, my sister's husband. What other Big Mike would I be talkin' about?" Jessica snapped.

Woo sat back and thought before he spoke, just in case she was on some shady shit and trying to set him up for Big Mike. "Why you wanna do that?" he asked cautiously, not wanting to let her know how game he was. He had thought about the same thing many times, but never had the guts to go through with it, fearing the consequences.

"I'm sick of that ho-ass nigga and his friend. They think they all that. And furthermore, Big Mike put his hands on me on New Year's Eve, so he needs to be taught a thing or two." Jessica picked the blunt up out the ashtray and lit it up again. She took a couple of puffs and put it out before straddling Woo's thin body.

"How we gon' do it?" he asked.

"Anyway you want to," she said seductively.

"I'm not talkin' about that," he said, pushing her off his lap.

"Anyway," Jessica said, rolling her eyes at his rejection. "I already know the code to the security system from goin' in and out with Sherry. And the other day I saw her go in the safe to get some money out to pay bills and I saw the combination. She didn't think I was payin' any attention, so when she left out the room to answer the telephone, I tried the combination to see if it would work for me and it did."

"How much did you get?" he asked. Now Woo's nose was wide open.

"I took two thousand out for myself," she said, smiling.

"How much money was in the safe?" Woo inquired.

"Man, it was mad thousands up in that bitch. It might have been at least fifty or sixty gees. He had stacks of hundreds."

Woo's mouth watered as he listened to Jessica talk about all the money Big Mike kept in the safe. "Well, what's the plan?"

Jessica cleared her throat before speaking. "Well, I heard Sherry tellin' Big Mike that she didn't like the new lawn-care guys, so he told her to hire some that she did like. So I'm gon' tell Sherry about a new lawn-care service that does an excellent job and that's where you come in at," Jessica said.

"Huh?" Woo said with a puzzled look.

"I'm gon' take Sherry to Cheddar's for lunch on Friday. I'm goin' to slip her door key off her key ring and then I'll excuse myself to go to the bathroom, but I'm really goin' to run next door to the drugstore and make a copy of the key. I need you to meet me there. Then I'm goin' to carefully slip it back on her key ring when she goes to the bathroom or something."

Woo became excited as he listened to Jessica's master plan. "And then what?"

"What do you mean *and then what?* I'm gon' give you the key, the security code, and the combination to the safe and you and one of your boys is gon' go up in the crib and hit the safe."

"We got a problem," Woo said.

"What is it?"

"Where am I gon' get a lawn-care truck from. You know I'm gon' need one, 'cuz if one of his nosy-ass neighbors see an unfamiliar black face lurkin' around that neighborhood house, you know they gon' call the police on me," Woo said.

"I know. That's why we have to make this look legit. We need the lawn-care truck, uniforms, the whole nine yards."

"Yeah, I like that." Woo smiled widely. "I still don't know where I'ma find a lawn truck."

"I don't know, either. Look, I'm doin' the hard part so the truck is on you. Anyways, I'm gon' make up an excuse why I have to leave the restaurant early and I'ma call you so you can bring me my money."

"Yo' money? Don't you mean our money?" Woo said.

"Yeah, whatever. Just bring me mines!"

"I don't know. The plan sounds fine and dandy, but where's Big Mike gon' be while I'm hittin' his safe, Einstein?"

"He's still mad at my sister for talkin' to me after I ruined their party, so he don't never be home anymore, but it's not like he was there in the first place."

"Just make sure he's not there," Woo said, while grabbing the back of Jessica's hair and kissing her violently. The thought of money was making him horny.

"Strip for me, bitch," he said, and Jessica happily obliged.

Twenty-four

"Dariel, Marcus is up here," Mrs. Daniels yelled into the basement. Dariel and his boys sat around the newly remodeled basement and played video games as Trouble read her book. Dante sat between Ta'liyah's legs as she braided his hair, while he beat the brakes off of Josh in the new *NBA Live*.

"Tell him to come on down, Momma," Dariel yelled back.

Ta'liyah's entire body tensed as she prayed that Marcus didn't say anything stupid.

"You okay, baby?" Dante turned around and asked Ta'liyah.

"Yeah, I'm fine," she lied.

Marcus walked down the stairs with a smile on his face until he reached the bottom step and jealousy invaded him. *What the fuck is this nigga doing sittin' between my girl's legs*, he thought.

"What's up, man? How come you didn't come to my party last night?" Dariel asked Marcus.

"My folks made me go to my grandparents' fortieth-anniversary party," Marcus said as he watched Ta'liyah braid some other nigga's hair.

"Oh, by the way, these are my dudes from back home," Dariel said as he proceeded to introduce them.

"Sup?" Darius said, taking the game controller from his brother and beginning to play the game.

"What's up?" Dante said as he rubbed the back of Ta'liya's calves as she greased his scalp.

Marcus shot Dante a dirty look, but he was so involved in the video game he never even noticed.

Ta'liyah noticed the look Marcus gave Dante and instantly became uncomfortable.

"You sure you're okay, baby?" Dante asked Ta'liyah again.

"Yeah, I'm cool," she said, letting out a nervous chuckle.

"So your grandparents been married for forty years, huh? That's a long time to be married to the same woman." Dante laughed, along with everyone else.

"Yeah," Marcus said, grimacing.

I wonder why Marcus keeps starin' at Dante like that, Dariel thought.

"Okay, I'm finished," Ta'liyah said. "I'm 'bout to go home and lay down for a little while, and I'll be back over later on."

"Come on, I'll take you home. I just hope I don't get lost on my way back," Dante said, standing up.

"I'll come with you," Josh said, laying the controller down on the table. "I need to stretch my legs after sleepin' in Nikki's twin-size bed all night," he said, laughing.

"No, I'm all right. I can walk," Ta'liyah said.

"Naw, baby, I'll take you. It's kinda cold outside," Dante said.

"Kinda cold? It's cold as hell," Josh said, putting on his First Down coat.

"Go'n and let him take you," Marcus said sarcastically.

"I said I'm cool," Ta'liyah huffed.

"All right, now don't say I didn't offer," Dante stated.

"I know," she said, smiling.

Dante kissed Ta'liyah on the lips.

"What the fuck is goin' on between y'all?" Marcus snapped.

"Marcus, don't start," Ta'liyah warned.

"Naw, fuck that! I don't know what type of games you playin', but you betta get it right."

"Marcus, go'n and get out my face with the bullshit," Ta'liyah said.

"What? This yo' girl, nigga?" Dante asked.

"Are you my girl, Ta'liyah?" Marcus asked.

Trouble was totally confused about all the commotion that was going on.

"No, I'm not your girl," Ta'liyah said.

"You wasn't sayin' that when I was all up in that pussy, now was you?"

"Go'n with that stupid shit, Marcus," Dariel said.

Trouble's eyes widened.

"You mean to tell me that you didn't tell your friends that I was still tappin' that ass?" Marcus asked Ta'liyah.

"What?" Trouble said in a whisper-like tone.

"Yeah. I'm still hittin' that," Marcus said, smirking. "And I bet you she didn't tell y'all about the abortion either."

The room got quiet, and at that particular moment, Ta'liyah wanted to die. *How could Marcus tell everybody our secret? I knew I couldn't trust that no-good-ass nigga*, she thought as tears streamed down her cheeks. She looked at everybody in the basement, who were staring back at her, before disappearing up the stairs and out the front door.

All the attention turned to Marcus. It felt like the walls were closing in on him. He wanted to run away, but his feet wouldn't let him. His face had that tight feeling to it. He was the one who wanted to embarrass someone, but in the end, he was the one feeling ashamed.

"Get out my house, man," Dariel said.

"Man, I'm sorry," Marcus pleaded. "I know that's your cousin and all, but—"

"You heard him, nigga, get out," Dante said as he stood in Marcus's face.

"Not in here, man," Josh said as he stood between the two.

Marcus looked around the room for some compassion but got nothing but cold stares. He hung his head down low and walked up the basement stairs.

"I gotta go," Trouble said, standing up.

"Where you goin', baby girl?" Dariel asked.

"I'm 'bout to walk over to see if Jyson is home," she replied.

"I'll take you," Dariel said.

"No, thank you. I need to walk, 'cuz I got a lot of shit on my mind," she said.

"But it's cold outside, at least take this jacket," he said, handing her one of his Nike windbreakers.

"I'll call you later," Trouble said, kissing Dariel on the lips.

I can't believe my best friend would do a thing like that, she thought as she walked down Wood Street. *How could she keep somethin' like that from me?* Tears formed in Trouble's eyes as she walked and badgered herself for answers. *I'm gon' call her ass as soon as I get home and cuss her ass out!* Trouble said to herself. *No I'm not. That's why she didn't tell me in the first place, 'cuz I'm always criticizin' her about everything. I'm gon' call her so we can talk.* Trouble picked up the pace as the wind began to tear through the thin windbreaker she was wearing.

"Hey, baby, can I get out and walk with you?" a light-skinned brotha rolled down his passenger-side window and asked.

Trouble kept up her stride, ignoring him as he drove alongside of her. She watched as the yellow Eldorado pulled beside her. "You ignorin' a nigga or somethin'?"

Trouble stopped and put her hands on her hips. "I'm tryin'a get home, 'cuz I got somethin' to do, if you don't mind."

"Can I at least take you to the crib? It's kinda cold out here," he said, smiling, melting Trouble instantly.

It was cold outside, but Trouble didn't know this guy from a can of paint and she wasn't about to take no chances with this stranger.

"No thanks, I'll walk. I only live—" Trouble stopped herself, not wanting this unfamiliar man to know anything about her.

"I'm not gon' bite you, damn. I just wanted to take you home since it's cold out."

Normally, Trouble would have cussed a brotha out from head to toe for sweating her the way this guy was doing, but for some strange reason, she kind of liked the attention she was getting from him. "Look, I hafta go. I have somethin' to take care of. Thanks for offerin' me a ride," Trouble said, smiling, before turning to walk away.

The canary yellow Cadillac pulled over, and the tall, slim light-skinned brotha got out of the car. "Hey, shorty," he called as he walked over to the passenger's side of his ride and leaned up against it.

Oh my goodness, this nigga just don't know when to quit, Trouble thought as she turned around to answer his call. "Yeah?"

"Come here for a minute," he said, smoothly in his mack daddy, *rico suave* voice.

"Didn't I tell you I had somethin' to do?" she huffed and walked over to him. As she got closer to him, his smile sent chills down her spine immediately because he looked a lot like Jyson when he showed off those pearly white teeth of his.

He rubbed his hand down his thin mustache. "Whatever you have to do must not be that important, 'cuz you came to see what I wanted," he laughed.

Dang, he even sounds like Jyson when he laughs, Trouble thought. Trouble felt embarrassed and out-witted by his remark, but she really wanted to know what he wanted with her. "What do you want?" she said, putting her hands on her hips, trying to act as if this brotha was bothering her.

"Can I call you later on?" he asked as he fell in love with her hazel eyes.

Trouble licked her lips teasingly. "No can do." Her hands fell freely to her side as she shifted her weight from one leg to the other.

"What? You don't think I'm worthy enough to have your phone number?" He smiled cooly.

"Look, I don't know if you're worthy or not. For one, I don't even know you, and for two, do you think I just go around and give my number to strangers?" she said.

"We can get to know each other," he stated as his eyes roamed over her entire body. *This girl is fine as hell! A little young, but fine,* Woo thought.

As much as Trouble would have loved to get to know this fine-ass nigga who had been recklessly eyeballing her body parts, she couldn't step out on Dariel, even if he might have a baby on the way by

some other girl. She couldn't find it in her heart to
mess around on him because she loved him and she
knew that he loved her as well. Besides, this fine piece
of meat she had standing before her reminded her too
much of her brother and he probably was a whore just
like Jyson and she didn't have the time nor the room
for that in her life.

"I'm kinda seein' someone," Trouble replied, wishing in the back of her mind that she wasn't.

Light-skin leaned close to her face as if he was
about to give her a kiss. "If you're *kinda* seein' someone, that means that you're not sure that the nigga is
gon' be around too much longer," he said, smirking.

Trouble had just had a taste of reality. How could
she let this nigga have that type of effect on her when
she didn't even know him? "I didn't mean it like that.
I am seein' someone that I love very much, and we
do plan on bein' together for a long time," she added.

Light-skin took a step back and walked around to
the driver's side of the car and opened up the door.
"Don't count on it," he said before getting into his car
and driving off, leaving her speechless and alone.

"Who do this nigga think he is?" Trouble asked
herself as she picked up her pace. "How could I let
him get to me like he did? And I wonder what he
meant by *don't count on it?* I do plan on bein' with
Dariel for a very long time," she said with an inch of
doubt. *That light-skin nigga treated me like I was
some type of naive schoolgirl,* Trouble thought as she
continued to walk.

Trouble couldn't get the mysterious guy off her mind. His face kept popping up into her head as she strolled down Glessner Avenue. "I don't even know his name. Oh well, that might be a good thing," she said out loud as she walked into the house.

Trouble threw her purse on the couch and walked into the kitchen to get herself something to quench her thirst. She leaned up against the counter and started replaying the entire conversation she had with this stranger that now she feared she had a crush on. Trouble thought about all the stuff she wished she would have said to him and some things she wished he would have said to her.

"What's up, sis?" Jyson asked, interrupting her thoughts.

"Hey, Jyson," she said, smiling, and took a seat at the kitchen table. "What's up?" she asked, finishing off her drink.

Jyson paced back and forth across the kitchen floor. "Trouble, I think I'm about to ask Michaela to marry me," he stated, and waited on a response from his little sister.

Trouble stared at her brother for a brief moment before speaking. "So, how did this come about?"

Jyson sat down at the table across from his sister. "I told you before that Michaela wants to finish college in Atlanta. So I'm gon' give up the dope game, buy us a house down there, and go to school," he said.

Trouble smiled and stood up from the table and placed her empty glass in the sink. She looked at her brother before wrapping her arms around his neck.

"Thanks, Trouble." Even though his sister said no words, he knew that her hug could have only meant happiness. And he needed someone other than himself to be proud of his decision to get his GED and attend college to fulfill his own goal of becoming a probation officer.

Trouble didn't say another word to her brother before exiting the kitchen. She just hoped her hug was enough to show how happy she was for him. She walked into her bedroom and plopped down on her unmade bed, then rolled over and grabbed the cordless phone out of its cradle. She could still smell the scent of Dariel's cologne on her sheets. As she lay there, phone in hand, she let her mind wander back to this strange light-skinned guy as she dialed Ta'liyah's phone number. She quickly came back to earth as Mr. Turner answered the telephone.

"Hello, Mr. Turner, is Ta'liyah home?" Trouble asked, promising herself that she wasn't going to criticize her friend for doing what she had done and for not telling her about her pregnancy.

"Yes, she's here, and how are you, Candria?" Mr. Turner asked.

"I'm fine," Trouble replied.

"Okay, hang on a minute. Hey, Candria?" Mr. Turner called out.

"Yes, Mr. Turner?"

"I'll holla." He laughed, trying to stay in touch with his hip side.

Trouble laughed at the fact that Ta'liyah's dad always tried his best to fit in with the young folks. Mr. Turner was always making Trouble and Ta'liyah laugh about something. Growing up, Trouble always wished that Mr. T was her dad but instead, she got stuck with a man that never stayed at home with them, never had family fun night, and didn't have a funny bone in his body. Trouble's dad's idea of funny was a corny knock-knock joke that he would get off the wrapper of a piece of Bazooka Joe bubble gum. Trouble adored the fact that Ta'liyah had both parents living in the same household, and they always did family things together. They played games together, they watched movies with each other, and they were always taking family vacations. When Trouble was younger, she always hoped that her mother would leave the drugs alone and her father would realize that he needed his wife and kids, and that they could all be a happy family. But the older she got, the more she came to accept that her Huxtable family dreams would never come true.

"Hey, Ta'liyah, this is Trouble," was all she could manage to say after Ta'liyah picked up the phone.

Like I don't know your voice after all these years of friendship, Ta'liyah thought. "Look, Trouble, if you called to criticize me, save your breath, 'cuz this time

I'm not goin' to listen. I know what I did was wrong and I'm the one who has to live with it, so I don't wanna hear what you or nobody else have to say."

Trouble listened as her friend vented, and she let her finish before she spoke. Normally Trouble would have cut her off and told her what she thought about the horrible thing she had done, but she sat quietly as Ta'liyah's voice became shaky.

"Ta'liyah, I didn't call to criticize you, I called to talk," she said.

Ta'liyah was speechless, because she was so used to Trouble taking over and leading a conversation. "What do you want to talk about?" Ta'liyah asked.

"Are your parents around you?"

"Nope. They're both downstairs paintin' the kitchen."

"Where's Tico?"

"He's at work, and he doesn't get off until seven o'clock."

"Cool. Well, let's talk then." Trouble paced her bedroom floor, not really knowing what to say. She didn't want to come off sounding too pushy so she approached the situation slowly. "Okay, how come you didn't tell me that you were pregnant?" Trouble asked with caution.

Ta'liyah took a deep breath before answering. "Because I didn't want you to try to talk me out of gettin' an abortion and I didn't want you to think less of me. You always said that I'm the one that's gon' end up with a houseful of kids at a young age. And you always used to say that I'm so promiscuous just because I was sexually active and you weren't. That kind of stuff hurt my feelings."

Trouble felt bad about the hurtful things she said to her best friend. *How could I have known that those things hurt her feelings when she never said anything before now?* Trouble thought. "I never meant to hurt you, Ta'liyah. I was just teasin' you."

"Everything is not meant to be turned into a joke, Trouble," she snapped. "You have always thought that you were better than everybody. You had to have the best clothes, the finest boyfriends, you just had to have the best of everything. You are so spoiled. If shit don't go your way, then it ain't the right way," Ta'liyah said.

Trouble didn't know what to say. She was the one who was supposed to be doing the criticizing, not Ta'liyah, but her friend had turned the tables.

"I never thought I was better than you," Trouble responded. "A little spoiled, yeah, but never have I thought I was above anything or anyone. Is somethin' wrong with wantin' to have the best of everything?"

"I guess not."

"And how did we switch the subject from you to me?" Trouble asked.

"Look, I'm sorry for not tellin' you that I was pregnant. I didn't want you to be mad at me for still fuckin' around with Marcus's stupid ass."

"Why would I be mad at you? If you wanted to continue to mess with him that was on you. But what I don't understand is how come you didn't come to me and talk to me after you found out you were pregnant by the nigga."

Ta'liyah sighed heavily. "Trouble, I really wasn't pregnant by Marcus. I told him that only so he could help me pay for the abortion," she admitted.

"What?"

"Trouble, I had to, 'cuz Andre said that the baby wasn't his so he wasn't givin' me no money for no abortion," Ta'liyah said with tears in her eyes. "So I had no choice but to blame it on Marcus."

Trouble knew her best friend was wild, but she didn't know she was sheisty too. But a girl has to do whatever she needs to do to get over and get by.

"First of all, who the fuck is Andre?" Trouble asked.

"You remember Andre. I met him at the mall a few months back."

"The dark-skin brotha with the good hair?"

"Yeah," Ta'liyah said, smiling.

"Guurrrl, he was fine," Trouble admitted. "Okay, finish tellin' me the story."

"Anyway. After I found out I was pregnant, I saw Marcus at the video store and I asked him if he would burn me a couple of CDs and he said sure. He invited me to his house while he burnt them. He started kissin' on me and one thing led to another. And that's when it dawned on me," Ta'liyah continued. "If I didn't mention protection, I could blame the baby on him."

"Scandalous," Trouble said.

"There you go criticizin' me again."

"I'm not knockin' the hustle. Hey, if the nigga fell for it, then that's on his stupid ass," Trouble said, laughing.

"I'm sorry about keepin' my secret from you," Ta'liyah said.

"It's okay, just don't let it happen again," Trouble said, smiling.

"It won't. I promise," Ta'liyah replied sincerely.

"Now that that's over with, tell a sista how good Andre was in the bed." Trouble laughed. Trouble and Ta'liyah talked on the phone a couple more hours, laughing and carrying on like usual.

Twenty-five

"The number you have reached is no longer in service," the recording said as Jessica dialed the number over and over again.

"What the fuck?" Jessica yelled and threw the phone on the bed. *This nigga done got his fuckin' number changed on me.* "Li'l Tony, get in here and call yo' grandma and ask her for your daddy's phone number," Jessica yelled at her oldest son.

"Damn, I was playin' *Mortal Kombat*," Li'l Tony huffed as he walked into his mom's room.

"Whatever, just call ya granny." Jessica dialed his grandmother's number in a hurry and handed her son the phone.

"Hello, Grandma?" he asked when she picked up the phone.

"Hey, baby, is this Granny's li'l stankum?" Woo's mom asked in a pleasant, grandmother-like tone.

"Naw, this is Li'l Tony," he replied.

"Oh. What you want, boy?" she huffed, mistaking him for one of Woo's other children. "I ain't got no money and tell ya momma no, I ain't babysittin' y'all."

Jessica rolled her eyes because she could hear all the shit that was coming out of Woo's mom's loud-ass mouth.

"I wanna speak to my dad."

"He ain't here and I don't know when he's comin' back. He took his ass off to Detroit," Woo's mom said.

"Ask for his new phone number," Jessica whispered in the background.

"Can I have his new phone number?" Li'l Tony asked.

"Now look boy, ya botherin' me. I'm tryin'a watch *The Young and the Restless,*" Woo's mom huffed as she dug in her purse for the piece of paper Woo had left his new number on. She rambled off the number and slammed the phone down. Ms. Walters wanted nothing to do with her grandson and it wasn't only because she couldn't stand his momma, it was also because he was so disrespectful and out of control. Ms. Walters used to keep all of Jessica's kids while she worked, even though only one of them was her biological grandchild. She would treat all of Jessica's children the same. She used to love keeping them until one day Jessica disappeared for a week and didn't leave the kids no food, money, or even a change of clothes. Jessica popped up at the door one day just like she had did nothing wrong. So after that, Ms. Walters washed her hands of Jessica and her children.

"Give me the number, boy," Jessica yelled as Li'l Tony hung up the phone.

"I am, shit. Don't be hollerin' at me," Li'l Tony said.

"You betta watch yo' mouth, boy. Yo' ass only twelve years old," Jessica yelled as she dialed Woo's new cell phone number.

"I'm grown," Li'l Tony retorted before walking out of his mother's room with a serious attitude.

Jessica listened as the phone rang.

"Hello?" Woo answered.

"Nigga, where the fuck my money at?" Jessica screamed into the phone receiver.

"Who is this?" Woo asked, already knowing.

"Dis Jessica, nigga. Don't play stupid with me! Now where's my half of the money?"

Woo pulled the heist off and it went smoothly as planned. Woo told his boys that it was like stealing candy from a baby. He made sure he crossed all his *T*'s and dotted all his *I*'s because there was no room for mistakes, especially in front of Big Mike's nosy-ass neighbors. The heist went so smooth that Woo had some of the neighbors trying to hire him to come cut their lawns. The only thing he didn't follow through with was giving Jessica half of the money. Instead, Woo took all the money and went back to his home-town of Detroit and splurged on any and everything he wanted.

"I don't know what you're talkin' about."

"Quit playin', Woo. Now, how much money did we get?"

"*I* got fifty-two gees," Woo said as he snorted a line of pure white cocaine.

"Fifty-two gees?" Jessica asked, excited. "Well, where's my cut?"

"I did all the work, so I don't think you deserve half."

"What? Woo, don't play with me," Jessica warned. "I'm the one who set the entire thing up."

"Thank you. And I'm not playing with you," Woo said in his best white man's voice.

"Well, how much of it do I get?" she asked.

"I'll send you a six-thousand-dollar check," Woo snorted again.

"Muthafucka, six thousand ain't shit. Hell, you eight thousand behind in child support," Jessica screamed.

"Well, after I send you this six gees, I'll only be two thousand behind." Woo laughed.

"Fuck you, Woo, and yo' six thousand dollars. You can keep it all! And I'm tellin' Big Mike you robbed him," she shouted.

Woo began laughing, because he knew damn well she had to be joking.

"Why the fuck are you laughin'? You ain't gon' be laughin' when that nigga kill yo' ass," she said, hoping to scare him.

"And what is he gon' do to you?" Woo asked with his voice dripping in sarcasm.

Jessica thought for a second. She knew damn well she couldn't tell, because her sister would never forgive her, and plus Big Mike would kill her ass too if he found out she had anything to do with him getting robbed or she could tell and hope and pray that Woo didn't mention her name, but she knew better than that. If Woo had to die, sure enough he was going to take her with him. "What about Li'l Tony? You ain't gon' send him no money?"

"I'm sendin' six thousand in the mail. You get three and give my son three," Woo said.

"Fuck you, Woo!" Jessica screamed.

"You can't afford to fuck me. And just for threatenin' to tell Big Mike on me, I ain't sendin' you shit," he yelled and hung up the phone.

Jessica dialed the number repeatedly, only to keep catching his voice mail. She tried blocking her number out so he would pick up, but he still didn't answer. Jessica got so desperate she ran down to the corner pay phone and called him from a different number, but still no answer. "Fuck!"

Twenty-six

Trouble stopped by Jyson's house on the way to Loretta's to see how her big brother was doing. His truck was parked in the driveway so she had Dariel drop her off while he went to his parents' house to get him some more school clothes to wear for the next day.

"Jyson," Trouble called out, but didn't get an answer. "Jyson, are you home?" Trouble walked from room to room looking for her brother but he was nowhere to be found. "He must of left with Big Mike or Michaela," she said to no one in particular.

Trouble walked into the kitchen to get something to drink and as she reached to get a glass, the telephone rang "Hello?"

"Hello, Trouble, this is Loretta, what are you doin' over to Jyson's? School isn't out yet," she said.

Trouble had to think quick. "School let out early today, so Jyson came and picked me up and brought me over here for a little while," she lied.

"Anyways, I was callin' Jyson to tell him and now I can tell you that Daddy just passed away," Loretta cried into the phone receiver.

Trouble's heart jumped into her throat. "What?" Tears formed in Trouble's eyes. "Okay, I'll let Jyson know," Trouble said.

"Where's Jyson at?" Loretta asked. " 'Cuz the family is about to go over to your daddy's house so we can make all the funeral arrangements."

"Okay, well, I'll be at the house when you get there and you can let me know when the funeral is gon' be."

"Your not comin' over to your dad's house? You must didn't hear me when I said the *family* was meetin' over there," Loretta said.

"I heard what you said. And no, I'm not goin' over to his house," Trouble said, knowing that their conversation was about to turn into a heated argument again.

"You know what, Candria? You are one of the most selfish bitches I've ever ran across. If things don't revolve around precious Candria, then it's not important. You just lost your grandfather and you don't have enough decency to go over to your dad's house with the rest of the family to pay your last respects," Loretta shouted angrily.

"Loretta, I know you just lost your dad and all, but you not gon' sit up here and talk all crazy to me. I'll go to the funeral to pay my respect to Poppy, dang." Trouble hung up the phone before Loretta could say anything else.

Trouble opened up the refrigerator and poured herself some juice. She leaned up against the counter and smiled. She was proud of the fact that she handled her aunt gracefully. If it wasn't for the passing of her daddy, she would have cussed Loretta inside out. Trouble started feeling guilty because she hadn't seen her grandfather in months. She really felt bad that she had chosen to go to Dariel's birthday party instead of going to her father's house to spend some time with her poppy, knowing he was sick. Trouble picked up the phone that hung on the kitchen wall and dialed Jyson's cell phone number.

"Jyson, Poppy passed away," she said to her brother when he answered his phone.

"Damn, that's deep," was all Jyson could say. "You okay, Trouble?" he asked.

"Yeah, I'm fine," she said as tears streamed down her cheeks.

"Well, look here, I got a couple of things to take care of and I'll be over to Loretta's to see you in about an hour," he said.

"Jyson, I'm not goin' over to Loretta's tonight, me and her just got into an argument and I don't feel like hearin' her mouth."

"I'll call Loretta and tell her your stayin' with me tonight," Jyson said, pulling into a gas station to get gas.

"Okay," she said, wiping her tears with the back of her hand. Trouble hung up the phone and went and lay across her bed. *I wish I could find Momma to let her know that Poppy passed away.* Trouble's heart was crushed because she felt like she had let her grandfather down by not going to visit him while cancer ate away at his body. She grabbed her teddy bear and cried until she drifted off to sleep, only to be awakened twenty minutes later by a knock at the door.

"Who is it?" she yelled as she headed toward the front door.

"It's Dariel, baby girl," he yelled back.

Trouble reached the door and opened it up. She knew she had to look a hot mess by the look on Dariel's face when he walked in.

"What's wrong with you?" he asked Trouble.

"My grandfather passed away," she said as tears formed in her eyes again.

"Sorry to hear that," Dariel said, grabbing her and hugging her.

Trouble buried her head deep into Dariel's chest and he rocked her body back and forth as tears flowed heavily from her beautiful eyes.

"It's gon' be okay, baby girl. I'm here for you and always will be, no matter what," he said, wiping her tears away with his hand.

Trouble was so relieved to have Dariel by her side in her time of need. She wanted nothing more than for him to always be there for her because he always made everything seem okay.

Dariel led Trouble to her bedroom and they both lay across her bed. He listened as Trouble cried and reminisced about the old memories she shared about her grandfather. Dariel tried to ease Trouble's pain away by massaging her scalp with his fingertips until they both fell off to sleep.

Trouble woke up again to the sound of a ringing cell phone.

"Dariel, your cell phone is ringin'," she said in a raspy voice.

"Answer it," he said and fell back to sleep.

"Hello?"

"Who is this?" the lady asked.

"Who is this?" Trouble asked her back.

"This is Janelle, Jameelah's mom. Where's Dariel?" she asked rudely.

"He's asleep, why?" Trouble asked.

"Well, tell the nigga to get up, 'cuz Jameelah just went into labor," Janelle said with a serious attitude.

"What?"

"You heard me!" Janelle snapped. "Jameelah just went into labor and I need Dariel to meet us at the hospital."

"Okay, I'll tell him," Trouble said.

"See that you do," Janelle said and slammed the phone down in Trouble's ear.

Trouble started not to tell Dariel shit just because of how rude Jameelah's mom was to her. Now she knew where Jameelah had gotten her bad attitude from. Like they say, the apple don't fall too far from the tree. Trouble let the news about the baby sink in before waking Dariel up. She knew that her relationship was about to make a drastic change. Everything was about to involve the baby, and Trouble would be put on the back burner.

Trouble got out of bed and walked into the bathroom and knelt down on her knees to pray. "Lord, I know this may seem like a selfish prayer, but give me the strength to deal with this situation. And Lord, please don't let our relationship change that much if this child proves to be Dariel's," she cried.

Maybe Loretta was right. Maybe if things don't revolve around me they're not important, Trouble thought as she got off her knees and washed her face before going back into her room to wake Dariel up. This day would be one of the hardest days of her life and it would be one of the happiest days of Jameelah's.

"Dariel, Jameelah's mom just called and said Jameelah went into labor."

Dariel jumped up. "What? Already? She still got two more months left before she's due." Dariel rolled out of Trouble's bed and grabbed his coat. "Come drive me to the hospital," he said.

Trouble's heart began to race as she became jealous. Reality had set in. Trouble couldn't believe that Dariel was really going to the hospital to be there for Jameelah when he didn't even know if the baby was his.

"Why do I have to drive you?" she snapped angrily.

Dariel could feel the tension fill the room. "Aren't you goin' over to Loretta's house tonight?"

Why do you care? You're takin' your ass up to the hospital with Jameelah, Trouble thought. "I'm stayin' over here tonight."

"Well, come drop me off and I'll call you when I'm ready to be picked up," he said, walking out of Trouble's bedroom.

Trouble was unable to move. She wanted to walk out to Dariel's truck but something kept her from moving from the spot she stood in.

"Are you comin'?" Dariel asked, walking back into Trouble's room.

Trouble followed Dariel out to the truck. They got in and rode in silence as Dariel sped down the busy streets. Trouble listened as Dariel talked on the phone to his mother.

"Son, are you on your way to the hospital?" Mrs. Daniels asked.

"Yeah, Mom, I'm on my way," he said, smiling.

Trouble wanted badly to slap his ass to sleep for having that big-ass smile plastered all over his face.

"I'll see you when I get there," he said, hanging up.

How can this nigga just leave me in my time of need? He knows my grandfather just passed away and he's gon' take his stankin' ass up to the hospital with Jameelah, Trouble thought. Tears fell down her cheeks as she looked out the window at the cars that passed by. Trouble kept her head turned because she didn't want Dariel to see her crying. She wanted to tell him how hurt she was behind him going to the hospital, but she was at a loss for words. Dariel's cell phone rang; again her chest tightened because she knew that it was probably Jameelah's mom again.

"Hello? Yes, I'm on my way, so calm down. We're almost there."

"Who is we?" Jameelah asked.

"Me and Trouble, Jameelah," Dariel said.

Oh, so it's not Jameelah's mom. It's the bitch, Jameelah herself, Trouble thought as she listened in on his conversation.

"You better not bring that bitch up here," Jameelah screamed as a contraction hit her.

"Don't start, she's just droppin' me off up there." Dariel pushed the end button on his cell phone and handed it to Trouble.

"What do you want me to do with this?" Trouble asked smartly.

"Put it in the glove compartment for me," he said.

"What was that call all about?"

"It was just Jameelah talkin' stupid, that's all."

"What the fuck would I want to come up to the hospital for? That baby doesn't concern me one bit," Trouble snapped.

Dariel couldn't believe that Trouble had the audacity to say something that cruel about a child, much less one that might be his. "If I concern you, then my child should too," he replied.

"You heard what I said," Trouble said and left it at that. Dariel pulled up in front of the hospital where his parents stood talking to Janelle.

"About time," Janelle said, grabbing Dariel's arm before he could get all the way out the truck.

"Hey, Candria," Mr. Daniels said, smiling as he walked to the passenger-side window. "How are you?"

"I'm fine," she said, holding back the tears.

"Hello, Candria," Mrs. Daniels said, walking over to the truck and standing by her husband. "How are you, sweetie?"

"I'm fine."

"You don't look fine. It looks like you've been cryin'," Mrs. Daniels said, noticing Trouble's puffy eyes.

"I lost my grandad earlier today," she said, letting a tear fall from her eye.

"I'm sorry to hear that, baby," Mrs. Daniels said.

"Me too," Mr. Daniels added.

Tears fell steadily from Trouble's eyes.

"Charles, can you excuse me and Candria for a minute?" Mrs. Daniels asked her husband.

"All right. I'm 'bout to go up to see if the baby been born yet. Now you take care, Candria, and come by the house later on 'cuz we're gonna celebrate. I'm makin' my famous barbecue," Mr. Daniels said.

Trouble forced a smile and replied, "I really don't have an appetite, Mr. Daniels. But I might."

"That man is always talkin'," Mrs. Daniels laughed. "Now back to you, Candria. I know that you are upset about your grandfather, but I also know that you are upset that Jameelah is about to have that baby." Tears rushed down Trouble's cheeks as she listened to Mrs. Daniels.

"I know at first you might feel left out, but, baby, you gon' have to share him if this baby turns out to be his. I know it's gon' be hard, but if you love Dariel, you are gon' hafta try to adjust."

This bitch got a lot of nerves, Trouble thought. "I know, Mrs. Daniels. And you're right, it's gon' be hard, very hard to accept the fact that Dariel might be a father. What makes it so hard is havin' to deal with Jameelah," Trouble admitted.

"It's up to you, baby, if you gon' stay around or not. I hope y'all can work through this. Dariel loves you and I know he would hate to lose you."

"I love him too. But it's gon' take a lot of time. Call me selfish if you want, I just don't know if I can handle it," Trouble sobbed.

"It's gon' be okay. Trouble, don't cry, baby." Mrs. Daniels hugged her long and tight. "Just give yourself some time, then see what happens. You know you are the best thing that has happened to my little D man, and Charles and I adore you. We want you to still come around even if things don't work out between you and my son."

"I will, Mrs. Daniels."

"Come on, Maggie, she's about to give birth," Janelle ran out the hospital door and yelled.

"Is she? I'm comin'. Take care, Candria, and come by the house later on if you feel like it." Mrs. Daniels shut the truck door and ran into the hospital with a huge smile on her face.

Trouble sat in front of the hospital for what seemed like eternity before pulling out of the parking lot. She had to pull the truck over several times because the tears that flowed from her eyes blurred her vision. Trouble pulled in the driveway and got out of the truck. She walked into her room and grabbed her robe off the back of her closet door.

Jyson came out the kitchen and yelled his sister's name. "Trouble, is that you?" he called out.

"It's me," she called out from her bedroom.

Jyson made his way down the hallway. He softly knocked on her bedroom door.

"Come in," she said, sounding drained.

"What's up?" he said, walking into her room.

"Nothin'," she said, sitting down on her bed, putting her head in her hands.

"That's messed-up about Poppy, ain't it?" he asked.

"Yeah it is," she said, holding her head up.

"Trouble, you don't look too good," Jyson said. "Are you feelin' okay?" he asked, walking over to his sister, feeling her forehead.

"I'm cool," Trouble sighed and got up off the bed and walked out of her room. Trouble made her way to the bathroom and turned the hot water on. She got undressed and slipped into the shower. The water felt good beating down on her weak body. *I cannot let myself go like this. I gotta get over it and move the fuck on with my life,* she thought as the water stung her body like bee stings.

Jyson walked out of his sister's room when he heard a knock at the door. "Who is it?" he yelled.

"It's Ta'liyah," she answered.

"What's up, Ta'liyah," Jyson said, opening the door.

"What's up, Jy? Is Trouble okay?" Ta'liyah asked.

"Yeah, she's okay. She's still upset because she didn't get to say good-bye to Poppy."

"Where did he go?" Ta'liyah asked, confused.

"He passed away. What else could Trouble be upset about?"

"Where is she?" Ta'liyah asked, ignoring his last comment.

"She's in the shower," Jyson said, pointing down the hallway toward the bathroom.

Ta'liyah made her way down the hall and walked into the bathroom without knocking. "Trouble, are you okay?" Ta'liyah asked.

"Yeah, I'm fine," she answered.

"You know, Dante came back in town last night, but he's leavin' today 'cuz he got some business to take care of," Ta'liyah said, making small conversation.

"That's cool. Well, go'n back over to Dariel's with Dante and tell him I said good-bye," Trouble said.

"What do you mean good-bye?" Ta'liyah asked as she snatched the shower curtain open. "You're not gon' kill yourself over this are you?"

"Damn, girl, you scared the shit outta me," Trouble yelled, snatching the curtain closed. "Hell naw, I ain't gon' kill myself. You did say that Dante was leavin' today, didn't you?"

"Yeah."

"Well then, tell him I said good-bye, dummy."

"My bad," Ta'liyah said, chuckling. "You had me worried there for a minute."

"This shit is serious, but it's not serious enough for me to kill myself over. Damn, girl, give ya sista some type of credit. I'm hurt but I ain't crazy."

"Give me a hug," Ta'liyah said, snatching the shower curtain open again.

"Would you stop doin' that?" Trouble yelled, and snatched the curtain back closed. "I'm not givin' you a hug, I'm naked."

"You act like I haven't seen your fat ass before."

"Excuse me?" Trouble opened up the shower curtain and stood with her hands on her hips.

"Not *F-A-T*, I'm talkin' 'bout, *P-H-A-T*, you know, *pretty, hot, and tempting,*" Ta'liyah said, laughing.

"I thought so. Come here, girl, and give me a hug."

Ta'liyah wrapped her arms around her friend and gave her a warm embrace. "Now, finish washing your stankin' ass. I'm 'bout to go out here and push up on yo' brother before I go back over to Dariel's with Dante." Ta'liyah laughed as she walked out the bathroom. Trouble shook her head and finished showering.

Ta'liyah answered her ringing cell phone. She listened as her aunt bragged about the baby. Ta'liyah hung up the phone and walked into Trouble's room. She hated to be the bearer of bad news, but she would rather tell her than for someone else to.

"Trouble, Dariel's mom called and said that Jameelah had a baby girl. She is four pounds and two ounces."

"She's a tiny little thing, isn't she?" Trouble said as tears filled her eyes.

"Yeah. She was a little early."

"I hope she'll be all right," Trouble said, sniffing.

"She will be."

"Did your aunt tell you the baby's name?" For some strange reason, Trouble needed to know.

"They named her Shayne Ne'cole Everson."

"Ne'cole? Ain't that about a bitch," Trouble screamed. "I wonder who gave her that name?"

"I don't know, but whoever it was must have had you on their mind."

"Fuck that! Should I feel privileged 'cuz the baby has my middle name? Well, I don't," Trouble yelled as her cell phone rang. She picked it up and looked at the number before tossing it on her bed.

"Who was that?" Ta'liyah asked.

"Nobody I wanted to talk to."

"Trouble, why are you trippin'?"

"Ta'liyah, you don't understand, that is supposed to be me up there layin' in the hospital holdin' Dariel's baby, not Jameelah." Trouble's phone rang again, but this time she didn't bother picking it up.

"Would you answer your damn phone?" Ta'liyah yelled.

"No, I will not."

"Well, let me answer it." Ta'liyah grabbed Trouble's cell phone from the bed.

"Give it here," Trouble screamed, snatching the phone.

"Answer it then."

"No," Trouble said, throwing the phone up against her bedroom wall and watching as it shattered into pieces.

"What you do that for?"

"I told you I didn't want to talk." The home phone began to ring as she argued with Ta'liyah. Jyson answered it.

"Trouble, telephone," Jyson yelled out.

"Whoever it is, tell 'em I'll call 'em back," Trouble responded.

"Trouble," Ta'liyah whined.

"Trouble said she'll call you back," Jyson said, following his sister's orders.

"All right," Dariel sighed, heavily. "I don't know what has gotten into your sister. Just tell her that it's a girl and she weighs four pounds and one ounce. She's in an incubator right now, and tell her that her name is Shayne Ne'cole," Dariel said, smiling, happily.

"All right, man, I'll tell her, and congratulations," Jyson said, hanging up the phone. "Trouble," he called, walking down the hall and into his sister's room without knocking.

"Boy, don't be just walkin' in my room. I could have been naked," Trouble screamed.

"Trouble, cut the games. It's gon' be all right," he said, walking over to her and wrapping his arms around his sister. She couldn't take it no longer and broke down as her brother ran his hand down her long silky hair.

Ta'liyah walked out of Trouble's room and into the bathroom to get her friend some tissue. Jyson held on to his sister, wishing he could take all of her pain away. But he knew the only thing that would ease her pain was time.

Ta'liyah laid the tissue on the bed and walked into the living room. She decided to call the hospital after finding the number in the phone book. "Can you connect me to Jameelah Everson's room, please?" she said to the operator who had answered the phone.

"Hello, Dariel?" Ta'liyah said.

"What's up? Who is this?" Dariel answered.

"Ta'liyah."

"What's up?"

"Who the baby look like?" she asked.

"Truthfully, she looks like me," Dariel replied.

"You still betta get a DNA test," Ta'liyah warned.

"We already got our mouths swabbed when they was runnin' tests on Shayne. They said it could take up to six weeks to get the results back."

"Dat's what's up."

"You just can't be too sure, and that's another reason why the baby don't got my last name, yet," Dariel said.

"Where's Trouble?"

"She's in her room cryin' and talkin' to her brother."

"Cryin' about what? What happened? Never mind," Dariel said. "Tell her that I love her and I'll call her when I'm ready to leave."

"All right, D, congratulations on your new baby girl," Ta'liyah said.

"Thanks," he said and hung up the phone.

"What was that conversation all about?" Trouble asked, leaning up against the living room wall.

Ta'liyah hadn't even heard Trouble come into the living room. "I was just talkin' to Dariel about the baby, that's all. He told me to tell you that he loves you and he'll call you when he's ready to leave."

"There's no need for him to call me, 'cuz we are about to go drop his truck off at the hospital," Trouble said.

"We?"

"Yes, you and me equals we."

"Are you sure about this?"

"Sure as ever. Let's go."

Jyson made his way down the hallway as Trouble and Ta'liyah were about to walk out the door. "I forgot to tell you that Dariel left you a message," Jyson said.

"That's nice," Trouble said, opening up the front door and walking out on the porch with Ta'liyah in tow.

"Do you wanna hear it?" he yelled after her.

"No thanks," she said as she walked off the porch. Trouble walked to Dariel's truck, got in and drove off as Ta'liyah got inside her brother's beat-up Pinto and pulled off after her.

Trouble parked the Escalade in the crowded hospital parking lot and walked into the hospital with keys in hand as Ta'liyah sat in the no-parking zone and waited for her.

"Hello, may I help you," a triage nurse asked as Trouble walked through the revolving doors.

"Can you please give these keys to Dariel Daniels? He should be in Jameelah Everson's room," Trouble stated politely.

"I sure can." The nurse smiled as she took the keys from her hand.

Trouble returned the smile before heading back out of the hospital.

The triage nurse looked on her computer to see what room Jameelah was registered to before heading toward the elevator. "Is there a Dariel Daniels in here?" the nurse asked once she walked into Jameelah's room.

"I'm Dariel," he answered. "Why?"

"Some young lady asked me to give these keys to you," she said.

"How long ago?" Dariel asked.

"Oh, maybe five minutes or so," the nurse replied.

"Thanks," Dariel said glumly. "Mom, I'll be right back."

"Where you goin'?" Jameelah asked before Mrs. Daniels could open her mouth.

"None of your business," Dariel snapped.

Mrs. Daniels shot Jameelah a dirty look and rolled her eyes. "Where you goin', son?" Mrs. Daniels asked.

"I'm going over to Trouble's house, but I'll be back."

"We just had a baby, and you're about to leave and run up behind that trick. You might as well stay here and be with your family," Jameelah said.

"Don't start with me, Jameelah. You are not my family and the test will tell if the baby really is," Dariel said harshly before walking out of the room and over to the elevator. Dariel pressed the down button and waited.

"Don't worry, Meelah, you don't need that no-good-ass nigga in ya life anyhow," Janelle spat.

Mrs. Daniels's head turned like Linda Blair's did in *The Exorcist.* "Excuse me, what did you just say about my son?" she asked.

"You heard me," Janelle responded with an attitude.

Mr. Daniels walked over and stood next to his wife because he didn't want her to do anything crazy. "Let's just go home, Maggie," he said, touching her on her shoulder.

"My son is and always will be the best thing that ever happened to your daughter. She is the one that's no good; out here sleepin' with all these different boys. And the only reason why me and my husband is up at this hospital is because Dariel admitted to us that he did have unprotected sex with your daughter. So there's a strong possibility that Shayne is our granddaughter!"

Dariel heard the commotion coming out of Jameelah's room and walked back in before the elevator doors opened up.

"Don't think I don't know how ya daughter get down," Mrs. Daniels continued. "Just 'cuz I don't go nowhere don't mean I don't know nothin'."

"Whatever," Janelle said, rolling her eyes into the top of her head.

"Let's go, Maggie, that's enough," Mr. Daniels said as he grabbed hold of his wife's hand.

"You know the only thing that has stopped me from jumpin' on you for talkin' trash about my son is the grace of God, 'cuz honey, if you would have caught me a few years ago, I would be stompin' these Rockports all over yo' head right about now," Mrs. Daniels snapped as her husband pulled her out of the hospital room.

Dariel stood in shock because he had never heard his mother talk or act this way before. He looked over at Jameelah and her mom and smiled before following his parents out into the hall.

"I told you that ya momma used to be roughneck back in the day." Mr. Daniels laughed as they rode the elevator down to the first floor.

If the DNA proves this child is Dariel's, I hope that hussy don't try to stop me from seein' my grandbaby, Mrs. Daniels thought as she followed her son and her husband to the car.

Twenty-seven

"You are not the father!" Jessica yelled at the televison as Maury read the DNA results of some homely looking girl that had the nerve to sit on his stage, knowing damn well she didn't know who the father of her baby was in the first place. "I told you, bitch, that wasn't none of his baby," she laughed.

"Here," Li'l Tony said, throwing the mail onto his mother's lap as he entered the room.

"Next time put it in my hand, you little fucka," Jessica yelled at her son.

"Naw, next time I'll just leave it in the mailbox and let yo' lazy ass get up and get it," he said, walking back outside to play with his friends.

"I can't stand that little bastard," she said, sorting through the pile of bills. She instantly noticed Woo's chicken-scratch handwriting on an envelope and quickly opened up the letter and began reading it. *See, if you wouldn't have ran your big mouth, you could be enjoyin' some of this money too. Give my son his three thousand dollars and let him buy whatever he wants. And you bet' not spend a dime on yourself or those other kids. Love, Woo.*

"Fuck you, nigga. I'm spendin' all this money on me," Jessica said, looking at the six money orders for five hundred dollars each. Jessica ran into her bedroom, grabbed her knockoff Gucci bag, and called a cab because her car had broken down two days ago. "Li'l Tony, I need you to babysit your brothers and sisters for me while I run somewhere," she said as she walked outside where he was playing in the yard with his friends.

"How much you gon' pay me?" he asked.

"I'll give you five dollars," Jessica said.

"I ain't babysittin' for no damn five dollars. Give me twenty and I'll do it."

"Okay, twenty dollars," she said. Li'l Tony held out his hand. "I'ma give it to you," she said, digging in her purse.

Li'l Tony held the money up to the sunlight to see if it had a strip in it and put it in his pocket. "Nice doin' business with you, come again," he said, smiling at his mother.

Fuck you, Jessica thought and would have said it out loud, but he might have changed his mind about keeping the kids.

She jumped in the cab when it arrived and headed straight to the bank to cash the money orders.

Trouble and Jyson had just walked through the door coming from their grandfather's funeral when the telephone rang.

"I'll get it," Trouble said, picking it up without checking the caller ID first.

"Trouble, what is wrong with you?" Dariel asked.

Trouble rolled her eyes in her head because she wasn't in the mood to talk to Dariel or nobody else. "There's nothin' wrong with me. Is there supposed to be?"

"Well, I been callin' you all day and you haven't answered the phone. I even called your cell phone and left a message. Explain that."

Trouble was upset that Dariel didn't remember her telling him that her grandfather's funeral was today. Lately he'd been so wrapped up in this baby it seemed like nothing she said to him mattered anymore. "I can't explain it. Look, I'm about to change my clothes, I'll talk to you later."

"I'll be over to bring you the truck, just in case you have some errands to run," Dariel said.

"No thanks, my brother will take me wherever I need to go."

"Well, I'll be over so we can talk, then."

"Didn't I tell you I had somethin' to do?"

"You said you had to change your clothes. How long is that gon' take?" Dariel asked sarcastically.

"Dariel, I don't feel like talkin'."

"Trouble, I'm on my way over," he said, hanging up the phone before she could say anything else.

"I hate when he hangs up on me!"

For some strange reason Trouble started to feel good. She wanted to talk to Dariel just as bad as he wanted to talk to her. She wanted to know where their relationship stood and if the baby was going to affect her being in his life.

"I bet not find out yo' tramp-ass sister had anything to do with me gettin' robbed. If I find out, I'm not only gon' take her job, but I'm gon' take her worthless-ass life too," Big Mike said to his wife without blinking an eye.

Sherry knew her husband meant every word that was coming out of his mouth. She knew that her sister had done some foul shit in her life, but she didn't think she'd be dumb enough to set up her own brother-in-law—or would she? Sherry ran upstairs and dialed her sister's phone number as fast as she could.

"Hello?" Jessica answered the phone, completely out of breath.

"What you outta breath for?" Sherry asked.

"Oh, I just ran in the house to catch the phone. I was just about to call you," Jessica said, smiling. "I was at the mall today and picked us up matchin' Coach bags." Jessica rambled through her many shopping bags as she talked to her sister.

"Where did you get money from to buy matchin' Coach bags?" Sherry asked suspiciously.

"Woo gave it to me. He's finally tryin' to catch up on his child support," she said, stretching the truth.

"Oh, 'bout time that nigga stepped up."

"What's up? Whatchu' call me for?" she asked, holding her new four-hundred-dollar Prada dress up to her body.

"I got a question to ask you, and I'm hopin' the answer is no. I'm just askin' you to make sure and to keep Mike's mouth shut."

Jessica already knew what her sister was about to ask her. "What is it, sis?"

"Did you have anything to do with Mike gettin' robbed? You know that's how you get down and all."

"Oh, my muthafuckin' goodness! No you didn't just ask me that bullshit. Why would I do that, Sherry? I know me and Big Mike don't see eye to eye all the time, but I wouldn't play him like that. And further-more, I know if he gets robbed, you get robbed too. And y'all do too much for me and the kids to fuck up our relationship like that," she shouted, remorseful about what she had done.

"I know, Jessica," Sherry said, trying to calm her sister. Sherry knew her sister wouldn't have done such a horrible thing like that to them. "I just needed to know. Now I can tell Mike to stop accusin' you of that bullshit."

"Please do."

"You're not mad at me, are you?" Sherry asked.

"No, I'm not mad. Call me later."

"I will, and thanks for the Coach bag."

"Anytime, sis." Jessica hung up the phone with her sister and guilt rushed over her. She felt horrible for the terrible thing she had done to her sister's hus-band. *How could I have done that shit to my sister?* Jessica thought as the tears flowed down her cheeks.

"Jyson, can I get a ride to Loretta's house? Dariel was supposed to come get me, but he never showed up," Trouble said.

"Are you ready to go home right now?"

Trouble shook her head yes. She wanted to cry because this was the third time Dariel had stood her up. He always came up with an excuse on why he couldn't take her to her aunt's house and Trouble was getting fed up. Ever since the DNA proved Shayne to be his, he had been spending less and less time with her and it was really beginning to get to her.

"Do you need a ride to school in the mornin'?" Jyson asked, grabbing his keys.

"Naw, Dariel is gon' take me," she hoped.

"All right now, if he don't come through, call me and I'll come take you," Jyson said, opening up the front door.

Trouble sighed heavily and followed her brother out to his truck. She sat in silence the entire ride to Loretta's. She listened as Jyson talked on his cell phone to Michaela. *They seem so happy together*, Trouble thought as her brother kept telling Michaela how much he loved her.

Jyson hung up his cell phone as he pulled in behind Loretta's beat-up Taurus. "You okay, sis?"

"I'm fine," Trouble said, hiding her hurt behind a weak smile.

"Are you sure?"

Trouble shook her head yes and opened up the truck door.

"Now don't forget to call me if you need a ride to school in the mornin'," Jyson said.

"I won't," Trouble said, getting out of the truck.

Trouble walked in the house and went straight to her bedroom.

"Trouble, is that you?" Loretta called out from downstairs.

Who else would it be? she thought as she pulled out a pair of pajamas from her dresser drawer. "Yeah, it's me," she answered.

"Okay, just checkin'," Loretta said before going back into the kitchen to fix herself a cup of hot tea.

Trouble walked into the bathroom and turned on the shower. She slid in and let the water beat down her weary body. After running all the hot water out, Trouble walked back into her bedroom and sat on the bed with her towel wrapped around her body. She put lotion all over her body before putting on her pajamas and crying herself to sleep.

The next morning Trouble took her sweet time getting dressed. Her cell phone that she had gotten to replace the one she had broken rang and she answered it.

"Trouble, I'm on my way. I overslept, the baby kept me up all night cryin'," Dariel said.

Trouble was too through about what Dariel had just told her. She was at a loss for words. "So you mean to tell me that the baby stayed all night over to your house?"

"No, Trouble, I stayed all night over to Jameelah's house," Dariel said as if it was no big deal.

"What?"

"It ain't like I slept with her, Trouble. Me and Shayne slept in the nursery."

"So the fuck what if you slept in the nursery! What happened to you comin' to get me to bring me back to my aunt's house last night?"

"I'm sorry, but Jameelah was in pain, so she needed me to take care of Shayne while she got some rest."

"Whatever, Dariel, just come get me," she said, hanging up the phone.

Trouble wanted to call him back and tell him to go to hell, but she didn't because she did still need a ride to school. She could have called her brother for a ride, but decided against it. She walked down to the kitchen and popped a piece of bread in the toaster and waited for Dariel's arrival.

A half an hour later, Dariel pulled up in front of Loretta's house and blew the horn for her. She gathered her book bag, grabbed a light jacket, and headed out the door. The ride to school was a long, silent one. Trouble had so much on her mind and there was so many things she wanted to say to Dariel but her pride wouldn't let her. She wanted to let him know how much she really loved him and how she was afraid of losing him, but she didn't want to come off sounding desperate so she just contined to ride in silence.

Trouble got out the truck with her pride in her pocket and walked into the school, leaving Dariel standing at the truck.

"Congratulations," Carla said to Trouble as she walked past her in the hallway.

Trouble gave her a confused look. "What are you congratulatin' me for?" she asked, clueless.

Carla smirked. "Didn't you and Dariel have a baby?"

Carla and the group of girls she stood with laughed. Trouble had had enough. She threw her book bag down on the floor and charged Carla like a raging bull, knocking her to the floor. Trouble climbed on top of Carla and pounded her in the face. She talked with every punch that connected with Carla.

"Somebody get her off me," Carla screamed, but no one moved, they just stood around watching as Trouble pulverized her.

"Trouble is down the hall beatin' the fuck outta Carla," Charlie ran up to Dariel and said.

Dariel ran down the hallway looking for his girl. "What the fuck is wrong with you, Trouble?" Dariel asked as he rushed through the crowd that had formed around the fight. Dariel pulled Trouble off of Carla. "What the fuck is goin' on?"

Trouble's shirt and jeans were both covered in blood. Carla lay on the floor crying as Dariel led Trouble out of the school building and back to his truck. "What the fuck is wrong with you, baby girl?"

Trouble used to love when Dariel called her *baby girl*. It used to feel like she mattered to him when he called her that, but at that particular moment, *baby girl* sounded more like *bitch* to her. Something had snapped in Trouble's head as she stood staring at Dariel. Rage had took over like a thief in the night. "You wanna know what's wrong with me? Muthafucka, I'll tell you what's wrong with me. You spendin' all your time over that bitch's house and actin' like it's supposed to be okay! Well, Dariel, it ain't!" Trouble snapped.

"Trouble, she is the mother of my child. What do you want me to do, not be around my daughter?"

"Did I say that?"

"You didn't have to, but that's what you're actin' like. As a matter of fact, you actin' like a damn child," Dariel said, grimacing.

"How in the world can you sit up here and say that I'm actin' like a child? Let's be reasonable, Dariel. If I got pregnant by someone else when we first got together, would you have pursued our relationship?" Trouble asked.

"Yes, and I would have been supportive, like I'm askin' you to be."

"How can I be supportive of you stayin' over to Jameelah's house? What sense does that make? Put the shoe on the other foot."

"No, I probably wouldn't like it if the father of your child was stayin' over to your house. That's only 'cuz I know how men are." Dariel had just stuck his foot in his mouth and didn't realize it.

"That's my point. You're a man, aren't you?"

"But it's different. I don't want nothin' to do with Jameelah. All I want to do is be around my daughter. That ain't too much to ask for, is it?"

"Just take me back to Loretta's house. I don't feel like bein' at school today, and plus I'll probably get suspended anyway," Trouble said.

"We can't leave school."

"Maybe you can't, but I am. I got a headache."

"Trouble, please, baby girl. I don't want to argue with you. Can we just go back to my house and talk?" Dariel begged.

"Look, I don't wanna talk about this shit no more. You don't even have to take me back to Loretta's. Drop me off over to my brother's house."

"Can we please talk, Trouble?"

"Whatever, Dariel, we can do whatever you want." Trouble sighed and got into the truck.

Dariel climbed in the truck and looked over at Trouble. "I love you, Trouble," he said, starting up the truck and pulling off. Dariel pulled into his parents' driveway and got out. He walked up on the porch and stuck his key in the door. Trouble followed behind him in silence. She hadn't said one word since they had left the school.

He walked in and looked around to make sure his parents were at work before he led Trouble to his bedroom. Dariel pulled off his jersey and threw it on the end of his bed.

"Let's talk," he said, sitting down on his bed.

Trouble didn't know how or where to start. All she knew was that she had so much on her chest that she wanted and needed to get off. "You brought me over here, so you start talkin'," Trouble said, standing by the door.

"I can do that," he said. "First off, ever since the DNA came back you've been actin' funny toward me."

"Dariel, I have to be honest with you, I don't know if I can handle you being a father to Jameelah's baby."

"Would it be any different if I was the father of someone else's baby? I don't get it. Is it Jameelah you got the problem with, or is it the baby?"

"That's just it, I don't know," Trouble said truthfully.

"You don't have anything to worry about, Trouble, when it comes to Jameelah. But I love my little girl and I can't and I won't let anyone come between that," Dariel explained.

"I don't wanna come between you and your daughter. But like I said, I don't know if I can handle it."

"Trouble, don't feel like that. We're gon' get through this like I said before. You're a part of my life and I want you to be a part of Shayne's life too."

"Dariel, I love you, but please understand how I'm feelin'. You wouldn't be happy for me."

"Can you at least try to be happy, 'cuz I don't wanna lose you, baby girl."

"I'll try, but I'm tellin' you now, if things start to get too hectic, I'm out, and I mean it," Trouble warned.

"Everything is gon' be fine. You'll see," Dariel said, walking over to her and kissing her on the forehead.

"I sure hope so."

"Trouble, I love spendin' time with my daughter. You just don't know how she makes me feel." Dariel's eyes glistened as he talked about his child.

"I can't knock you for wantin' to spend time with your daughter. It's just knowin' you're around Jameelah is what bothers me," Trouble admitted.

"What? Trouble is threatened by another female?" Dariel joked.

"Dariel," Trouble said, hitting him on his shoulder.

"I'm sorry." He laughed.

"It's not that I'm threatened by her. I don't know what it is." Trouble walked over to the dresser and leaned against it. "I can't put my finger on why I feel so insecure about Jameelah."

"I don't know why either, 'cuz you have no reason to be." Dariel walked over to the dresser and stood next to her.

"I know I don't, and furthermore, why would you leave all of this for her?" she said, turning around, showing off her well-rounded backside.

"You damn right about that," Dariel laughed and wrapped his arms around her, cupping her ass in his hands. "I love you, baby girl, and I want to spend the rest of my life with you."

Trouble was speechless as tears formed in her eyes. Of all the times Dariel told her that he loved her, she knew if he never meant it before, right at that particular moment, she knew his love for her was real. "I love you too, Dariel."

Dariel leaned down and kissed Trouble with heated passion. He picked her up and carried her to his bed, removed her clothes and his, and they made sweet, passionate love until they both fell off to sleep.

Twenty-eight

Trouble walked through the door and went up to her room to change her clothes. She put on a pair of old jogging pants and a T-shirt before going downstairs to fix herself a ham sandwich while she waited on her brother's arrival.

"Who is it?" Trouble yelled to whomever it was on the other side of the door.

"It's Jyson," he answered.

Trouble put her cup of juice down on top of one of the coasters on the coffee table before letting Jyson in.

"What's up, sis? Has Loretta made it home yet?" Jyson asked, walking through the door.

"Not yet. You know we gotta give her some time to get from the bank," Trouble said. "It's a damn shame that I can't get my own money," she said, sitting on the couch.

"Yeah, that's fucked-up that Momma and Loretta is the only ones allowed to cash your check." Jyson shook his head. "What chu' gon' do with all that money?"

Trouble smiled. "Well first, I'm gon' take you on a shop-pin' spree like I promised when we were younger."

"You know one hundred gees is a lot of money for a girl your age," Jyson said.

"Yeah, I guess it is. But I'm gon' do the right thing with it. I'm gon' put some up for college, of course, even though I know I'm goin' to get an academic scholarship. I'm still gon' need money for clothes and a nice-ass ride, though," Trouble said, smiling.

Jyson heard a car pull up in the driveway and looked out the window as a late-model Mitsubishi Eclipse pulled up. "Who is this in this car?" Jyson asked Trouble.

Trouble got up off the couch and ran over to the window. "I don't know," she said as Loretta stepped out the car, struggling with about seven or eight shop-ping bags. "It ain't her payday, so I know this bitch did not spend any of my money," Trouble snapped, taking her earrings off.

"Calm down, sis," Jyson said to Trouble right before Loretta stepped up on the porch.

"Hey y'all," Loretta said as she walked through the door smiling—something neither Jyson or Trouble had seen in a long time.

"Where my money at?" Trouble said, getting straight to the point. "I hope you didn't buy that car with my money," she warned.

"Girl, don't start with me," Loretta said. "I got your money." She handed Trouble an envelope and walked into the kitchen with her bags.

Trouble opened up the envelope and looked at the seventy-five-thousand-dollar bank receipt. "Hold on, I'm supposed to have a hundred gees here," Trouble huffed.

"I borrowed some money to pay off my bills, I paid cash for the car, and I put a little money in my savings account for a rainy day," Loretta said nonchalantly as she walked out of the kitchen.

"What the fuck do you mean? So in other words, you did what you wanted to do with my money before consultin' with me?" Trouble asked angrily.

"How in the fuck you just gon' spend her money without askin' her first?" Jyson argued. "That money was not for you, it's for Trouble," he spat. "If Poppy wanted you to have some of his money, he would have left you some."

"Trouble lives here rent- and bill-free. She don't buy no groceries or nothin' else. That little bit of money I took didn't hurt her any," Loretta said.

"You know what, bitch, I lived here by force, not by choice," Trouble snapped, her eyes filling with tears of anger.

"You better watch your mouth talkin' to me like that," Loretta warned.

"Fuck you," Trouble spat. "Bitch, I'm about to get my shit and raise the fuck up outta here before I do somethin' to yo' ass," Trouble said.

Loretta didn't care one way or another. She got what she wanted so there was no more need for Trouble's spoiled ass to stay with her. "This is my house, and I'm not gon' let you talk all crazy to me," Loretta shouted.

"How could you take my money, Loretta?" Trouble asked, still not believing her aunt had the audacity to spend her money without asking.

"You owed me that money for stayin' here," Loretta said.

"I'm gettin' the fuck up outta yo' house and I don't give a fuck about you callin' children services, bitch. And I'll tell you one thing, if they come knockin' at Jyson's door, you gon' have some problems," Trouble threatened Loretta.

Loretta had no intention of calling children services; she got a car, some new clothes, and money for her savings account. Her mission had been accomplished.

Trouble was on fire as she stormed up to her room. *How could this bitch take my money without askin'?* she thought as she stuffed her clothes in suitcases and trash bags.

Loretta dialed her brother's phone number and as soon as he answered she started telling on Trouble. "Ronnie, let me tell you about your smart-mouth-ass daughter. She got her money from Daddy and when I went and cashed it, I bought me a car. I didn't think she would mind, bein' that my car was on its last leg," Loretta explained. "I came home and gave Candria the rest of her money and she started callin' me outta my name and makin' threats on my life."

"What? I know my muffin wouldn't do a thing like that. Where is she?" Trouble's father said into the phone receiver.

"Her and Jyson are upstairs packin' her clothes."

"Put her ass on the phone," he said, becoming angry.

Loretta headed up the stairs to Trouble's room and stood in the doorway. "Trouble, ya daddy on the phone," she said, throwing the phone on the bed, making sure she didn't get in Trouble's way.

"Yeah?" Trouble said, grabbing the phone.

"What's your problem, girl?" her father asked.

"Problem? I don't know what you talkin' about."

"Ya auntie told me you was over there disrespectin' her."

"That bitch spent my money and spent it without askin' me, so you damn right I'm disrespectin' her ass," Trouble yelled, looking over in Loretta's direction.

"Trouble, she's your aunt. You shouldn't be mad 'cuz she spent some of Daddy's money. You live there rent- and bill-free, so you shouldn't be mad. You know she needed a new car to get back and forth to work so she can pay those bills for y'all."

"She ain't payin' no bills for me. I'm hardly ever here. And how dare you talk about respect? This bitch stole from me, how can I respect her?"

"Respect her and me. You done got too grown for ya britches, girl. All that cussin' you doin'."

"Respect? Nigga, I don't even respect my own damn momma, so you should know that you and this bitch Loretta ain't got shit comin' in the respect department," Trouble said, hanging up the phone.

Five seconds later the phone rang and Jyson answered it this time.

"Jyson, why are you over there lettin' your little sister act up? You're supposed to be a role model to her," their father said.

"Well, what type of role model are you? Loretta was dead wrong for spendin' Trouble's money. That's why Uncle Jimmy left her, 'cuz her ass was money hungry on top of bein' bossy," Jyson said.

"How dare you say that about me?" Loretta shouted.

"Fuck you. Trouble, let's get your stuff so we can get the fuck outta here," Jyson said as he hung the phone up and helped Trouble with her things.

Trouble and Jyson toted all of her belongings to Jyson's truck as Loretta stood by watching. *Never will I step foot back in this house again*, Trouble thought as she and her brother pulled off, leaving misery behind.

Loretta stood in the doorway smiling as she watched her niece and nephew pull off. She wanted to call children services just to be spiteful, but she thought about the threat Trouble had made and decided against it. She had gotten a car, jewelry, and some new clothes out of the money, plus her checking account was no longer in the negative, so she was satisfied with that. "Farewell, my darlin' niece, and thanks for the money." Loretta smiled as she waved good riddance to Trouble and Jyson.

Twenty-nine

Spring break rolled around and Trouble was glad. No teachers, no books, and sadly, no Dariel for ten whole days. *I'm gon' miss my baby*, she thought as she twisted a piece of her hair. She felt at ease being back at home with her brother. She could finally relax. The only thing that worried her was the thought of Loretta calling children services, but Loretta was no dummy; she knew Trouble would do anything in this world to protect her brother from harm. Trouble got out of bed and pulled her hair up into a ponytail, cleaned her room, and fixed herself something to eat. She lay across her bed after she ate and thought about what she was gon' do with herself while Dariel was down in Atlanta. Trouble thought long and hard until she finally drifted off to sleep. She woke up two hours later feeling relaxed and refreshed. She got out of bed and walked into the bathroom. The phone rang while she flushed the toilet. She hurried into her room to answer the ringing phone. "Hello?" she said into the phone.

"Trouble, we're leavin' a day early for Atlanta, so I'm about to come and get you so we can spend some time together," Dariel said.

Trouble began feeling sad all over again. "That's cool. I'll be ready when you get here," she said.

"I'll be there in about twenty minutes," he said, hanging up the phone without saying anything else.

"Ooooohhhh, I hate when he does that!" she shouted.

Trouble and Dariel walked through the front door and to Trouble's surprise, Jameelah was sitting on the couch holding Shayne.

"There's Daddy," Jameelah spoke in a childlike voice.

Trouble rolled her eyes.

"Hey, Candria," Mr. and Mrs. Daniels said simultaneously.

"Hey, how y'all doin'?" Trouble smiled from ear to ear. *Now bitch, they like me too,* Trouble thought.

Dariel kissed Shayne's chubby cheek as he took her from Jameelah and held her close to his body.

"Gimme Grandma's baby," Mrs. Daniels said, taking the baby out of Dariel's arms.

"What is me and Shayne gon' do while you gone?" Jameelah asked Dariel.

"I don't know. I told you to let me take her with me," Dariel said.

"I told you she can't go unless I go too," Jameelah replied.

Trouble shot Jameelah a dirty look and then looked at Dariel and waited on his response.

"I told you that you ain't goin'," Dariel said.

"I got family in Atlanta. I could take Shayne down there to see 'em," said Jameelah.

Mrs. Daniels and Trouble both looked at Dariel.

"Heck naw, girl. What I look like takin' you to Atlanta with me when I ain't even takin' my woman. And for your information, this is a family trip, you're not a part of this family so you can't come," Dariel said.

Trouble let out a little chuckle before taking a seat on the couch.

"Trouble, how come you're not comin' with us?" Mrs. Daniels asked.

"I told Dariel I would have went with y'all, but I'm about to start my driver's education classes this week," Trouble said, smiling.

Jameelah was crushed and Trouble could see it all over her face. *How dare they ask that bitch to go to Atlanta with them. I'm the one who had their grandchild*, Jameelah thought.

"Do you have all your clothes packed, Dariel?" Mrs. Daniels asked. "Here, take this girl, she done pooped in her pants." Mrs. Daniels handed Dariel the baby so he could change her diaper.

"No ma'am, not yet," Dariel said, turning up his nose. He kissed his daughter on the cheek and handed her to Jameelah.

"Dang, she's your child too," Jameelah yelled with emphasis, as if to let Trouble know that Shayne was his daughter.

"Petty," Trouble mumbled, shaking her head.

"Come on," Dariel said.

Jameelah stood up, smiling. "Where we goin'?"

"I'm talkin' to Trouble, not you," he said.

Trouble couldn't help but laugh as Jameelah sat back down on the couch and changed the baby's diaper.

"We'll see who has the last laugh," Jameelah retorted as Trouble and Dariel walked up the stairs.

For the next ten days Trouble kept herself busy with things like sorting through her clothes and giving the ones she didn't want to the homeless shelter. She switched her bedroom around two different times along with the living room. She watched *Baby Boy* over and over again, and wished Dariel were there to watch it with her.

After taking a nap, Trouble woke up and washed her hair and put on a new outfit because today was the day Dariel and his family would be home. Trouble smiled at the reflection in the mirror as she sang the words to one of New Edition's old cuts. Trouble's heart pounded as her cell phone rang. She smiled because she knew it was Dariel because he had his own ring tone.

"Hello?" she said, smiling.

"I'm home, baby girl, and I can't wait to see you," Dariel said.

"I can't wait to see you, either," she cooed.

"Is Jyson at home?" he inquired.

"No, so come on over, big boy," she said seductively.

The only thing Trouble heard next was the dial tone.

"I hate that!" she screamed.

Dariel got to Trouble's house and she answered the door buck-ass naked. He picked her up and carried her off to her bedroom and they made wild, nasty love for hours.

Thirty

Summer had arrived and school was finally out. Trouble and Dariel spent almost every day together. And when Trouble wasn't taking lifeguard lessons at the local YMCA, she and Dariel did a lot of things with Shayne, like taking her to the park and to the mall. Dariel already had her spoiled at the tender age of four months. She had every pair of shoes; she had Baby Phat, Sean John, Ecko, you name it. If it came in Shayne's size, Shayne had it. Trouble had one problem and that was Jameelah wouldn't stop popping up over to Dariel's house every time they were over there and she constantly blew up his cell phone. She would always call and say stuff like, Shayne wants to talk to her daddy, knowing damn well the baby couldn't talk. Trouble kept her composure every time the phone rang, but she could feel herself about to explode at any given moment.

Trouble answered her ringing cell phone. She smiled because it was her baby on the other end of the line. "Hello?"

"Let's go to dinner and a movie tonight," Dariel said.

"Would you like for me to call Jameelah to see if her and Shayne want to go too?" Trouble asked sarcastically.

Dariel grimaced. "Why would you do that?"

"Shit, we ain't gon' get to eat dinner in peace anyway, 'cuz Jameelah is gon' blow ya damn phone up," Trouble said.

"Trouble, don't start, okay?"

"Well, I'm tellin' the truth, Dariel. We can't even have sex without her callin' your cell phone. We can't even go over to your house and chill or to the mall without her poppin' up. I'm beginnin' to think the ho is stalkin' you."

"Come on, Trouble."

"I'm serious, Dariel. I'm gettin' real sick and tired of it too. I can't believe she didn't pop up at Cedar Point when we went. If she had a ride, she probably would have been standin' by the Magnum waitin' on us."

Dariel laughed. "You crazy, baby girl."

"No, I'm serious."

"Well, I'll be to get you in about an hour. Be ready and I'll see you then." Dariel hung up the phone before Trouble could say anything else.

She shook her head and walked into the bathroom to get ready for her date.

Dariel pulled up and Trouble was standing on the front porch taking in some of the warm summer air. The breeze was feeling good blowing through her long hair. The moment was just right as the night air sent chills down her spine.

"Are you comin' or what?" Dariel yelled out the window.

Trouble smiled and walked off the porch and got into the truck with her man.

"You smell nice," he said, making small conversation.

"Thanks," she replied, saying nothing else.

Trouble and Dariel pulled up in front of Logan's steak house. The parking lot was full. They had to park next door at Circuit City just to get a parking space. Dariel got out of the truck and walked around to the passenger's side to open up the door for his lady. She got out and they walked into the restaurant hand in hand.

"It's nice and cozy in here," Dariel said as they waited to be seated.

"Yeah, it is," Trouble agreed. The sound of Dariel's cell phone instantly triggered an attitude with her. *I knew it was too good to be true. That phone ain't rang the entire ride to the restaurant*, Trouble thought.

Dariel looked at the caller ID and pressed the ignore button, and after about five minutes the phone started ringing again.

After ordering and receiving their food, Trouble sat at the table and picked at her salad.

"What's wrong, baby girl?" Dariel asked.

"Nothin'," she said as his cell phone rang again.

"I gotta go to the bathroom," Dariel said, excusing himself from the table. When he came back he picked up his fork and continued eating. "Sorry it took so long, there was a long line in the bathroom," he lied. The real reason was Jameelah kept calling his phone asking him his whereabouts and making him feel bad because he was spending time with Trouble instead of Shayne.

Trouble was mad as hell because she knew Dariel was lying. "Dariel, don't lie to me. Do you think I'm dumb? I know you was talkin' to Jameelah on the phone," she leaned over and whispered, not wanting to cause a scene in the crowded restaurant.

Dariel hung his head down. "I'm sorry. She keeps callin' me."

"Well, get your fuckin' number changed," she whispered a little louder.

"I can't. What if somethin' happens to Shayne?" Dariel's phone rang again and he ignored it.

"Answer your damn phone!" Trouble demanded.

Dariel hesitated before answering his phone. "Hello?"

"Dariel, Shayne is sick," Jameelah started in.

"What's wrong with her?" he said, panicking.

"Where you at?"

"I'm eatin'," he said. "Now what's the matter with my baby?"

"Who are you eatin' with?" she picked.

Dariel became angry because the shit Jameelah was talking was irrelevant. All he wanted to know was if his baby was all right. "I'm with Trouble, who else? What's wrong with Shayne?" he asked.

"She has a summer cold and she needs some Children's Tylenol."

"Well, have your mom go get her some. I'm out with my girl," he said in hopes of cheering Trouble up, but it didn't work.

"Look, nigga, my momma didn't lay down with me and make this baby, so it ain't her responsibility to get her some medicine. Your triflin' ass is at a resturant spendin' money on food for you and ya trick, but you can't spend six punk-ass dollars on some medicine for your daughter?"

Dariel sighed. "I didn't say that I couldn't. I just asked if your mom could go get it and I'll pay her back after I get finished eatin'," Dariel said.

"And I told you no. Are you gon' go get it or does your daughter have to suffer?" Jameelah knew that remark would make him feel guilty. "And hurry up!" she said before hanging up the phone.

Dariel cut his cell phone off and looked at Trouble. "Let's finish eatin'," he said, smiling.

"I'm not hungry anymore. Matter of fact, I'm ready to go home," Trouble said.

"What's the matter with you, baby girl?"

Trouble was furious and her whisper grew into loud, obnoxious words. "I don't know what done happened to you. You are not the Dariel I fell in love with. You have lost your fuckin' mind. I don't know how come you can't see that the bitch is usin' that baby against you. And you are stupid enough to keep lettin' her do it!"

"It ain't like that, Trouble," Dariel pleaded as he tried to get Trouble to calm down.

"You act like that ho put roots on yo' ass or something. Have you been eatin' her spaghetti or did you leave a pair of yo' draws over her house?" Trouble asked.

Dariel was stunned by Trouble's words. "Calm down. Check please," he said, motioning for the waiter.

Trouble grabbed her purse and threw it up on her shoulder and rushed out of the restaurant, leaving Dariel behind feeling confused and embarrassed. The ride back home was a silent one for her. Every now and then Dariel would say a few words to her, but he would get little or no response at all.

Trouble felt bad after she thought about the scene she had caused in the restaurant, but it felt good to release those bottled-up feelings she held inside. She didn't want to push Dariel away, but she couldn't deal with Jameelah and her childish games any longer. Shit was going downhill and Dariel was so wrapped up in his daughter, he didn't even realize it.

"Trouble, we can go to the movies after I drop Shayne's medicine off to Jameelah," Dariel said.

"No thanks, I just wanna go home."

He pulled up in front of Trouble's house and looked over at her. He knew she was mad, he could see it all over her face. He had to do or say something to make up for it quick. "Well, we can always go to the movies tomorrow. I'll be back in about an hour. I'ma go check on Shayne, okay?"

"No, don't worry about goin' to the movies tomorrow or comin' back in an hour." Trouble got out of the truck and slammed the door behind her.

"Trouble, what do you want me to do? My daughter needs some medicine."

Trouble turned around, looked Dariel in the face, and said, "You know what I want you to do? I want you to get a fuckin' backbone and realize that Jameelah is playin' you for a straight fool," and she turned around and walked into the house.

Dariel parked the truck and knocked on Trouble's door.

"Who is it?" she yelled, knowing darn well it was Dariel.

"Quit playin', you know who it is," Dariel said as he waited on her to open up the door.

Trouble opened up the door and sat back down on the sofa and picked up the *TV Guide*.

Dariel stood in the doorway watching every move she made. Usually when he was in Trouble's house, he felt comfortable, but this particular time he felt like a stranger.

"What you standin' up for? You makin' me nervous," Trouble said, laying the *TV Guide* back on top of the coffee table.

"I didn't know if you wanted me to sit down or not."

"Nigga, if I didn't want you to sit down, I wouldn't have let you in my house."

Dariel reluctantly sat on the couch next to his woman. He picked up her legs and laid them them across his lap and removed her shoes. Trouble's head tilted back as he began massaging her feet. She let out a little moan, and Dariel knew what that meant. He stopped massaging her feet and stood up from the sofa. He reached his hand out for her and led her to her bedroom where he made sweet love to her.

"Dariel, we really need to talk," Trouble said, running her hand down his bare chest.

"Damn, baby girl, we just got finished makin' some good love, and now you wanna mess up the mood by arguin'."

"I wanna talk, not argue. There's a big differnece," Trouble said. She sat up in the bed and smiled at her handsome man.

Dariel sighed and sat up too. He listened as Trouble complained about Jameelah and all her phone calls. She felt sort of bad for having to get involved in the way Jameelah had been acting, but she figured why should she have to sit around and be miserable while Jameelah got all the excitement?

Dariel promised his baby girl that he would handle Jameelah, and as the weeks went by he did just what he had promised. He laid down the law to her. The phone calls didn't stop completely, but they did slack off some, which was fine, for right now. Jameelah stopped popping up unannounced and Trouble was happy for the moment. But . . . on the other hand it worried her, because she was no dummy when it came to psycho broads. She knew that Jameelah took some time off from stalking Dariel only to sit back and plot on her next move. And it bothered Trouble because she didn't know when or where it would be.

Thirty-one

It was the hottest day of the summer and the park was packed with niggas standing around shooting dice as the ladies kept their eyes glued on the brothas that were running up and down the baskeball court acting like the next Michael Jordan. Trouble had finally gotten herself a job at the neighborhood swimming pool as a lifeguard. She loved being in charge of something and that's what made her decide to take lifeguard training in the first place. As she sat in that high lifeguard chair with the whistle wrapped around her neck, she was now in charge of every life that swam in that pool.

"Hey, boo." Dariel smiled as Trouble hollered at him from the lifeguard chair.

"Hey, baby girl," he replied.

"Hang on for a minute, it's almost time for my break," Trouble said.

Trouble spotted Jameelah walking toward Dariel with Shayne in her arms. She rolled her eyes at the same time Dariel did.

"Here's Daddy," Jameelah said as she approached him.

"Hey, baby," Dariel said, smiling, as he took his daughter from Jameelah's arms. He planted a sloppy kiss on her cheek.

"Hey, Shayne," Trouble said, smiling down at the baby.

Jameelah rolled her eyes.

Trouble laughed as she blew the whistle to clear the pool.

"What you gon' do later on?" Jameelah asked Dariel.

"I've got plans, why?" he said.

" 'Cuz, I need a babysitter, that's why," Jameelah stated.

"Well, I'm doin' somethin'. You got to find someone else."

Trouble was happy that her man was finally standing up for himself. She let out a little chuckle and Jameelah looked up at her and rolled her eyes. Trouble called out to Dariel. "Hey, baby, this is for you," she said as she dived into the pool, looking like a professional diver as her body hit the water without making a big splash. People cheered as she came from under the water. Trouble got out of the water and walked over to where Jameelah and Dariel stood talking. He wrapped his left arm around her shoulder as he held Shayne in his right.

"Hi, Shayne," Trouble said, kissing her on her chubby cheek. Shayne squealed with laughter and that pissed Jameelah clean off.

"Gimme my baby," Jameelah said, snatching her daughter from Dariel's arm.

Trouble blew it off with a smile.

"I'm 'bout to go wash my truck and get ready for tonight," Dariel said.

"What do you got up your sleeve?" Trouble asked suspiciously, knowing her man was leaving for basketball camp in two days.

"Don't worry about it. I'll be here to pick you up at seven o'clock."

"Can you take me and Shayne home?" Jameelah asked.

"How did y'all get here?" Dariel questioned.

"Don't even worry about it. We'll just walk in the hot sun," she said, knowing good and well Dariel wouldn't let his daughter be out walking in the blazing sun. Jameelah knew that she was getting under Trouble's skin and she was loving it. *You'll get tired of me sooner or later and want to leave my man alone. I'll be here waiting for him to come back to me so we can raise our child as a family,* Jameelah thought as she went to gather her and Shayne's things.

Jameelah was right, Trouble was fed up with her always depending on Dariel for every little thing. "This shit is gon' hafta stop," Trouble said under her breath as she watched Dariel and Jameelah walk off with Shayne. "The line is drawn here."

Dariel had his mother pack him a picnic basket and he drove Trouble out to Mifflin Lake and they had a nice romantic picnic while they watched the sun go down. Dariel made sure he brought plenty of candles to keep the mosquitoes away as they lay on the blanket and enjoyed each other. He wanted the night to be perfect without interruptions so he left his cell phone in the truck.

"I can't believe you're goin' to basketball camp," Trouble said, looking over at Dariel.

"I've been goin' since the fourth grade, Trouble," he said, laying back on the blanket.

"I know. But what am I gon' do for the two weeks that you're gone?" She moved closer to him and lay her head on his chest.

"You know I'm gon' call you every day," he said, rubbing her head as she listened to the beat of his heart. "You can go shoppin', go over to Ta'liyah's. You'll find somethin' to keep your time occupied. Just make sure it ain't no nigga occupyin' your time," Dariel joked.

"Never that. You know you are my one and only," Trouble said, kissing Dariel on the lips.

"I betta be!"

Trouble got up, ate breakfast, and combed her hair before heading to the mall. She didn't know what she was gon' do while Dariel was away so she took his advice and went shopping. She went into All Dat and got her hair and nails done. She sipped on some French vanilla coffee while sitting back listening to all the latest gossip about who was fucking who and who was the biggest ballas in the neighborhood. Jyson's name came up a few times, but not as many as Big Mike's. Trouble was proud that her brothers had a rep, even though she wished it wasn't for selling drugs.

"You are so lucky to have two big brothers with money, girl," Sonya said as she crimped Trouble's hair.

"I know," Trouble said, smiling.

"Girl, hook a sista up wit' Jyson," Carmella, one of the other beauticians, said.

"He got a girlfriend. And besides, you ain't his type," Sheedy, the gay beautician, replied.

"Shit, I know if he fucked with Jessica, he'll fuck with just about anything," Carmella said.

"Jessica who?" Sheedy asked, putting his hand on his hip.

"You know, old hood rat Jessica that lives out on King Street in the jets," Carmella said as she flatironed her customer's hair.

"Gurrrl, say it ain't so," Sheedy said, snapping his fingers with every word.

"Now-now, y'all can't be discussin' my brother's business while I'm up in here," Trouble said.

"We'll finish talkin' when she leaves," Sheedy said, smacking his lips.

"That'll be y'all's best bet, 'cuz y'all know my girl, Trouble, will set it off up in here," Sonya said, laughing.

"That's right," Trouble laughed as Sonya proceeded to finish up her hair.

After spending hours in the salon, Trouble strolled around the mall, going in and out of every store. She had so many shopping bags she had to make a trip out to Dariel's truck to put them in the trunk. She was grateful that he left her his truck so she could get around.

"Well, well, well, look who we have here. I thought you moved outta town," a male voice said.

Trouble didn't recognize the voice. She turned around, and to her surprise it was the light-skinned cat that drove the yellow Cadillac. *Damn, he look better now than he did back when I first saw him,* Trouble thought, giving him the once-over.

"Hello, hazel," he said, smiling.

"Hazel? Why you call me that?"

"The color of your eyes are hazel, aren't they?" he said, smirking.

"Oh yeah," Trouble said, embarrassed. *How dumb can I be?* she thought.

"What nigga got you out spending' up all his money?"

"I'm spendin' my own money. I don't need no nigga to take care of me," Trouble replied.

"Okay, Miss Independent. I like that," Light-skin said, smiling.

"That's right."

"Well, I don't wanna hold you. I'm gon' let you go'n and finish shoppin'," Mr. Light-skin said, walking off.

Trouble stood and watched as he disappeared into Finish Line. Something inside of her wanted to follow

him, but she shook the feeling off and walked into
Macy's instead. She searched for a shirt to go with the
new pink capris she had just purchased from Saks.
She walked around the store until she found a clear-
ance rack, then rambled through the rack of clothes
and found three more outfits. She took her outfits up
to the register and waited patiently while the cashier
rang up her purchase.

"It'll be forty-five dollars even," the cashier said,
smiling.

"I got it," Light-skin said, handing the cashier a
hundred-dollar bill.

"Thanks, but I can pay for my own stuff," Trouble
said.

"I know. Just consider it a gift." Light-skin smiled,
took his change and walked away, leaving Trouble
stunned. She grabbed her bags off the counter and
caught up with this fine yellow piece of meat.

"Hey, what type of game are you tryin'a run?"
Trouble asked.

"Game? I don't play games, shorty," he said.

"Ne'cole is the name," Trouble replied, not wanting
him to know her real identity.

"Ne'cole, huh? Niggas call me Woo," he said, smiling.

"Woo? What kinda name is that?" Trouble asked,
twisting up her mug.

"Oh, you gotta problem with my name?"

"Naw. I just wanted to know."

"Has anybody ever told you that you were nosy?"

"All the time," she laughed.

"Let's go," Woo said.

"Go where?" Trouble asked as she followed Woo out of Macy's.

"To Victoria's Secret," he said, smiling wickedly.

Trouble stopped dead in her tracks. "For what?" she asked, putting her hands on her hips.

"Come on, shorty, don't trip. Don't every woman match their panties and bras up with their clothes?"

He called me a woman instead of a girl. Trouble smiled at the thought. She followed as Woo led her into panty and bra heaven.

"Here, I want you to have these, these, and those over there," he said, pointing to all the nice and lacy lingerie in the store.

Shit, if the nigga is gon' pay for all this shit, I'm gon' take advantage of it, she thought as she picked out the most expensive shit on the racks.

"You got everything?" he asked after about twenty minutes of shopping.

"Yep," Trouble said as she walked to the register and laid her belongings on top of the counter. The cashier rang up the purchase and Trouble looked at Woo and waited on him to pull his money out of his pocket.

"What? I know you ain't waitin' on me to pay. Didn't you just tell me that you can pay for your own stuff, Miss Independent?" Woo said, laughing.

Trouble wanted to die right on the spot. She tried to play this nigga, but in return she got played. She looked around the store to see if there was a table that she could run and hide underneath, because them had been her exact words, but she didn't have enough money in her purse to pay for all the panties and bras she had picked out. *How embarrassing is it gon' be for me to have to put all this shit back,* she thought as she dug in her purse, knowing damn well she only had fifty dollars left out of the six hundred she had brought to the mall with her.

"Naw, I'm just playin'," Woo said, laughing, pulling out two more hundred-dollar bills. "I had you scared, didn't I?"

"Scared for what? If you wouldn't have paid, I was just gon' hafta pay for the stuff myself," she lied.

"Oh, I keep forgettin' I'm dealin' with an independent woman."

Trouble loved the fact that Woo realized she was more of a woman than a little girl. Her age might have been young, but her mind, body, and soul were something different. "That's right, and don't you forget it," Trouble said, smiling, melting Woo's heart.

Trouble and Woo walked around the mall for a couple more hours, laughing and talking.

"Oh well, it's gettin' late. I think I better be headin' home," Trouble said, not really wanting to leave because she was enjoying his company so much.

"Can I take you?" Woo asked.

"I got a ride, but thanks anyway."

"Can a nigga get yo' phone number then?" Woo asked.

"It all depends on what nigga you talkin' about."

"This nigga here," Woo said, pointing at his chest.

Trouble hesitated. *I can't give this nigga my number. What if he calls while Dariel is around?* she thought.

"Oh, you still with yo' dude?"

"Somethin' like that." *Where did that come from?* she thought. *How come I didn't just tell this nigga yes that I am still with my man?*

"Girl, give me your number. And if I ever call when he's around, just tell me I got the wrong number or somethin'," Woo said.

"How many times you think he's gon' fall for the wrong-number bit? My man ain't no dummy, you know," Trouble said.

"You gon' give me your number or not?"

Trouble pulled a receipt out of her bag and scribbled her cell phone number on it, kinda hoping that he couldn't read it. She then handed him the piece of paper.

"Okay, I'll call you," he said, smiling.

"Do that," she said, smiling back. Trouble walked back to Dariel's truck with a big smile on her face. "Calm down, girl, Dariel is still your man," she said as she got into the truck and started it up.

For the next week Trouble talked to Woo on the telephone until the wee hours of the morning. A few times she caught herself getting mad when Dariel would beep in on the line and interrupt their conversation. Woo kept Trouble laughing, sounding just like her brother. She felt herself falling for this brotha, but had to check herself time and time again because she did still belong to Dariel. Trouble wished she could introduce Woo to Ta'liyah, but she knew even though Ta'liyah was her best friend, Dariel was still Ta'liyah's cousin, and Trouble was a firm believer that blood was thicker than mud.

"Let's go to the movies tonight, shorty," Woo said.

"I don't know about all that. What if someone sees us?" Trouble worried.

"Won't nobody see us. We'll go to the last show and we'll even go in separate cars," Woo suggested.

"I still don't know. I can't let nobody see my boyfriend's truck parked at the movies. I'll tell you what, if I decide to go, I'll catch the bus."

"Stop worryin' so much. I don't care how you get there. Just be at the late show at Cinema Ten," he said.

"What are we gon' see?"

"We'll figure that out when we get there," he said.

"Whatever you say."

"Okay, I'll see you later on."

"All right," Trouble giggled like a little schoolgirl. She jumped off her bed and ran into the bathroom to get ready for her date.

Thirty-two

Jyson pulled up in the McDonald's parking lot and got out of his truck wearing a big hoodie and a pair of sweatpants. He walked in and strolled over to the counter. "Hello, welcome to McDonald's, may I take your order please?" the girl behind the register said, smiling. "Yeah, let me get a double cheese-burger and a large fry," Jyson said, smiling back.

"Would you like somethin' to drink, sir?"

"No thanks. Can you tell me where the bathroom is?" he asked.

"Yes, it's right around the corner," the girl said, pointing.

"Thanks." Jyson waited on his food and then walked to the bathroom. He nodded his head at a young man who sat at a table eating alone. Jyson walked into the bathroom and emptied the food into the trash can. He walked into a stall with his empty bag and lifted up his hoodie, then untaped the six ounces of pure cocaine he had strapped to his body and placed them in the bag. He checked to make sure his nine was cocked as he walked out of the stall, balling up the bag and throwing it in the trash can. Jyson turned on the water and began washing his hands. The young gentleman who sat alone at the table walked in and nodded at Jyson. Jyson nodded back. The young man threw a bag in the trash can and stood beside Jyson and began washing some left-over ketchup off his fingers. Jyson reached in the trash and picked up the bag the young man had thrown away. He looked in the bag, nodded an approval, and then exited the bathroom and headed out the McDonald's exit door.

"Thank you, and come again," the girl yelled as Jyson walked out the door.

Jyson got in his truck and began counting the money. "Six thousand," he said, placing the money back in the bag and then pulling off.

"Hello?" he said, answering his ringing cell phone.

"What you doin'?" Big Mike asked.

"I'm on my way to my apartment. Why? What's up?"

"Let's go to the club to celebrate," Big Mike said.

"What's the occasion?"

"Sherry is pregnant," Big Mike said, smiling.

"Straight up? Congratulations. As soon as I drop this money off I'll swing by the club to celebrate," Jyson said, smiling.

"Cool," Big Mike said as he hung up the phone.

Jyson's smile soon turned to a frown as he thought about how happy he had felt when Michaela told him that she was pregnant. He began wondering how good of a father he would have been to his child and what the child would have looked like. He shook the bad memories out of his head as he pulled up into his apartment complex.

Trouble and Woo laughed as they walked out of the movie theater.

"That was a good movie, wasn't it?" Woo asked.

"Yeah, it was. You know Marlon and Shawn Wayans are always makin' some funny shit," Trouble said.

"I can't believe you really caught the bus," Woo said, looking into Trouble's mesmerizing eyes.

"I told you I was. I better get out of here before I miss my bus," she said, heading toward the bus stop. "See you later."

Woo followed behind her. "I can't let you stand out here alone and wait on the bus, it's too late for that. Do you mind if I wait with you?"

He is so considerate, she thought. "I don't mind," Trouble said, smiling.

Trouble and Woo sat on the bench and talked until she spotted the bus coming.

"I know you got a man and all, but can I get a kiss, please?"

"Woo, I got a man."

"I didn't ask you to stick your tongue in my mouth. All I want is a small kiss, shorty."

Trouble thought for a second and as soon as the bus pulled up, she agreed. "Okay, but just one small kiss," she said.

Woo licked his lips and Trouble leaned in and planted a nice friendly kiss on him. He grabbed her around the waist and stuck his tongue in her mouth. Trouble was in complete shock but she didn't stop him; in fact she enjoyed it.

"Well, well, well, look at what we have here. Like they say, when the cat's away the mice will play," Jameelah said out the bus window.

Trouble took a quick step back and looked up at Jameelah.

"Does Dariel know about your little friend?" Jameelah said, smirking while pointing at Woo.

"No. I mean, not yet," Trouble said.

"Oh, he will now. Bye-bye," Jameelah said, waving as the bus pulled away.

Trouble was in a state of shock. *What are the chances of somebody catchin' me kissin' another nigga?* she thought.

"Are you all right, Ne'cole?" Woo asked.

"Yeah, I'm fine," she lied.

"Well, why did you just let the bus pull off?"

"I don't know."

"Who was that girl on the bus? Was she a friend of yours?"

"No, she's my boyfriend's baby momma," Trouble said.

"Do you think she's gon' tell ya dude on you?"

"Hell yeah. I know she can't wait to get home and call him."

"What do you think he's gon' do to you?"

"I ain't for sure. The worse thing that could happen is he'll break up with me," Trouble said sadly.

"He ain't gon' put his hands on you, is he?" Woo asked, concerned.

"Naw, he doesn't hit women."

"You never know, shorty, what a nigga might do when he finds out his girl is cheatin' on him."

"I'm not cheatin' on him. All I did was come to see a movie with you, that's all," Trouble assured him.

Woo shook his head and laughed. "Come on, so I can take you home."

"No thanks. I'll wait on the next bus," Trouble said, not wanting to be anywhere around Woo ever again.

"Suit yourself," Woo said, walking away. "Hey, shorty," he called over his shoulder.

"What, Woo?" Trouble sighed.

"You do know that was the last bus, don't you?" he laughed and continued walking to his car.

Trouble let out a pitiful sigh and followed Woo to his car. She didn't open her mouth the entire ride, except for when she gave him directions to where she stayed.

"Which street do you live on?"

"I live on Main Street," Trouble lied. "Just keep drivin'."

"What house?"

"Just drop me off at the gas station right there," Trouble said, pointing. "I need to get a few things out of there," she lied.

"I'll wait on you," Woo said, pulling into the gas station parking lot.

"No need. I'm fine."

"I'll call you tomorrow," Woo said before Trouble got out of the car.

"Woo, look, I had a good time while it lasted, but I can't see you or talk to you anymore," Trouble said, getting out.

Woo shook his head. "I feel you, shorty. But if the nigga break up with you, don't hesitate to call," he said, smiling.

Trouble smiled back and closed his car door.

"Damn, I was feelin' shorty. That's okay, though, I'll run into her again, and next time I'm gon' make her mines," Woo said as he pulled out of the gas station parking lot.

Trouble walked into the gas station and bought a pack of Big Red gum and stood around for five minutes just to make sure Woo had pulled off. She ran out the door and down the street. When she reached her house, she walked up on the porch and stuck her key in the lock. She ran in her room and ripped off her clothes and fell back on her bed.

Of all the people in the world, how was it Jameelah that caught me kissin' another nigga? Trouble thought.

Thirty-three

Trouble was a nervous wreck the day Dariel arrived home from basketball camp. She was waiting on him to call her and tell her to never speak to him again. He called Trouble and told her that he would be over to her house as soon as he woke up from his nap.

Dariel walked up on the front porch and knocked on Trouble's door.

Her nerves were shot. She started not to answer the door, but he already knew she was in the house.

"Hey, baby girl, I missed you," he said, kissing his woman on the lips.

"Hey, Dariel, how was camp?" she asked, pulling away from him.

Dariel brushed it off. "It was horrible."

"Why?"

"Because you weren't there," he said, kissing her again. "You just don't know how much I missed you."

"I missed you too," Trouble said, walking over to the couch and taking a seat.

"What did you do while I was gone?" he asked, walking over and taking a seat next to her.

"Nothin'," she snapped. "What makes you think I was doin' somethin'?" she asked nervously.

"Damn, I was just askin' what you did to occupy your time while I was gone. Don't be so defensive, it ain't like I was accusin' you of messin' around on me," Dariel said.

"I know," Trouble said, relieved. *Shit, I better calm down before I end up tellin' on myself,* she thought.

"Come on in your room and let me make love to you," he said.

Trouble smiled. "Let's go," she said, leading the way. *That bitch didn't even tell Dariel she seen me kissin' Woo*, Trouble thought. *This bitch got somethin' up her sleeve. She got me just where she wants me and I don't like it, not one bit!*

For the next week, Trouble avoided going over to Dariel's house because she feared that Jameelah would pop up over there and expose their little secret. Trouble didn't want to do nothing to make Jameelah mad, so in order to keep things tight between them, she just stayed away.

"Hey, girl, it's your break time," Teena, another lifeguard at the swimming pool said, climbing up the ladder.

"Okay," Trouble said, smiling. "Clear the pool," she said, blowing her whistle. She watched as everybody scurried out of the water. Trouble looked over at the entrance door and her heart jumped into her throat as she watched Jameelah walk through it, pushing

Shayne in her stroller. Trouble shook her head and dived off the chair into the deep end of the pool and wished there was a trapdoor at the bottom she could escape through.

"Looka here," Jameelah said, smiling at Trouble when she came up from underneath the water.

"Leave me alone, Jameelah," Trouble said, getting out of the pool.

"What I do to you? I haven't even begun to bother you, yet," she said, smirking.

"Do what you gon' do. I don't care," Trouble lied, hoping that Jameelah would just forget about what she had seen.

"So you tellin' me that you don't mind if I tell Dariel that I saw Mommy kissin' Santa Claus?" Jameelah laughed.

"I don't understand why you haven't already told him. I don't know what your plans are but whatever you gon' do, I wish you would go'n and get it over with," Trouble said, wiping the excess water from her face.

"What would I tell on you for? I'm not cut like that. Dariel is a good-ass nigga, Trouble, and I know if I tell him about you kissin' someone else, he would be crushed. True enough, I still love Dariel and I want to be with him, but the last thing I wanna do is tell him somethin' that's gon' hurt him."

This bitch makes a lot of sense, Trouble thought as she listened to Jameelah talk.

"See, it's girls like you that give girls like me a bad name," Jameelah continued. "I'm not gon' tell on you, broad, 'cuz eventually the guilt will eat you up and you'll tell on yourself." Jameelah looked at Trouble as if she disgusted her before walking away.

The rest of the day Trouble felt horrible because she knew Jameelah was telling the truth. She did feel guilty about running around with another nigga while her man was away at basketball camp. But how was she gon' break down and tell him the truth? How was he gon' react?

At seven o'clock Trouble's shift was over. She looked out into the parking lot at Dariel, who was waiting to give her a ride home from work. She walked to his truck and climbed in.

"Hey, baby girl, what's the long face for?" Dariel asked, noticing Trouble had a worried look. "Did you have a bad day at work?" Trouble shook her head no. "Well, what's wrong then?" he asked as he pulled out of the parking lot.

"Dariel, we need to talk," Trouble said as tears ran down her cheek.

"Okay," he said, pulling over to park.

"Dariel, I'm sorry," she sobbed, heavily.

Dariel's heart raced because he didn't know what was going on. "Sorry about what, baby girl? What did you do?"

"I cheated on you while you were away at basketball camp," she cried.

Dariel didn't make a move. He was silent for a long time. He didn't know what to say. He held his head down and shook it slowly. "With who, Trouble?" he whispered.

Trouble didn't answer him, she just looked out the window and cried.

"Who did you mess around on me with, Trouble?" Dariel asked again, but this time his voice was dripping with anger.

Trouble still didn't open her mouth to answer.

"Answer me dammit!" Dariel yelled while pounding his fist on the dashboard. "Don't I deserve to know who you were fuckin' around with?"

Trouble was afraid because she had never seen this side of Dariel before. And the comment Woo made about not knowing what a man would do once he found out his girl was cheating popped up in her head. "His name is Woo, Dariel. And I didn't fuck him, I just kissed him," she said as the tears streamed down her face.

"Oh, so you didn't fuck him?"

"No, Dariel, I didn't fuck him. I went to the movies with him and I gave him a kiss."

"I can't believe you, Trouble. I go away to camp and yo' ass runnin' around with another nigga? Ain't that about a bitch!"

"Dariel, I'm sorry, baby," Trouble pleaded.

"Don't *baby* me. Was I yo' baby when you was runnin' around with that nigga?"

"Dariel, I'm sorry, please forgive me," Trouble cried.

"So when did you meet this nigga?"

"I met him the day I walked home from your house. The same day Marcus busted Ta'liyah out about havin' that abortion."

"You mean to tell me you've been conversatin' with this nigga all this time?"

"No. I just saw him again the day you left for camp. I was at the mall and he started talkin' to me and we talked on the phone a few times and he asked to take me to the movies and I said yes," Trouble explained, hoping Dariel would understand that it was nothing more to it than that.

Dariel's heart was shattered. He pulled off and drove Trouble home as quick as he could. He ran stop signs and even ran a couple of lights. He didn't want to be nowhere around her. He pulled up in front of her house and put the car in park.

"You comin' in?" she asked.

Dariel shook his head no.

"Why not?"

"I'm tired, Trouble, okay?"

"Okay," she said, opening up the door and getting out.

"I'll call you tomorrow." Dariel sped off with the door still open, but once he turned the corner it closed.

Trouble walked into the house and grabbed the cordless phone and dialed Dariel's cell phone.

"Hello?" Dariel said, flatly.

"I fucked up, didn't I?" Trouble asked.

"What do you think, Trouble?"

"I don't know. I said I was sorry."

"All right, Trouble, I'll talk to you tomorrow," Dariel said.

"Why you gettin' off the phone? You don't wanna talk to me?" Trouble whined.

"I said I'll talk to you tomorrow," Dariel said, irritated.

"What you 'bout to do?"

"I'm about to go see Shayne."

"I thought you were tired?" Trouble asked.

"I am. But I haven't seen my daughter all day, so I'm goin' to see her before I go home and go to bed."

"Whatever, Dariel. You probably goin' over there to see Jameelah," she retorted.

"That would just make us even, don't you think?" he said sarcastically.

"Whatever." Trouble hung up the phone and sat hoping that Dariel would call her right back, but he didn't. She prayed to God that her relationship wouldn't end.

Thirty-four

"Dariel, Shayne is asleep. You should have brought yo' ass over here ealier, while you was up in that bitch's ass all day," Jameelah spat as Dariel stood at the doorstep.

"Didn't I ask you not to talk about my girl like that?"

"Yo' girl, please." Jameelah laughed.

"Well, I'll be over here in the mornin' to get Shayne."

"Where you takin' her?"

"I don't hafta tell you where I'm takin' my damn child."

"Yes the fuck you do! I'll tell you one thing, I don't want my baby around that ho no more."

"I told you to stop talkin' about my damn girl," Dariel warned.

Jameelah was jealous because Dariel kept referring to Trouble as his girl. "If the bitch was yo' *girl*, why did I see her kissin' another nigga while you were away at basketball camp?" Jameelah said, hoping to break Dariel's heart so he could come running back to her and she would be right there waiting with open arms.

"She already told me about that, now," Dariel said. He hesitated for a moment then looked over at Jameelah.

"How did you know that?"

" 'Cuz I seen her when she kissed the nigga."

"Where were you at?"

"Oh, you tryin'a keep tabs on me now?"

Dariel sucked his teeth. "Please. For what?"

"Well, if you really must know, I was on the bus comin' home when it pulled up to the bus stop they were standin' at," Jameelah said.

"Why was Trouble at the bus stop when she had my truck?"

"I don't know. That's a question you should be askin' yo' *girl,* or whatever she is," Jameelah said, snickering.

"Did Trouble see you?" Dariel asked angrily.

"Yeah, she saw me. That's why the bitch ain't been trip-pin' lately. She thought I was gon' tell on her dumb ass. But like I told her, I wasn't gon' tell you shit. I made the ho tell on herself," Jameelah said, laughing.

"I'm out. I'll be over here to get Shayne in the mornin'."

"Dariel, wait. Don't you wanna stay a little while longer?" she asked.

"No thanks. I'm tired, and besides, I got a lot on my mind."

"Ya girl got cha' mind all fucked-up. Just remember if you need to talk, I'll be here," Jameelah said sincerely.

"Thanks," Dariel said. *I guess Jameelah ain't really all that bad of a person*, he thought. *Shit, she just argue too damn much for me. If she'd stop all that damn bickerin', she wouldn't be so bad. I can't believe Trouble left out the fact that Jameelah saw her kissin' dude. That's probably the only reason she broke down and told me. She must have thought Jameelah was gon' tell on her. Slick ass!*

After leaving Jameelah's house, Dariel went home and went to bed. He tossed and turned all night. He didn't even know what this nigga Woo looked like, but all he kept imagining was Trouble lip-locking with him. "I can't believe this shit," he shouted as he lay in bed. Dariel rolled over and reached for his cell phone and dialed.

"Hello?" Trouble answered, still half asleep.

"Wake up, Trouble, we need to talk," he said.

"Who is this?"

"Who you want it to be? Oh, I'm sorry, was you waitin' on Woo to call you?"

"Dariel, don't start. It could have been Jyson or Big Mike," Trouble said.

"Or Woo, huh?"

"Dariel, please, it's three o'clock in the mornin', so I know you didn't call me to talk about Woo."

"No, as I matter of fact I didn't. I called you to talk about the reason why you failed to mention that Jameelah seen you kissin' that nigga."

Trouble sat up in her bed. "I forgot. And besides, it wasn't that important."

"How in the hell did you forget that your worst enemy seen you kissin' someone else? Trouble, you so full of shit."

"No, I'm not, Dariel. I told you what happened, didn't I?"

"Yeah, but you just so happen to forget the part about Jameelah seein' you. Trouble, I'm beginnin' to think that if you wouldn't have been caught kissin' that nigga, you probably would have never told me."

"That's not true, Dariel. I tell you everything," Trouble pleaded.

"I don't know if I can trust you. You used to sit up and talk about Jameelah messin' around on me, shit, you ain't too much better than her," Dariel said angrily.

That remark stung. "How can you say that about me, Dariel? I didn't cheat on you. Oh, just 'cuz I went to the movies with a male friend and gave him a kiss I cheated?"

"Well, what do you call it, Trouble?" She didn't have an answer for him. "That's what I thought. In the real world, baby girl, it's called cheatin'!"

"Dariel, call it what you want. Me and you went to the movies when you and Jameelah was together, remember? Was you cheatin' on her?" Trouble asked. "And we kissed," she said in a matter-of-fact tone.

"You know what, yeah, I did cheat on her. I cheated on her with the girl I thought that I wanted to spend the rest of my life with. When I got with you, I planned on bein' with you forever, not just for a couple of months or so," Dariel said.

"That still didn't make it right. Look, Dariel, I said I was sorry. What more do you want me to do?"

"It's all good."

"No, it's not. Dariel, look, please let's just get past this," Trouble begged.

"Just let it go, huh? You think it's that damn easy? You right. I'm gon' let it go, but don't bother callin' me tomorrow night, 'cuz I'm takin' a female friend to the movies," Dariel said, hanging up the phone.

"Oooohhh, I can't stand him!"

Trouble and Dariel's relationship was going down-hill quick. They didn't spend nearly as much time to-gether as they did before Dariel found about her and Woo. Trouble couldn't remember the last time Dariel had satisfied her sexually. He was fucked-up behind that kiss; he didn't know if he could ever trust his baby girl again, but the fucked-up part about it was he still loved her to death.

Jameelah spent all day in the hair salon getting her hair and nails done. Ever since Dariel had got mad at Trouble, he had been spending a lot of time with her and Shayne, and she wanted to look good at all times for her soon-tobe man. Jameelah knew she couldn't hold a candle to Trouble when it came to looks and style, but she wasn't too far behind. She kept up with all the latest styles and made sure she kept her weekly hair appointment with Sonya. Jahmeelah was as happy as a fag trapped in a cave with a bag of dicks. She just knew one day soon, Trouble would be out of the picture for good and Dariel would be all hers again.

"Hello?" Jameelah answered her cell phone with a smile because she knew it was her king.

"Hey, take Shayne over to see my mom. I'm not gon' be able to pick her up 'cuz I'm at the park playin' in the Brooks and Holmes basketball tournament," Dariel said, out of breath.

"Okay, well, what time will you be at home?" Jameelah asked.

"I'll be there around eight," Dariel said, hanging up the phone.

Jameelah smiled from ear to ear. *I told that bitch a long time ago to have her fun with Dariel while she could, 'cuz I was gonna get him back!* Jameelah thought.

Dariel walked into the house and went straight up the stairs. He could hear singing coming out of the bathroom.

"Itsy-bitsy spider went up the water spout, down came the rain and washed the spider out," he heard Jameelah sing.

Dariel smiled as Jameelah sang to their daughter while giving her a bath. "What y'all doin' in here?" Dariel asked, interrupting her song.

Jameelah looked up from Shayne and smiled. "Oh, your mom asked if she could stay all night and I told her yeah. So I came up here to give her a bath and put on her pj's before I leave."

"Where is my mom?" Dariel asked.

"She was down in the basement doin' laundry," Jameelah said as she dried Shayne off.

"Oh." Dariel watched as Jameelah handled their child with great care. She put lotion on Shayne before putting on her diaper and pajamas. They walked out of the bathroom and into Dariel's room. Jameelah sat in the rocking chair and began singing to Shayne so she could fall asleep.

"I'll be back. I'm goin' to get in the shower," Dariel said.

"Okay," Jameelah said, smiling, as she continued to rock the baby.

Mrs. Daniels heard the doorbell ring and went to go answer it. "Hello, Candria," Mrs. Daniels said, smiling. "I haven't seen you in a while."

"I know," Trouble said, walking through the door. "Is Dariel home?"

"I haven't seen or heard him come in. But I've been in the basement doin' laundry so he might be here," Mrs. Daniels said, smiling.

"I see his truck parked outside," Trouble said.

"Well, then he must be home. Go'n upstairs and see if he's up there," Mrs. Daniels said before walking back into the basement to put the clothes in the dryer.

Dariel stood in his room with a towel wrapped around his wet body. "You sure are a good mom."

"Thanks," Jameelah said, smiling. She lay the baby in her crib and when she turned around, Dariel was standing directly behind her.

"You need somethin'?" Jameelah asked nervously.

"Yeah," Dariel said, pressing his lips to hers and kissing her passionately.

"Dariel, you in there?" Trouble called out as she walked into his bedroom. Trouble then got the biggest shock of her life. She looked at Dariel and then at Jameelah as they made love with their lips. Dariel turned around and his face hit the floor. Trouble's eyes filled with hurt on top of hatred. She couldn't say or do anything except turn around and walk back downstairs.

Jameelah had a huge smile on her face as she watched Trouble walk out of the room.

"Trouble," Dariel called out desperately as he followed her down the stairs. His towel fell away from his body as he chased her but he kept right on moving behind her. Trouble moved as fast as she could. She nearly knocked Mrs. Daniels over as she ran out the front door.

"Where's your clothes at, Dariel?" Mrs. Daniels asked, confused, as her son stood in the middle of the living room in his birthday suit.

Dariel was so busy chasing Trouble, he didn't even realize that he was standing buck naked in front of his mother. "Trouble," he ran on the front porch and called out, but she ran down the dark street as fast as she could. "Fuck!"

Thirty-five

An entire year had passed and it was still hard for Trouble to cope with the breakup between her and Dariel. She literally became sick to her stomach every time she saw him walking down the hallway in school with Jameelah by his side. She had heard rumors of them getting back together, but Ta'liyah denied it all. Trouble never looked for another boyfriend, even though plenty of guys tried to get at her. She just couldn't bring herself to deal with anyone else after Dariel. She had went out on a few dates, but she let the brothas know from the get-go that all she wanted to be was friends. Dariel missed Trouble just as bad as she missed him and he wanted her back in his life, but he couldn't face her after he got caught kissing Jameelah. At first he looked at it as payback and then he realized that he took her through a lot of shit when he found out about her kissing Woo and he couldn't deal with the guilt.

Trouble was now a senior in high school and she didn't worry about anything but graduating and getting out of Mansfield. She gave up on Jyson doing anything positive with his life, 'cuz he was still out in the streets clockin' dollas. Michaela also gave up on him moving her to Atlanta to finish school because her man couldn't seem to leave those streets alone. Jyson was the big boy in town and he got mad respect, and if a nigga didn't give it, he made sure he took it. He wasn't ready to move away and leave all this money and respect behind.

Trouble sat at the kitchen table doing her trigonometry homework when Jyson walked in puffing on a blunt.

"What's up, sis?" Jyson asked, blowing smoke out of his mouth.

"I thought you were gon' get your GED a long time ago, boy?" Trouble said to Jyson.

"I'ma get it, I'ma get it," he said, sitting down at the table across from his sister.

"You ain't gon' never do right, big head," Trouble said, getting up from the table and walking into the living room.

"Yes, I am," he said, following behind her.

"When, Jyson?"

"Next week. Watch and see."

"Shit, been watchin' and seein' for the past year and you still haven't done anything different than before. What happened to you buyin' a house in Atlanta and movin' Michaela down there?" Trouble asked.

"Michaela understands what her man is out here doin'," Jyson said. "And I have done somethin' different. I have more money, I got a different ride, and I'm buyin' you more expensive clothes," Jyson replied.

Trouble rolled her eyes. "Shut up, boy. You ain't gon' never change. You gon' be just like Big Mike, ninety years old and still out in the streets slangin' dope," she said, laughing.

"Oh, you gettin' yo' Dave Chappelle on, huh?"

"Don't I always? But seriously, you would have thought that Big Mike would have settled down a little bit after he made Sherry have that miscarriage," Trouble said.

"Yeah, that was some foul shit."

"You know he was dead wrong for slammin' that girl, knowin' she was five months pregnant," Trouble said, shaking her head.

"That was crazy. All because she found a phone number in his pants pocket and confronted him. I told that nigga that he betta be glad she didn't press charges on his dumb ass," Jyson said.

"I love Big Mike and all, but she should have. His ass would have been sittin' in prison for murder."

Jyson shook his head in disgust. "I'm 'bout to bounce. Call me if you need me." He grabbed his coat and opened up the front door.

"Are we still goin' to New York Saturday to get my prom dress?" Trouble asked.

"How many times do I have to tell you yes?"

"I gotta keep tabs on you. You know how forgetful you are," Trouble said, laughing.

"I'm gettin' old, sis, I'm gettin' old."

"You're not gettin' old, nigga, you gettin' wise."

"Jyson, I have somethin' to tell you," Michaela said.

"What's up, baby?" Jyson asked as he played the *Madden* 2008 on the PlayStation 3.

"Can you turn the game off for a minute?" she asked, as she rubbed her hands together.

"Right after this play, baby."

"Jyson, turn the game off now!" Michaela demanded.

Jyson let the controller fall from his hand. "What's yo' problem, girl?"

"Jyson, I'm pregnant," she blurted out.

Jyson didn't know whether to jump for joy or cry tears of pain, because he didn't know if she was going to keep it. Jyson wanted to be a daddy more than anything in this world. He knew that if he became a father, the streets would no longer be his main priority because he would have a child to live for. The only thing that kept going through his mind was if she was going to have another abortion or not. If she did, he would leave her and never look back.

"Did you hear me, Jyson?"

"Yeah, I heard you. What you gon' do?"

"What do you mean, what am I gon' do? You helped make this baby too."

"I helped make the last one too, but I didn't have a say, remember?"

"I got two years of college left and baby, that's when my life begins," Michaela explained. "I can become the pediatrician I've always wanted to be."

"Your life began twenty-seven years ago. When you graduate from college is gon' determine how you gon' live your life. Michaela, please, you took one child away from me, don't take another one," Jyson begged.

"Jyson, let me explain somethin' to you. I have put my life on hold for you too many times before. We were supposed to have moved to Atlanta a long time ago, but where are we? Still in Mansfield. I tried to accept the fact that you are young and caught up in them streets, that's why I quit pressin' you about movin' a long time ago, but Jyson, we are not gettin' any younger and it's time for you to get your shit together."

"Please, Michaela, I want this baby. I need this baby to help me get my shit together," he said.

"How is this baby gon' help you get your shit together?"

"I'll stop sellin' drugs, get my GED, and I promise we'll move out of Mansfield so you can finish school and become the pediatrician you've always wanted to be." Jyson got down on both knees and wrapped his arms around Michaela's waist and laid his head on her stomach to see if he could feel any movement.

"What are you doin'?" she asked.

"I just wanna feel my baby move."

"It's too early for all that, dummy," Michaela said, laughing.

"Do we have a deal or not?" Jyson asked.

"Now you promised you were gon' get your shit together if I keep this baby, right?"

"Hell yeah," Jyson responded.

"Then we have a deal," Michaela said.

Jyson was one happy camper. He stood up and picked up his pregnant woman and carried her off to her bedroom and made love to her.

Jyson did what he promised Michaela he was going to do. He signed up for his GED class and he went faithfully. He sold the rest of the dope he had left. Jyson even went as far as calling some real estate agents in Georgia to find them a house.

"Wow, Trouble, you look beautiful," her momma said as Trouble walked out of her bedroom dressed in a cream form-fitting Gucci dress with the cream pumps to match. Trouble just shook her head, because Momma had a way of just popping up. Even though she was still shooting her regular and looking a hot mess, she wouldn't have missed seeing her daughter on her prom night for all the cocaine in Peru.

"Who has the honor of escorting my beautiful daughter to the prom?"

"I was gon' go by myself, but Ta'liyah begged me not to.

She's makin' me go with Darius since she's goin' with Dante, if you really must know."

"When did you decide on this?" Jyson asked. "The last you told me, Regina was messin' with Darius."

"She was, but she's not comin' to the prom, because she had to get her tonsils taken out two days ago," Trouble explained.

"Man, Dariel is gon' hit the floor when he sees you walk into the prom with his boy on your arm," Jyson said, laughing.

"No he's not. Darius already told him that he was takin' me. What can Dariel do anyway? He has a woman," Trouble said.

As soon as Dante, Darius, and Ta'liyah arrived, Michaela took plenty of pictures of the couples for her photo album. Momma was so happy to be able to see her daughter off to the prom, she cried when the limo pulled off.

"You all right, Momma?" Jyson asked, wrapping his arms around her.

"I'm fine, son. It's just I've missed so much of y'all's lives growin' up," she cried.

"It's okay, Momma, you'll have the chance to make it up to us once we get to Georgia," Jyson said, smiling.

"What's in Georgia?" Momma asked.

"We will be real soon."

"And you takin' me with you?" she asked.

"Why wouldn't I? It's time for us to get our shit together, Momma. We ain't gettin' no younger," Jyson said. Michaela smiled at Jyson as he tried to talk some sense into his mother just like she did him.

"I know, son. But what am I gon' do down there? Georgia is so big," she said.

"For starters, we gon' get you into a drug rehab," Jyson said.

"I'd like that," Momma said, smiling.

"And then we'll see what happens after that."

"I'm gon' hafta get me a job so I can help pay some bills. You know I can't live nowhere for free," Momma said.

"We'll worry about that when the time comes. For right now, let's focus on gettin' you clean," Jyson said.

"I can't wait," Momma said, smiling, and kissed her oldest child on the cheek.

Trouble, Darius, Dante, and Ta'liyah got out of the stretch limo looking like movie stars. Trouble held her head up high as she walked past the crowd of people who stood outside the prom taking pictures. Trouble knew she was the shit, and she was glad she didn't have to worry about nobody showing up at the prom with a dress on like hers. Darius was dressed in an all-cream tux with an aqua vest underneath, and he sported a pair of cream gators. Nobody at the prom could top Darius's ensemble. Trouble and Darius walked through the door, and what do you know, Dariel and Jameelah were the first couple she laid eyes on.

Don't they look cute, she thought. Dariel had on a black tux with a yellow vest underneath, and Jameelah sported a yellow dress that Trouble knew she had seen in the JCPenney catalog. But other than that, they matched.

"What's up, Dariel?" Darius said, giving his friend a firm handshake and a hug.

Dariel stared at Trouble before speaking. *Damn, she looks good as hell!* he thought. *And she's wearin' the hell outta that dress.*

"You lookin' good, boy," Darius said to Dariel.

"You lookin' mighty sharp yourself." Dariel shook his head in approval while looking at Trouble.

Damn, Dariel is so damn fine, Trouble thought as she licked her lips. *And his broad still looks plain.*

"Hey, Darius," Jameelah said.

Darius nodded his head.

"You do look good," Jameelah said.

"Thanks," Darius replied.

"How you been, Trouble?" Jameelah asked, trying to be funny.

"Can't you tell by the way I look?" Trouble asked sarcastically.

"Come on, baby, this is our song, let's dance," Jameelah said, pulling Dariel's arm and leading him to the dance floor.

Trouble instantly felt sick to her stomach as she watched Dariel and Jameelah on the dance floor.

"You wanna dance?" Darius asked Trouble.

"Sure, why not?" she said, smiling, and walked over to the dance floor.

Dariel couldn't keep his eyes off of Trouble as she and Darius danced. As soon as the song went off, Dariel walked over by the punch bowl and stood by Dante. "I'm still in love with that girl," Dariel said to him.

"Go getta then, nigga."

"Man, that girl will never take me back. After all the shit I put her through, then I turn around and do the same jackass shit," Dariel said.

"Ya nevah know."

Dariel must have drank a cup of courage, because he got up enough nerve and walked over to the dance floor and tapped Darius on his shoulder. "May I?" Dariel said, nodding toward Trouble.

"Fa' sho'," Darius said, stepping to the side, already knowing his dude still had mad love for Trouble.

Dariel didn't know what to say. He really didn't know if he should open his mouth at all, so he just danced to the music.

"You look nice," Trouble said, breaking the awkward silence between them.

"Thanks. And so do you," he replied.

Trouble already knew that she was fly as all get up, so she smiled at Dariel and kept on dancing. "I see you and Jameelah are still hangin' in there."

"It's not what it seems," Dariel said.

"How's Shayne?" Trouble asked.

"She's gettin' big and bad," Dariel said, laughing.

"Are your parents okay?"

"They're fine too. They still ask about you."

"Well, tell them I said hello."

"I sure will."

When the song went off neither one of them wanted to leave the dance floor. "You wanna dance to this song?" Dariel asked.

"Sure."

Jameelah was hotter than a firecracker as she watched Trouble on the dance floor with her man. *I can't believe he's out there dancin' with that bitch*, she thought as she walked over to the dance floor and tapped Dariel on his shoulder.

Dariel grimaced and turned around to see who was fucking up his mood. "What's up?" he said upon seeing Jameelah.

"Why are you out here dancin' with her?" Jameelah huffed.

Trouble shook her head and laughed.

"We ain't doin' nothin' but dancin'. You act like I'm out here fuckin' her! Don't start, Jameelah," Dariel warned.

Jameelah stormed away as fast as she could.

"Look, Dariel, I ain't tryin'a start no shit with you and ya girl, so I'll see you later," Trouble said.

"Later when?" Dariel mustered up enough nerve to ask.

"Later whenever, Dariel," she said, smiling.

"Later like in tonight?" Dariel pressed his luck and asked, hoping he didn't get rejected.

Trouble smiled and shook her head yes.

"Is the number still the same?" Dariel asked anxiously.

Trouble turned around, walked away, and shook her head yes.

Yeah, booooy! Dariel thought.

Jameelah was so upset about Dariel dancing with Trouble she called her mom and left the prom early. Later on that night, Trouble and Dariel went to the hotel room that was intended for him and Jameelah and made love all night long. True to form, Jameelah had continuously blew Dariel's cell phone up until the wee hours of the morning.

Thirty-six

"Are you ready to give your valedictorian speech today?" Dariel asked Trouble over the phone.

"You know it," Trouble said, smiling.

"Okay, baby girl, I'll see you at the graduation," Dariel said, hanging up.

"Man, I hate when he does that!"

Trouble, Jyson, Michaela, and Momma all piled up in Jyson's Envoy and headed to the graduation. Momma had been coming around more often and trying harder to stay clean since Jyson had asked her to come to Atlanta with them. She had even begun putting on a little weight. They pulled up into the crowded parking lot and got out. Trouble walked over to Regina and Ta'liyah and began talking while Jyson, Michaela, and Momma went on in to find themselves some good seats. Before they started handing out diplomas the principal called out Trouble's name. She got up out of her seat and headed toward the stage.

"Let's give a round of applause for our class of 2008 valedictorian," the principal said as Trouble walked up onstage.

Trouble grabbed the microphone and adjusted it. "Hello, family and friends," Trouble started her speech. "Today is the last day of our childhood, tomorrow our adulthood begins. Our lives will be filled with bigger decisions and better choices. We didn't make it this far in life to lose sight of our goals for a better future. I was guided here today by two wonderful people, and before I go on I would like to thank those two people.

"First off, I would like to thank God for guiding me and protecting me. The second person I would like to thank is someone who has been my mother, father, and my best friend all wrapped up into one. That special person is none other than my big brother, Jyson. Thank you, Jyson, for believing in me when I didn't believe in myself. And thank you for staying by my side when everybody else decided to leave me." Tears fell from Jyson's eyes as his sister read the rest of her speech. Her mother cried too, because she knew she had let her beautiful daughter down her entire life. Trouble finished her speech, accepted her diploma, and walked back to her seat with a smile the size of Mt. Rushmore plastered on her face.

"That was a beautiful speech, Trouble," Ms. Carter said, giving Trouble a hug. "There's no doubt in my mind that you are gon' be very successful in life. Good luck, Candria."

"Thank you, Ms. C, for everything." Trouble smiled and walked away to catch up with her family and friends.

"Well, we gotta get goin', Trouble," Michaela said. "We gotta finish gettin' the club set up for y'all's graduation party."

Michaela left for the club while Jyson took Trouble to the car lot so she could pick out her graduation gift.

Michaela watched the caterers as they maneuvered around Club Brittney's blowing up ballons, placing bottles of sparkling grape juice on all the tables, and putting the rest of the decorations up. The place looked nice for Trouble's graduation party.

"Yes, everything's done," Michaela said, sitting her tired and pregnant body down on one of the bar stools.

Ta'liyah and Regina walked in early. "Where's Trouble?" Ta'liyah asked.

"Trouble is with Jyson, pickin' up her new car," Michaela replied.

"The place looks good," Big Mike said, walking from behind the black curtain.

"Thanks," Michaela said.

"Now y'all know, I'm gon' miss out on a lot of money tonight, 'cuz I'm shuttin' down the club and lettin' y'all have this graduation party," Big Mike said, laughing.

"Dang, you must love us if you gon' miss out on yo' money," Ta'liyah said.

"Y'all all right," Big Mike joked.

DJ Danny walked over to his turntable and started getting his music together for the big party tonight.

"Man, you got a lot of music," Regina said.

Danny smiled and kept digging through his large collection without saying a word.

"Sing somethin' for us, Regina," Ta'liyah yelled.

"Can she sing?" Big Mike asked.

"Can she? She can blow," Ta'liyah replied.

"Hook her up with somethin', Danny," Big Mike said, walking over to the mircrophone.

Danny dug through his CDs. "What'll it be?" he asked.

Regina didn't know what to sing. Singing was her specialty so whatever he played she could sing.

"Sing some Alicia Keys," Michaela said.

Regina closed her eyes to gather all the words and waited on Danny to play the insrumental. Regina sang her heart out. She hit every note without missing a beat. Singing was her life. It was her only way to let the world know what she was about. When she finished the song, she opened her eyes and smiled at her small audience.

"You can blow, girl," Michaela stated.

"I told y'all," Ta'liyah boasted.

"You need to be on somebody's record label. You have a beautiful voice. I gotta give Alicia Keys her props, but she ain't got nuttin' on you," Big Mike said.

"Thank you," Regina said, blushing.

"Watch out, world, for the next Whitney Houston," Michaela shouted.

"That's all fine and dandy, but just make sure you leave Bobby Brown at home," DJ Danny said. They all laughed.

Thirty-seven

Big Mike and Woo sat at the bar drinking. "Where yo' brother at?" Shady Sue asked Big Mike. "I don't know where he at. Let me page him." Big Mike pulled out his cell phone.

"Here, give me the number, go'n and talk to Sue and I'll page him. What's his number?" Woo asked. Jyson had changed his number since he last dealt with Woo.

Big Mike rambled off Jyson's pager number. "And put six nine behind the callback number, that means meet me at the club." Big Mike was so caught up in his new stripper, he never paid any attention to Woo writing down Jyson's new pager number.

About an hour later, Jyson walked though the door. "What's up, Jyson?" Big Mike asked, giving his brother a hug. "What's up, Mike? I see you sloppy drunk, big boy." "Naw, I'm feelin' real good though," Big Mike replied. Jyson took a seat.

"What's up, Woo?" "Sup?"

"When y'all plannin' on leavin' for Atlanta?" Big Mike asked.

"Michaela is flyin' out on Wednesday to go take a look at this house one of the Realtors found for us."

"About time yo' ass leavin'. It's been what, 'bout ten years since you been sayin' you leavin'?" Big Mike joked.

"Naw, nigga, but it's been a minute," Jyson said, laughing. "But now that Michaela is pregnant, I wanna change my life and start livin' right for my child," he explained.

"What you gon' do? You gon' get in the game down there or what?" Big Mike asked before taking a sip from his drink.

"Naw, man, I promised my girl. I'm gon' enroll in college and get my shit together. I'm 'bout to marry Micheala," Jyson said.

"Hold off a while before jumpin' the broom. Test the pussy in Atlanta first. 'Cuz they got some bad bitches down there!" Big Mike said, excited.

"I ain't tryin'a get caught up. Don't get me wrong, though, if opportunity knocks, I'm gon' open up the door," Jyson said, laughing.

"I hear ya, baby boy. Here, I got a little goin'-away present for you. I've been meanin' to give it to you, but you've been so tied up in them GED classes I didn't have the chance," Big Mike said, pulling a briefcase from underneath the table and handing it to his little brother.

"What's this?" Jyson asked.

Woo listened and watched closely.

"It's only fifty gees, nigga," Big Mike informed him. "It ain't much, but it's a little somethin' just in case you hit hard times. And you know there's always more where that came from."

"Man, I can't take this money from you," Jyson said.

"Why not?"

" 'Cuz I got money, man."

"It's a gift, nigga. So stop arguin' with me and take the damn money. Matter of fact, put it in a savings account for my niece or nephew."

I'll take it, Woo thought.

"Man, I can't," Jyson said, shaking his head.

"If you don't, my feelins' are gon' be crushed."

"If you say so, thanks, man." Jyson took the briefcase and set it beside him.

A light went off in Woo's head. He needed to get up outta there with the quickness. "I'm out, y'all," Woo said, finishing off his drink and then standing up from the table, exiting the club.

"Man, why you still fuck wit' that police-ass nigga?" Jyson asked Big Mike. "I don't trust him."

"Man, I keep tellin' you that Woo is an all right cat. He 'bout his business," Big Mike responded. "And as long as he don't cross *us*, he's cool."

Jyson threw his hands up in the air. "Whatever you say, man, I still ain't fuckin' wit' him."

"I feel you," Big Mike replied.

"I'm 'bout to bounce. I promised my mom, Trouble, and Michaela that I would take them out to eat," Jyson said, standing up.

"That's cool. Tell them I said hello," Big Mike said.

Jyson grabbed the briefcase in one hand and gave his brother some dap with the other. "Good lookin' out, man. I owe you."

Big Mike sucked his teeth. "Nigga, the only thing you owe me is a drink."

"No problem. Shady Sue, give my brotha a drink."

"You leavin'?"

"Yep. I gotta go," Jyson said.

"You don't wanna stick around and have some fun with me?"

"I'm gon' hafta pass. I gotta go home and pick up my three favorite girls and take them out to dinner. Maybe next time." Jyson winked at Shady Sue and walked out the door, bumping into Woo who stood outside the club puffing on a cigarette. "My bad."

Woo looked down at the briefcase and then back up at Jyson. "Man, let me ask you somethin': was you fuckin' my girl?"

"Who's your girl?" Jyson asked, puzzled. "I done fucked so many hoes, ain't no tellin'."

"Jessica."

"Man, I fucked that hood rat a long time ago. That's old news. I know you ain't tryin'a check me 'bout that ho?"

Woo really couldn't have cared less about Jyson fucking Jessica, he just needed some type of an excuse to have beef. "That's fucked-up, man. How you gon' fuck my baby momma? You wouldn't like it if I fucked Michaela's fine ass, now would you?" Woo said, smirking.

"For one, I don't even think you could handle Michaela. But look, nigga, I ain't about to stand out here and argue with you about no bitch. I'll holla at you when you got somethin' important to talk about." Jyson walked away, leaving Woo feeling insulted.

I'ma get that bitch-ass nigga, Woo thought to himself. *I'm gon' rob him and then beat the shit outta him.* Woo pulled out his cell phone and called his cousin Kyron in Detroit.

"Kyron, this Woo," he said into the phone receiver.

"What's up, nigga?" Kyron asked.

"I got another lick for us to hit," Woo said.

"Look, man, I hope you don't need another lawn-care truck, 'cuz the judge is givin' up mad time for carjackin' and I ain't tryin'a go back to prison," Kyron said.

"Naw, I'm cool on the truck," Woo said.

"Well, how good is the lick?"

"Real good. I'm talkin' at least fifty gees, fa' sho'."

"Is it gon' be easy like the last one? You know hittin' that nigga Big Mike was like taking candy from a baby," Kyron said, laughing.

"Yeah, it was. But . . . um, this lick might be just a little bit harder, but you know I'll come up with some type of plan."

"Well, count me in. Just let me know what's up and hit me back when you get it all together," Kyron said.

"Bet." Woo hung up the phone with a smile on his face.

I'm like the boogeyman, I'm comin' to get you, Jyson, he thought and busted out laughing.

"How come you didn't tell me you and Jyson was fuckin'?" Woo said to Jessica as he sniffed a line of powder off the mirror that lay on the coffee table.

"I didn't know I needed your permission to sleep with somebody other than you. Do you call me and ask me if you're allowed to fuck other girls? And plus, that shit was a long-ass time ago," Jessica said, sniffing a line of the powder.

"Why you choose that nigga of all people?" Woo asked, sniffing another line.

"What's wrong wit' Jyson? He got money, he's cute, and he got a big old dick," she said, rubbing her nose.

"Fuck that nigga!" Woo became angry. "I'ma do that nigga in. I saw Big Mike give that nigga a briefcase with I know at least fifty grand in it, and the dumb-ass nigga tried to give it back to him. So I know that nigga is paid in full," Woo said.

"I bet you he is paid. He don't got no kids. He lives in that tiny apartment and he don't got no family that can beg from him. Only person he's takin' care of is Michaela," Jessica said.

"You right. That nigga ain't got no family to support so I'm gon' get some of his money, if not all. You game?" Woo asked.

Jessica stood up from her knees. "Nigga, please. You will never get another chance to play me like you did when you robbed Big Mike."

"I'm sorry." Woo stood up behind her and kissed the back of her neck. "I promise we'll split it fifty-fifty this time."

"I don't know, Woo. I can't trust you."

"Come on, baby, I'ma do right. I'll bring the money right over to you so we can split it."

Jessica thought as Woo seduced her.

"So what's it gon' be?" he asked, lifting up her shirt and sucking on her nipple.

"I'm cool. I ain't gettin' in it. I'm done playin' niggas like that. All that shit is gon' come back on us," Jessica said. "I still feel bad about settin' up Big Mike."

Woo stopped sucking on Jessica's nipple. "Fuck you then, bitch!" Woo screamed angrily. He shoved her on the couch and began punching her in the face.

"Get the fuck off me, Woo!" Jessica screamed at the top of her lungs. Woo wrapped his large hands around her neck and choked her until she nearly passed out.

"I don't need your help, bitch. I'ma get the money myself, and don't ask me for shit." Woo let Jessica's neck go, grabbed the rest of the powder off the table, and walked out the door, slamming it behind him. Jessica used to be Woo's right-hand girl back in the day. They had set up dope boys all over the map and now she wanted to turn her back on him. Woo jumped in his car and pulled out his cell phone and called Kyron.

"Hey, Ky, I'm still workin' on it," Woo said into the phone receiver.

"Like I said, let me know. And don't call me back until you're ready for me to come to Mansfield," Kyron said, hanging up the phone.

Jyson and Big Mike had the U-Haul filled with all of Michaela's belongings from her apartment. He had left all the of his things in the house for his Aunt Rachel to use since he was going to be renting the house out to her. Jyson planned on furnishing their new house with all new furniture and appliances. He wanted to leave all his old things behind and start over fresh because he didn't want anything to remind him of his past.

"I'm sure gon' miss this house," Jyson said, looking around. "We've had a lot of good memories here."

"And bad," Trouble added.

"I can't believe I'm finally leavin' Mansfield."

"I'm happy for you," Trouble said. "I can't hardly wait until school start in August so I can get up outta Mansfield myself."

"You need to come on and go to Atlanta with us and go to school down there," Jyson said wishfully.

"No thanks. I'm gon' stay right here with Auntie Rachel until it's time for me to leave for Washington," Trouble said. "But you know I'll be in Atlanta every chance I get."

"I already know," Jyson said, smiling.

"I'm so glad that Mommma decided to go with y'all."

"Yeah, me too. It didn't take much for her to agree. Trouble, whether you know it or not, Momma is tired of them streets," Jyson said. "And goin' to a big city will give her the opportunity to do something different."

"I'm happy for her," Trouble said, smiling.

Jyson looked at his Movado watch. "Big Mike better come on so we can go'n and hit the highway."

"There he is right there," Trouble said, pointing.

When Big Mike pulled up he got out of his truck and walked over to Trouble and Jyson. "You ready to roll?" he asked.

"I'm as ready as I'm gon' get," Jyson replied.

"Let's go, then." Big Mike was going to start out with the driving so he got into the U-Haul to adjust the seat and the mirrors.

"Take care of Momma and Michaela while I'm gone," Jyson said, giving his sister a hug.

"You know I will," Trouble said, smiling. Trouble walked up on the porch and watched as Jyson and Big Mike pulled away.

Jyson and Big Mike hit the highway going as fast as the U-Haul would let them. Once they got to Georgia, their plan was to get everything set up in the house so when Michaela and Momma came down, they wouldn't have to lift a finger. Since the ladies did a lot of work in Michaela's apartment, packing and cleaning up, Jyson decided that he would repay them with a full week of pampering. He had rented them a room at the Radisson Hotel where they would be able to swim, enjoy the Jacuzzi, and get a massage whenever they wanted one, and they were loving every minute of it. He also promised his little sister that when he returned home, he would take his three favorite ladies out to a restaurant of their choice.

"Momma, where you goin'?" Trouble woke up and asked.

"Nowhere, baby. I was just goin' to sit by the pool. You wanna come?" she answered.

"Sure," Trouble said, smiling, as she climbed out of bed and followed her mother to the hotel's outside pool.

Trouble and her mom sat on the edge of the pool with their feet in the water.

"Momma, do you ever get the urge to start smokin' again?" Trouble asked as she moved her feet back and forth in the water, watching the tiny waves.

"Yeah, I do, baby, all the time. I get the urge all the time to get back out in the streets and find the nearest crack house."

Trouble was happy with her mother's honesty. "Well, how come you don't go, Momma?"

Momma took a deep breath. "Because, baby, do you remember the speech you made on your graduation day?"

Trouble shook her head. "Yeah, what about it?"

"It touched my heart, but it made me sad at the same time."

"Why, Momma?" Trouble gave her mother a concerned look.

"Because, me and ya daddy was supposed to be there for you to keep you on the right track in life, but instead we left it up to ya brother. And it wasn't fair to him or you." Tears streamed down Momma's face and fell onto her robe.

"But Jyson didn't care, Momma." Tears began to form in Trouble's eyes also.

"Have you ever asked him if he cared, Trouble? I know it had to be hard on him. Havin' to raise his little sister on his own since he was ten or eleven years old. He was still a kid himself," Momma cried.

"I didn't have to ask him, Ma. If he would have cared about takin' care of me, he wouldn't have made sure I had everything I needed. He could have left me home alone or easily made me go stay with somebody else, but he didn't. Momma, my big brother got out in them streets and sold drugs to keep me and him together, and I love and respect him for that, 'cuz he didn't have to," Trouble cried.

"I love and respect the both of y'all." Momma hugged Trouble, and for the first time in a long time, Trouble hugged her back and it felt good.

"Am I interruptin' somethin'?" Michaela asked, walking toward them.

"Naw, come on, big momma," Trouble said, laughing, and helped her down. "We ain't supposed to be out here anyway, 'cuz the pool is closed." They all sat around the pool laughing and talking until the wee hours of the morning.

Thirty-eight

Jyson and Big Mike took their sweet time setting up the new house. "This is home," Jyson said, looking around his new house. "Yeah, this is it, baby boy. And it's one helluva home," Big Mike added.

"The contractor is supposed to be comin' in the mornin' to dig the hole for the pool. I hope they don't take all day, 'cuz I'm ready to get back to Mansfield to see my babies."

"What babies?" Big Mike asked.

"Trouble, Michaela, and my momma," Jyson laughed.

"Boy, you somethin' else," Big Mike laughed.

When Jyson and Big Mike returned from Atlanta, Jyson handed his sister a plane ticket.

"What is this, Jyson?" Trouble asked.

"It's a first-class ticket," he answered.

"For what?"

"Open it up and see."

Trouble opened it up and smiled. Jyson was sending her on an all-expense-paid trip to Washington so she could tour Howard University. "Thank you, Jyson," Trouble said, hugging her brother.

"No problem. I'm proud of you, sis."

"I'm proud of you too," Trouble said as she embraced her brother.

Trouble enjoyed the entire week she had spent in Washington. She visited the campus and she had taken some of the savings that her grandfather left her and went on a straight shopping spree. She had so many clothes, she had to buy three extra suitcases to put them in. Trouble had to stay dressed to impress; especially now that she would be going to college, she had to step her dress game up.

"Trouble will be home today," Jyson said as he rubbed Michaela's aching back.

"I know she enjoyed herself. All them fine college boys," Michaela said.

"Is that what you gon' be down in Atlanta lookin' for, a fine college boy?" Jyson asked.

"For what? I already got a fine college boy," she said, smiling.

"You better had said that." Jyson kissed his woman on the lips.

"Stop that, y'all. That's how y'all got that baby," Momma said, laughing, as she watched Jyson and Michaela cuddle on the couch.

Trouble arrived home the day before Regina and Ta'liyah were set to leave for California.

"This is our last time together for a long time," Ta'liyah cried.

"I know, let's make a toast," Regina said to Trouble and Ta'liyah, holding up her glass of white Zinfandel.

"To friendship," they all said.

"I'm really gon' miss y'all," Trouble said as tears rolled down her cheeks.

"I'm gon' miss you too," Regina said, wiping tears away as well.

"I'm gon' be comin' to California to see y'all when I'm not down in Atlanta visitin' my brother. Now I want y'all to find me a good-lookin' man."

"We sure will," Regina said, smiling.

"Have you talked to Dariel?" Ta'liyah asked.

"Nope. Not since that night we stayed together. I wanted to call him, but I decided against it. I'm not tryin'a be a home wrecker," Trouble stated.

"Fuck that! Dariel is yo' man and always will be," Ta'liyah said.

"Yeah," Regina added.

Trouble smiled and shook her head. "Let's go before y'all miss the plane."

Trouble was happy that her two best friends were also leaving Mansfield. Ta'liyah had decided to move to California with her aunt for a change of scenery and she invited Regina to go along with her so she could try to pursue her singing career. Ta'liyah made Regina promise that if she did get a contract, she would have to make her the manager, and Regina happily agreed. Trouble hugged her girls and sat in the airport watching them board the plane. She watched as their plane took off before hurrying home to get dressed for dinner. Jyson was taking his girls out to celebrate them all leaving Mansfield.

"What's up, Kyron? It's on tonight," Woo said into the phone receiver.

"Cool. I'm 'bout to hit the highway right now. Let's get that dough."

"It's on," Woo said, hanging up the phone and then snorting a half ounce of powder to calm his nerves.

"Trouble, I'm leavin' in three days. I want you to keep an eye on my safe until I come back to get it," Jyson said.

"I sure will. How much money you got in there?" Trouble asked.

"You still nosy as hell," Jyson laughed. "I'm gon' give you the combination. And if anything should happen to me while I'm in Atlanta, I want you to give Michaela half of everything and give Momma a little bit too."

"Boy, ain't nothin' gon' happen to you in Georgia."

"You never know, sis."

"Stop talkin' like that and let's go, I'm hungry," Trouble said.

"All right. Go see if Momma and Michaela are ready and I'll be right back." Jyson ran out to his truck and took his 9 mm from under the driver's seat. He took it into the house and put it in his safe. *I can't be ridin' around with this while I got my girls in the truck with me,* he thought to himself.

Jyson pulled up in the crowded parking lot of Red Lobster. He got out of the truck and opened up the door for his ladies. Once they were seated, they all sat around and reminisced as they sipped on virgin daiquiris.

"I'm so proud of my children," Momma said, smiling.

"Thank you, Momma," Jyson and Trouble said, smiling.

"In a few years I'm gon' have a dentist, a doctor, and a probation officer," Momma said.

"That's right, Momma. When you get sick, Michaela can hook you up with some health care, and as you get older and start losin' the rest of yo' teeth, I can hook you up with some partials, and when you get into trouble, Jyson can be your probation officer," Trouble said.

They all sat around and laughed. Jyson looked into Michaela's sparkling eyes and pulled a box out of his pocket.

"Oh no, Jyson," Momma said with tears in her eyes.

Tears rolled down Michaela's cheeks as Jyson opened up the little black box, revealing the two-karat diamond engagement ring.

"Michaela, will you marry me?" he asked her.

"Yes, yes, I will marry you," she cried.

Tears rolled down Trouble's cheeks as Michaela cried tears of joy. She started imagining how she would react if it were Dariel asking her to marry him. She shook the thought out of her head and gave her brother a hug. They celebrated the engagement before returning home to get some rest.

Later that night Trouble sat on the couch while everyone else slept, staring at the wall.

"What chu' still doin' up?" Jyson asked, as he walked into the living room and took a seat next to his sister.

"I can't sleep," she replied.

"Why not?" he asked, laying his cell phone and car keys on top of the table.

"I got a lot on my mind, that's why," she sighed, heavily.

"Dariel?"

"How did you know?" she asked.

"Sis, I'ma tell you like this, if you love him, go get him before it's too late. There's no reason for you to be sittin' around here miserable and there's no reason for him to be in a relationship that's makin' him miserable as well," Jyson said.

"I know, but it's not that easy."

"Y'all need to work this shit out, Trouble, and get it together, 'cuz evidently you really love this nigga, 'cuz it's been a year and you haven't moved on yet."

"You think it's a chance me and him can work this out?"

"I know y'all can, sis. Y'all just got to let the past stay in the past and move the fuck on."

Trouble smiled at her brother. "Thank you, Jyson."

"Anytime, sis. That's what I'm here for. Now try to get some sleep."

"I will and thanks again."

"No problem. I love you, Trouble."

"I love you too, Jyson."

"I love you more."

"Get outta here."

Jyson laughed as his pager went off. He pulled it from his pants pocket and looked at the number.

"Who's pagin' you this late?" Trouble asked.

"Damn, you nosy, girl."

"You know it."

"Look, I'll be back. Big Mike just paged me again and he wants me to come down to the club," Jyson said, putting his pager back into his pocket.

"This late? It's three o'clock in the mornin'," Trouble said.

"Big Mike is probably laid up in the club with one of his strippers and he need me to take him home so Sherry can think he's been with me," Jyson said, laughing, as he picked his car keys up off the table.

"You right about that," she laughed too.

"All right, I'll see you when I get back. And if my wife wakes up, tell her I love her and that I went to go see about Big Mike."

"I sure will."

"Oh, before I forget, the combination to my safe is your birthday," Jyson said.

"Shoot, if I would have known that, I would have been hittin' the safe a long time ago."

Jyson shook his head and laughed at his sister as he walked out the door. He got in his truck and turned the radio to a smooth jazz station before pulling off. Once he arrived at the club he didn't see a car in sight.

"Damn, I don't even see Big Mike's truck," he said.

"Maybe he parked in the back," he said to himself as he pulled around the back of the building. "He ain't back here either. Let me call this nigga." Jyson put his truck in park and searched for his cell phone. "Damn, I left it on the coffee table."

Jyson put the truck back into drive and attempted to back out, but he was blocked off by a black Intrepid, so he pulled forward and a blue minivan blocked him in. "What the fuck? Blue minivan and black Intrepid, these are the same niggas that's been robbin' all the soldiers." Jyson reached up under his seat to get his nine, but remembered that he took it out earlier and put it in his safe. "Shit!"

Two masked men jumped out, one from each car, and ran up to Jyson's truck. One had a .38 pointed at Jyson's head as he screamed, "Get out the fuckin' truck, nigga!" Jyson did what he was told.

The second guy searched all of Jyson's pockets and his truck while the first gunman kept his gun pushed tightly into Jyson's temple.

"Where the money at?" the first gunman screamed as he held onto a sawed-off shotgun.

"I don't got no money. You can take my truck, my jewelry, and whatever else, just don't kill me. Man, I gotta baby on the way," Jyson pleaded with the two masked men.

"Shut the fuck up, nigga, and take us to the safe," the second masked man yelled.

"I don't have no safe," Jyson assured them.

"Stop lyin', bitch-ass nigga, before I blow yo' fuckin' head off!" the first gunman yelled.

"I ain't lyin', man," Jyson replied, damn near in tears. The thought of not being around for his firstborn and his sister sent chills down his spine as he stood there begging for his life.

The second gunman got mad and hit Jyson in the head with the butt of the sawed-off shotgun, knocking him to the ground. Jyson felt the top of his head as the blood gushed down his face. All he could keep thinking about was Trouble, Michaela, and his unborn son.

"Come on, man, let's go. He said he ain't got no money," the first gunman yelled.

"Naw, fuck that! I know this nigga got some money," the second gunman said to his partner. He then turned his attention back to Jyson. "I ain't gon' ask you no more, where's the fuckin' money?" he yelled and began stomping Jyson in the face.

Jyson was dazed. His eyes started rolling in the back of his head. He struggled to get off the ground but was unsuccessful.

"Come on, Woo, that's enough," the first gunman yelled, looking around to see if anyone was watching.

"Woo, why man?" Jyson moaned in pain. "I'ma get you nigga."

"Fuck you, bitch! And get this," Woo screamed and shot Jyson once in the heart.

"Man, what the fuck you do that for?" Kyron said, panicking.

"Fuck him, nigga. He was lyin'. I know that bitch had some money," Woo said, pacing back and forth.

"Why you kill him, man? You didn't hafta kill the nigga," Kyron said. "I can't be goin' to prison for murder."

"He knew who I was, nigga! You shouldn't have called my damn name," Woo screamed.

"What we gon' do?" Kyron asked.

"Leave his ass," Woo said as he jumped in the black Intrepid and sped off.

Thirty-nine

"Dang, Jyson, why you beatin' on the door like you the police?" Trouble yelled. "You need to start makin' sure you got your key." She opened up the door to find two police officers standing there with stern looks on their faces.

"May I help you, Officers?" Trouble asked nervously.

Michaela got up from the couch and walked over to the door and stood next to her soon-to-be sister-in-law.

"May we come in?" the tall officer asked.

"For what?" Trouble asked.

"Please, ma'am, this is important," the short, fat officer said.

"Yeah, come in, what's wrong?" Trouble asked, stepping aside for them to enter.

"Don't tell me that Jyson is in jail again?" Michaela smiled to hide her nervousness.

The tall officer looked down at his short, fat partner.

"Ma'am, could you two please have a seat?"

"What's goin' on?" Auntie Rachel asked, coming out of the kitchen with Momma on her heels.

"We need for all of y'all to sit down," the tall officer replied.

They all did what they were asked, everyone except for Trouble. She didn't like the feeling these two officers were giving her.

The short, fat officer cleared his throat. "I'm afraid there has been an accident. Is your son Jyson Lewis?"

"An accident?" Trouble asked, almost near tears.

"Yes, he is my son. What happened to him?" Momma asked frantically.

"We found Jyson's body in an alley behind Club Brittney's," the officer stated.

"Oh, noooo! Is he okay?" Michaela jumped up and screamed.

"I'm sorry, ma'am, but he's dead," the tall officer replied. "We need someone to come to the hospital to identify the body, please."

"Noooo, not my brother!" Trouble screamed.

"How do you know it was him?" Michaela asked, hoping it was a case of mistaken idenity.

"We didn't find any ID on him so we ran the license plates on the truck and it came back in his name," the short officer answered.

Michaela's body went limp and she hit the floor and held her stomach.

"Get an ambulance," the tall officer yelled.

Trouble watched as everyone hovered over Michaela's body. She wanted to go over and help, but her feet wouldn't let her leave the spot she was in. Trouble stood motionless. She couldn't think straight, all she could do was take a seat on the couch, pick up a pillow, and put it up to her face and scream.

"Ma'am, are you okay?" the tall officer asked, walking over to Trouble.

"I need to call someone." Trouble's mind went blank as she stood up and paced the living room floor. "I don't know who to call. I don't know anyone," she said as her mind played tricks on her.

"Who would you like for me to call, ma'am?" the officer asked.

"I don't know. Call Ta'liyah, no, call my daddy, no, never mind, call Dariel." Once Trouble remembered his phone number, she rambled it off to the officer. "Tell him to meet me at the hospital."

"Hello? Is this Dariel?" the officer asked.

"This is he. Who dis?" Dariel asked in a sleepy voice.

"This is Officer Thompson, I'm with the MPD. This young lady wants you to meet her at the hospital."

"What young lady?" Dariel said, panicking.

"What's your name, ma'am?" the officer asked Trouble.

"My name? Um, it's Trouble—I mean Candria," Trouble answered.

"Her name is Candria," the officer told Dariel.

"What's wrong wit' her? Is she okay?" Dariel asked nervously.

"Yeah, she's fine, sir, but I'm afraid her brother isn't."

"What's wrong wit' him?"

"He was found dead behind Club Brittney's," the officer explained.

"Ahhh naw," Dariel said, jumping up.

"Damn, you didn't have to push me off of you," Jameelah huffed.

"I gotta go. Tell her that I'll meet her at the hospital in ten minutes." Dariel scrambled around the room for his clothes.

"Where you goin'?" Jameelah demanded, standing up and blocking the doorway.

"Trouble needs me," he said, fighting back tears.

"Trouble needs you? Huh? Well, me and Shayne need you too. And how you gon' just jump out of bed with me and run to that bitch?" Jameelah asked.

"Look, if you don't get the fuck out of my face with that bullshit, I'm gon' do somethin' to you," Dariel said, pushing Jameelah out of his way.

"Fuck you, chump. Go'n and be with that bitch then," Jameelah yelled as Dariel walked down the stairs and out the door.

Trouble stood outside the hospital waiting for Dariel while the rest of her family was upstairs tending to Michaela. Trouble paced back and forth as the Escalade pulled up. A part of her wanted to smile because she knew that even though he was still mad at her about Woo, he would never let her down when she needed him. Trouble watched as Dariel jumped out of the truck and ran over to her. He wrapped his strong arms around her body and she broke down into tears. Even though the time was not right, it still felt good being held by him. He still made her feel safe and secure and she missed that feeling. She thanked God silently as Dariel comforted her. Tears rolled down Dariel's eyes on top of Trouble's head as she cried an unfamiliar cry. A cry of hurt, pain, and agony all mixed up into one.

"You can't park there, sir," the security guard said as he walked toward them.

"Okay," Dariel said, wiping the tears away. He kissed Trouble on the forehead before going to park his truck. He rushed back over to her side and listened as she held a phone conversation with Ta'liyah.

"It's gon' be okay, baby girl," Dariel said when Trouble got off the phone. Dariel wrapped his arms around Trouble again and it felt even better than before. He missed everything about her. Her laugh, her smile, the way she smelled. It had been a very difficult year living without her in his life. Every time he had seen her at school, he wanted to rush over to her and grab her and tell her how much he missed her and how bad he wanted her back, but he knew that once he fucked up with a girl like Trouble, there was no getting her back. Jameelah nor any girl could compare to his baby girl in any shape, form, or fashion.

"I'm ready to go in," Trouble said, wiping away her tears.

"Let's go," Dariel said, grabbing her by the hand and leading her into the hospital.

Dariel and Trouble walked over to the elevator, and once they reached the second floor, they walked over to the nurse's station and asked to be directed to Jyson's body.

"Who are you?" an officer interrupted.

"I'm his sister and this is his brother," Trouble replied.

"I'm sorry about your loss, and as soon as we find out something, we will be getting in touch with the family. We will be keeping the pager and his truck for evidence," the officer said.

Trouble responded with a shake of her head as one of the nurses walked from behind the counter and pointed toward Jyson's room. Trouble and Dariel followed behind her as she led the way.

They walked into Jyson's room. The nurse walked over to Jyson's body and pulled the white sheet from over his head. "He looks 'sleep," Trouble said as she cried and laughed at the same time. "My brother still looks good," she said as she rubbed her hand through his soft, curly hair. "Why did they take you away from me?" Trouble spoke to Jyson. "You were all I had. I don't know what I'm gon' do without you. I can't make it in this world alone. Please Jyson, I need you," Trouble cried. Dariel walked up behind Trouble and tried to hug her. "Get off me!" she screamed. "Don't you see my everything layin' here dead? What am I gon' do, Dariel?" she asked rhetorically. "I need him here with me. How could you do me like this, Jyson? You promised that you would never leave me!

Why?" Trouble cried so hard that a couple of the other nurses and the officer came running into the room.

Dariel cried as he watched Trouble stand over her brother and unfold. She was pouring her heart out to Jyson and Dariel wanted to wrap his arms around her and rock her pain away like he used to.

Big Mike jumped out the bed as someone beat on the door like the police. "Who is it?" he yelled nervously.

"It's me, Jessica. Let me in please," she screamed hysterically.

Sherry came running in the living room past her husband and opened up the door for her sister. "What's wrong, Jessica?" Sherry said, panicking.

"Jyson's dead!" she screamed.

"What the fuck?" Big Mike said, grimacing.

"Where did you hear that from, Jessica?" Sherry asked.

"I got a call from Tamika, she works at the hospital. She called and said they found him behind Club Brittney's shot to death." Just as Jessica finished with what she heard, Big Mike's cell phone rang.

"Hello?" he answered quickly.

"Mike, this is Trouble," she wailed.

"What happened, li'l sis? Tell me what happened to my muthafuckin' brotha?" Tears fell down from Big Mike's eyes.

"All I know is that he was found behind your club dead," Trouble cried.

"Ahhh naw, did they have any witnesses?" Big Mike said, sobbing.

"They don't have no suspects or no witnesses."

"Where you at?" Big Mike asked.

"I'm at the hospital. Momma and the rest of the family is up here too."

"Where's Michaela?" Big Mike asked.

"She's up here too. She fainted and fell on her stomach," Trouble answered.

"I'm on my way up there," Big Mike said, hanging up the phone.

When Big Mike and Sherry arrived at the hospital, he walked over to Trouble and hugged her tight. "Where is he?" Big Mike asked.

Trouble pointed to his room. Big Mike took a deep breath before walking into Jyson's room. He walked over to the bed and touched his arm. He looked as if he were asleep. Tears rolled down Big Mike's face, one after the other.

"Man, this wasn't supposed to happen," Big Mike cried to Jyson. "We was supposed to sit on yo' front porch and drink shots of Hennessy together until we both were old and gray. You were supposed to be my probation officer. But somebody took that away from me. I promise, nigga, that whoever took you from me is gon' pay dearly, that's on my life."

Denise and a police officer walked in as Big Mike was talking to Jyson.

"Who are you?" the officer asked.

"Who are you?" Big Mike asked him back as he wiped away his tears, only to have more follow.

The officer had his gun holster ready when he asked Big Mike again, "Who are you?"

"This is my other son," Momma shouted as tears ran down her cheeks.

"Oh, I just needed to make sure," the officer said, putting his gun back into the holster.

"Do y'all know who done this?" Big Mike asked, pointing down at Jyson.

"Not yet, son," he replied.

"I bet if my brotha was white, y'all would have all kinds of leads to his murder," Big Mike retorted.

"Listen here, son, it ain't no black-and-white thing with me. Whoever committed the murder planned it out to a T. We'll get 'em, though. We always get our bad guys," the officer said.

"Yeah, whatever," Big Mike said.

"Trust me, son, we're on the job," the officer tried to assure Big Mike, but he wasn't having it.

"For one, quit callin' me *son*. Do I look like the little boy that sits at your dinner table at night? And for two, I hope y'all catch the muthafucka before I do."

"You better watch what you say, son."

"You heard what I said." Big Mike was furious. He walked out of Jyson's room and took a seat in the lobby with the rest of the family and cried like a newborn baby.

Denise walked out into the lobby and wrapped her small arms around Big Mike's husky body. Sherry stood back and watched as her musclar husband sobbed. She wanted to reach out to him and help him, but she didn't know how. Of all the years they'd been together, she had never once seen her husband shed a tear.

"How's Michaela, Ma?" Big Mike asked through tears.

"She's asleep. To tell you the truth, I really don't think she realizes what's really goin' on. Before she fell asleep, she kept on askin' me to go out in the hallway to get Jyson for her. I didn't have the heart to tell her that he was gone," Momma cried.

"Don't tell her. She'll find out soon enough," Big Mike stated.

"Are you okay, Ma?" Trouble walked over to her mother and asked.

Momma shook her head yes. She needed to get high real bad to calm her nerves, but she knew that she couldn't walk out on her daughter at a time like this. She sat in the chair and watched her beautiful daughter as she stood around reminiscing with the family and wondered how Jyson's death was going to affect her. She knew right then and there that she had to be strong and stay strong on the strength of her only child and grandchild.

"How you holdin' up, Trouble?" Loretta had the audacity to ask.

Trouble shot her a dirty look. "I don't even know why you're up here. You didn't give a fuck about my brotha," Trouble shouted.

Big Mike got out of his chair and walked over to Trouble. "This ain't the time, sis," he said, wrapping his arms around her, pulling her away.

"How dare you say that?" Loretta shouted.

"Loretta, please," Trouble's father said. "This is not the place for this."

Trouble wanted to slap the shit out of Loretta, but she knew that Big Mike wasn't going to let her go until Loretta was out of her sight. She contined talking to some of the other members in her family before they all went back to Aunt Rachel's house to make the funeral arrangements.

Forty

When Trouble and her family arrived at the church there was barely enough room to pull the stretch Hummer limos up in front of the church. There were cars and people everywhere. You would have thought that you were pulling up at a Janet Jackson concert the way all the people stood in line trying to get into the church. Trouble noticed a lot of women crying and the funeral hadn't even started. A couple of them were his ex-girlfriends. Trouble didn't know her brother had so many friends. But she knew that everyone wasn't here to pay their last respects but to see if her brother was really dead. Once inside the church, Trouble and her family were escorted to the front to be seated. Trouble listened as the preacher preached Jyson's eulogy. Tears would not stop falling from her eyes. Rev. Larson called Trouble up to the front of the church. She wiped away her tears and walked up to the microphone.

"I would like to take the time to read a poem I wrote for my brother," Trouble said, looking out at all the people that attended the funeral. She cleared her throat and wiped the tears away from her eyes. "My poem is called 'Jyson.'"

> *I won't get mad because this earth Jyson has left behind. I know I will see him again, it's just a matter of time. The love I have for Jyson will never cease. I'm just satisfied that his soul is now at peace. There's no more suffering and no more pain. There's no more cloudy days and no more rain. Jyson held on to God's unchanging hand. And he led my dear brother into the Promised Land. I'm here crying on the inside and don't have him here to stop me, But my heart is at ease, because I know he's up there with Poppy. All I ask of you is that you wait for me by the gate. I promise to be on time because to see you I can't wait. I'll never forget him and I'll always remember the stories that we shared. I'll hold him close in my heart because for me he always cared. I'll never forget that he was so strong and bold. The love I have for my big brother I will always hold. Rest now, Jyson, you have fought the battle long enough. And when days get long and times get rough, I will think of you to see me through, but nothing can take the place of me being there with you.*

"I love you, Jyson," Trouble cried. There was not one dry eye in church after Trouble finished reading her poem. Trouble could hear Loretta shouting for God to take her and bring Jyson back. *I wish it was you instead of him,* she thought as Loretta performed for the family.

The preacher motioned for Regina to come up and sing one of Jyson's favorite church songs, "His Eye is on the Sparrow." Regina closed her eyes and sang from the heart. She had Jyson's family and friends standing on their feet as she poured out her heart and soul to Trouble through song. Regina touched a lot of people's lives with her voice in that church; she even had some people wanting to get saved after she sung.

Trouble broke down as she watched Michaela rock back and forth. She screamed Jyson's name over and over while holding her round belly. Big Mike wrapped his arms around Michaela's shoulders and they cried together. Trouble couldn't take it any longer, she had to leave. She couldn't take looking at her brother laying in that pearl-white casket with hundreds of white and peach roses surrounding him. She stood up and headed toward the back of the church. Her father touched her hand as she walked past him. She quickly snatched it away and ran into the church's hallway and took a seat on the bench.

"Trouble, are you all right?" Dariel came out in the hall and asked.

"I'm fine. I just had to come out here to get some fresh air, that's all," she replied.

"There you are. I wondered where you disappeared to," Jameelah said, walking into the hall.

Trouble was disgusted by the sight of Jameelah.

"If you need anything, don't hesitate to call me," Dariel said. Jameelah shot Dariel an evil look.

"Thanks." Trouble forced a smile on her face and walked back into the church.

Dariel came over every day and waited on Trouble hand and foot. He did everything he possibly could for her and she appreciated every minute of it.

"Dariel, I hope you're not comin' over here 'cuz you feel sorry for me," Trouble said.

"Trouble, I'm comin' over here because I want to and because I miss havin' you in my life."

"So what are you sayin', Dariel?"

"I'm sayin' that I want you back in my life."

"How can that be possible when you're still with Jameelah?"

Dariel got down on his knees and looked Trouble in the eyes. "Trouble, I don't wanna be with Jameelah, I want you. I still love you. I'm still in love with you. I can't shake these feelings. I tried time and time again, but I can't."

"I don't know what to say, Dariel."

"Just say you still love me too, and you want to be with me as much as I want to be with you."

"You took the words right outta my mouth," Trouble said, smiling happily.

Trouble lay in her bed with Dariel by her side. She tossed and turned all night. *Why can't I sleep?* she thought. Trouble then eased out of bed and went into the living room and picked up the phone and dialed Big Mike's number.

"Hello?" Big Mike asked, still half asleep.

"Did I wake you?"

"Naw, I was just layin' here," Big Mike lied. "What's the matter, Trouble? Are you okay?" he asked.

Trouble took a deep breath before speaking. "I just wanted to hear your voice, that's all," she said.

Tears instantly formed in Big Mike's eyes. He knew now that Jyson was gone, he would have to step up and be the big brother Trouble was used to having around. "Do you need me to come over so we can talk?"

"Naw. I'll be okay."

"Are you sure?"

"Yeah, I'm sure. Are you still comin' over in the mornin' to take Momma and Michaela to Georgia?"

"Yeah, I'll be over there bright and early," Big Mike replied.

"Okay, we'll talk then. Good night."

"Good night," Big Mike said.

Trouble walked back into her room and walked over to her dresser and picked up the picture of her and Jyson on her graduation day. She hugged the picture and imagined it was Jyson she held in her arms. Tears ran down her cheeks, landing on her nightgown. She took a deep breath, wiped away her tears, and climbed back into bed. She wrapped Dariel's limp arm around her waist before drifting off to sleep.

The next morning Trouble got up bright and early and waited for Big Mike to arrive.

"Good mornin', Momma," Trouble said as she entered the kitchen.

"Mornin', suga," Momma said, smiling, as she stood at the stove cooking breakfast.

"Mom, do you remember the time Jyson got up early one morning on Mother's Day and wanted to surprise you by cooking you breakfast, but the only thing he ended up cooking was the kitchen?" Trouble said, laughing.

Momma smiled while tears ran down her face. "Yep, that boy set the whole kitchen on fire. He meant well, like always. That's one reason me and ya daddy didn't punish him."

"Momma, I'm gon' miss y'all," she said, walking over to her mother and giving her a hug.

"I'm gon' miss you too, baby girl."

Trouble heard a loud knock on the front door. "That has to be Big Mike," she said as she went to answer the door.

"What's up, li'l sis? You all right?" Big Mike asked when Trouble opened the door.

"I'm maintainin'," Trouble replied.

"You about to go off to college in about two weeks, ain't you?"

"That's what I wanted to talk to you about last night when I called. I decided I wasn't goin' to college," she said.

"What do you mean, Trouble? You have to go to college. Girl, are you outta yo' mind?"

"I'ma go, but not until January or sometime later."

"Trouble, why?"

"I got somethin' to do first," she said.

"What could be more important than goin' to college? You know Jyson would be real upset if he knew you weren't goin' to college," Big Mike said.

"Mike, I have somethin' else I want to tell you."

"Don't tell me you're pregnant," Big Mike said, frowning.

"No, I'm not pregnant."

"Hey, Mike," Michaela said, walking into the living room.

"Look, we'll talk when you get back from Georgia," Trouble said, walking back into the kitchen.

Two weeks had passed and Trouble didn't know what to do with herself. Jyson was dead, Ta'liyah and Regina were back in California, and Dariel was on an airplane to North Carolina to start his freshman year of college. He offered to stay in Mansfield with her, but she insisted that he go on with his life because she didn't want to hold him back from getting an education. Trouble stayed up all night crying. Some days she didn't know whether she was coming or going. Suicide had even crossed her mind a few times. She couldn't take it anymore so she picked up the phone and called Big Mike.

"Hello?" he answered.

"Mike?" Trouble cried.

"What's the matter, li'l sis?" he said, panicking.

"Mike, I can't eat or sleep. All I do is sit up in my room and cry."

"Trouble, you gotta get out and do somethin'," Big Mike suggested.

"Do what? Jyson is gone, Ta'liyah gone, and Dariel is gone, so what am I gon' do?" Trouble asked desperately.

Mike didn't have a clue. "Anything, sis. Just do some-thin' besides sit up in your room."

"Mike, would you please do me a favor and find out who took my brother away from me?" Trouble cried. "That's the only way I'm gon' be able to move on with my life," she said.

"Sis, I already got my niggas on it. And they know what to do as soon as they find out who the nigga is."

"No, don't let ya boys kill 'em."

"What do you mean, Trouble? Somebody killed our brother and you don't want them dead?" Big Mike asked, puzzled.

"You don't understand. I want 'em dead, but I want them to suffer the way that Jyson did. I've got a plan," she said.

"What kinda plan you talkin' 'bout, sis?"

"When you find out who took my brother's life just let me know, then leave the rest up to me, please," she begged.

"I don't know, Trouble. This shit could get real ugly. And besides, what do you have in mind?"

"I don't know yet, but I'll think of somethin'. I can't function, Big Mike. And it ain't fair for me to have to suffer. So promise me you'll call ya boys and tell them don't hurt the niggas that killed our brother."

Big Mike took a deep breath, and as bad as he wanted to tell Trouble no, he couldn't. When he finished talking to her, he called his jump out boys and told them to stay on top of finding out who murked his little brother, but to leave the niggas unharmed.

Forty-one

Jessica walked up on her sister's front porch, pulled out her cell phone, and dialed her number. "Hello?" Sherry answered. "Sherry, I need to talk to you," Jessica said. "Are you okay, sis? Where you at?" "I'm outside your front door, talking on my cell phone. Can you please come let me in?"

Sherry walked over to the front door and let her sister in. Jessica walked in looking like she hadn't bathed or eaten in weeks. She had lost so much weight, and her hair was matted to her head.

"Jessica, you look horrible. Are you snortin' that shit again, girl?" Sherry asked, concerned.

Jessica shook her head. "No. I've been up for the past three days straight. I got a lot on my mind."

"What's the matter with you?" Sherry asked.

"Sherry, I have somethin' to tell you, but you gotta promise not to tell Big Mike," Jessica said desperately.

"I won't tell him," Sherry assured her sister.

Jessica closed her eyes and took a deep breath. "I know who killed Jyson," she said in a whisper-like tone.

"Who?" Sherry asked, surprised.

"You gotta promise me that you won't tell Big Mike."

"Jessica, please tell me you didn't have anything to do with Jyson's death," Sherry said, panicking.

"No, Sherry, I didn't. But I know who did," she said with tears forming in her eyes.

"Who, Jessica? Who killed Jyson?"

"Woo killed Jyson," Jessica sobbed heavily.

"What? He's one of Mike's right-hand men. Are you sure it was Woo?"

Jessica shook her head. "Yes, I'm sure. And he's not one of Big Mike's right-hand men either. He was the one rob-bin' all of Mike's and Jyson's soldiers, and he robbed Big Mike too." Jessica's entire body trembled as she spoke.

"Hell naw!" Sherry exclaimed. "How did you find all of this out?"

" 'Cuz I'm the one who set the whole thing up," Jessica admitted.

"What?" Sherry asked, surprised. "You mean to tell me that you set my husband up after all the shit he has done for you and those kids?"

"Sherry, I'm sorry. I didn't mean it," Jessica sobbed heavily.

"You damn right, Jessica, you are sorry, now get the fuck outta my house and don't come back, ever!" Sherry yelled.

"Sherry, please, don't tell Big Mike, he'll kill me!" Jessica frantically begged for her life.

Sherry walked up into her sister's face and pointed her finger in it. "You know what, bitch, you deserve to die. But it wouldn't be fair for Momma to have to raise your brats while your ass is layin' in the cemetery worry-free. I'm gon' let you slide this time, but I don't ever want you to step foot back into my house again, you understand? If you do, I'm gon' tell Big Mike everything. I'm gon' even make up some shit if I ever hear from you, now get the fuck out!"

"Sherry, I'm sorry," Jessica said as she tried to hug her sister.

Sherry took a step back and pointed to the door. "Get the fuck out!" Sherry screamed at the top of her lungs. Jessica hung her head low and walked out the front door with her feelings and her pride crushed into a million tiny pieces.

"Trouble, if you're there, pick up the phone," Big Mike yelled into the answering machine. Trouble could hear urgency in his voice but still decided not to pick up the phone. She just laid there in her bed crying. "Okay, then, call me when you get this message, I've got some good news. My boys found out who killed Jyson."

"Who?" Trouble quickly picked up the phone before Big Mike hung up.

"How come you didn't answer the phone the first time?"

"I don't know. Who killed Jyson?" Trouble asked, desperately needing to know. She sat up and waited on Big Mike to tell her who took her brother away from her.

"This bitch-ass nigga named Woo."

Trouble's head began to spin as her stomach balled up into knots. "Who did you say?" she asked, just to make sure her ears weren't playing tricks on her.

"This nigga named Woo. You know him?" Big Mike asked.

"I've ran into him in the past. And now it's time for me to give Mr. Woo a visit," Trouble said.

"Trouble, Woo can be dangerous. That's why I kept the nigga by my side, 'cuz he had heart," Big Mike explained.

"He couldn't have had too much heart, 'cuz he took my brotha away from me," Trouble said as tears rolled down her cheeks. "I got somethin' in store for that nigga," she said as her tears turned into anger.

"Trouble, what do you plan on doin'? I don't know if I can let you get close to Woo," Big Mike said.

"I'm not the one you should be worried about, you better worry about Woo," Trouble said angrily.

"Trouble, whatever you plan on doin', you better have it planned out to a T, 'cuz Woo is no dummy," Big Mike said.

"Oh, don't worry, it will be planned. Just give me a couple of days and I'll get back with you," Trouble said.

Big Mike sighed and hoped that he'd made the right decision by letting his little sister handle Woo. "Okay, Trouble, I love you," he said.

"I love you too," she said and hung up the phone.

"Shit!" Big Mike yelled before closing his eyes and praying to God that Trouble knew what she was about to get herself into.

Trouble got out of bed and paced back and forth as she contemplated on how she was going to pay Woo back for killing her brother. She thought about nothing else for days.

Trouble got up early one morning and put on a pair of the shortest Daisy Dukes she could find and a halter top. She went to the shop and got her hair and nails done and headed to the park where they were holding the basketball tournaments. She knew that everybody that wanted to be somebody would be at the park, including Woo. She searched the park high and low, but Woo was nowhere to be found. Left feeling defeated, Trouble headed home.

"Hey, girl?" she heard a familiar voice call out.

After looking up and seeing that the voice calling her was Woo, she smiled. "Hey, Woo, long time no see."

"Yeah, I know. The last time I talked to you, you told me to kick mud." He laughed, sounding just like Jyson.

It took everything in Trouble to try to stay calm. "My bad. I was just goin' through some things."

"You sho'll look good," Woo said, licking his lips. *Man, she done lost a lot of weight*, he thought as he admired her still nicely shaped physique.

"Thank you, and you don't look bad yourself," Trouble said, smiling. *But you would look even better dead,* she thought.

"Come on, Woo, we gotta bounce," a tall slender cat yelled from a brand new Hummer.

"Look, shorty, I gotta go. Can I call you sometime?"

"That'll be nice," Trouble said, smiling.

"Is the number the same?" Woo asked, pulling out his cell phone.

Trouble nodded yes. "I'll call you later," Woo said and smiled as he got into the truck.

"Yeah, do that," she said, smiling back.

Woo winked at Trouble as the truck pulled away. Trouble watched as they drove down the street, waiting until they were out of sight before she broke down into tears.

Trouble and Woo kept in contact by phone for the next couple of months. Woo always wanted to take Trouble out somewhere, but she always declined. She didn't want to get too close to him until she came up with the ultimate plan. She told Woo that she wanted to take things slow between them because she had just gotten out of a relationship and he understood.

Trouble spent all day in the shop getting her hair and nails done. Thanksgiving break was a couple days away, and she wanted to look extra good when Dariel came home for the holiday.

Once Dariel arrived at the airport, he called Trouble to make sure she was all right. He hadn't talked to her in a while; he still felt guilty about going all the way to North Carolina during a time when she really needed him. He thought about sneaking into town without her knowing, but he knew that wouldn't have been right. He still loved her whether she felt the same way about him or not.

"Hello?" Trouble said, answering her ringing cell phone.

"Hey, baby girl, how are you?"

"I'm fine. What about yourself?"

"I'm doin' okay, I guess," he said.

Silence fell between the two. They both had so much to say but were afraid of how the other might react. At that particular moment, they both felt like total strangers to each other.

"I ran into your mother at the store last week," Trouble said, breaking the silence.

"You know Moms, she's always shoppin'," Dariel said, laughing.

"She told me you were comin' into town," Trouble said, switching the phone from one ear to the other.

Dariel was relieved that he had made the right choice and called Trouble. How would he have explained to her later on him coming home and not bothering to call her?

"Can I take you out to dinner tonight?" Dariel asked her.

"Sure," she said, smiling.

"Okay, I'll pick you up at eight."

"Oh, you have your truck?"

"That's right, I don't."

"Then I'll pick you up at eight," she said.

"Okay, baby girl, I'll be waitin'." Dariel hung up the phone and smiled.

Trouble got dressed and went and picked up Dariel. The ride to the restaurant was a quiet one. Dariel just figured that Trouble had Jyson on her mind and didn't want to talk. Once they arrived at the restaurant, they waited to be seated. Dariel smiled every time his eyes met with hers.

"You look nice tonight," he said.

"Thank you," she said, smiling.

"College is way better than high school," he said, making general conversation. Dariel instantly regretted mentioning college because he could see the hurt in Trouble's eyes. He knew her lifelong dream was to go away to college so she could get out of Mansfield, but someone took that ambition away from her when they killed her brother.

Trouble looked into Dariel's eyes. "Dariel, I have some-thin' to tell you."

"Trouble, please don't tell me you're in a relationship with someone. I can't go through this shit with you again," he said.

"I'm not messin' around with anyone. I just wanted to tell you that they found out who killed Jyson," she said.

"Ahhh man, that's great. Is the nigga in jail?"

"No, Dariel, he's not."

"Why hasn't he been arrested yet?" Dariel asked, puzzled. "Who is the nigga?"

Trouble hesitated at first. "Woo," she sighed.

That name instantly brought back bad memories no sooner than it rolled off of Trouble's tongue. "We're not talkin' about the same Woo we broke up over, are we?" Dariel asked.

"We didn't break up because of Woo, Dariel. We broke up because you couldn't talk to me about how you really felt about me and Woo kissin'. Instead, you went and tried to pay me back by fuckin' around wit' Jameelah, but that was so long ago, I don't wanna talk about it," Trouble said, pushing the memory of the kiss out of her head.

Dariel agreed and changed the subject. "How come Big Mike ain't took that nigga out the game yet?"

"We got everything under control." Trouble told Dariel that she had plans on setting Woo up.

"You gotta be outta yo' fuckin' mind. You think I'm gon' be here waitin' around on you to finish fuckin' with this nigga?" Dariel snapped.

"Dariel, it ain't like that. I don't have no feelings for Woo," Trouble desperately tried to explain. "He killed my brother."

"You gon' be fuckin' this nigga, and you expect me to still have dealings with you? What type of dummy do you take me for?"

"It ain't all about fuckin' him, Dariel. I'm doin' this for Jyson."

"So you are gon' be fuckin' the nigga?" Dariel's feelings were crushed. "Bitch, I shoulda known you wasn't about shit from the get-go." Dariel got up out of his seat and walked away.

"Dariel, wait," Trouble said, causing a scene in the restaurant. "Please, don't do this to me. Bear with me, baby," she said, following behind him.

"So you sayin' you want me to bear with you while you spend time with another nigga? Fuck you, Trouble."

Trouble grabbed Dariel by the arm. "Please, Dariel."

Dariel yanked his arm away from Trouble, only to be grabbed by her again. "Get the fuck off of me and go find Woo," Dariel said angrily before he slapped blood out of her mouth.

Trouble grabbed the side of her mouth. She couldn't believe Dariel had just put his hands on her. Dariel shook his head as he walked down the street, in disbelief himself that he had put his hands on a woman—Trouble of all people.

Trouble tried calling Dariel everyday for the next two weeks but he wouldn't answer her calls. She left several messages for him to call her, but he never did. She still loved Dariel and wanted to be with him, but if he couldn't understand that she had to get close to Woo in order to get revenge for her brother's death, then piss on him. For the next several weeks, Trouble spent most of her time with Woo, trying to find out everything she could about him. She wanted to know his favorite hangout, all his likes and dislikes, even his favorite food. She had to know all of these things so she could come up with a plan to take her brother's killer out of the game for good!

"What we gon' do today?" Woo asked Trouble as they strolled through the mall.

"Whatever you want," Trouble said, smiling.

Woo grabbed Trouble's hands and held them tightly in his. "I want you to meet my momma."

Trouble pretended to feel special and couldn't wait to meet her. "I'd like that," she said, smiling from ear to ear. *Maybe she can die right along with you,* Trouble thought as she held onto her fake smile.

Woo drove Trouble to his mother's house for her to meet his new friend. As they walked in the house, Trouble could smell the aroma of some good old down-south cooking.

"Momma, you home?" Woo called out. Woo's mother walked into the living room from the kitchen. "Momma, I would like for you to meet Ne'Cole."

"Hey, baby," Woo's mother said, smiling.

"Hello," Trouble said, smiling back.

"Y'all come on in the kitchen, 'cuz y'all just in time for dinner," Woo's mother said, walking into the kitchen and fixing two plates of fried chicken, macaroni and cheese, collard greens, and hot water cornbread.

Trouble's mouth watered as Woo's mother set the plate down in front of her. Trouble couldn't remember the last time she had a good home-cooked meal. She picked up her fork and began eating just like she was at home. When she finished, she was so full she had to unbutton her jeans.

"Thank you, Ms. Walters, the food was delicious," Trouble said as she got up to take her plate to the sink.

"Thank you, Ne'cole. I'm glad you liked it."

After dinner they all sat in the living room laughing and talking while eating on pound cake. Ms. Walters asked Trouble about her family a time or two, but after she kept avoiding the questions, Ms. Walters figured Trouble just didn't want to talk about her family. Woo and his mother made Trouble feel so comfortable. She missed that feeling and could get used to it all over again. Trouble couldn't understand how a person as vile as Woo could end up with a sweet mother like Ms. Walters. She was the type of mother Trouble always dreamed of having.

"Come on," Woo said, holding out his hand.

"Where we goin'?" Trouble asked, taking his hand.

"Up to my room."

Trouble's eyes widened. "For what? And what is yo' momma gon' say?" she asked.

Ms. Walters smiled. "It's okay, baby, y'all are both adults."

Trouble still hesitated at first and then gave in. She followed Woo up the stairs and into his bedroom.

When she walked in, she looked around at all the pictures he had of him with all these different girls. Trouble recognized one of the girls in one of the pictures. "Who is she?" Trouble pointed at the picture.

"That's a hood rat named Jessica. I fucked around and had a baby by the ho," Woo said.

That's the bitch Jyson was fucking, Trouble thought. Trouble took a seat on Woo's neatly made queen-size bed. She looked around at the stack of shoe boxes in one corner and the stack of CDs in the other and it reminded her of how Jyson used to stack up his shoe boxes and his CDs. Trouble took her mind off of Jyson by staring at the picture of Halle Berry that hung on Woo's ceiling right above his bed. "Your room is nice," Trouble said.

"Thank you." Woo walked over to his stereo and turned it on. He played with the dial until he found a station, turning to a smooth jazz station. And it just so happened, Jyson's favorite jazz song by Boney James was playing.

"Please, turn this off," Trouble said, not wanting to be reminded of Jyson again.

"Why? You don't like jazz music?" Woo asked as he bobbed his head to the music.

"No, I don't."

Woo turned the radio station to 93.1 WZAK and walked over to his bed, taking a seat next to Trouble. He smiled as he looked into her hazel eyes.

"What you smilin' at?" she asked.

"You."

"What about me?" she asked.

"You are so cute," he said, rubbing his finger down the bridge of her nose.

I know, she thought. "Thanks," she said bashfully.

"Look, I'm full so I'm 'bout to take a nap. You're welcome to take one with me," Woo said, taking off his shoes and lying down on his bed. Trouble felt the same way so she took her shoes off and lay down beside him. Woo wrapped his arm around her waist as they both lay there.

"Ne'cole?" Woo whispered.

"Yes, Woo?" she answered.

"Would you be my girl?" he asked sincerely.

Trouble's body tingled on the inside. Even though her whole motive was to make Woo pay for what he had done to her brother, she couldn't help but accept his offer. Trouble was so used to being wanted, it felt good knowing that someone still wanted her to be a part of their life. She turned to face him and said, "Yes, Woo, I'll be your girl."

Woo pressed his lips against hers and he slowly kissed her before undressing her. The inside of her thighs throbbed with excitement. It had been a very long time since anyone had dove into her chocolate waterfall, too long to be exact. Trouble had never imagined anyone other than Dariel between her legs, but since he hated her, why not let Woo take care of her needs? Woo grabbed both of her breasts and licked her nipples at the same time. That drove Trouble crazy. He worked his way down south and feasted upon her Garden of Eden. She went buck wild, moaning and panting like a little puppy. Dariel was good at what he used to do to her, but Woo was something like an expert.

Woo kissed his way back up to her mouth. He leaned over, opened up his nightstand drawer, and pulled out a condom. Woo eagerly slid the condom on and entered all eight inches into her tight walls that he quickly loosened up. Trouble was tense at first, but she got into the groove of things as Woo put in work. She thought she had lost it, but once Woo began putting it down, it all came back to her. She moved her hips just like Dariel had taught her and she could tell it was driving Woo wild.

"Damn, shorty, you so tight and wet," he moaned as he managed to stroke the inside of her walls about ten more times before he exploded.

That's it? Trouble thought as her wet pussy pulsated.

"My bad, shorty. The pussy was too good and too wet. I'll make it up to you when I wake up," Woo said, before he turned over and fell asleep.

Damn, I just had sex with my brother's killer, Trouble thought as she drifted off to sleep herself.

Forty-two

Trouble lay across her bed waiting on Woo to call. She couldn't get enough of him. It was like she had to be around him everyday. He treated her like a queen. Dariel treated her good and all, but Woo treated her like royalty. He was everything she was used to having but more.

Trouble rolled over and answered the ringing telephone. "Hello?"

"Trouble, this is your dad," the caller said.

"I buried my dad a few months ago," she responded.

"Look, Trouble, this is hard enough as it is. I wanna do better as a father. I've lost one child, I'm not tryin'a lose another. I think we should start over and work this shit out," her father stated.

"What do you mean you don't wanna lose two children? What you fail to realize is, you lost us both when your triflin' ass walked out on us," Trouble snapped.

"I didn't walk out on y'all. I didn't have any other choice but to leave. Your momma started smokin' dope and she was stealin' from me. I told her to get her shit together or I was leavin'. She chose not to, so I left. She didn't want to get off of the crack. I tried my hardest to stay by her side. I even tried gettin' her help, but she wouldn't accept it." He cried as the memories came back and hit him like a ton of bricks.

This was the first time Trouble had ever known for her father to cry. She couldn't even remember seeing him cry at his own father's funeral. She began crying too because she felt kind of sorry for her daddy.

"Trouble, the hardest thing for me to do was to leave my two babies with a crackhead, but I had no choice," he explained.

Trouble wasn't aware of anything her father had just told her. She and Jyson were both under the impression that their mother started smoking after their father had left. Trouble got quiet, not knowing what to say.

"Hello, Trouble, are you still there, baby?"

"Yeah, I'm still here. Are you tellin' me that Momma started smoking crack before you left?" Trouble asked to make sure.

"Yes, she did. Did you think she started after I left?"

"That's what we were told," Trouble admitted.

"After I left she made it look like I was the reason she started usin' drugs," he explained.

"Daddy, I didn't know. I'm so sorry," Trouble cried.

"It's okay, baby. Don't cry, 'cuz you didn't know any better. You and ya brother were just kids then," he said in a soothing tone.

"What I don't understand is if you knew Momma was on drugs, why did you leave us with her?"

"I told her I was gonna take her to court to get custody of y'all. And she told me that if I tried to take y'all from her, she would take y'all and leave the state. And you know how ya momma is, she would have done it. So I didn't wanna take the risk of losing you and your brother for good," he informed.

Trouble was outdone. *How could I have believed what Aunt Trina said about my daddy, her own brother*? Trouble thought.

"Who told y'all I was the reason why ya momma started smokin'? Never mind, I don't even wanna know. All I wanna know right now is if we can start over."

Trouble smiled. "I'd like that, Daddy." Trouble began trying to fill her father in on everything he had missed in her and Jyson's lives. She told him about the ups and downs in her and Dariel's relationship. She tried to fill him in on everything in the three hours they spent on the phone. Before hanging up, her father made her promise not to be mad at her mother for the mistakes she had made in the past, and Trouble happily agreed.

"You got a fine-ass girlfriend," Kyron said as they sat around Woo's bedroom smoking on a blunt.

"I know," he boasted. "I'ma marry that young girl," he said, taking the blunt from Kyron.

"She got a sister?" Kyron asked.

"Nope, she's an only child."

"Damn, you lucky, man. You always be gettin' them fine-ass bitches. Look at Jessica's fine ass."

Woo grimaced at the sound of her name. "Don't mention that bitch in my presence. I told you how the bitch played me about that nigga Jyson, remember?"

Kyron laughed. "Yeah, but she still fine as hell."

"She's fine all right, but the bitch is all used up," Woo said, laughing.

"Yeah, she do gotta lot of miles on that pussy," Kyron agreed. "She give some good head, though."

Woo frowned at his cousin and shook his head.

"You picked a winner this time," Kyron said.

Woo gleamed. "Yeah, and I'ma make sure I keep her far away from yo' ass."

"Shit, I couldn't stop Jessica from givin' me head. Yo' ass was passed out from all that coke you snorted so she moved on to the next best thing," Kyron said, laughing. "As soon as yo' head hit the pillow, the bitch was all over me." Kyron laughed again.

Woo was getting angrier every time his cousin laughed.

"It's all good, man. You got you a good girl this time," Kyron said.

Woo smiled. "Yeah, you right. I got the bitch sprung with the pearl tongue," he bragged.

"Man, you gon' fuck around and have that young girl's nose wide open."

"It's too late. Her nose is opened like Interstate Seventy-one. She asked me if I wanted to use her brand new Chrysler 300 to go look for a job."

"Nigga, you know you ain't about to get no job," Kyron laughed.

"Hell naw, I be pickin' up my other bitches ridin' them around. I be perpin' like it's my shit," Woo said, laughing. "You know I'm a playa, nigga. She be arguin' every time I come in the house at two or three in the mornin'. I'ma hafta put it down on her," Woo said.

"You gon' hafta do her like you did all them other bitches."

"Start kickin' that ass," Woo and Kyron said in unison.

"Ne'cole, I'll be back," Woo said, grabbing her keys off the coffee table. Woo had been using Trouble's car ever since the engine blew up in his and it was beginning to make Trouble mad. Every time she had something to do, Woo was gone in her car.

"I got somethin' to do, Woo," she said, walking into the living room.

"Well, do it when I get back," he snapped.

"No, Woo. Me and my daddy is goin' out to lunch today," she huffed.

"Fuck yo' daddy, bitch. I said I'll be back!" Woo said as he walked out the door.

"No, give me my keys," Trouble said, following behind him. As Woo stuck the key in the door to unlock it, Trouble jumped on his back.

"Get off me, bitch," he said, and slung her to the ground.

Trouble got up, dusted herself off, and charged him again. This time Woo punched her in the eye. She had never been hit so hard in her life. She grabbed her eye and took a step back.

"See what you made me do to you? Now get yo' ass in the house and I'll be back," Woo yelled angrily before getting in her car and pulling off.

Trouble walked back into Woo's mother's house and went into the bathroom to get a cold towel to put over her eye. "I can't believe this nigga hit me," she said to the reflection in the mirror. *I shouldna' hit him first. He said he would be right back,* she thought as she lay across his bed with the towel over her eye.

Four hours later Woo returned home drunk as hell with a bouquet of flowers in hand. He tapped Trouble on the shoulder as she lay in the bed sound asleep. "Get up, shorty, these are for you," he said, shoving the flowers in her face.

Trouble pushed the flowers out of her face, sat up, and felt her swollen eye. "Look what you done to my eye, Woo," she snapped.

Woo looked at the black-and-blue ring around her eye and said, "Well, the next time I tell yo' ass that I'll be right back you better listen or there's more where that came from." Woo took off his Timbs and crawled into bed and fell fast asleep.

Over the next couple of months, Woo had been whooping Trouble's ass on a regular basis. He basically began dictating her life. He told her what kind of clothes she could and could not wear, he made her wear her hair in a certain style, and he even went as far as making her stay away from her father because he said he was the only man she needed in her life. Every time Woo put his hands on her, Trouble promised herself that she would put her plan in effect, only to give up after Woo bought her an outfit, begged for forgiveness, and promised to never put his hands on her again. Trouble was a straight sucka for Woo and she knew it too. She tried to desperately fill the empty space that used to be filled with the love that Jyson and Dariel showered her with. That was the only reason why she stayed by Woo's side, she told herself. And if accepting an ass-whooping here and there would get her the love she needed to feel, so be it, because getting negative attention was better than getting no attention at all—so she thought. Trouble called Big Mike every other day to check in and let him know that her plan was almost complete. Big Mike was starting to get impatient with Trouble and told her that she'd better get things in order quick or he would have his boys go ahead and handle Woo.

Forty-three

February had rolled around again and it was another sad month for Trouble because Dariel's birthday was a couple of days away. She wanted to call him to wish him a happy birthday but she knew he wouldn't answer her call. Woo had made Trouble move all of her things from her aunt's house into his mother's house. Ms. Walters didn't mind because whatever made her only son happy, made her happy as well. Trouble loved being a part of a real family again. The only thing she hated was the ass-kickings Woo was handing out. Woo had gotten to the point where he wasn't even coming home at night and then he would waltz his happy ass in the next morning smelling like sex and cheap perfume. Trouble wouldn't open her mouth because she was too afraid of what the outcome was going to be, so she would just sit back and let Woo dog and disrespect her. Big Mike was fed up because Trouble was taking too long to get shit in order. Trouble had gotten to the point where she would avoid Big Mike's phone calls in hopes of stalling the plan. As much as Trouble hated to admit it, she had fallen in love with her brother's killer.

What the fuck am I doing? Trouble thought as she lay in the bed beside Woo, as he slept peacefully. *Oh well, whatever it is, it sure feels good*. Trouble smiled, and drifted off to sleep, right next to her man.

"Girl, I haven't heard from you in ages!" Ta'liyah yelled into the phone receiver. "Where the fuck have you been?"

"I been around. I been workin' on a project," she said. The real reason Ta'liyah hadn't heard from her was Woo didn't allow her to use the telephone except to call her mother once a week to let her know she was doing all right. She had to sneak to call Ta'liyah while Woo was out riding around in her car.

"Trouble, are you okay?" Ta'liyah asked suspiciously. "I called your cell phone and it said your phone had been disconnected. What's up with that? You know back in the day, you couldn't live without your cell phone."

"I got it cut off, 'cuz I couldn't afford to pay the bill," Trouble lied. "You know I can't live high on the horse no more since Jyson died." The only means of communication Trouble had was the prepaid cell phone Big Mike had bought to keep in contact with her when he needed to know how close she was coming to putting her plan in effect.

"Trouble, you're scarin' me," Ta'liyah said.

"I'm fine, Ta'liyah, stop worryin'." Trouble heard the front door open. "I have to call you back," she said and hung up the phone before Ta'liyah could say anything else.

Spring break was right around the corner and Trouble knew that if it was the last thing she did in life, she was going to make it her business to see Dariel while he was home on break. She would have to come up with one hell of an excuse for Woo on why she had to leave the house, but she loved and missed Dariel so much, she knew she would come up with something without getting caught.

"You know my birthday is in two weeks, girl," Woo said to Trouble as she massaged his tense shoulders.

"I know," she said, smiling, happily. "What do you want for your birthday?" she asked.

"I already got it," he said, smiling. Woo's cell phone rang. He checked the caller ID and grabbed Trouble's keys off the dresser. "I'll be back."

Where the fuck you goin'? Trouble's head asked, but her mouth said, "Okay." She sat around the house bored to death while Woo and his friends rode around smoking blunts and drinking in her car. Trouble pulled her prepaid cell phone out from underneath the bed and checked her messages. She had twenty-six missed calls from Big Mike. She knew sooner or later she would have to talk to him, but she would have preferred it to be later. Just her luck, the phone rang and she reluctantly answered it.

"Hello?" she said.

"Sis? Why haven't you been answerin' your phone?" Big Mike yelled. "My patience is wearin' real thin, Trouble. I see I'm gon' hafta handle this shit myself!" Big Mike snapped angrily.

"I'm gon' handle it. I promise," Trouble lied.

"I'm not gon' wait too much longer, I done waited long enough."

"Okay," she said sullenly.

"You act like you in love wit' this nigga!" Big Mike said. Trouble fell silent. "Are you? You done got caught up?"

"No. No, I'm not in love or caught up," she lied again.

"All right then, I'm just makin' sure. But just remember time is runnin' out," he said, hanging up the phone.

Trouble put the phone back underneath the bed in her hiding spot. She got off her knees and sat on the bed. She didn't know what else to do so she started cleaning up Woo's bedroom. "Damn, I gotta stop eatin' so much, my clothes are gettin' too tight," she said, unbuckling her pants. *How can I set him up now when I'm in love with him?* she thought. Trouble began feeling sick to her stomach just thinking about her dilemma.

She stopped cleaning and lay across the bed. After a few minutes passed she sat up and when she did, she threw up all down the front of her clothes. Her stomach had been bothering her a lot lately. She went and took a shower and walked back into the room with a towel wrapped around her body. As she was pulling a long white T-shirt out of the drawer, something fell to the floor. Trouble bent down to pick it up and noticed it was someone's license. She knew it wasn't Woo's because he didn't have one. Trouble looked at the picture and quickly dropped it on the floor, instantly becoming dizzy and stumbling over to the bed. She took two deep breaths and went back over and picked the driver's license up off the floor and read the name out loud. "Jyson D. Lewis," she said. Tears streamed down her face as she held the license close to her trembling body. Why?" she screamed loudly. "Why did he have to kill you, Jyson?" she asked the picture on the license. "You didn't deserve to die," she cried. At that particular moment, it dawned on Trouble that she was letting her brother down. Jyson had her back since day one and she had turned hers on him by falling in love with the nigga that killed him. Trouble's tears turned into straight, uncut anger. "Jyson, don't be mad at me for not doin' what I had set out to do. I'm sorry that I got off track and fell in love with the nigga that took you away from me. I'm human, big bra'. But now I know it's time for me to handle my business," she cried.

Trouble felt a burst of strength come from somewhere. She wrapped the license back in the shirt and put it neatly in the drawer. She gathered all of her things and set them by the door. She fixed herself something to eat and watched *Baby Boy* as she waited patiently for Woo's return.

"What's up, shorty?" Woo said, smiling, and attempted to kiss her when he finally returned home.

Trouble blocked his face and got prepared for whatever was about to come her way. "Nothin'. Keys please," she said, holding out her hand. Woo put the keys in her hand.

"Where the fuck do you think you about to go?" he snapped angrily. Trouble didn't answer.

Normally, Trouble would have flinched by the tone in Woo's voice, but it didn't faze her one bit and Woo could tell that she wasn't bothered by his demanding tone. "Was I gone too long?"

"Nope." Trouble began toting all of her belongings to her car, and when she opened the door, the aroma from the many blunts Woo and his friends had smoked hit her dead smack in the face.

"Where you goin'?" Woo yelled from the doorway.

"Home," Trouble replied.

Trouble got in the car and started it up. She looked at Woo with a disgusted look and headed to her Aunt Rachel's house. She walked into the house and paced back and forth. Trouble was so angry with herself for letting Woo dog her the way that he did. She had never let a man do her the way Woo had done and right then and there she made a promise to herself that she would never let it happen again.

Trouble pulled out her prepaid cell phone and called Big Mike to let him know her plan.

"That's smart thinkin', li'l sis. I'm all the way down with that," he said, smiling. "It took you long enough."

"I had to make sure the time was right," Trouble said.

"I feel you, sis."

"Mike?"

"Yes?"

"I love you."

"I love you too," Big Mike said sincerely.

As much as Trouble hated Woo, she had to make up with him in order for her plan to go right. She called him and asked if she could come over so they could work out their problems and he agreed. Once she arrived at his house, he had a nice candlelit dinner waiting on her. But this time it didn't faze her one bit.

"Woo, I wanna have you a birthday party in Detroit," Trouble said as she picked at her salad.

"Why in Detroit?" Woo replied.

" 'Cuz, you're always up there with Kyron and most of your family lives there. I want it to be more of a family thing with a few of your friends," Trouble said.

Woo smiled. "That's why I love you, girl. You're always doin' somethin' special for me."

"I love you too." *Till death do us part*, she thought.

Trouble asked Woo's mother for a list of his family and friends in Detroit so she could send them invitations to his birthday party. Ms. Walters helped Trouble find a nice hall to rent out. Trouble was happy that Ms. Walters was willing to help her plan everything. She had even offered to help Trouble with decorating the hall. Trouble went to the bank to withdraw some of the money her grandfather had left her and hired a caterer, bought decorations, and she sent Woo's cousin some money to buy the liquor and hire a DJ. She had vowed not to touch her savings unless it was something important, but what could be more important than watching her brother's killer die a slow and miserable death? The following Friday, Trouble had Woo's mother rent them a car and they hit the highway and headed to Detroit.

Woo and Trouble checked in at the Westin Hotel in Detroit. Trouble was tired and anxious all at the same time so she decided to try and lie down for a nap. Woo had other plans for them. He called up Kyron and his friend Doc to come by the hotel and kick it in their executive suite.

"This party is gon' be jumpin' tonight," Woo said as he passed the blunt to Kyron.

"I know it's gon' be some fine bitches up in there," Kyron said, laughing, taking a pull and inhaling the smoke.

"I'm hip," Doc, Woo's childhood friend, agreed. "I hope them niggas from the west side don't show up or it's gon' be some problems."

"Baby, I hope ya boys don't think they gon' be bringin' no guns up in the party," Trouble said. "I have already hired some bouncers to walk around and there will be somebody at the door with a metal detector, checkin' everybody that comes and goes."

"That's cool, baby," Woo said and then turned his attention back to his boys. "Y'all niggas can't bring no heat up in the party. My girl went through a lot of trouble gettin' this party together for her man, ain't that right?" he said, patting her on her ass.

Woo's touch made Trouble's skin crawl, but she only had to play it cool for a few more hours. "That's right, baby, and I don't want it messed up with no drama between hoods, y'all hear me?" Trouble said dramatically.

"What the fuck ya girl mean, we can't pack no heat?" Doc said, grimacing. "I ain't feelin' that shit at all," he complained.

"Y'all can pack 'em if y'all want to, but y'all gotta keep them in y'all's cars," Trouble warned.

"That's cool," Kyron agreed.

"That's more like it," Doc said.

Trouble grabbed her clothes out of her suitcase and excused herself to go to the bathroom to get dressed for the party. When she finished getting dressed she walked out and gave Woo a kiss on the cheek. "I'm 'bout to go pick up your mother so we can go finish decoratin' the hall," she said.

"I'll ride with you so you won't get lost. I'll just get dressed over Kyron's house." Woo walked over and grabbed his suitcase and they all left the hotel together.

Ms. Walters and Trouble arrived at the hall around the same time as the caterers. The DJ was setting up his music while some of Woo's family helped set up everything else.

"This is gon' be a nice party," Ms. Walters said, smiling at Trouble.

"I know it is," Trouble smiled back. "And I know it's gon' be packed."

"Yeah, I know. That's why I'm not stayin'. I'm goin' back over to my sister's house," Ms. Walters said.

"At least stay for the dinner," Trouble insisted. "Please?"

"I guess I can," Ms. Walters agreed as they finished decorating and guests started to arrive.

The party was packed with Woo's family and a lot of his friends from his old neighborhood. The DJ was spinning the latest tunes as everyone sat around laughing, eating, and drinking. Trouble spotted Woo in a corner with his arms wrapped around some girl's waist and his tongue halfway down her throat.

"Who is this, Woo?" Trouble asked as she approached them with her feelings crushed. Even though she hated him and was finally about to make him pay for Jyson's death, he wasn't going to be disrespecting her in his final hour.

"Bitch, didn't I tell you about askin' me questions?" Woo screamed. "And besides, she's my cousin," he lied.

Trouble shook her head. "I'm goin' to the corner store up the street to get some more ice," Trouble said to him.

"Yeah, go somewhere," Woo said, waving her off and turned back around to pick up where he had left off.

Trouble walked up to the corner store and pulled out her prepaid cell phone. "You have ten minutes for this call," the electronic operator said. Trouble dialed Woo's cell phone as tears ran down her cheeks.

"Hello, Woo," Trouble said.

"Where you at with the ice?" Woo asked, irritated, as soon as he heard Trouble's voice. "Muthafuckas hot up in here," he yelled.

"I'm on my way back. But first, I have somethin' to tell you."

"Can't it wait until later?" he asked.

"Nope. Woo, I'm pregnant."

"All right, and? I'll take care of it," he said nonchalantly. "Now hurry up with the ice."

"You know it sounds good, but I don't plan on keepin' it."

"Come on, Ne'cole, it's my birthday. Let's talk about this bullshit later."

"I'm not keepin' it, Woo."

"Why not?" he sighed, not really caring if she kept the baby or not.

" 'Cuz it's gon' be hard raisin' a baby on my own. I sit back and look how hard it is for Michaela and I don't wanna go through the same thing."

"Who?"

"You know who Michaela is. Her baby's father won't be around to see his first son bein' raised."

"Why not?" he asked, getting irritated by this entire conversation. Woo had planned on dumping

Trouble as soon as they got back to Mansfield anyways because he was tired of her mood swings and he needed a change.

"Cuz you took his life," she said while tears fell from her hazel eyes.

"Who's life did I take, Ne'cole?"

"You took my brother's life away from me and his family. And now it's time for me to do the same to you and yours."

With phone in hand and time running out, Trouble walked back toward the hall and nodded her head at the bouncer that stood at the front door. She got in the rental car and watched from across the street.

"What are you talkin' about, Ne'cole?"

"Bye Woo," she said, hanging up the phone, wiping her fingerprints off of it and tossing it out the window. She jumped as gunfire rang throughout the dance hall.

"Oh shit," Woo yelled as three bullets hit his chest backto-back. The bouncers that Trouble hired were Big Mike's boys from St. Louis. They shot and killed Woo and everybody else who happened to be in the line of fire.

Trouble waited in the rental car until the police arrived. She got out and ran across the street.

"What happened?" Trouble questioned.

"Ma'am, you need to step back," an officer yelled.

"But my boyfriend is in there. I need to see if he's okay," Trouble screamed as fake tears clouded her vision.

A tall white officer talked to one of Woo's aunts as blood dripped from her arm. She was giving the officer names of all the people she knew that didn't make it out alive.

"What's your boyfriend's name?" the officer asked.

"Anthony Walters," Trouble answered.

The officer looked on the list and shook his head no. "I'm sorry, ma'am, he didn't make it. Whoever planned this massacre, did a damn good job."

Trouble wanted to say thank-you to the officer but decided against it. She stood behind the police tape and watched as they wheeled out all the dead bodies. She saw an arm hanging out from under one of the white sheets and recognized the sleeve on Ms. Walters's dress. Trouble had a crooked smile on her face. *Payback is a bitch!* she thought.

Trouble caught a cab back to the hotel. She asked the driver to wait for her while she grabbed her suitcase. She toted her bag to the car and had the driver drop her off at the nearest bus station, then walked up to the counter and purchased a one-way ticket to Mansfield. The entire trip home, she cried. She was relieved that Woo paid the ultimate price for taking her brother away from her, but she felt bad his mother had to pay for her son's mistakes also. Trouble arrived in Mansfield at 4:45 a.m. and stood in the bus station and watched as all the happy couples embraced one another with hugs and kisses. Trouble walked over to the pay phone and put in fifty cents.

She took a deep breath and closed her eyes before dialing Dariel's phone number.

"Hello?" he answered, half asleep.

"Hello, Dariel, this is Trouble."

"Trouble?" Dariel said sitting up, rubbing his eyes.

"Could you please come and get me?" she cried.

"Where are you? Are you okay, baby girl?" he asked.

"Not really. I'm at the bus station."

"Well, stay put, I'm on my way," he said, hanging up the phone before she could say anything else.

"Ugggg!"

Epilogue

"Trouble, y'all almost finished with y'all's homework?" her mother asked.

"Almost, Momma. Why what's up?"

"'Cuz me and Michaela is about to take junior to the Dairy Queen and I wanted to know if you and Dariel wanted to tag along."

"I don't care. You wanna go, Dariel?" she turned and asked him.

"Let's go," he said, smiling at his pregnant girlfriend. "Daddy's gon' feed that baby some ice cream," he said to Trouble's round belly that held the offspring of the man who killed her brother.

"No you're not. She wants a salad," Trouble said, laughing.

"I love you, Trouble," he said.

"I love you too, Dariel."

Dariel took his fiancé by the hand and kissed her on the forehead. Although Trouble had a hard time at first accepting Dariel's child with another woman, he had no problem at all accepting her child by another man. That's just how strong he loved her.

Love is

Love is something that cannot be broken. Love is not a word that can be spoken. Love is an action, it's something that you do. Love is something that's shared between me and you. Love is not bad, love is good. If you never had the chance to love, I recommend you should. Love is something that makes you smile. Love is something that makes living life worthwhile. I love love, it's my heart and my desire. I love love, because it sets my soul on fire.

Coming Soon

December 2014

Powder Blu

by Brandi Johnson

Chapter 1

Powder Blu

I live on Eighty-third and Ellis Street in Chicago. Every day I'm awakened by these crack heads knocking on the damn door all night long, feigning for that morning fix. Along Seventy-ninth was the hot spot, but the raw shit was here, plus, Momma sold hers cheaper than anybody else in the hood which made alotta' of the dope niggas mad. "Who is it?" I yelled as someone banged on the door like the police.

"It's me, you got somethin'?" I heard someone say.

"Who is me?" I said getting up from the couch, still half asleep.

"Me, Bart," he answered in a slight whisper.

I walked over to the door and looked through the peep hole to make sure it really was Bart on the other side of the door and not just some random fein my momma never fucked with. My momma was real particular about the hypes she served. She wasn't trying to get caught up again. She already had one dope case pending that she was going back and forth to court for. For the life of me I don't understand why she won't give up selling dope and get herself a real job. Sure enough it was Bart's dusty ass standing there scratching the skin off his dirty-ass neck.

"Hang on, let me go get my momma," I said, and slowly turned to walk away. I made my way down the hall and lightly knocked on my mother's bedroom door. Not, getting an answer I bent down, looked through the keyhole, and the sight nearly floored me. I saw my momma on her hands and knees like a dog with her eyes shut tight, titties hanging, while her new big fat-ass boyfriend, Troy was behind her moving back and forth. They looked like two big hippos during mating season. I instantly got sick to my stomach. I didn't know if it was from the Chinese food I ate late last night or the sight that made me throw up all over my momma's freshly waxed hardwood floors. I guessed the sound of me regurgitating right outside her door, alerted her that someone was watching.

"Blu, is that you?" she called out.

I stood quietly, afraid to move.

"Is that you, Blu?" she repeated.

"Ummm yes, it's me," I answered hesitantly while wiping the liquefied leftovers from my mouth.

"Are you out there throwin' up all over my damn floor, girl?" she yelled.

"Yes, ma'am," I answered, hesitantly. I knew she was gon' be mad because she spent all day on her hands and knees waxing. The crazy thing was she only cleaned up to try to impress Troy any other time the house was fucked up. It wouldn't be long before Troy saw the real.

"You gon' clean that shit up," she fussed. "I just waxed them damn floors!"

"Okay," I answered.

"What the fuck you doin' outside my door in the first place?" she continued to yell.

"Somebody at the door," I answered as I looked down at the pool of vomit.

"Who is it?" Momma asked.

Bring yo' ass out here and find out, I wanted to say. "Bart," I answered instead.

"Ask him how much," she moaned, still never coming to answer the door.

"How much what?" I asked smartly.

"Just go do what the fuck I said!" she yelled, slightly annoyed with my presence.

"Oh . . . ok." As I walked toward the front door, I knew what my momma was having me do. I didn't mind because I wanted to see what it felt like to be a drug dealer just like my momma, and my brother's best friend, Budz. With the bottom of my pajamas soiled, I unlocked the chain and opened the door to get a good look at Bart. I wanted him to see my face. I wanted him to know that I was in charge of the deal that was about to go down.

"How much?" I asked as my voiced echoed in the hallway.

"Girl, lower yo' damn voice," Bart whispered, looking around to see if anyone had heard me. "You tryin'a get ya' momma cased up again?" he asked with a frown.

"No," I shook my head, embarrassed because Bart knew I was inexperienced.

"Now go tell ya' momma I need a quarter ounce."

"Huh." I asked, confused.

"Quit lookin stupid and go tell her what I said," he said stepping in, closing the door behind him." As I walked away, I heard Bart mumbling. "Stacey shouldn't be lettin' no li'l-ass kid do her job . . . ol' dumb bitch, that's how she got busted the last time."

I continued to walk back toward my mom's room keeping what Bart just said to myself because I knew if I told her she would be on Bart's ass like back pockets. All these fiens and these niggas around the hood knew my mom didn't play. That's why they never tried to fuck her over 'cuz they knew she would pop a nigga in a heartbeat if they ever tried to cross her. What some people was 'sleep to was me and my brother were both born while my momma was locked up in the penitentiary. My aunt Shanican before she had passed away used to tell us that my brother was a felonious assault baby and I was a drug possession baby. That was just a few of the cases my momma had caught during her fifteen-year stent she'd spent in and out of the joint.

I stepped over the puddle of vomit and knocked on my momma's door again. "Momma!"

"What?" she snapped.

"He said he want a quarter ounce."

"Aiiiight," she said, still refusing to get up off the dick long enough to handle her own business. Blu, are you listenin' to me?" she yelled from the other side of the door.

"Yes ma'am," I answered.

"Go look under the kitchen sink, there's a carton of Epsom salt. Open it up and give him only one ball out of there, you hear me? Only give him one," she repeated.

"Yes ma'am," I replied before turning to walk away. I couldn't believe that I was going to actually make my first drug transaction at the age of fifteen. I was super excited as I walked into the kitchen and did what my mother had told me to do. I followed her directions carefully because I wanted to show her that I wasn't a little girl anymore and was ready to get into the dope game for myself. I pulled out a clump of white stuff from the Epsom salt box the size of a golf ball, examined it for a few seconds before walking back into the living room and sticking my hand out.

"What you got ya' hand out for?" Bart asked.

"Gimme' the money first," I said in a demanding tone. The last thing I needed was for this fein to run off without giving me my money. I would never hear the end of it.

"Awwww, I ain't gon' try to beat you outta no money," Bart fussed as he handed me $125. I really couldn't add all that well, but one thing my momma made sure of was me and my brother knew how to count and add money so nobody could ever beat us out of any. It wasn't like I was dumb; I just didn't take the time to learn anything in school whenever I decided to go. I had other shit to do, like hangin' on the block wit' my older brother, and his sexy ass best friend, Budz or kickin' it wit' my girls, Nikki and Sierra. One thing for sure two for certain sitting in somebody's classroom was the last thing on my mind!

"Aiiiight, tell ya' momma I might be back later on," Bart said, before turning to walk back out the door.

Without responding, I closed the door behind him, put the chain on and headed off to my room to count my money. The feeling I got from my first drug deal had me feeling on top of the world. It was easy as hell! If handing a mutha' fucka some crack and them giving me money is all I had to do in this dope game, I'm 100 percent sure I could do this shit for a living wit' no problem.

Whoa, I just made my first $125, I thought with a smile as I recounted my money. The sound of my momma's heavy footsteps coming down the hallway startled me.

"Blu, where is my money?" she busted into my room and yelled.

"But momma, I just made this all by myself," I grimaced.

"Girl, you betta give me my shit, or I'ma stick my foot down yo narrow ass." She warned. My momma played about a lot of things but her money damn sure wasn't one of them so I couldn't do anything at this point, but give her the shit.

"I can't believe yo' ass tryin' to keep my damn money," my momma ranted as she counted her money, stuck it in her robe pocket, and headed out of my room. "And bring yo' ass out here and clean that damn shit up from in front of my bedroom door I almost stepped in it!"

"But I'm the one who sold Bart the stuff," I argued as I followed her. "So rightfully the money belongs to me."

My momma stopped dead in her tracks and turned to face me. My first thought was she was about to haul off and slap the shit out of me, but to my surprise she pulled the wad of money out of her robe pocket and peeled off a bill.

"Here," she said, shoving a five dollar bill into my hand.

I looked at the money as if it was a foreign object.

"Five dolla's?" I frowned. "This all you gon' give me?"

"If you don't want it, give it back," she said, and headed into the kitchen.

I looked around the living room and instantly got a straight attitude. "Now, everybody wanna get their asses up, smelling like old sex and stale pizza," I said frowning while looking at Troy and my older brother, Miguel as they both sat on the couch eating a bowl of cereal looking like two fat-ass pigs."

"Troy told me momma let you serve yo' first hype," my brother said smirking. "Growin' up in the world, huh?" he asked sarcastically

"What's it to ya'? I didn't see you gettin' yo' fat ass up to answer the door."

"That's 'cuz I don't sell crack, I sell weed," Miguel responded before sticking a spoonful of cereal into his mouth.

"I heard that shit you sell is bunk anyway," I teased.

"Shit, I sell nothin'but killa'," my brother said.

"That ain't what I heard," I antagonized, getting under his skin.

"Fuck what ya heard, I know my shit is the bomb," Miguel said, defensively.

"You betta' watch yo' mouth, boy," my mother warned coming out of the kitchen while scratching her ass.

"But, mom she always got somethin' fly to say," Miguel whined. "You don't neva' say nothin' to her!"

"Quit all that damn whinin', nigga. You sound like an ol' bitch," my mother yelled as she walked over to the coffee table and shook a cigarette out of the pack.

"Act like one too," I mumbled, hoping my mom didn't hear me.

"You always takin' her side!" Miguel huffed, smacking his lips.

"Stop all that damn lyin' and you betta' watch yo' mouth like I said! Nigga you only seventeen, remember I'm the only adult in this house. You hear me, boy?"

"Yes ma'am." Miguel answered, slowly.

I looked over at my brother and smirked. We always laughed at each other when one of us got in trouble by Momma. Miguel couldn't have looked any worse with his bottom lip damn near hanging to the floor. His eyes squinted like a Chinese person as he stared me down. I already knew if my momma wasn't home he would try to give me some work. I knew my boundaries when she wasn't around but it was fair game when she was.

Miguel had always thought he was the boss because of the times my mom would ask him to watch me while she hit her out-of-town runs. He would bully me with threats if I told her about all the girls him and Budz had in his room. I couldn't understand for the life of me what girls saw in Miguel. Now Budz on the other hand was fine as fuck. He was wanted by damn near every chick in the hood, including me. I guessed Frenchie whoever she was had his heart, because her name was tattooed on the side of his neck. He had a lot of hoes in his stable though. I tried my best to become one of his prize-winning ponies but he always told me I was too young and he looked at me like a little sister. That never stopped me though; I still always shot my shot, hoping one day he would give in. Miguel was my brother and I loved him, but he was fat, black, and ugly just like his daddy with a big mole on the left side of his nose. He had gay tendencies to me, but he had so many girls how could he be. Unless he was undercover. Hell who knew? My only thought was he had to be payin' these girls for pussy.

Bored with taunting my brother, I cleaned up the vomit and decided to go to my bedroom, get dressed, and get up outta the house to see what was poppin' off in the hood. I walked over to my dresser and pulled out a pair of cut-off jean shorts and a shabby T-shirt with Tupac on the front of it. You woulda thought with all the money my momma made selling drugs, she would at least make sure her children were laced, but instead she spent her money on all the different niggas she fucked. Even at the young age of fifteen I knew that niggas only fucked with her because she paid them too. My momma wasn't the prettiest person in the world, but she wasn't the ugliest either. She was short, black as fuck, overweight and kept a scarf wrapped around her nappy-ass head at all times. Thankfully the only thing I'd inherited from her was her color. I got my slim build, height, good hair and my good looks from my daddy who was part Creole and Puerto Rican. I really couldn't remember him since he'd left my mom when I was little. I didn't have no memories, no pictures no nothing. Only thing I had was a baby doll named Gi-Gi that he'd bought me for my first birthday; other than that I had nothing to remember him by. According to my aunt and maternal grandmother that was more than enough; they'd always told me I wasn't missing much. I still felt like a piece of me was missing. I was always jealous because Miguel had his father in his life and I didn't and he constantly reminded me that Rick was his father and not mines.

I grabbed my robe off my bed and headed to the bathroom. After getting undressed, I examined my boyish figure in the mirror. I was tall, dark and skinny. Miguel always made fun of me callin' me Ms. Six O'Clock 'cuz I was built straight up and down, with no curves at all. My momma said once I started having sex my curves would eventually come, I guess I would never get any 'cuz I was never having sex. After my shower, I quickly got dressed, brushed my hair into a ponytail and headed toward the door.

"You betta' be yo' ass home before dark," my momma warned as I opened up the front door.

"Yea aiiiight," I responded and continued on my way.

"Fast-ass hefah," I heard her say as I closed the door behind me.

I jumped on the elevator and rode it down to the first floor. I held my breath the entire time because I couldn't stand the putrid piss smell every time I got on. I stepped off and ran into Budz and some other random niggas who were having a dice game in the hallway.

"Hey, Budz," I smiled widely as my heart skipped a few beats.

He looked up briefly from the dice game and smiled. "Hey, sis, wassup?"

I hated when he called me sis. "Nothin', bouta' go blow somethin'. I need to get my mind right," I said, trying to sound grown.

"Blow what? Some candy cigarettes?" He laughed, making the other niggas laugh too.

"Some weed, what else you think I'm gon' smoke?" I answered, embarrassed while rolling my eyes, knowing damn well I didn't know anything about smoking weed.

"You need to have yo' ass in school," he said before rolling the dice.

"I go to school," I lied.

"Whatever," Budz said hitting a quick lick before grabbing his money off the floor and standing up. "Miguel home?" he asked, counting his winnings.

"Yeah, his fat ass up there," I joked.

Budz shook his head and smiled before pressing the button on the elevator. I watched as he stepped on. He hit the number seven button and winked at me as the doors closed.

With chills running up and down my spine, I hurried out of the apartment building to go brag to my girls Nikki and Sierra about how Budz just tried to get on with me!